THE AENEID

THE AENEID

Virgil

WORDSWORTH CLASSICS

This edition published 1995 by
Wordsworth Editions Limited
Cumberland House, Crib Street, Ware,
Hertfordshire SG12 9ET

ISBN 1 85326 263 3

Printed and bound in Great Britain by
Mackays of Chatham plc, Chatham, Kent
Typeset in the UK by R & B Creative Services Ltd

INTRODUCTION

The Aeneid was commissioned by Augustus Caesar in celebration of the Battle of Actium in 31BC which had left Augustus as master of the Roman world. Initially reluctant to accept the commission, Virgil took several years to write and re-write the poem, dying before he had finished the final draft. Virgil left instructions for *The Aeneid* to be burnt, but Augustus evidently considered the poem a fitting eulogy, and his wish was countermanded.

Virgil's choice of Aeneas rather than Augustus as the hero of his epic was inspired. Aeneas was already worshipped by Romans as the founder of their race, and Virgil wanted to relate the luxurious Roman civilisation which he felt was on the brink of degeneration to her heroic past, and to inspire belief in an equally glorious future. Writing for the survivors of a long and savage civil war, he constructed a fairy tale modelled on the epics of Homer. Intellectually challenging and tragic in its view of the world, *The Aeneid* roused the Romans' pride in their past and upheld Roman ideals. Yet Virgil's narrative is laden with moral implications. Aeneas ultimately learns that imperialism cannot be achieved without war and the traditionally heroic aspects of this are duly shown, but they are set against a vision of war as something monstrous. The limitations of reckless bravery and the excesses generated by war are copiously illustrated throughout the epic. Set one thousand years before Augustus, the poem alludes directly to the emperor in prophecies and visions throughout the narrative, subtly suggesting that after a century of decline, Augustus will engender the recovery of Roman fortunes.

Starting at approximately the point where Homer left off in *The Iliad*, *The Aeneid* tells of how Aeneas, urged by benevolent deities, leads survivors of the fall of Troy westwards around the Mediterranean through a series of adventures in search of a new kingdom in Italy. The goddess Juno obstructs his progress and he faces many trials, the greatest of which is the tragic outcome of his love affair with Dido, Queen of Carthage. During a descent into the underworld, Aeneas is allowed a preview of Roman history and sees his own mighty descendants. Virgil illuminates the relationship between the gods and man by showing time and again that Aeneas' happiness is of no concern to the gods, that he must always submit dutifully to their will and that he may not deny the destiny that has been decreed for him by Jupiter.

Written in Latin hexameter, *The Aeneid* is divided into twelve books. Virgil exploits the characteristic journeys, divine intervention, battles, speeches, and extended similes that are the stock-in-trade of Hellenistic epic verse. But though his style also derives from that tradition, in *The Aeneid* Virgil extends his range, drawing on earlier stylistic sources and creating a highly individual method of presentation. As a document, *The Aeneid* is central to Roman culture and is hence of significance to all Western cultures which derive from Rome. Borrowings from Virgil's works can be found throughout European literature where his influence is all-pervading.

The poem is given universal and timeless relevance by the broad sweep of Virgil's narrative which encompasses the lives of ordinary folk, and recognizes with heartfelt compassion that the Roman empire was bought with their suffering and deprivation. *The Aeneid* is a story full of individuals who behave as real people still do. Virgil maintains an ambivalent view of the ideals and achievements of Augustus and gives a balanced account of imperialism. The poem is a profound meditation on every aspect and implication of power.

There have been many English translations of *The Aeneid*, some of the most notable being by the Scottish poet, Gavin Douglas, in 1553, by John Dryden in 1697, and by Henry Howard, whose 16th century translation of books II and III is the earliest example of English blank verse. John Jackson's lucid prose translation made in 1908 renders this masterpiece accessible to every reader.

Virgil (Publius Vergilius Maro), was born near Mantua in 70BC. He was educated in Cremona, Milan and Rome, but early life on his father's farm was central to his education. His first major work, the Eclogues *or* Bucolics *(37BC) idealized rural life whilst in his next work, the* Georgics *(30BC), he created a realistic and didactic rural poetry. He spent the rest of his life on his most famous work* The Aeneid, *an epic poem in twelve books, and one of the greatest long poems in world literature. Virgil died in Brindisi in 19BC. His works influenced poets of the Renaissance from Dante onwards.*

Further reading:
An Introduction to Virgil's Aeneid, W.A. Camps, Oxford, 1969
Virgil's Aeneid, Kenneth Quinn, London, 1968

THE AENEID

BOOK I

Aeneid

epic theme

ARMS I SING, and the man, who first from the shores of Troy
came, Fate-exiled, to Italy and her Lavinian strand – much buffeted he on flood and field by constraint of Heaven and fell
Juno's unslumbering ire; much suffering in war, withal, ere he
could found him a city and bring his gods to Latium; – author of
the Latin race, and the sires of Alba, and the walls of lofty
Rome!   *obligatory invoking of the muse*

Sing, Muse, the cause! Wherein was her godhead affronted,
what anger was at her heart, that the Queen of Heaven drave a   *Juno (Hera)*
hero – the soul of piety – to wade through such manifold disaster
and encounter such manifold toil? Can heavenly spirits cherish
resentment so dire?

There stood a city of old time – settlers from Tyre its habitants, Carthage its name – fronting Italy and Tiber's mouth from
afar, rich in all wealth, and fiercest of the fierce in the pursuits of
battle. This single town, they tell, Juno favoured over all lands
else – not Samos itself so dear. Here were her arms, here her
chariot, and that here (did the Fates allow) should arise an
empire of the world, was even then her celestial goal and the purpose of her heart. Yet had she heard that a line was springing
from Trojan blood, which, in days to be, should overthrow her
Tyrian towers, and that from those loins should issue a nation
broad-realmed, war-renowned, to the destruction of Libya: for
such the cycle the Sisters ordained! This the child of Saturn
feared, and still was mindful of the old war she waged aforetime
under Troy-town for her beloved Argos; nor yet had the causes
of her wrath, nor her hot resentment, faded from her soul. Deep-   *beauty contest*
written in her heart the judgement of Paris remained, and the
outrage to her slighted beauty, and that hated stock, and the glories of ravished Ganymede. Therefore, with this fuel for her
flames, she drove the Trojans – poor relics of Grecian conquest
and a stern Achilles! – storm-tossed over all the main; and far
from Latium she held them, while for many a year they wan-

dered, Fate-driven, about every sea. So vast was the struggle to
found the Roman state!

Scarce out of view of Sicilian soil, glad-hearted they were
spreading sail to the deep, their brazen prows lashing the brine
into foam, when Juno, cherishing the eternal canker at her heart,
thus communed with herself: 'And am I vanquished? Must I
flinch from my settled purpose, and fail to turn this Teucrian
king from Italy? The Fates, forsooth, forbid me! And Pallas
could fire the Argive fleet, and drown its crews fathom-deep, all
for the sin of one and the frenzy of Oïlean Ajax! With her own
hands she hurled Jove's rushing bolt from the clouds, flung their
vessels abroad, and upheaved the ocean-floor with her gales –
seized the wretch in her whirlwind, as he yet gasped the flames
from his pierced breast, and impaled him on a jagged rock! But I
who move through Heaven, its empress, sister and wife of Jove,
year after year wage war with a single people! And is there one
left to adore the deity of Juno? or, henceforth, will any pay the
suppliant's homage upon her altars?' ~ wants an apology?

With these thoughts surging the while in her fevered heart,
the goddess came to Aeolia, home of the storm-cloud – a region
whose womb is rife with the wild southern blasts. Here, in his
dreary cavern, king Aeolus lords it over rebellious winds and
piping storms, and curbs them with chain and dungeon. Indignant they rave round their prison-walls, while the mountain
murmurs in loud response: in his citadel aloft sits Aeolus, sceptre
in hand, chastening their spirit and taming their ire – else would
they whirl, in their fleeting course, earth and sea and the cope of
heaven, and sweep them through the void! But, in dread thereof,
the Father omnipotent hid them in sunless caves and whelmed
them under mountains massy and tall. And a king he gave them,
who should know, under settled covenant, to tighten their reins
or loosen them at his bidding. To whom Juno then addressed her
suit: 'Aeolus – for to thee the Sire of gods and King of men has
granted power by thy winds to lay the waves and raise them – a
nation that I loathe sails the Tuscan sea, bearing Ilium and its
vanquished gods to Italy. Breathe fury into thy blasts; sink and
overwhelm their ships; or drive them abroad and strew the deep
with their bodies! Twice seven Nymphs I have of radiant beauty,
and the loveliest of all is Deiopea. Her I will join to thee in stable
wedlock, and make her thine own for ever, that, for thy faithful
service, she may live out her years at thy side and her fair children call thee father!'

Then Aeolus: 'Thine is the task, O queen, to explore thy will: for me it is meet that I do thy behest! Thou hast won me my little kingship, my sceptre, and a gracious Jove: thou hast given me to sit at the feasts of Heaven, and hast made me lord over storm-cloud and storm.'

So said, he turned his spear against the hollow mountain, and smote on its side. Like legions of war, the gales poured through the opening gate, and swept their whirlwinds across the earth. They fell upon the main, and all from its uttermost deeps they heaved it – East banded with South, and South with the storm-fraught West – chasing the league-long waves to the strand. Straight rose a shouting of men, and a creaking of cables. Incontinent the clouds blotted sun and sky from the Teucrians' view, and midnight brooded over the sea. Thunder sounded from pole to pole, the heavens glittered to the fast-flashing levin, and all things that are menaced the heroes with instant doom. At once Aeneas' limbs were loosened in the chill of fear; groaning he uplifted either palm to Heaven, and thus spoke: 'O happy, thrice and again, they whose lot it was to bleed under the towers of Troy before their father's eyes! O Tydeus' son, bravest thou of the children of Greece, why might I not fall on the Ilian plains, and resign this spirit beneath thy right hand, there where mastered by the Aeacian spear fierce Hector lies low, with great Sarpedon at his side, and Simois whirls under his rolling flood so many a shield and helm of the brave, so many a stout, heroic frame?'

As wildly he bewailed him, a squall howling from the North struck full on the sail, and tossed the surge to the stars. The oars shivered, the prow swung round, the side lay bare to the billows, and down there bore, all in a mass, a mountain of water precipitous. Here the seamen hung on the crested wave, there the yawning flood shewed them earth betwixt the watery walls, and everywhere brine and sand raged commingled. Three vessels the South snatched and hurled on a lurking reef – that mid-ocean reef which Italy styles *The Altars*, a vast ridge scarce overtopping the foam; – three the East drove from the deep, a sight for tears, to the shallows and quicksands, dashed them on the shoals, and left them begirt with a rampart of sand. One, that convoyed the Lycians and trusty Orontes, a great sea, crashing from aloft, smote on the poop full before the chieftain's eyes. The helmsman was flung forth; headlong he rolled into the main; and three circles his barque made in the self-same place, amid the swirling billows, then plunged beneath the dizzy eddy. Here and there in the wastes of ocean a swimmer was seen – weapons of war, planks of ships and treasure of Troy all broadcast over the flood! – And now the tempest had mastered the stout vessels of Ilioneus and valiant Achates, with that wherein Abas sailed, and that which held the old Aletes: the bolts of their timbers were riven, and all, cracked and agape, were fast drinking in the fatal tide.

Posidon

Neptune, meanwhile, grew ware that the deep was turmoiled with sullen roar, the tempest abroad, and the still waters seething up from their nether pools. With quickening anger he heard, lifted his majestic brow above the brimming flood, and looked forth upon the main. He saw the fleet of Aeneas scattered over ocean, the Trojans whelmed under the billows and wrack of heaven, and the guile and wrath of Juno were plain to a brother's eye. East and West he summoned to himself, then opened his lips: 'And rest ye such trust on your race? Is the hour come, when, sans my godhead, the winds dare embroil earth and heaven, and raise these watery mountains? Whom I – but better to calm the insurgent waves! In time to come ye shall atone me your transgressions with other penalty. Flee and tarry not, and bear this word to your king: not on him did the lot confer the lordship of ocean and the dread trident, but on me! His empire is bounded by those dreary rocks – the home, Eurus, of thee and thine. In that palace let Aeolus vaunt him, and there let him reign, but see that his dungeons be shut!'

on the Trojans' side

He spoke, and – sooner than said – lulled the swollen waters, scattered the embattled clouds, and recalled the sun. Cymothoe, withal, and straining Triton tugged the galleys from the jagged rock; their master raised them with his trident, he opened the vast quicksands, he soothed the sea, and on light wheel skimmed the summit of the tide. – And as oft in some great concourse, when Sedition lifts her head and the nameless vulgar kindles to rage, – when brands and stones are already flying, and fury ministers arms, – if they chance to behold a man of reverend goodness and worth, on the instant all are mute; and about him they stand with listening ear, while he sways their spirit by his word and allays their passion: – even so sank all that tumult of ocean, when Father Neptune looked forth on the waves, and, floating under a cloudless heaven, guided his steeds and flew onward, giving rein to his speeding car.

But Aeneas' weary comrades made all effort to run to such strand as was nighest, and turned toward the Libyan coast.

There, in a deep bay, is a roadstead, which an island forms by its jutting sides. On those sides every wave from the deep breaks, then parts into the winding hollows: on this hand and that are vast rocks, and twin cliffs frowning to heaven; and beneath their peaks, far and wide, the peaceful seas are silent. From the height hangs a background of waving forests, and a grove of dim and tangled shadows. Under the fronting crags is a rock-hung cave – haunted by the Nymphs – and, within it, sweet water and seats from the living rock. Here no chains fetter the wearied ships, and no anchor with crooked fang restrains them. – Hither, Aeneas came, with but seven ships mustered out of the full tale. Yearning for their mother-earth, the Trojans landed. The long-hoped beach was theirs at last, and they laid their brine-drenched limbs on the sand. And first Achates struck a spark from the flint, nursed the fire in leaves, set dry fuel around, and quickened the flame in tinder. Anon, weary and worn, they brought out their wheaten store, all marred by the billows, with the armoury of the mill, and set themselves to parch the rescued grain and bruise it under the stone.

Meanwhile Aeneas ascended the cliff and searched the whole wide watery prospect, if perchance he might mark a storm-tossed Antheus with his Phrygian galley, or a Capys, or Caicus' arms on the stately poop. Not a ship met his view; only three stags, that strayed on the beach while all the herd followed in their rear – a long array browsing through the vales. He halted, snatched his bow and winged shafts (loyal Achates bore the weapons), and first laid low the chieftains, high-headed with branching antlers, next the commonalty, and through the leafy woods drove the whole rout in confusion before his arrows. Nor stayed he his victorious hand, till he had stretched on earth seven huge bodies, and the number tallied with his ships. Then, repairing to the haven, he apportioned them to his comrades. Next he allotted the wines, wherewith good Acestes had laden his casks on the Sicilian strand (the hero's parting gift), and thus spoke comfort to their sorrowing hearts: 'Friends – for 'tis long since we made acquaintance with grief – friends, that have endured yet heavier blows, God will grant an ending even to this! Ye have looked on the rage of Scylla, and her hollow crags reverberant: ye have braved the Cyclops' cliffs. Recall that spirit of yore; a truce to your doubts and fears! The day may dawn when this plight shall be sweet to remember. Through manifold chances, through untold hazards, our way lies to Latium, where Fate promises a home of peace. There Heaven wills that our Trojan realm should rise again! Then endure for a while, and live for a happier day!'

So he spoke, sick at soul under his weight of care, feigned hope on his brow, and stifled grief in his heart of hearts! His men girt themselves to the quarry and the banquet to be, stripped the hides from the ribs, and bared the carcasses. Part carved the still quivering flesh, or pierced it with spits: part set cauldrons on the beach and supplied them with names. Then all fell to and renewed their strength, couched on the sward and sating themselves with old wine and rich venison. But when hunger had yielded to their feasting and the boards were removed, long-discoursing they yearned for their lost companions, hovering betwixt hope and fear – should they deem them to live, or to have suffered the last pang and to hear not the voice of the caller. But, more than all, good Aeneas bemoaned his fallen friends – now bold Orontes, now Amycus, and now the cruel doom of Lycus, with Gyas the stout, and Cloanthus the brave.

And now all was ended, when Jove looked down from his ethereal height on the sail-set sea and its shores, on the lowly lands and their broad peoples, and, looking, halted on the peaks of Heaven, and fixed his gaze on the kingdoms of Libya. And him, while such care exercised his soul, Venus bespoke, sadder than her wont, her starry eyes tear-dimmed: 'O thou who governest, under sceptre eternal, the world of men and of gods, and affrightest them with the thunderbolt, what sin so heinous could my Aeneas – could my Trojans – sin against thee? Yet, though so many a man hath bled, all the globe is shut against them for Italy's sake! But surely thy word went forth, that hence, as the years rolled onward, *Rome* should arise, and that from Teucer's renascent line should spring captains of war, to hold the sea and all lands under their sway! What counsel, sire, hath changed thee? In this hope I found solace for fallen Troy and those tearful ruins; and ever I balanced fate against opposing fate: but now the same fortune hounds my heroes through infinite ill. What term, great king, dost thou set to their toils? Antenor, escaped from the Argives' midst, availed to thread the Illyrian gulfs, and to win unscathed past Liburnia's inmost realms and the fount of Timavus, where, to the hill's echoing roar, the sea bursts forth through nine mouths and whelms the fields under its resonant flood. Here, spite of all, he set his Patavian town and his Teucrian home, and now, amid peace and calm, he rests and is still; while we thy children, we to whom thy nod has promised the citadel of Heaven – oh the shame and sorrow! – our ships all lost are betrayed for the anger of one, and sundered afar from the shores of Italy! And thus is piety honoured? Thus dost thou restore us to our kingship?'

With a smile on that countenance wherewith he calms sky and storm, the Sire of gods and men printed a father's kiss on her lips, then spoke: 'Spare thy fears, Cytherea: the fate of thy heroes remains thee unmoved. Thou shalt see thy city and the promised walls of Lavinium. Thou shalt bear aloft thy great-hearted Aeneas to the stars, nor hath any counsel changed me! He – for, if this care gnaws at thy heart, I will speak and unroll the latest pages of Destiny with their mysteries – he shall wage a great war in Italy, and he shall bruise her fierce peoples: he shall give laws to the nations, and he shall build walls to their cities, till the third summer shall have seen him king in Latium, and the third winter shall have viewed his camp since the Rutulians fell. But the child Ascanius, now named by another name *Iulus* (Ilus he was while the Ilian state stood and was a kingdom), shall fulfil in sovereignty thirty full circles of the sun, as the months roll onward; he shall unseat his rule from Lavinium, and in might he shall strengthen Alba the Long. There for thrice an hundred years the crown shall be worn by Hector's people, till Ilia – priestess and queen – shall bear, to the loins of Mars, twin children. Then Romulus, exultant in tawny hide of the fostering wolf, shall receive the nation, found the War-god's walls, and call his lieges by his own name – the *Romans*. For them, I set no bounds to their fortunes, nor any term of years: I have given them empire without ending. Nay, Juno, that now wearies earth and sea and sky with her fears, for all her bitterness, shall change her counsels for the better, and, with me, cherish the Romans – lords of the world, people of the gown! Such is my pleasure. And the time shall come, as the lustres glide past, when the house of Assaracus shall hold in bondage Phthia and famed Mycenae, and be lord over conquered Argos. A prince shall be born of the fair stock of Troy, that shall bound his empire by ocean, his fame by the stars – CAESAR of the Julian line, name inherited from great Iulus! Him, in days to be, secure thou shalt receive in Heaven, all burdened with the spoils of the East; and men shall call on him also in their prayers. Then war shall be laid aside, and the harsh world soften to peace: white-headed Faith, and Vesta, and Quirinus, with brother Remus at his side, shall be lawgivers: the accursed gates of Battle shall be shut with iron bar and clenching bolt; and godless Frenzy shall sit within upon the weapons of savagery – behind her either hand chained in a hundred brazen bonds, shrieks issuing from those ghastly, bloody lips!'

So said, he sent down Maia's son from above, that the lands and towers of nascent Carthage might open in welcome to the Teucrians, nor Dido drive them from her realm, unwitting of Fate. Through the ocean of air he sped upon beating wing, and alighted incontinent on the Libyan strand. Quickly he did his errand, and the rugged Tyrian hearts softened at the will of Heaven; and foremost their queen received a gentle spirit and gracious thoughts for Troy.

But good Aeneas pondered much through the night, and, so soon as the kindly day was come, his resolve was made: he would go forth, explore the strange land, learn to what shores the wind had brought him, who their habitants – man or beast; for waste was all he beheld! – then bring back sure intelligence to his comrades. His fleet he hid under a hollow rock amid overarching woods, encircled by trees and tangled shadows, and himself walked abroad, Achates his sole companion, brandishing two steel-shod spears of broad point. In the heart of the forest his mother confronted him, wearing a maiden's aspect and garb, and a maiden's arms: Spartan she might have been, or Thracian Harpalyce, when she outwearies her steeds and outstrips the fleet Hebrus in her course. For a huntress she seemed, and huntress-wise she had slung a light bow from her shoulder and given her locks for the winds to scatter: her knee was bare, and the waving folds of her kirtle were gathered in a knot. And, first, 'Ho, warriors,' she cried, 'if perchance ye have seen sister of mine roving here, girt with quiver and the fell of some spotted ounce, or calling her hounds hard on the heels of a foaming boar, show her to me!'

Thus Venus, and thus in answer the son of Venus began: 'No sister of thine have I seen or heard, maiden – but how shall I style thee? For thine is no earthly face, and thy voice rings not of mortality! O goddess manifest! – sister of Phoebus? Nymph by line? – show thou grace to us, lighten our toil, whosoever thou art, and teach us under what sky, in what regions of earth our stormy lot is cast! We are wanderers, witless of place and people, hither driven by the wind and dreary wave. Say, and many a victim shall fall before thy altars under our right hand.'

Then Venus: 'For me, I claim not such honour. We maidens of Tyre use to carry the quiver, and high on our ankles we bind the buskin of purple. Thou seest the realms of Carthage – Tyrian the people, Agenor's the city. But the country is Libya, a nation stubborn in war. Here Dido holds sway, fled from Tyre to escape her brother. The tale of injury is long, long its windings, but for thee I will skim its summits. She had a spouse, Sychaeus, whose domains were broadest in all Phoenicia. Him she loved with a great and disastrous love: for on him her father bestowed his virgin daughter, and wedded her to him in those rites that she then first knew. But her brother Pygmalion swayed the sceptre of Tyre, a monster the blackest of mankind, and a frenzy came between the two kinsmen. For with traitorous steel, blinded by the lust for gold, godlessly he did the unwitting Sychaeus to death before the altar, with never a thought for his sister's love. And for long he hid the deed, and, by many a wile, mocked the heart-sick, yearning wife with the shadow of hope. But the spectre of the tombless dead came itself in her dreams, uplifting her husband's countenance ghastly-pale, bared the altars of cruelty and the sword-pierced breast, unveiled all the secret villany of the house, then bade her tarry not, but flee and go forth from her country, and drew out from earth his old-time treasures – an untold weight of silver and gold – to speed her on the way. Dido, aghast, prepared for flight and rallied her friends. All foregathered who loathed the tyrant either in savagery of hate or bitterness of fear. They seized upon a fleet that chanced to stand ready, and bore the wealth of covetous Pygmalion over the main, – a woman the head of their emprize. To these regions they came where now thou seest arise the giant ramparts and citadels of nascent Carthage, and bought of the soil – Byrsa they called it in token thereof – so much as they could encircle in a bull-hide. – But, tell me, who are ye? From what shores are ye come? Or whither bend ye?'

She asked; and thus with a sigh he answered, summoning each word from the depths of his breast: 'O goddess, should I trace the tale from beginning to ending, and thou have leisure to hearken our annals of disaster, too soon would the star of eve close Olympus and lay the day to rest! From ancient Troy – if Troy's name hath been borne to thine ears – we sailed over distant seas, till the random tempest drove us upon the shores of Libya. I am the good Aeneas whose fame overtops the stars. On board I bear my gods, rescued from the sword, and I seek my native Italy, and my forefathers, the begotten of Jove. With twice ten ships I gat me on the Phrygian main: my goddess-mother showed the path, and I followed the oracles of Fate. Scarce seven, shattered by wind and wave are left to me! Myself, unknown, unfriended, exiled of Europe and of Asia, I tread the Afric deserts.'

No farther Venus endured his wail, but, in his mid-tide of grief, broke in on him: 'Whosoever thou art, methinks, not unloved of Heaven thou drawest the breath of life, since thou art come to this Tyrian city. Only go thy way, and betake thee hence to the threshold of the queen. For, save my parents were false, and vain the augury they taught me, I tell thee of comrades returned and a recovered fleet swept into safety by veering gales. Look on those twelve swans and their joyful train: but now the bird of Jove, stooping from the regions of air, chased them in rout across the open firmament; now, thou seest, in long array, either they choose their ground, or – the choice already made – gaze down upon it. Even as they return glad-hearted, and, flocking, circle the sky and sing, so thy barques and the company of thy friends are either safe in port or entering its mouth with bellied sail. Do thou but go thy way, and turn thy steps where the path shall lead thee!'

She said, and, as she turned away, flashed on him with roseate neck. From her head her ambrosial tresses breathed a fragrance celestial, her raiment fell waving to her feet, and the goddess indubitable was revealed in her step. He, when he knew her for his mother, followed her vanishing form with pursuant voice: 'Why, cruel with the rest, mockest thou thy son these many times with counterfeited semblance? Why may we never clasp hand in hand, and hear and speak the words of truth?' – He made his plaint, and bent his way to the ramparts. But Venus shrouded them, as they went, in a mist of darkness, and, with celestial power, shed round them a great mantle of cloud, that none might see them, none lay hand upon them, nor any man question the cause of their coming and beget delay. Herself she fled on high to Paphus, and, glad in heart, reviewed the home of her love, where her temple stands and a hundred altars glow with Sabaean frankincense and breathe the perfume of fresh-twined garlands.

Meantime, with the path for guide, they hastened on their way. And now they were scaling the hill, that lowers giant-like over the city, and gazes from its pinnacle on the fronting towers below. Aeneas marvelled at the vast structures, – huts erewhile, – marvelled at the gates, at the din, and at the paved highways. Hotly the Tyrians were pressing their toil: part raised walls, laboured at the citadel, and, by force of hand, rolled up rocks to the summit;

part chose the ground for their dwellings, and enclosed it by a furrow. Here were workers hollowing out a roadstead; there others, laying the theatre's deep foundation, and hewing from the cliff great columns – stately ornaments of the stage to be! Such the tasks that employ the bees in the flower-spangled meadows when summer is new, when they march forth the young manhood of the race, or press the liquid honey, and fill the distended cells with nectarous sweets; or receive the burdens of them that enter, or, in battled array, cast out the drones and their idle bands from the homestead while all is fervent with toil and the fragrant honey is redolent of thyme. 'O happy they, whose walls are already rising!' cried Aeneas, and lifted his eyes to the city-towers. Cloud-veiled he entered – wondrous to tell! – into their midst, and mingled with the throng, yet was seen by none.

In the heart of the town there stood a grove of luxuriant shade, marking that site where the wave-worn, storm-tossed Tyrians first dug forth the sign that imperial Juno foreshowed – the head of a gallant steed, in token that so should their people be valiant in battle, and their life unstinted throughout the ages! Here Sidonian Dido was rearing a vast temple to Juno, dowered with abundant offerings and the especial presence of her deity. The steps led upward to a threshold of brass; brass-bound were the posts, and the hinges creaked under brazen doors. In this grove a vision was first vouchsafed to charm fear away: here Aeneas first dared to hope salvation, and rest a surer trust on his darkened star! For while he swept his gaze round all in the ample shrine, till the queen should come, – while, with inward wonder, he mused on the gracious destiny of the city, on the bands of craftsmen, and their toil-fraught works, he descried the battles of Ilion ranged scene upon scene, and all the wars that Fame, even in that day, had blazoned through the ends of earth, – Atreus' sons, and Priam, and Achilles, the feared of both. He stayed his foot, and, 'Achates,' he cried, 'is there any place, is there any land of all the lands, that is not yet rife with our tale of sorrow? Lo, here is Priam! Even here, virtue hath her rewards, and mortality her tears: even here, the woes of man touch the heart of man! Dispel thy fears; this fame of ours is herald to some salvation.' He said, and sated his soul with the barren portraiture; and oft he sighed, and his cheeks were wet with the welling floods. For here he saw the Greeks, that warred round Pergamus, driven in rout, with Troy's warrior-youth hard upon them: and there Phrygia fled, and plumed Achilles followed fast in his car. Nor far away, weeping he saw the pavilions of Rhesus, and their snowy canvas, betrayed by the first hour of sleep, and Tydeus' son, red from a great carnage, laying them waste and driving the fiery steeds to his camp, ere they could taste the grass of Troy and drink of Xanthus. Elsewhere Troilus fled – ill-starred boy, that fronted Achilles with unequal arm! – His weapons were lost; his coursers whirled him on, as he clung, face upturned, behind the chariot, yet still clutched at the reins, while his neck and hair trailed along the plain, and the dust was scored by his inverted spear! Meantime the daughters of Ilion were moving to the shrine of an unpropitious Pallas. Suppliant and sad, with tresses dishevelled and hands beating on breasts, they bore the Robe: but the goddess was turned from them, and her eyes were fixed on earth. – Thrice round the ramparts of Troy had Achilles whirled Hector, and was bartering his breathless clay for gold. Then deep, in truth, was the sigh that arose from the hero's heart of hearts, when he saw the spoils, saw the chariot, saw the very corpse of his friend, and Priam outstretching his weaponless hands to the slayer! Himself, too, he knew, mingled in the mellay amid the Achaean van; and he knew the embattled East, and the arms of swarthy Memnon. Last, wild Penthesilea led her Amazon hosts with their crescent-shields. In the midmost thousands she raged, one naked breast bound with circlet of gold, – a queen and warrior, a maiden that braved the battle against men.

While Dardan Aeneas looked and wondered, while spellbound he stood, rooted motionless in one set gaze, queen Dido moved in radiant loveliness to the fane, a great throng of banded youths encircling her. Such as Diana is, when, on Eurotas' banks or along the peaks of Cynthus, she leads the dance, and a thousand attendant Oreads muster on either hand; but she, the quiver on her shoulder, towers, at every step, over the goddesses all, while Latona's mute heart is thrilled with joy: – even such was Dido, and so she gaily moved through the throng, intent on her labours and the empire to be. Then, in the sacred portals, under the temple's central dome, she took her seat, fenced with steel and enthroned on high. Thence she meted justice and laws to her lieges, adjusted their burdens of toil in due proportion, or assigned it by the lot, when, lo, in the heart of a great concourse, Aeneas saw approaching Antheus, and Sergestus, and stout Cloanthus, with other of his Teucrians, whom the black whirlwind had scattered over ocean and swept far away to diverse shores. In amazement he stood – and in amazement Achates stood – under the shock of joy and fear. Eagerly they burned to clasp hand in hand; but the mystery unread perturbed their souls. Therefore they dissembled, and, draped in the sheltering cloud, looked forth to learn what fortune was with their friends, on what strand they had left their fleet, and wherefore they came: for, the chosen of every vessel, they advanced to sue for grace, and amid clamour repaired to the shrine.

So soon as they had gained entrance, and audience was granted before the throne, Ilioneus, their eldest, began with unruffled breast: 'O queen, whom Jove hath willed to found a new city and to bridle the proud peoples with law, we – ill-starred sons of Troy, whom the winds have borne over every sea, – prefer our prayer: ward the dreadful flames from our ships! We are come not to waste with the sword the homes of Libya, nor to drive the prey we have reft to the strand. Such fierceness fits not our hearts, nor such insolence the vanquished! There is a country that Greece styles Hesperia, an immemorial land, strong in battle and rich of soil. Oenotrians were they that held it: now, Fame tells, a new generation has named the country with the name of their leader – *Italy*. Thither we voyaged, when stormy Orion rose with a sudden swell and swept us upon the ambushed shoals. And afar he scattered us, over billows and trackless rocks, with his boisterous gales and the tyrannous seas, till hither we drifted – a poor remnant – to thy shores. What race of men is this? What home of savagery smiles on these dealings? They deny us the bare welcome of the sand: they unsheathe the sword, and forbid us to plant foot on the verge of their soil! But if ye contemn the children of men and the arms of mortality, yet bethink you of the gods – that they will forget neither the good nor the evil! We had a king, Aeneas, peerless in justice and goodness, as in the weapons of war. If him the Fates have preserved, if he breathes the air of heaven, and lies not yet in the unpitying ghostly realm, then we fear not: nor shall it rue thee that thou wert foremost in the strife of courtesy. In the fields of Sicily, also, there are cities and swords, and a prince of Trojan line – Acestes the glorious! Grant us to beach our wind-buffeted barques, to shape us planks in thy forests, and to strip boughs for our oars, that so, if it shall be ours to sail for Italy with king and comrades recovered, to Italy and Latium we may fare, glad of heart; but, if our salvation be cut off, and thou – oh noble soul, father of Teucer's people! – if the Libyan main possess thee, and the hope of Iulus be no more, then we may seek at least the Sicilian seas, whence we bore hitherward, and the mansions prepared for us, and king Acestes!'

Thus Ilioneus, and all the Dardans, with one voice, cried assent.

Then Dido made response, briefly and with eyes downcast: 'Men of Troy, unburden your hearts of fear; lay aside your cares! Harsh necessity and the infancy of my realm constrain me to use such caution, and to set watch and ward through the breadth of my boundaries. Who could be stranger to the fame of Aeneas' people, to Troy town, her heroes and their deeds, and the flames of that great war? Our Tyrian breasts are not so sluggish, and the Day yokes not his steeds so far from our Tyrian city! Whether broad Hesperia and the fields of Latium shall be your choice, or whether the region of Eryx, and king Acestes, I will send you forth safe under my guard, and I will aid you of my wealth. Or will ye settle, peers with me, in this kingdom of mine? The city I build me is yours! Beach your ships: Trojan or Tyrian – all shall be one in my sight. And would that your king had been driven with you by one and the self-same gale, and Aeneas were here! Yet will I send faithful messengers through my coasts, and bid them scour the ends of Libya, if it chance that he wanders an outcast in forest or town.'

With spirit exalted by her words, brave Achates and father Aeneas long had burned to break forth from their cloud; and first Achates addressed Aeneas: 'Goddess-born, what counsel now stirs in thy soul? Thou seest that all is safe, – thy fleet and thy comrades restored! But one is wanting; and him our own eyes saw engulfed: all else tallies with thy mother's word.' Scarce had he spoken, when suddenly the investing cloud disparted and was purged into the open sky, and in its place stood Aeneas, glittering in the lucent day, godlike in aspect and frame: for the mother had breathed on her son, and his locks were beautiful; he was clad in the rosy light of youth, and his eyes were lustrous and glad: – as when the artist-hand lends loveliness to the ivory, or when silver, or Parian stone, is enchased in the yellow gold. Straight he turned to the queen, and, unforeseen by all, spoke on the instant: 'He that ye seek is in your midst, – Trojan Aeneas, snatched from the Libyan wave. O thou, who alone hast pitied the unutterable travails of Troy, who wouldst fain take this remnant, that Greece hath spared, – outworn by every disaster of land and of sea, bereft of all – and make it one with thee in city and home – Dido, no power of ours, no power of all the children of Dardanus, wheresoever they stray, scattered through the wide

world, can pay thee the thanks thou hast merited! But if piety
still have regard in Heaven, if justice and a mind conscious of the
right yet be aught on earth, may God give thee due reward!
What happy age saw thy birth? What glorious parents gave being
to such a child? While the rivers shall run to ocean, while the
shadows shall move in the mountain valleys, while the sky shall
feed the stars, always shall thy honour, and thy name, and thy
glory abide, whatever the lands that beckon me!' – He said, and
grasped his friend Ilioneus with his right hand, Serestus with his
left, and the others in their turn, – with them, brave Gyas and
brave Cloanthus.

Sidonian Dido sat in amaze, first at sight of the hero, soon at
thought of disaster so deep, and thus she opened her lips: 'What
fortune, goddess-born, hounds thee through such infinite peril?
What violence has thrown thee on our barbarous shores? Art
thou that Aeneas whom gracious Venus bore to Dardan Anchises
by the wave of Phrygian Simoïs? And, in truth, I remember how
Teucer came to Sidon, an exile from his native fields, to win a
new realm by Belus' aid – Belus, my sire, who then was ravaging
Cyprus and its wealth, and held it by his conquering sword.
From that early day have I known the fall of Troy town, and thy
name, and the Pelasgian kings. Foeman though he was, yet he
extolled the Teucrians with signal praise, and fain would vaunt
him sprung from the ancient Teucrian line. Come then, ye warriors, and enter my doors. I, too, have been storm-tossed through
seas of trouble by a fortune such as yours, that only in this land
has willed that I should find peace. Not unschooled in woe do I
learn to succour unhappiness!' She spoke, and with the word led
Aeneas into her queenly halls, and commanded a solemn sacrifice
in the temples of Heaven. Nor less, meantime, she sent to his
comrades on the strand twenty bulls, a hundred great swine with
bristled backs, and a hundred fatted lambs with their ewes, to be
her gift and their joy on that festal day.

But the inner palace they decked in the splendour of royal
state, and prepared the banquet in the midmost halls. The coverlets of princely purple were embroidered by master-minds, massive silver stood on the boards, and on gold were chased the high
exploits of their sires – a long historic line, traced through many
a hero from the old-world origin of their race.

Aeneas – for a father's love suffered not his heart to rest – sent
Achates hot-footed to the ships, to bear the tidings to Ascanius
and escort him to the town – Ascanius, in whom was centred all

his dear parent's care. Gifts, moreover, he bade him bring, rescued from the ruins of Ilium; a pall, stiff-rustling with figured gold, and a veil with woven border of yellow acanthus – adornment, once, of Argos' Helen, that she brought from Mycenae, a wondrous guerdon from her mother Leda, what time she sailed to Troy-towers and her unblest bridal; – the sceptre, too, which Ilione had swayed in other days, eldest-born of Priam's daughters, and a pearl-strung collar for the neck, and a double diadem of gems and gold. – Such commands to speed, Achates was bending his way to the fleet.

But Cythera's queen revolved new wiles, new purposes, in her breast – how Cupid, changed in form and lineaments, might come in lieu of sweet Ascanius, kindle the royal dame to frenzy by his gifts, and flood her veins with fire. For she feared that house of unfaith, and the double tongue of Tyre; Juno's cruelty was flaming torment, and her dread returned with returning night. She spoke, then, to her winged Love, and said: 'My son, my sole strength, my effectual might – my son, who scornest the Titan bolts of our sovereign Father – to thee I come for succour, and, suppliant, implore thy deity! How thy brother Aeneas is driven over the main round every shore by Juno's relentless malice, thou knowest full well, and often hast thou sorrowed with our sorrow. Now Phoenician Dido holds him in her keeping, and enchains with soft words; and I fear me whither this welcome of Juno shall tend – for she will prove no laggard when the wheel of Fortune is thus on the turn! Therefore my purpose stands to strike the first blow, to take the queen in my toils, and encompass her with a wall of flame, that she change not under any constraint, but be bound to me in the strong bond of Aeneas' love. Hear now my thought, how thou mayest achieve this end! The princely boy, my dearest care, makes ready to go to Sidon's city at summons of his loved sire, in his hand such gifts as have survived the waves and a burning Troy. Him I will lull in sleep and hide in my hallowed dwelling above Cythera's peaks or in Idalium, that he may neither learn our wiles nor intervene to thwart them. For a single night – and no more – do thou simulate his form, and, boy thyself, assume a boy's familiar traits, that so when Dido, in the fullness of her joy, shall take thee to her lap, amid the kingly feast and the flowing wine, and shall throw her arms about thee and imprint sweet kisses, thou mayest inspire the lurking flame and betray her with thy poison.' Love yielded to his dear mother's prayer, put off his wings, and tripped gaily with

Iulus' step. But Venus shed the quiet dews of sleep over Ascanius' limbs, and bore him on her warm celestial breast to the towering groves of Idalia, where the soft amaracus cradled him in flowers and the breathing fragrance of its sweet shade.

And now Cupid, obedient to the word, was on his way, bearing the royal gifts to the men of Tyre, and blithe under Achates' guidance. When he came, the queen already had laid her down on her golden couch, beneath the proud awnings, and assumed her place in the midst. Now came father Aeneas, now the warriors of Troy, and all reclined on the outspread purple. Servants proffered water for the hands, ministered bread from baskets, and brought cloths of shorn nap. Within were fifty maids, their task to replenish in ordered course the great stores of cheer and to keep the hearth ablaze; and, with them, a hundred more, and pages as many of equal years, to pile the boards with viands and range the goblets. Nor less the Tyrians came thronging through the festal halls: for they, too, had their appointed seats on the embroidered couches. Admiring they surveyed the gifts of Aeneas, admiring surveyed Iulus, and the god's glowing cheeks, and his counterfeited words, and the pall, and the veil with border of yellow acanthus. But, above them all, Phoenicia's ill-starred queen, doomed to the destruction to be, could not sate her soul, but looked and burned, spell-bound alike by the child and by his gifts! He, for a little space, nestled in Aeneas' arms and hung on his neck, filling the hungry heart of his feigned sire, then took his way to the queen. With soul and eye she clung to him, and ever and again fondled him on her breast. Hapless Dido, little did she know how great a god she clasped to her aching heart! But he, mindful of his Acidalian mother, began line by line to efface the image of Sychaeus, and did his all to surprise by a living love that mind so long unstirred, that breast so long untenanted.

So soon as the feasting had pause and the boards were cleared, they set the huge bowls in their places and crowned the wine. The palace grew loud with din, and voices rolled through the ample halls; kindled lamps hung from the gold-fretted roof, and night fled before the flaming torches. Then the queen called for a cup, ponderous with gems and gold – that cup which Belus used, and all the kings from Belus onward – then filled it with unmixed wine, and, silence imposed throughout the hall: 'Jove, for they say thou givest laws to host and to guest, may it be thy will that this shall be a day of gladness for Tyrian and Trojan

exile, and that our children's children may tell of it! May Bacchus, the giver of joy, and kindly Juno be in our midst; and ye,
my Tyrians, be gracious and honour our gathering!' She said,
and poured forth the liquid offering upon the board, and, libation made, first touched the cup with her lips, then passed it with
jesting challenge to Bitias. Valiantly he drained the foaming
bowl, and drenched him from the brimming gold: then, after
him, his peers. Long-locked Iopas, whom mightiest Atlas taught,
made music on his gilded lyre. He sang of the wandering moon
and the travailing sun, of the birth of man and beast, of rain and
of fire, of Arcturus and the rainy Hyads, and of the twin Bears:
why the wintry suns so hasten to lave them in ocean, and what
the delays that impede the laggard nights. The Tyrians pealed
applause, and the Trojans followed. Nor less the unhappy Dido
lingered out the night in interchanging converse, and drank deep
draughts of love. Much she asked of Priam, much of Hector; and
now would know what the arms wherein came the son of Dawn;
now, how seemed the steeds of Diomede; now, how great was
Achilles. 'Nay,' she cried, 'come, our guest, and tell us, from
their first beginnings, of Grecian treachery, the fall of thy
people, and the wanderings of thyself. For already the seventh
summer bears thee a pilgrim over every land and sea!'

BOOK II

EVERY TONGUE WAS STILL, every face turned rapt upon him,
when thus from his couch aloft father Aeneas began:
    'Too deep for words, O queen, lies the sorrow thou bidst me
renew, to tell how Greece overthrew the power of Troy and her
tearful realm, – all the deeds of woe mine eyes have beheld, and
those whereof I was no small part! What Myrmidon or Dolopian,
what swordsman of the stern Ulysses, could tell that tale and
refrain from tears? And now dewy Night falls precipitate from
heaven, and the setting stars counsel sleep! Yet, if such thy yearning to learn our disasters and to hear in brief the last agony of
Troy, though my spirit shudders at remembrance and hath
started backward at the pang, I will take the word.
    'War-shattered, fate-repulsed, the Danaan chieftains, now that
so many years were fled and fleeing, built them, with Pallas'
celestial skill to aid, a horse, mountain-huge, and inwove its
flanks with hewn pines – an offering, they feigned, for their safe

return: and so the bruit went forth. In those dark sides they prisoned by stealth the flower of their chosen heroes and their great
frames, and filled the vast and cavernous womb with weaponed
soldiery.

'In sight of Troy lies an island, far-famed in story, Tenedos by
name – rich in all wealth while Priam's kingship endured, now
but a bay and a traitorous roadstead. Thither they sailed, and
hid them on the solitary strand, while we deemed they had
flown and were running before the wind to Mycenae. Therefore
all Teucer's land melted from her long sorrow into joy. The
gates stood wide, and pleasant it was to go view the Doric camp,
and the empty places and forlorn shore. Here, we mused, were
the Dolopian bands, there cruel Achilles pitched his tent: here
stood their fleets, there they fought in battled line! Part stood
amazed before the death-fraught-offering to maid Minerva, and
marvelled at the steed's huge bulk: and first Thymoetes urged
that it be drawn within our walls and set in the citadel – whether
his was the voice of treachery, or whether the fates of Troy
already wrought to this end. But Capys, and they of sager counsel, bade hurl to ocean these Danaan wiles, these sinister gifts,
burn them with subject flame, or pierce and explore the hollow
ambuscade of the womb: the fickle multitude swayed betwixt the
opposing causes.

'Then, foremost of all, with heart aflame, Laocoon came running from the summit of the citadel, a great troop of men hard
on his steps, and thus cried from afar: "My ill-starred countrymen, what height of madness is this? Trust ye the foe is
departed? or think ye that any Grecian gifts may be guileless? Is
it thus ye have proved Ulysses? In the hiding of this wood there
are Achaeans imprisoned; or it is an engine of war, devised
against our walls, that shall overlook our homes from above; or
some deceit lurks therein. Men of Troy, trust not the horse! Be it
what it may, I fear the Danaans, though their hands proffer
gifts!" So said, he hurled his mighty spear with strong arm full
against the monster's flank, and into the curved and jointed belly.
And then, had not the will of Heaven, had not our own minds
fought against us, he had moved us to hack the Argive coverts
with our steel, and Troy would still be standing, and ye lofty
towers of Priam – ye still would rise!

'But, lo, in the meantime, came a band of Dardan shepherds,
dragging to their king, amid clamorous outcry, a youth whose
hands were bound behind him. A stranger, he had thrown himself

of free will in their path, that he might compass this very end and leave Troy naked before Achaea – unappalled in soul, and nerved to either event, whether to spin his toils, or to fall under death inevitable! From this hand and that our Trojan youth came streaming round, and mocked the captive with rivalry of insult.

'Now hearken to Danaan guile, and from a single crime know the nation! For, as he stood in full view, unweaponed, confused, and swept his gaze round the Phrygian lines, "Alas!" he cried, "what land, what sea, now shall give me haven? or what remains at this hour to my misery? I have no place amid the Greeks, and the very Trojans, no less, prove foes and cry for the penalty of blood!" At his moan our mood was changed and all violence quelled, and we bade him say of what lineage he sprang, and what his message, and declare the trust of his captivity.

' "For me," he began, "O king, I will confess thee all in truth, be the issue as it may. Neither will I deny me of Argive race – this first – nor, though Fortune have fashioned Sinon to misery, shall all her malice fashion him to knavery or deceit! If it chance that speech has brought to thine ear some echo of Palamedes from Belus' line, his name and his storied fame – Palamedes, whom under monstrous impeachment, because he forbade the war, Greece delivered to death on the lying charge of treason, and mourns him now that he sees not the light – as his comrade and his kinsman my needy sire sent me hither to battle in my early years. While he stood secure in his kingship and was strong in the counsels of the princes, we, too, bore some name and repute. But when, by the jealousy of false-hearted Ulysses (no obscure tale!), he was banished from the realms of day, prostrate I dragged out my life in darkness and sorrow, and my soul was hot within me for the fate of my guiltless friend. And – fool that I was! – I unlocked my lips, and vowed that, if ever Fortune should bring it to pass, and I return conqueror to my native Argos, I would arise his avenger: and my speech roused his bitter hatred. Thence for me the first plague-spot of disaster: thence Ulysses ever held me in terror by slander upon slander, scattered words of double import among the vulgar, and sought his weapons with guilty fear. For he rested not, till, with Calchas for tool, – but why unroll these unwelcome pages to no avail? or why linger? If ye account all the Greeks of one likeness, and the name, but heard, suffices you, – then exact your tardy vengeance! This would the Ithacan pray, and the sons of Atreus purchase at a great price!"

'Then, in truth, we burned to inquire and explore the cause: for we knew not that blackness of crime, nor the arts of Greece. In fear and trembling he took up the tale, and spoke from his lying heart:

' "Time and again the Danaans longed to compass their return, to abandon Troy and flee from the weariness of that long strife – and oh that they had so done! Time and again the fierce, storm-swept sea debarred them, and the southern blasts affrighted them as they set forth. And most, when this horse already stood with its texture of maple-beams, the storm-clouds thundered through all the firmament. Bewildered, we sent Eurypylus to question the oracles of Phoebus, and from the shrine he brought us this woeful response: *With blood and a maiden slain ye appeased the winds, when first, Danaans, ye came to the shores of Ilium. With blood shall ye buy your return, and grace shall be found by an Argive life.* When that utterance reached the vulgar ear, all were stricken in soul, and a chill horror pierced them to the very bone – whom would the Fates doom? whom would Apollo call? Then he of Ithaca, with loud clamour, dragged Calchas the seer forth into the host; and hotly he questioned him, what meant that revela-tion of the celestial will. And even then many there were foretold me the pitiless crime of that master-craftsman, and in silence viewed the event. For twice five days the prophet was mute, and wore his mask: his tongue should betray no man, nor deliver him to death! Hardly, in the end, overborne by the Ithacan's clamour, he broke into the words of their pact, and destined me to the altar. All cried assent; and the fate, that each feared for himself, they brooked full lightly when it turned to blast one poor wretch!

' "And now the accursed day was come: the holy rites were almost ready, and the salted meal, and the garlands for my brow, when – hear my avowal! – I fled from the slayer, burst my bonds, and, screened by the sedge, lay all night in a miry swamp, till they should have sailed, if sail they would! And now I hope not to see my old-time country, nor the children of my love, nor the father of my yearning. Nay, it may be, Greece will exact the penalty of our flight at their hands, and atone my guilt by their hapless lives. Therefore, by the heaven above us, by the powers that have cognizance of truth, by unstained faith, if any there be yet lingering in any land among men – pity, I implore thee, calamity so deep, pity a soul that suffers where it has not sinned!"

'To his tears we accorded life, and, with life, compassion. Priam himself was first to command that his manacles and drawn fetters be undone, and thus spoke in tones of amity: "Whosoever thou art (for henceforward think not of the Greece thou hast lost!), ours thou shalt be; and answer truth to this my question: to what end have they raised the fabric of this huge horse? Who was father to the thought? or what seek they? for what service of Heaven, or what engine of war was it devised?" He said; the captive, with treachery and Pelasgian guile at his call, raised his unchained hands to the stars: "Ye eternal fires," he cried, "and your inviolate godhead, ye altars and cursed knives that I fled, ye sacred garlands that I wore for the sacrifice – I call you to witness: I sin not that I annul the fealty I swore to Greece, I sin not that I hate her sons, and bring to light all things soever that they hold secret; and no laws of country bind me! Do thou, Troy, but abide by thy word, and, preserved, preserve thy faith, if I shall speak truth, if I shall recompense thee in full!

' "All the hope of the Danaans, all their trust in the war begun, stood always in the aid of Pallas. But, from the day when Tydeus' impious son and Ulysses, the author of crime, ventured to ravish her fateful Palladium from the hallowed sanctuary, slew the warders of the citadel-height, bore the sacred image away, and dared to lay ensanguined hands on the virgin fillets of the goddess – from that day the Danaans' hope began to ebb, to slip, and to recede: their strength was broken and the heavenly heart was turned from them! And Triton's maid gave sign thereof by no dubious portents. Scarce was the effigy lodged in the camp, when glittering flames flashed from her uplifted eyes, a salt sweat stood on her limbs, and thrice – tale of wonder! – she sprang of herself from earth, bearing her buckler and quivering lance. Straight Calchas raised his prophetic voice: the main must be traversed in flight; for never should Troy-towers be razed by the Argive steel, till they sought them auspices once more from Argos, and brought again the favour of Heaven, that they bore across the seas in their crooked keels! And now, that they have run to their native Mycenae before the wind – it is but to muster arms and attendant gods, and, the wave recrossed, they will be here unforeseen. So Calchas expounds the omens. This image they have reared at his warning in place of the Palladium, to atone for deity affronted and expiate the guilt of sacrilege. But Calchas bade them raise it to this vast bulk with oaken texture, that so it might not find entry through the gates, nor be drawn within the walls, nor shelter its people under their ancient worship. For if hand of yours had profaned Minerva's offering, then, said the seer, a dire destruction –

Heaven send that the omen light first on himself! – should fall upon the kingdom of Priam and upon the Phrygians. But if it ascended by your hands into your city, then Asia should turn again, and fare to the walls of Pelops with wide-wasting sword; and such the fate that awaited our children's children!"

'These wiles, and the arts of forsworn Sinon, won credence for his tale, and fraud and forced tears took captive them whom neither the son of Tydeus, nor Larissa's Achilles, nor ten years of battle, nor a thousand ships could subdue!

'But now another portent, greater and far more terrible, met our woeful gaze, and turmoiled our unprophetic spirit. Laocoon, whom the lot had drawn to be priest of Neptune, stood by the wonted altars in act to slay a great bull: but, lo, over the peaceful deep from Tenedos – I shudder at the word! – twin serpents lay along the main with immeasurable coils, and side by side they moved to the strand. Their breasts were reared amid the waves, and their sanguine manes overtopped the billows: the rest of them swept the sea behind, wreathing the huge rolling length of spine; and the foaming waters roared beneath. And now they had gained the plain, and, with burning eyes blood-shot and fire-shot, were licking their sibilant jaws with flickering tongues! Bloodless and pale at the sight, we scattered: they, with unfaltering march, sought Laocoon. And, first, either serpent, encircling the tiny frames of his two sons, bound them fast, and, with gnawing fang, preyed on their hapless limbs. Next they seized the sire, as, weapon in hand, he ran to the rescue: in their vast folds they chained him; and now they had twice encompassed his waist, twice had flung their scaly bodies about his throat, and were towering above him with head and uplifted neck. His fillets bedewed with gore and black venom, at one and the same time he strove to sunder their knots by the strong hand, and raised fearful cries to the stars – like the bellowings of some wounded bull, when he has fled the altar and dashed the frustrate axe from his neck! But the two dragons fled sliding to the temple on the height, and sought the tower of Triton's pitiless maid, there to find refuge under her celestial feet and the orb of her buckler.

'Then, in truth, a strange dread thrilled every trembling breast, and the word passed how Laocoon had but paid the merited penalty of his crime, in that he had profaned the holy wood with his spear, and hurled his sinful javelin against the flank. With one voice men cried that the image be drawn to its sanctuary, and prayers preferred to the goddess and her deity.

'We cleft the walls, and laid open the town within. All bent to
the work, set beneath the feet wheels whereon to glide, and
stretched hempen bonds about the neck. Fraught with battle,
that fateful engine scaled the ramparts. Around it boys and
unwed girls chanted sacred hymns, and joyed to lay hand upon
the rope. Upward it moved, and rolled with menacing front into
the heart of our city. – O my country, O Ilium, home of the
gods, and ye war-famed battlements of Dardanus' sons! four
times on the very threshold of the gate it halted, and four times
arms clashed in its womb! Yet, heedless and frenzy-blinded, we
pressed on, and set the accursed thing in the holy citadel. Then
Cassandra, too, opened her lips to the coming doom, – lips, that,
by behest of Heaven, Troy never credited! We, the unblest, we,
for whom that day was to be the last, in every street hung the
sanctuaries of the gods in festal boughs.

'Meantime the skyey sphere turned, and Night rushed down
over Ocean, involving in deep shadow earth, and heaven, and
Myrmidon guile. Throughout the city the Teucrians lay and
were still, and sleep embraced their weary limbs. And now the
Argive array was moving, with marshalled vessels, from Tenedos,
through the friendly silence of the mute moon, in quest of the
familiar strand, when the royal galley flashed the signal, and
Sinon – screened under the partial doom of Heaven – stealthily
unbarred the pine-built prison, and enlarged the Danaans pent in
its womb. Wide-opened, the steed restored its freight to the air,
and, from the hollow timbers, exultant there issued Thessander
and Sthenelus in the forefront and cursed Ulysses, sliding down
the pendent rope, Acamas and Thoas, and Neoptolemus of
Peleus' line, Machaon, with the first, and Epeus himself, who
wrought the treason. They rushed upon the city, as it lay buried
in slumber and wine, slew the sentinels, welcomed all their comrades through the wide-flung gates, and united their confederate
hosts!

'It was the hour when the first sleep of suffering mortality
begins, and, by the grace of Heaven, steals on its sweetest errand
of mercy: and, lo, as I slept, methought Hector stood in great
sorrow before my eyes, and wept with a rain of tears. Such he
was as erst when rapt by the car, black with blood and dust, and
with swollen feet pierced by thongs. Ay me, what a sight was
there! How was he changed from that Hector, who wended
homeward, clad in the spoils of Achilles, or fresh from hurling
the fires of Phrygia upon the ships of Greece! His beard was foul,

his locks matted with gore, and he bare those wounds innumerable that he gat round his native walls. And it seemed I also wept, and prevented him, and spoke with sorrowing utterance: "O light of Dardania, O hope most constant of Troy, what delay so great hath held thee? From what shores, Hector, comest thou, the long-awaited? How these weary eyes behold thee – after the fall of many a friend, after woes untold of citizens and city! What unworthy cause hath marred the calm of thy countenance? or why view we these wounds?" He answered not, nor regarded my vain questionings; but, drawing a heavy sigh from his heart of hearts: "Ah, flee," he said, "goddess-born, and snatch thee from out these flames! The foe holds the ramparts: Troy crashes from her pinnacles! Thou hast paid in full to thy country and Priam: if those towers could be saved by mortal hand, they had been saved even by this! Troy bequeathes to thy keeping her holy things and the gods of her homes: these take, that they may share thy destiny: for these seek those stately walls that thou shalt establish in the end, when all the seas are traversed!" He said; and, in his hands, brought forth from the inner sanctuary the image of dread Vesta, her fillets, and the immortal fire.

'Meanwhile the town was convulsed with woe crying on every side; and, though the palace of Anchises my sire stood apart, sequestered under embowering trees, yet louder and louder the din waxed, and the alarm of battle drew nigher. I started from sleep, mounted the sloping roof, and stood with intent ear: – even so, when the flames fall upon the standing corn while the South is raging, or a rapid torrent with mountain-spate whelms the fields, whelms the smiling crops and the labours of the oxen, and sweeps the forests headlong before it, the unwitting swain stands in amazement, listening to the roar from a craggy eminence! Then, in truth, was proof manifest, and the Danaan wiles were plain to read. Already the palace of Deiphobus had fallen in spacious ruin before the overmastering element, already neighbour Ucalegon burned, and the broad waters of Sigeum were glittering to the flames. There rose a shouting of men and a braying of trumpets. Madly I snatched at my arms – nor snatched with enough of reason, but my spirit blazed to rally a troop for battle and charge to the citadel with my comrades! Frenzy and anger urged me precipitate to the resolve, and meseemed it was good to die in arms!

'But, lo, Panthus, escaped from the Argive spears – Panthus, the son of Othrys, priest of the citadel and Phoebus, – came dragging with his own hand his holy vessels, his vanquished gods, and his tiny grandson; and distraught he raced to my door. "Where stand our fortunes, Panthus? What fortalice do we seize?" Scarce had I spoken, when groaning he answered: "The last day, the inevitable hour, is come for the Dardan land! Trojans we are no more, Ilium is no more, and the great glory of the Teucrians is departed! Tyrant Jove has borne all to Argos, and Greece is mistress in the town she has fired. The Horse, towering and erect in the city's midst, disgorges warriors in harness, and conqueror Sinon scatters flame and insult. There are men by the swinging gates – all the thousands that ever came from great Mycenae – there are men besetting the narrow ways with fronting spears: the edge of the sword stands drawn, and the point glitters athirst for the slaying! Scarce the first sentinels at the gate assay the battle, and resist in aimless mellay." Thus the son of Othrys; and his words and the will of Heaven swept me to the fire and the steel, whither the fell Fury, whither the din and sky-challenging clamour called me. Comrades joined me, – Rhipeus and Epytus, great in war, whom the moon revealed, Hypanis and Dymas – all rallied to my side, with young Coroebus, Mygdon's son. In those days, it fell, he had come to Troy, fired by wild yearning for Cassandra, and bore a son's aid to Priam and his Phrygians – hapless he, that he listed not the bidding of his frenzied maid! When I saw them banded and nerved to the fray, thereon I began: "Warriors, hearts stout in vain, if your desire to brave the uttermost be fixed to follow me, ye see the plight of our fortunes! One and all, the gods by whom this realm stood are departed, and forlorn are shrine and altar. The city ye would succour burns. Let us choose death, and plunge in the heart of battle! There is but one safety to the vanquished – to hope not safety!" At this, their young valour was spurred to madness, and anon, like ravening wolves in a black mist, when hunger's lawless rage has driven them blindly forth and their deserted cubs await them with parching throats, we went through spears and spearmen to death indubitable, and held our way to the heart of the city, while sable Night hovered above us with overshadowing pinions. – What tongue shall unfold that night's havoc, that night's slaughter? what eye match our disasters with tears? An ancient city was falling, a queenly city for many years, and helpless frames lay without number, scattered in streets and homes and the hallowed precincts of Heaven. Nor was Troy alone amerced in blood: times there were when valour returned

to the hearts of the vanquished also, and the victorious Danaans
fell. Cruel woe was everywhere, everywhere terror, and death in
infinite shapes!

'First Androgeos, amid a great troop of attendant Greeks,
crossed our path – for he deemed in his ignorance that we were
allied bands! – and hailed us with friendly voice: 'Haste ye, warriors! What sluggishness hath held you thus late? Others harry
and sack a flaming Troy; and come ye but now from the tall
ships?" He said, and, on the instant (for, in truth, we made no
assuring answer), he was ware that he had fallen into the
enemy's midst. Aghast he checked word and foot: and as one,
who toils through a thorny brake, tramples, unthinking, a serpent upon the ground, and with sudden start shrinks before its
rising ire and puffed azure neck – even so Androgeos trembled
at our view and recoiled. Onward we rushed, amid the thick-
volleyed spears, and on all hands we cut them down; for they
knew not the place, and fear had seized them! Thus Fortune
smiled on our first assay.

'And here Coroebus, flushed with gallantry and success: "O my
friends," he cried, "where Fortune first points the way to salvation, and proves her gracious, there follow we! Let us change our
shields and assume the badges of Greece. Fraud or valour, who
shall ask, when his aim is the foe? Themselves they shall give us
arms!"

'He said, and, with the word, donned the waving helm of
Androgeos and the fair cognizance of his shield, and girt an
Argive blade to his side. Thus did Rhipeus, thus Dymas also, and
thus joyously did all our company, each accoutring himself in the
new-won spoils. Mingled with the Danaans we went, under the
favours of an alien Heaven, and many a battle we joined as we
charged in the blackness of night, and many a Greek we sent
below. Part scattered for the ships, and raced towards their faithful strand: part, in craven fear, scaled the giant horse again, and
hid them in the familiar womb.

'Alas, it boots not to trust in the gods, when the gods will not
be trusted! Behold Priam's daughter, maiden Cassandra, dragged
by her streaming tresses from the holies of Minerva's fane, lifting
her flaming eyes to the regardless heavens – her eyes, for manacles pinioned those tender hands! Coroebus, with soul infuriate,
brooked not the sight; but into their midmost array he flung him
to his death. We followed to a man, and closed with serried
battle. Here first we were whelmed under the javelins of our

countrymen from the temple's tall pinnacle, and a piteous carnage arose through the aspect of our harness and error engendered by our Grecian crests. Then, groaning and raging that the maiden should be reft them, the Danaans rallied from this hand and that, and made their onslaught – Ajax, fiercest far, Atreus' either son, and all the Dolopian host: as oft, when a hurricane bursts its bonds, the adverse winds give battle, West, and South, and East, exultant on the steeds of the Morn, and the forests shriek, while foaming Nereus rages, trident in hand, and wakes the waters from their nethermost deeps! All, furthermore, whom, in the dimness and darkness of night, we had routed by our guile and driven through the breadth of the city, appeared; and at once they knew our bucklers and lying arms, and marked the alien tones on our lips! Instant their numbers overbore us: and first Coroebus fell by the altars of the Queen of Battle under Peneleus' hand; with him Rhipeus bled – just above all in Troy, and most zealous for the right, but Heaven's thought was otherwise! Hypanis and Dymas died pierced by friendly spears: nor could all thy piety, Panthus, nor Apollo's garland, shield thee! – Ye ashes of Ilium, thou death-fire of my people, bear witness: when your star set, I shunned neither sword nor any peril, and, had Fate willed me to fall by a Grecian hand, I had merited to fall! We were plucked from the scene, Iphitus and Pelias with me – Iphitus already burdened with years, Pelias halting, withal, from Ulysses' brand. For the shouting urged us farther to Priam's palace.

'There, in truth, we saw a great slaughter, as though all the battles else nowhere had being and no man was dying in all the city: so grim the fray we beheld – Danaans streaming to the roof, and the threshold beset by the driven mantlet! Ladders were clinging to the walls, and by the very doorways men clambered up the rungs: with their left they opposed the protecting buckler to the missiles, with their right they grasped the battlements. The Dardans, on their part, tore up turrets and all the palace-roof. Thus armed – for they saw the end! – they prepared to defend themselves even in the extremity of death, and rolled down the gilded rafters, the stately ornaments of their father's old-world days! Others had beset the doorways below with naked steel, and held ward in serried array. Our spirits were quickened to save the dwelling of our king, to relieve the warriors by our succour, and to furnish force to the fainting.

'There was an entrance, a secret portal, a thoroughfare travelling Priam's halls, a postern-gate forlorn in the rear, by which the hapless Andromache, while the kingdom endured, would ofttimes take her way, companionless, to the parents of her spouse, and lead child Astyanax to his grandsire. I mounted to the roof's sloping summit, whence the doomed Teucrians were flinging their unavailing missiles. There a tower stood on a sheer descent, with its topmost coping built to the stars, whence erstwhile we could view all Troy, and the Danaan fleet, and the tents of Achaea. With iron we assailed its circumference, where the highest storey tottered at the joining, wrenched it from its aery eminence, and heaved it below. With sudden downfall, it crashed in thunderous ruin, and lit on the Grecian hosts far and wide. But others filled their place; nor, meanwhile, ceased the hail of stones and of weapons in every shape.

'Hard before the portal, on the threshold's verge, Pyrrhus raged exultant, flashing in arms and lucent bronze: as a serpent fed on poisonous herbage, whom the icy winter held swelling under earth, at last lifts his breast and rolls his smooth frame to the light, in the splendour of youth regained, slough cast off, head to the sun, and three-forked tongue flickering from his jaws! With him giant Periphas and armour-bearer Automedon, who drove the steeds of Achilles, – with him all the flower of Scyros pressed to the palace, and flung brands to the roof. Himself in their van, he snatched a twy-bill, and set him to shatter the stubborn doors and to unhinge the brass-bound posts: and anon he had cut through the planking, hewn out the solid oak, and broken a huge gaping breach. The inner palace stood plain, and the long halls opened on the view: the inner chambers of Priam and the kings of old stood plain, and they saw armed men on the threshold's verge!

'But, farther within, the house was a turmoil of moaning and woeful tumult, the vaulted rooms wailed with the lament of women, and the cry struck upon the golden stars. Fearful matrons were straying through the vast halls, clasping the doors in their embrace, and printing kisses upon them. With his father's fury Pyrrhus pressed on: not the bars, not the very guards, could abide the brunt: the gate reeled under the recurrent ram; and, wrenched from their hinges, the posts fell flat. Force found its way! The entrant Danaans hacked a passage, slew the foremost, and their soldiery thronged the spacious places: – more gentle the foaming river, when, barriers burst, it goes forth, overbears the opposing mounds in its tide, and rushes with infuriate mass on the fields, sweeping the cattle and the stalls of the cattle over every plain! These eyes saw Neoptolemus drunken from blood, and the twin sons of Atreus upon the threshold! Hecuba they saw, and her hundred daughters, and Priam amid the altars, befouling with his gore those fires himself had hallowed! Those fifty bridal-chambers, – fair hope of children's children, – regal with barbaric gold and the spoils of battle, were fallen to earth, and Greece was mistress where the flames spared!

'Perchance thou wouldst ask what was Priam's end. – When he saw the fall of his taken city, saw the doors of his palace shattered, and the foe midmost in his chambers, with aged hands bootlessly he set the harness, so long disused, about his time-palsied shoulders, girt him' with useless blade, and rushed to his death amid the horded foemen! In the central palace, under the naked cope of heaven, stood a massive altar, and at its side an ancient bay-tree, drooping over the altar and enfolding the Home-gods in its shade. Here, like doves driven headlong down by some gloomy tempest, Hecuba and her daughters sat vainly about the stones of sacrifice. But when she saw Priam's self arrayed in the armour of his youth, "My poor husband," she cried, "what unblest resolve has driven thee to assume these arms? or whither wilt thou rush? The hour calls not for such succour, nor such defenders: nay, not were my own Hector now with us! Come hither, late though it be: this altar will shield us all; or, dying, thou wilt die with us!" She said, and received the white-haired king to herself, and lodged him in the consecrated place.

'But, lo, escaped from the sword of Pyrrhus, came Polites, one of Priam's sons, fleeing through javelins and foes along the spacious colonnades; and bleeding he traversed the forlorn courts. In his rear, with imminent steel, followed the fiery Pyrrhus, and ever and anon his hand seemed to clutch him, and his spear was hard upon him. At length he issued before the eyes and visage of his parents, and fell with life streaming forth in torrents of blood. At this, Priam, though even then he sat in the midst of death, yet refrained him not, and curbed neither voice nor anger: "Nay," he cried, "if there be any righteousness in Heaven to regard such deeds, may the gods pay thee worthy thanks, and render thee due requital for this thy crime and the sin thou hast dared, who hast made me to see my son bleed before my face, and hast polluted a father's eyes with the sight of murder! But not he, of whom thou feignest thee begotten, – Achilles was not as thou when he dealt with Priam for foe: but he reverenced the suppliant's right and trust, he rendered Hector's bloodless clay to the sepulchre, and he sent me back to my kingdom!" Thus spoke the old king, and cast his warless spear, and wounded not: for the clanging bronze flung it back incontinent, and idly it hung from the buckler's unpierced boss. To him Pyrrhus: "Then shalt thou bear thy tale and go messenger to Peleus' son, my sire! And forget not to rehearse my bloody deeds and his degenerate Neoptolemus: now die!" Thus saying, he dragged him to the very altar-stones, trembling and slipping in the blood that gushed from his son, wreathed his left in his hair, with his right drew out the glittering sword, and plunged it to the hilt in his side. – Such the close of Priam's fortunes, such the allotted ending that took him off, seeing, as he went, Troy in flames and Troy-towers fallen, – who once ruled over Asia, proud in the kingship of so many a people and land. A great trunk he lay on the shore, a head torn from its shoulders, a body without a name!

'For me, then, as never before, a grim horror beset me. I stood aghast, and there rose before me the semblance of my dear sire, as I saw a king, old as he, gasping out his life under the pitiless stroke: Creüsa forlorn rose before me, my home despoiled, and my little Iulus left to fate! I turnéd and looked what force was about me. All had quitted me outworn, and cast themselves precipitate to earth, or delivered their weary limbs to the flames.

'And now I alone was left, when I descried Tyndareus' daughter, sheltered in the house of Vesta and crouching mute in the secret fane: for the glowing fires gave me light, as I wandered and swept my gaze on this hand and that over all. She – for her fears foreshewed Troy embittered for her fallen towers, the vengeance of Greece, and the wrath of the consort she fled – had hidden herself (common Fury of her motherland and ours!) and sate abominable by the altars. Fire blazed out in my soul, and passion came upon me, to avenge my falling country and exact the penalty of sin: "Shall this woman, forsooth, look unscathed on Sparta and her native Mycenae? and shall she go a queen in the triumph she has won, and behold her spouse and her father's house and her children, with a throng of Ilian matrons and Phrygian handmaidens in her train? And shall Priam have fallen by the sword? Shall Troy have burned with fire? Shall the Dardan strand so many a time have sweated blood? Not so! For though there be no memorable renown in a woman punished, and the victory yield not praise, yet shall I be lauded that I cut off villany and took retribution whence it was due: and joy it will be to have filled my soul with avenging fire and slaked the ashes of my people!"

'Thus I raved, and was swept onward with infuriate heart, when my gracious mother, never erst so bright to my eyes, offered herself to view, and in pure radiance flashed through the night – goddess confessed, in beauty and stature such as she uses to seem in Heaven. And she took me by the hand and checked me, and thus pursued from roseate lips: "My son, what fierce resentment rouses this ungoverned anger? Why thy frenzy? Or whither is fled thy care for us? Wilt thou not rather look where thou hast left Anchises thy father under his burden of years – look whether Creüsa thy wife remain to thee, and Ascanius thy son? Round them all, on this hand and that, range the battalions of Greece, and, did not my care stand ward, the flames already had reft them, and the enemy's sword devoured them! Not the loathed beauty of Spartan Helen, nor Paris, though all men blame him, but Heaven and Heaven's inclemency overthrow this wealth of power and lay Troy low from her pinnacles! Behold, for I will purge from thee all the cloud that is now drawn before thine eyes, blunting thy mortal vision and spreading dank and dim about thee – and fear not thou any behest of thy mother, nor be loth to do her command! – behold, where thou seest sundered masses, boulders torn from boulders, and smoke eddying amid columns of dust, there is Neptune, shaking the ramparts that his mighty trident hath loosened, and upheaving all the city from her base! Here Juno, sternest far, stands foremost by the Scaean Gate, and, steel-girt, calls in fury her confederate bands from the fleet. Even now Tritonian Pallas (turn but and see!) is stationed on the topmost towers, effulgent in frontlet and dread Gorgon. The great Sire himself bestows on Greece spirit and strength for victory: himself he rouses Heaven against the Dardanian battle! My son, secure thy flight, and set the seal to thy struggles: I will quit thee nowhere, and I will set thee in safety on thy father's threshold!" She said, and vanished in the dense shadows of night. Dire faces rose to view, and the high gods warring against Troy!

'Then, in truth, it seemed to me all Ilium was sinking into flames, and Neptune's town tottering from her foundations – even as when the straining husbandmen toil to uproot on the mountain-summits some ancient ash, hewn about with steel and many a stroke of their axes, and ever it threatens descent, and, all tremulous, nods the tresses on its shaking crown, till little by little the wounds overmaster it, and it groans its last, and, uptorn from the crag, comes down in ruin. I descended, and, Heaven my guide, passed through flames and foes: spears gave me place, and flames receded!

'And now, when I had reached the threshold of my father's house and our ancestral home, my sire – he for whom was my first longing, that I might take and bear him to the mountain-heights – he for whom was my first quest – refused to linger out his days or to endure in exile when Troy was cut down. "Ye," he said, "whose blood is young as your years, whose strength stands confirmed in its native power – compass ye your flight! For me, if those above had willed that I should live on, they had preserved me this abiding-place. Enough, and more, that I have once looked on destruction, and once lived through a taken city! Say farewell to this clay, laid as it is – as it is, I beseech you – and wend your way! My own hand shall find me death: the foe, in his mercy, will covet my spoils, and lightly can I lack a tomb! For long I have clogged the years, heaven-hated and useless, since that day when the Sire of gods and King of men breathed upon me with the wind of his thunderbolt and scathed me with his flame."

'Thus, persistent, he spoke, and stood by his resolve. We, in other sort, melted in tears – Creüsa, my wife, Ascanius, and all the household – that he, our father, would not ruin all with himself, nor lend his weight to the crushing burden of doom. But *nay* was all his word, and he was rooted to purpose and home! Again I rushed to battle, and in my misery made death my choice: for – counsel or chance – what now was left us? "Father, and didst thou deem I could desert thee and go forth? and did word so monstrous fall from my sire's lips? If it is the will of Heaven that nothing be left from so great a city – if this resolve is fixed in thy soul, and thy pleasure is to add thee and thine to the hecatomb of Troy – the door stands wide for the death thou cravest, and Pyrrhus will be here anon, fresh from the streaming gore of Priam – Pyrrhus, who slays the son before the face of the father, the father before the altar-stones! For this, gracious mother, didst thou bear me through sword and fire, that I might behold the foe in the heart of my home, and Ascanius, and my father, and Creüsa at their side, slaughtered each in the other's blood? Arms, my men – bring ye arms! Their last hour is calling the vanquished. Suffer me to revisit and restore the battle: never on this day shall we all bleed unavenged!"

'Straight I girded on my sword again, and was fitting my left into the buckler's clasp, in act to rush without; but, lo, on the threshold, my wife embraced my feet, and clung to me, holding little Iulus up to his father: "If thou departest to death, take us also with thee to whatever shall betide! But if, from trial made, thou restest somewhat of hope on the unsheathed blade, then first guard this house! To whom is little Iulus, to whom is thy sire – to whom am I, that was once called thy wife – abandoned?"

'Thus she cried, filling all the palace with lamentation, when a sudden portent arose, strange beyond speech. For, betwixt the hands and before the countenance of his woeful parents, behold, on the crown of Iulus' head a light crest of fire streamed and shone, its lambent flame flickering hurtless round his waving tresses and straying about his brows. Trembling with awe and fear, we strove to shake free his locks from the burning, and to quench the holy fire with water. But my father Anchises raised joy-lit eyes to the stars, and uplifted hand and voice to Heaven: "Jove omnipotent, if thou bowest to any prayer, look upon us (we ask no more!), and, if our piety hath merited, then grant us a presage, and confirm these signs!" Scarce had the old man spoken, when thunder pealed with sudden crash on the left, and a falling star shot with gleaming trail through the night amid a flood of radiance. We watched it gliding high over the palace-roof, and gilding its path through heaven, till it sank resplendent in the forests of Ida: the furrowed wake glittered through all its long line, and the region around reeked with sulphur. On this, in truth, my father was overcome, and, lifting himself towards the sky, addressed the gods and adored the hallowed star: "No longer, no longer, will I delay! Gods of my country, I follow, and, where ye lead, there am I! Preserve my home, preserve my grandson: yours is this omen, and on your godhead Troy rests! For me, I yield and refuse not, my son, to accompany thy flight."

'He ceased, and now the fire through the city was louder in our ears, and the flame rolled a nigher tide. "Then come, dear my father, place thyself on my neck! These shoulders shall hold thee up, nor will such burden oppress me. Let Fortune fall as she will, our peril shall be one and common, our salvation one for both! Little Iulus shall walk at my side, and my wife shall follow our steps at distance. And ye, my henchmen, lend ear to my words. As men go forth from the city, there is a mound and temple of old time to forlorn Ceres, and at its side stands an ancient cypress-tree, that the piety of our fathers hath guarded through many years. To this one station we shall come by diverse paths. Do thou, my sire, take the holy vessels in thy hand, and the Home-gods of our country. For me, who have come from battle so grim and am new from the shedding of blood, it were sin to touch them, till I have laved me in the living stream."

'Thus saying, I spread my broad shoulders and subject neck with the covering of a tawny lion's hide, and stooped beneath my burden. Little Iulus clung to my right, and followed his father with unmatched step, while my spouse came on behind. We travelled through the shadowy places, and I – whom erewhile no volleyed spears, nor Greece massed in fronting battle, could move – now trembled at every breeze, and started at every sound, unnerved and timorous alike for my companion and my burden!

'And now I was nearing the gates, and meseemed I had traversed all my journey, when suddenly a trampling of feet, as we deemed, broke upon our ears, and, peering through the dark, my sire cried: "My son, my son, flee! They draw nigh: I see the glitter of shields and the gleam of bronze." On this, in my bewilderment, some unfriendly power confounded and snatched away my judgement. For while I threaded the untrodden paths and departed from the highway's familiar line, alas, to crown my sorrow, Creüsa my wife was lost to me – whether, torn away by Fate, she halted, or wandered from the road, or sate her down in weariness, I know not – nor ever after was she restored to these eyes. And I looked not back to her who was gone, nor turned my thought to her, ere we had come to the mound of ancient Ceres and to her sacred dwelling: there, at length, when all were mustered, she alone was lacking and failed comrades, and son, and lord. Whom did my wild censure spare, whether of earth or heaven? What calamity more poignant did I behold in the fallen town? To the care of my friends I committed Ascanius, Anchises my father, and the gods of our Teucrian hearths, and hid them in a winding glade. Myself I sought the city once more and girt me in, flashing steel. My resolve stood fast: I would brave all perils anew, return through all Troy-town, and again set my life on the hazard.

'First I took my way to the battlements, and the dim portal of that gate through which I bent my departing steps, and with watchful eye scanned my footprints, as I traced them back through the gloom. Everywhere horror thrilled my soul, and the very silence was fraught with terror. Thence I repaired to my house: – perchance, perchance, she had turned her foot thither-ward! The Danaans had streamed within, and were thronging the halls from end to end. Incontinent the devouring fire rolled wind-fanned up to the topmost pinnacles: victory was with the flames, and the blazing tide raved to the skies. Onward I went, and once more sought Priam's home and the citadel. – And now, in the forlorn colonnades of Juno's sanctuary, chosen warders – Phoenix and curst Ulysses – stood guard over the prey. Thither from all hands they brought and upheaped the treasures of Troy, ravished from burning fanes – hallowed boards, bowls massive with gold, and captive vestments. About them, in long-drawn lines, stood boys and trembling matrons!

'Nay, I dared to send abroad my voice through the night and filled the streets with my cries; and, again and again, from the agony of my heart I called upon Creüsa, and echoed her name in vain.

'As I sought, and, in frenzy, ranged incessant amid the houses of Troy, a tearful vision – the shade of very Creüsa – appeared before my gaze, in semblance greater than I had known. I stood aghast; my hair rose, and my voice clove to my throat. Then so she began to speak, and with these words to assuage my sorrow: "What avails it, my dear lord, to yield indulgence thus great to thy madness of grief? This issue comes not save by the decree of Heaven: it were sin for thee to bear Creüsa hence at thy side, nor does he who reigns in Olympus above assent thereto. Thou shalt sail to long years of exile, thou shalt plough the vast floor of ocean, till thou come to the Western land, where, through the rich fields of a warrior-race, Lydian Tiber flows with his gentle stream. There happiness, and kingship, and a queenly bride, are prepared for thee. Bid thy tears for loved Creüsa be dry! I shall view not the proud seats of Myrmidon or Dolopian: I shall go not as handmaiden to any matron of Greece – I a daughter of Dardanus, I who was wedded to the seed of Venus! – but the great Mother of Heaven holds me with her in these climes. And now farewell, and cherish thy love for thy son and mine!"

'This said, she left me to my tears and the many words I would fain have spoken, and vanished into thin air. Thrice, then, I strove to throw my arms round her neck: thrice the form, that I clasped in vain, fled through my hands, light as the winds and fleet as the pinions of sleep. – Thus it was that, with night out-worn, I beheld my friends again.

'And there, admiring, I found that a vast company of new com-

rades had streamed to join us – matrons and men, a band mustered for exile, a melancholy folk! From all hands they were
come, ready with heart and wealth to seek any land soever,
whereto I would lead them over the main. And now the Morn-
ing-star was rising over the heights on Ida's crown and ushering
in the day, and the Grecian leaguer held the entry of every gate,
nor was any hope of succour vouchsafed us. I yielded the struggle, took up my sire, and journeyed to the mountains.

BOOK III

AFTER HEAVEN'S DECREE had brought low the fortunes of Asia
and Priam's guiltless people, after the pride of Ilium was fallen
and all Neptune's Troy smouldered in the dust, we were driven
by celestial warning in quest of distant exile and untenanted
realms: we built our fleet fast beneath Antandros and the hills of
Phrygian Ida, knowing not whither Fate was tending, nor where
haven should be granted us; and there we gathered our company.
Scarce had the first blush of Summer come, and father Anchises
was urging me to spread my sails to destiny, when tearfully I
quitted the shores and harbours of my country, and those plains
where Troy was once a city. An outcast I fared forth to the deep,
with my comrades and my son, my Home-gods and divinities of
power.

'Far away lies the War-god's land, and the peoples of its limitless plains (Thracians they who till them), where of yore fierce
Lycurgus reigned – bound to Troy by age-long kindness and fed-
erate worship, before our star was set. Thither I bore and
founded my earliest town on the winding strand, Destiny frowning on my emprize, and named its people by my name – the
Aeneadae.

' I was paying the holy rites to my mother, Dione's child, and
the rest of Heaven, that they might watch over the work begun,
and was standing on the beach in act to slay a shining bull to the
high King of gods. A mound, it chanced, stood nigh, on whose
summit rose cornel-shoots and a myrtle horrent with serried
shafts. I approached, and assayed to uproot the verdant growth
from its soil, that the leafy boughs might veil my altars, when a
sight of fear, passing speech, met my view. For, from the first
tree I uptore from its broken roots, trickled gouts of black blood
staining the earth with gore. A chill palsy shook my limbs, and

my frozen blood curdled with horror. Again I set myself to sunder a second reluctant bough and to probe the lurking mystery; and again from a second bark followed the crimson stream. With many a thought surging through my brain, I paid worship to the rural Nymphs and the sovereign Lord of Battle, warden of the Getic fields, that duly they would prosper this portent and lighten the heavy omen. But when, with greater effort, I assailed the third sapling, with knee pressed against the resisting sand – shall I speak or hold my peace? – a moan laden with tears reached me from the nethermost mound, and a speaking voice was borne to my ear: "Aeneas, why rendest thou this unhappy frame? Spare the sepultured at last: spare to pollute those dutiful hands! Troy bore me not an alien to thee, and not alien is the blood that flows from this stem! Alas, flee this land of cruelty; flee this shore of covetousness: for I am Polydorus! Here I lie transfixed, and a forest of steel has encased me and shot forth into trenchant javelins."

'Then, in truth, I stood aghast, my hesitant soul laden with dread: my hair rose, and my voice clove to my throat. This was the Polydorus, whom, in other days, unhappy Priam had secretly sent, with a vast weight of gold, to be nurtured by the Thracian king, what time he began to distrust the Dardan battle, and saw his city beleaguered. He, so soon as Troy's might was shattered and her fortune departed, followed the star of Agamemnon and his victorious powers, severed all sacred ties, slew Polydorus, and laid violent hand on the treasure. O cursed lust of gold, to what canst thou not compel the heart of man!

'When the terror had quitted my breast, I revealed the celestial portent to the chosen princes of the people, and to my sire before all, and besought their counsel. In all there was but one mind: that we should depart from this sin-stained land, abandon this slaughter-house of guests, and admit the breeze to our sails. Therefore we paid new obsequies to Polydorus, heaped earth upon his mound, and raised altars to his ghost, all mournful in dark fillets and gloomy cypresses; while about them stood the daughters of Ilium, their tresses unloosed, as ritual ordains. We brought to him bowls that foamed with warm milk, and cups of sacrificial blood, laid his spirit in its sepulchre, and called him with the last loud cry.

'Then, so soon as there was faith in the deep, and the winds had lulled the waters, and the gently rustling South called us to the main, my comrades launched our vessels and thronged the strand. Forth from the harbour we voyaged, and lands and cities grew dim.

'There is a sacred country lies in mid-ocean, beloved by the Nereids' mother and Neptune the Aegean's lord, which the dutiful Archer-god, as it strayed round coasts and shores, chained from high Myconos and Gyarus, and granted that it should be a habitation unmoved and should contemn the gales. Thither I bore; and in all peace the island welcomed our weariness in sure haven. Landing, we paid our homage to the city of Apollo. King Anius – king alike over men, and priest of Phoebus – his brows bound with fillet and hallowed laurel, moved to greet us, and in Anchises owned an old-time friend. Host and guest, we clasped hand in hand, and entered his abode.

'In act of worship, I stood before the temple and its venerable stone: "God of Thymbra," I cried, "grant us a home that shall endure, grant the weary their walls, a nation, and an abiding city! Preserve these nascent towers of Troy – these relics of a conquering Greece and a stern Achilles! Who shall be our guide? Whither wilt thou that we go? Where wilt thou that we fix our seat? O father, vouchsafe a sign, and let thy presence fill our souls!"

'Scarce had the words left my lips, when on the instant all things seemed to quiver, the portals and the laurels of the god, and all the hill about shook, and the tripod moaned from the opened shrine. Prone we sank to earth, and a voice was borne to our ears: "Ye stout sons of Dardanus, the land that first bore you from the stock of your sires – that land shall receive your returning feet on its fruitful soil. Seek ye your mother of old. There the house of Aeneas shall be lord over all climes, and his children's children, and they that shall be born of them!"

'Thus Phoebus, and a wild and tumultuous joy sprang up in our hearts: and all men asked, where was the promised city, whither Apollo called the wanderers and bade them return! Then my father, pondering the legends of old-world men: "Hear," he cried, "ye princes, and know your hopes! In the mid-seas lies an island, Crete, the home of great Jove, where mount Ida stands, and the cradle of our race. There men dwell in a hundred proud cities – a realm most fruitful – and thence Teucer, our first sire, if I recall the tale aright, sailed in the beginning to the Rhoetean shores and chose a place for his kingdom. For not yet had Ilium and the towers of Pergamus arisen, but they dwelt in the lowly valleys. Thence came the Mother, who tenants Cybele, and the

Corybants with their cymbals, and the grove of Ida: thence the mysteries' faithful silence, and the yoked lions stooping under the chariot of their Queen. Then come, and, where the behest of Heaven leads, there let us follow. Let us appease the winds, and seek the kingdoms of Gnosus! They are distant no long course: let but Jove be with us, and the third dawn shall see our fleet on the Cretan strand!" He said, and offered due sacrifice on the altars – a bull to Neptune, a bull to thee, fair Apollo; a black lamb to the Storm, a white lamb to the favouring Zephyrs.

'A bruit went forth, that Prince Idomeneus had fled an exile from the realm of his fathers, that the shores of Crete were forsaken, its dwellings void of foes, and an abode standing tenantless to our hand. We left the havens of Ortygia, and flew over the main, – left Naxos and its bacchante-haunted peaks, green Donysa, Olearos, glittering Paros, and the Cyclades strewn along the deep, and threaded those seas, gemmed with so many an isle. The cry of the sailors rang clear, as they strove in their changing tasks, and my comrades' burden was ever: *Onward to Crete and our forefathers!* A breeze, freshening from the stern, followed us as we went, and at last we rode by the Curetes' immemorial shores.

'Eagerly, then, I built the walls of my chosen city, called it Pergamea, and bade my people, who joyed in their title, love their hearths and rear the high-coped towers. And now the work was almost done: the fleet was beached on the dry strand, wedlock and their new-won domains claimed the care of our youth, and I was assigning laws and dwellings, when suddenly the expanse of heaven was tainted and a wasting malady lighted on the limbs of men, a piteous blight on tree and crop, and a season of death. Part resigned the sweet breath of life, part still wearily dragged their plague-stricken frames: soon the Dog-star was burning the fruitless fields, the grass was athirst, and the sickening corn denied its sustenance. Back to Ortygia's shrine over the remeasured main, was my father's counsel, there to implore grace from Phoebus, and seek what bourne he designed to our languid fortunes, what succour he would bid us assay to our suffering, – whither he would have us bend our course!

'It was night, and sleep possessed all creatures that breathe upon earth, when the holy images and the gods of our Phrygian homes, whom I had borne forth with me from Troy, out of the heart of the flaming town, seemed, as I lay in slumber, to rise before my vision – radiant in the flooding light, where the full-orbed moon streamed through the inset windows. Then thus they began to speak, and with this utterance to assuage my sorrow: "What Apollo shall tell thee when thou hast voyaged to Delos, he revealeth here; and, lo, he hath sent us unsought to thy threshold! We who have followed thee and thy arms, since our Dardan realm sank in flame, we who under thy ward have gone down to the swelling deep in ships – we shall exalt to the stars thy children hereafter, and we shall bestow empire upon their city. Do thou but build great walls for the great, and abandon not thy long labour of exile! Change thine abode: not these the shores of Delian Apollo's counsel: not Crete the land where he bade thee rest! There is a region that Greece styles Hesperia – a country of old time, strong in battle and of fruitful breast. Oenotrians were they that held it: now, fame tells, a new generation has named the people with the name of their leader – *Italy*. There is our abiding-place: thence sprang Dardanus and father Iasius, from whom our race descends. Tarry not, but rise, and in gladness of heart rehearse this our message indubitable to thy grey-headed sire: that he seek Cortona and the Ausonian soil. Jove denies thee the fields of Crete!"

'Amazed at such vision, amazed at the celestial voice – for it was no sleep, but meseemed I knew their countenance before my countenance, their locks fillet-crowned, and their visage in very presence, and a cold sweat streamed over all my frame – I leapt from my couch, raised voice and hand to heaven, and poured on the hearth my pure libation. This sacrifice rendered, gladly I bore my message to Anchises, and expounded the tale in order. He avouched our doubtful descent and our twofold ancestry, and owned that those ancient lands had enmeshed him in novel error! Then he spoke: "My son, who hast wrestled so long with Troy's destiny, Cassandra, and none else, foretold me this fortune. For now I remember, she shewed this fate in store for our race; and oft she called on Hesperia, and oft on the kingdoms of Italy. But who should believe that Teucer's people would visit the Hesperian strand? or whom, in those days, could Cassandra among the prophets move? Come, yield we to Phoebus, and follow, at his warning, a wiser course!"

'He said; and rejoicing we all obeyed his word. Once more we resigned our home, and, leaving a remnant, set sail and sped over the great deep in our hollow barques.

'Our fleet had made the high seas, and no land more met the view, but everywhere the sky, and everywhere the main, when a gloomy cloud halted overhead, fraught with night and tempest, and ocean was ruffled by the dark. Straight the winds rolled up the flood, the great waves arose, and we were scattered and flung over the waste of waters. Clouds invested the day, the drenched night blotted out the heavens, and the recurrent levin leapt from its bursting womb. Driven from our course, we staggered through the viewless waters. Palinurus' self avowed that he knew neither day nor night in the firmament, nor could read his path in the mid brine. Three full days, that we knew not from night in the blinding mist, we wandered over the foam, and as many nights with never a star. Only with the fourth dawn we saw land rise at last, revealing hills in the distance and sending up wreaths of smoke. Our sails dropped down; we rose to the oars, and, unlingering, the seamen bent to their toil, scattering the spray and sweeping the blue.

'Delivered from the wave, I found my first welcome on the shores of the Strophads – Strophads they are named by Greece, islands standing in the broad Ionian sea, wherein dwells dire Celaeno with her sisterhood of Harpies, since the day when the house of Phineus was shut against them, and they fled afraid from their wonted boards. Fellest of abominations, no fiercer plague, minister of Heaven's vengeance, ever lifted head from the Stygian stream. Birds they are, virginal of countenance, foul-bellied, claw-handed, pinched always by the pallor of hunger.

'Thither borne, we entered the harbour; and, lo, we beheld fair herds of kine studding the plains, and bearded flocks warderless along the green. Steel in hand, we assailed them, and called the gods, with Jove himself, to part and lot in the spoil; then, on the winding beach, piled couches, and feasted on the bountiful fare. But, with sudden swoop and horrible, the Harpies were upon us from the hills, their beating wings clanging loud: they plundered our banquet, befouled all with unclean touch, and their ghastly screech was heard amid the noisome stench. Once more, in a long recess under a hollow cliff, we decked our boards and restored the flame to the altars: once more, from a quarter diverse of heaven, the noisy rout issued from ambush, – their talons hovering above the prey, their lips defiling the feast. Then I called to my comrades to take arms, and war on the accursed tribe. As I said, so they did: – laid their swords in the covering grass, and hid their shields from the view. Thus, when the foe descended, shrieking along the sinuous shore, Misenus, obser-vant from a tall cliff, sounded the alarm on brazen horn. On rushed our band, and assayed the strange fray – to mar with the steel those obscene fowls of ocean. But their plumes foiled our strength, their frames our wounds, and incontinent they soared in flight to the skies, leaving their part-devoured prey and revolting trail. Alone Celaeno, prophetess of evil, lit on a skyey crag, and thus the words broke from her soul: "War, even for slain oxen and butchered steers, – war prepare ye to wage (true seed of Laomedon!) and to banish the guiltless Harpies from their native kingdom? Then hear this my saying, and let it sink into your souls: What the Father omnipotent foretold to Phoebus, and Phoebus Apollo to me, that do I, eldest of the Furies, reveal to you. That ye may reach Italy ye sail the seas and ye invoke the winds. To Italy ye shall go, and ye shall enter her havens: but never shall ye wall the promised city, till the curse of hunger and the sin of your onslaught on us shall constrain you to grind with your teeth your half-eaten boards!" She said, and on fugitive pinion soared again to the woods. For my comrades, their blood froze with the chill of sudden terror; their spirits fell, and they urged me no more to seek peace at point of sword, but by vows and prayers. And father Anchises, his palms outstretched from the shore, called upon sovereign Heaven, and enjoined meet sacrifice: "Ye gods, thwart their menace; avert such disaster, and of your grace preserve the pious!" He ceased, and bade sunder the rope from the strand and shake loose the sheets. The South swelled our sails, and we sped over the foaming waves, whither wind and steersman called our course. And now, in the midmost flood, tree-crowned Zacynthus rose to view, and Dulichium, and Samê, and Neritus, craggy and tall. We fled the rocks of Ithaca, where Laertes reigned, and cursed the region that fostered pitiless Ulysses. Soon the cloud-capped peaks of Mount Leucata opened on our sight, and their Apollo, the mariner's dread; to whose shrine we sailed outworn, and came to a little city. Anchor was flung from prow, and our barques stood ranged on the beach.

'Thus, our feet at length on unhoped soil, we purified ourselves in honour of Jove, lit the altars with votive fires, and made merry the Actian strand with our Ilian games. Stripped and sleek with oil, my men plied their country's wrestling: and there was joy in the thought that scatheless we had passed so many a city of Greece, and had won our way through the heart of the foe.

'Meanwhile the sun circled the great year, and icy Winter began to ruffle the waves under his northern blasts. A buckler of hollow bronze, borne once by giant Abas, I nailed to the fronting doors, with a verse to note my deed – *These arms Aeneas from victorious Greece* – then bade my comrades quit the haven and seat themselves on the thwarts. Zealously they smote the main, and swept the watery level: and anon the towering Phaeacian hills were vanished, and we skirted the shores of Epirus, entered the Chaonian harbour, and drew to Buthrotum's high city.

'There a tale, surpassing credence, assailed our ears: – how Helenus, Priam's son, reigned over Grecian towns, lord of Aeacian Pyrrhus' bride and sceptre, and Andromache had passed again to a compatriot spouse! I was lost in amaze, and my heart burned with strange yearning to win speech of my friend and knowledge of this mysterious chance. Leaving fleet and shore behind, I went forth from the haven, at the hour, as it fell, when, in a great grove before the town, by the wave of a counterfeit Simoïs, Andromache was offering the wonted feast and her libation of sorrow to dust and ashes, calling on the dead by Hector's grave, – a tenantless mound of green turf that she had consecrated to him with two altars, to her a well-spring of tears. When she descried my coming, and, distraught, saw Trojan steel about her, fear-stricken at the marvellous vision, she froze in mid gaze, and the warmth forsook her limbs. Swooning she sank, and hardly, at long last, spoke: "A veritable form – a veritable messenger – dost thou come to me, goddess-born? Livest thou? Or, if the kindly light hath left thee, where is Hector?" She said, and melted in tears, and her wailing filled all the place around. To her frenzy of sorrow scarce I made brief response, and, confused, unlocked my lips in broken accents: "I live indeed, and draw out my life through all extremity of evil. Forbear to doubt: thy vision belies thee not! Alas, what estate receives thee, fallen from such a spouse? or what fortune, meet for her, smiles once more on Hector's Andromache? Bride of Pyrrhus endurest thou yet?" She cast down her eyes, and answered with faint voice: "O happy, sole above all, Priam's virgin daughter, whom they doomed to die by her foeman's grave under the towers of Troy, – who bare not the lot's arbitrament, nor, captive, knew the couch of a tyrant conqueror! We sailed over distant seas from the ashes of our country: in servitude and motherhood, we bowed to the insolence of youth and the pride of Achilles' seed; till, suitor for a Spartan bridal, he turned to Leda's Hermione, and passed me to Helenus, – slave mated with slave. But him Orestes, aflame for his stolen bride and goaded by the Furies of his guilt, ambushed and slew by his father's altar. Pyrrhus dead, part of his realm duly fell to Helenus, who named these plains *Chaonian*, and *Chaonia* all the land, from Chaon of Troy; and Pergamus is this Ilian tower that he has set upon the cliff. But thou – what winds, what fates, have wafted thy course? or what god has driven thee unknowing to our shores? What of child Ascanius, whom to thee erstwhile at Troy. . . . ? Lives he yet? Breathes he yet the upper air? Aeneas and Hector – sire and uncle – do their names spur him to the valour of his line and the spirit of manhood?" Thus her words flowed and her tears fell; and ever and again she broke into long agonies of weeping, when, lo, from the city-walls came hero Helenus, Priam's son, amid a great retinue, and knew us for his countrymen, and gladly led us to the palace, with eyes streaming at every word.

'On I went, and saw a little Troy, a Pergamus mimicking the great, and a waterless brook styled Xanthus, and embraced the portals of a Scaean gate. Nor meanwhile had my Teucrians less joy of their sister city. The king gave them welcome in his ample colonnades: goblet in hand, they made libation of wine in the central hall, and the feast was set on gold.

'And now a day, and a second day were sped; the breezes wooed our sails, and our canvass was big with the swelling South, when thus questioning I bespoke the seer: "Thou son of Troy, interpreter of god to man, who art cognizant of Phoebus' power, of the tripods and the bays of Claros' lord, who readest the stars, and the speech of birds, and the message of their presaging wing, speak, I prithee, – for fair was every voice of Heaven that declared my course, and every god gave celestial counsel, that I seek Italy and assay her distant shores; alone the Harpy Celaeno forebodes a strange portent unutterable, and denounces the terrors of vengeance and the horrors of famine, – speak and say: What perils first shall I shun? or what guidance shall avail me to cope with labours thus arduous?" Then Helenus first implored the peace of Heaven with ritual sacrifice of steers, loosed the fillets of his consecrated brows, and himself led me by the hand, thrilled with the presence of deity, to those portals, Phoebus, of thine: then, from his priestly lips, spoke inspired:

' "Goddess-born, clear is the warrant that under auspices most high thou sailest the flood: for thus it is that the King of gods allots the fates and ordains their succession, and thus the cycle revolves. Few things, therefore, out of many, my word shall reveal to thee, that so with the greater safety thou mayest traverse the stranger seas and find rest in Ausonia's haven. What remains the Sisters forbid Helenus to know, and Saturnian Juno seals his lips. And, first, that Italy, which even now in ignorance thou deemest at hand, thinking to enter a neighbouring port, a far path and pathless estranges from these our far realms. Your oars shall be bent in the Sicilian wave, your barques shall traverse the floor of the Ausonian main, and view the ghostly lake and the isle of Aeaean Circe, ere it be thine to build a sure city in a safe land. I will give thee tokens, and hold thou them treasured in thy mind: When, in an hour of trouble, thou shalt find by the waters of a sequestered stream a huge sow recumbent under the holms by the river's brim, with a litter of thirty heads, – white as she reclines on earth, and white the young at her teats, – there shall be the site of thy town, there shall thy travailings surely cease. And fear not the boards whereat ye shall gnaw: the Fates will find a way, and Apollo come to your call. But these lands, and the strip of Italian shore laved by the tides of our sea, shun thou: not a city but is habited by our enemies of Greece! There the Locrians of Naryx have built their ramparts, and Lyctian Idomeneus beset the Sallentine plains with spearmen: there is the seat of Philoctetes, Meliboea's prince, – little Petelia leaning on her wall. More, when thy fleet shall have made its passage across the waters and come to station, and, altars raised, thou payest thy vows on the strand, veil thy locks in covering of a purple cloak, that no hostile form may break upon the holy fires, in the worship of Heaven, and trouble the omens. This mode of sacrifice observe both thou and thy comrades, and by this rite let thy children's children devoutly abide. But when, on departure, the gales shall waft thee to the shore of Sicily, and the straits of narrow Pelorus broaden on the view, then seek – long though the circuit – the land on thy left and the seas on thy left, but eschew the coast to the right and its waters. These regions, men tell, in other days sprang asunder, convulsed with violent ruin and vast, though then either land was one and continuous: thus puissant for change are the ageing centuries! The main came surging between: its waves severed Hesperia's strand from Sicily's; and betwixt fields and cities, apart on confronting coasts, it flowed with narrow tide. Scylla guards the right: on the left is insatiate Charybdis; and thrice, day by day, in the lowest eddies of her abysm, she sucks the mountainous billows sheer down, and disgorges them alternating to the light, scourging the stars with spray. But Scylla a cavern confines in viewless ambush, whence oft she darts forth her mouths, and draws ships upon her crags. Above she wears a human face, to her waist a maiden with beauteous breast: below she is an ocean-monster, with dolphin-tails linked to her wolf-encircled belly. Better, lingering, to make Trinacrian Pachynus thy goal, and round it to bend thy winding course, than once to have looked on grisly Scylla in her drear cave, and those cliffs echoing to her sea-hounds' bay! Farther, if any foresight dwell in Helenus, if any credence be due to his seerdom, if Apollo fill his mind with truth, one charge, o Goddess-born, – one charge in lieu of all, – I will lay upon thee, and again, and yet again, admonish thee: To sovereign Juno's divinity let thy first prayers ascend, to Juno chant thy willing prayers, and overcome her imperial soul by thy suppliant offerings! This do, and at length thou shalt quit Trinacria, the victory won, and gain the confines of Italy. And when, thither voyaged, thou shalt approach the Cymaean walls, and the mystic lakes, and Avernus, loud with murmuring forests, thou shalt behold the frenzied prophetess, who sings the behests of Fate deep beneath her crag and commits to leaves the written word. And every prophetic verse that the maid inscribes thereon she ranges in due succession and leaves secluded in her cavern. Motionless they hold their station, and quit not their sequence: but when, on turning of the hinge, a breath of air has lit upon them, and the swinging door disturbed their light foliage, never more has she care to capture them as they flit through her cavern, nor to restore their ranks, nor to order her songs; but the questioner departs unanswered and curses the Sibyl's shrine. Count not thou the hours there lavished over-precious, – though thy comrades murmur, though the voyage urge thy sails to the main, and occasion be thine to fill thy sheets with a fair breeze, – but approach the prophetess and entreat her oracles with prayer, that herself she will utter her presages, and deign to unclose her lips in speech. She will reveal to thee the peoples of Italy, and the wars that shall be, and how thou mayest flee or abide each trial; and, duly besought, she will grant thee a favouring course. – Such the warnings that this voice of mine may give thee. Go thou, and let thy prowess exalt Troy in might to the stars!"

'When the seer's kindly lips had so spoken, next he commanded that gifts, ponderous with gold and carven ivory, should be borne to the ships, and burdened our holds with massive silver and caldrons of Dodona, – a hauberk, of linked mail and triple tissue of gold, and a casque with cone and waving plume, accoutrement once of Neoptolemus. My sire, also, had guerdons of his own. He gave us steeds, and he gave us guides: he completed the tale of our rowers, and my crews he equipped with arms.

'Meanwhile Anchises was bidding us hoist sail on the fleet, that the fair-blowing wind might not meet delay. Whom thus, with all reverence, the minister of Phoebus bespoke: "Anchises, – thou who wast honoured by Venus' high wedlock, thou the care of Heaven, the twice rescued from a fallen Troy, – behold Ausonia's land! Let thy sails hasten to possession! Yet this shore it behoves thee to skirt and quit not the wave; that region of Italy is afar, which Apollo reveals. Go"; he said, "blest in thy son's love! Why proceed my words, and impede the freshening breezes?"

'Nor less Andromache, all in sorrow for our last parting, brought robes figured with embroidery of gold, and a Phrygian mantle – equal its splendour! – for Ascanius; loaded him with presents from her loom, and so spoke: "Receive these also, child, that they may be memorials of my hands to thee and bear witness to the undying love of Andromache, Hector's wife! Take the last gifts of thy kindred, o thou the sole semblance that is left me of my Astyanax! Such were his eyes, such his hands, such his mien; and now in like years he would be growing with thee to manhood!"

'With welling tears, I addressed them in act to go: "Live and be happy: the course of your fortune is run, while we are summoned from fate to fate! Ye have won your peace: ye have no watery plains to cleave; ye have no Ausonian fields, ever vanishing, to seek. Your eyes look on a mimic Xanthus, and a Troy that your hands have builded, – builded, my prayer is, under kindlier auspices, and better shielded from Greece! If ever I shall enter Tiber, and the plains that verge on Tiber, and behold the walls promised to my people, thereafter, from our kindred cities and neighbouring nations, Epirot and Hesperian, – who share a common author in Dardanus and a common lot, – we will fashion one Troy single-souled: and may that care await our children!"

'Onward along the deep we fared past the nigh Ceraunian cliffs, whence the way leads to Italy and the voyage is briefest across the foam. Meantime the sun fell, and the shadows darkened on the hills. So soon as the lot had chosen who should abide by the oars, we laid us down by the waves, on the breast of the welcome earth, and all along the waterless strand rested our frames, while the dews of sleep sprinkled the limbs of the weary. Nor yet had Night, driven by the Hours, ascended to her mid sphere, when Palinurus, undelaying, started from his couch and explored every breeze, and listened to every breath of air. All the stars he observed, that floated in the silent firmament, – Arcturus, and the rainy Hyads, and the twin Bears, – and he gazed on Orion in his panoply of gold. When he saw that all was calm in the cloudless sky, he sounded his clear signal-note from the stern: we removed our camp, assayed our journey, and unfurled the winged sails.

'And now the stars were fled, and the Dawn rose blushing, when we descried the dim, distant hills and lowly coast of Italy. *Italy*, Achates cried the foremost: *Italy*, the crews shouted in joyful acclaim. Then father Anchises wreathed a mighty bowl in a chaplet, filled it with wine, and called upon Heaven, as he stood aloft on the poop: "Ye gods of ocean and earth, ye lords of the tempest, send us a smooth voyage before the wind, and breathe on us with gracious breath!" The gales freshened to his prayer: the haven, closer now, opened clear to our gaze, and we saw a shrine to Minerva on the cliff. The mariners furled sail, and turned their stems to the strand. There a roadstead sweeps curving from the eastern wave in semblance of a bow: invisible itself, before it stand rocks foaming with salt spray, while turreted crags stretch arms of stone like a double wall to the beach, and the temple recedes from the sea. Here, for our first omen, I saw four coursers on the sward, browsing at large through the plain, all white as the snow. Then Anchises my sire: "War, o stranger land, is thy offering: for war is the steed armed, and war these steeds menace! Yet the same four-footed kind is wont, in time, to stoop to the chariot and to bear yoke and bit in concord: hope there is of peace also!" Then we prayed to the sacred power of steel-clashing Pallas, who first had received us in triumph, veiled our heads before her altars in Phrygian cloak, and, obedient to the precepts of Helenus, that he gave expressly, kindled duly the sacrifice prescribed to Argive Juno. Without delay, so soon as our vows were paid in order, seaward we turned the horns of our canvass-spread yards, and quitted the dwellings of the children of Greece and their mistrusted soil. Next we descried the bay of Tarentum – Hercules' town, if Fame speaks truth – while over against it rose the goddess of Lacinium, and the hills of Caulon, and Scylaceum, the home of shipwreck. Soon, on the horizon, Sicilian Aetna appeared towering above the flood, and we heard from far the giant moaning of ocean, the crags sea-scourged, and broken murmurings along the beach, as the waters leapt up and the surf embroiled the sands. Then father Anchises: "Surely here is Charybdis: these are the cliffs, these the awful rocks of Helenus' burden! Save yourselves, comrades, and rise in unison to your oars!" As he commanded, so they did, and foremost Palinurus turned his griding prow to the waters on the left; and to the left swung all our company under stress of oar and sail. On the crested billows we were tossed to the skies, and again, with the receding wave, we sank to the Shades beneath. Thrice the cliffs roared among their rocky caverns, and thrice we saw the foam upheaved and the stars bedewed with spray.

'Meanwhile breeze and sun abandoned our weariness, and, in ignorance of the course, we drifted to the Cyclops' shores. There a haven lies, unapproached and unshaken by the winds, and spacious indeed: but hard at hand Aetna thunders with hideous ruin, and now hurls skyward dark clouds, fuming with pitchy tempest and white embers, and uplifts globes of lambent flame flickering to the stars, – now belches aloft rocks and her mountain-entrails uptorn, flings, moaning, to day masses of molten boulders, and seethes up from her uttermost deeps. Under that pile, Fame tells, lies whelmed the frame of Enceladus, scathed by the thunderbolt, while vast Aetna, set above him, breathes fire from her bursting furnaces; and – oft as he turns his weary side – all Sicily trembles and murmurs, and the heavens are veiled in smoke. All night long we lay under shrouding forests, enduring those dread portents, nor beheld the cause of the sound. For the stars had kindled not their lamps, and the pole shone not with its empyreal lights, but clouds lowered over a sable sky, and midnight prisoned the moon in mist.

'And now the second day was rising with renascent morn, and Aurora had withdrawn the weeping shades from the firmament, when suddenly from the woods there issued the strange form of an unknown man, lean with the extremity of famine, and piteously clad; and, suppliant, he stretched his palms to the shore. We turned to gaze. His squalor was foul, his beard hung down, and thorns clasped his vesture; yet in all else he was a Greek, and once he had sailed with his country's battle to Troy! When he saw from afar our Dardan habit and Trojan harness, for a while, fear-stricken at such sight, he stood rooted to earth and checked his step, then rushed precipitate to the strand, weeping and praying: "By the stars, by the gods, and by this light of heaven that ye breathe, I adjure you, Teucrians, – receive me! Take me to any land soever: it will suffice. I know that I am one from the Danaan fleet: I own that I bore sword against your Ilian hearths. For which – if so black be the guilt of my crime – scatter my limbs to the waves, and sink me in the unfathomed deep. If I die, it will be good to die by the hand of man!"

'He ceased, and clung to us, clasping our knees, and prone at our knees. We bade him declare his name, the lineage whence he was sprung, and to reveal what malice of fortune had pursued him since then. My father Anchises delayed not long, ere he proffered his hand to the youth, and reassured him by that potent pledge. He, his terror at length assuaged, thus began:

' "I am a henchman of Ulysses, the evil starred, – Ithaca my country, Achaemenides my name, – and I sailed for Troy from the poverty of Adamastus my sire. And oh that my fortune had so remained! Here, while hastily they fled from that merciless threshold, my comrades, oblivious, abandoned me in the vast Cyclopian cave – a house of blood and murderous feastings, sunless within and immeasurable. Its giant lord towers to the stars – may Heaven sweep that scourge from earth! – and no eye may lightly behold him, nor any tongue accost him. His food is the flesh and black gore of miserable men. Myself I saw how, supine in the heart of his den, he seized in huge hand two of our number, and broke them upon the rocks till the crimsoned floor swam in blood: I saw how he champed their members, streaming with red corruption, while the warm flesh quivered under his teeth. Yet not without requital! Ulysses brooked not that deed; and, in the extremity of evil, the Ithacan was still himself! For when, satiate with feasting and buried in drunkenness, he pillowed his drooping neck and lay along the cavern in monstrous length, disgorging in his slumbers foul humours and gobbets of meat commingled with blood and wine, we prayed to high Heaven and allotted each man his office; then from every hand streamed upon him, one and all, and with pointed weapon pierced the eye that lurked, single and enormous, under his stern brow, like buckler of Argos or orb of Phoebus! And thus, in the end, we avenged in triumph the spirits of our companions. – But flee, ye unhappy band, – flee and sunder cable from strand! For in fierceness and stature like to Polyphemus, as he pens the fleecy herds in the hollows of his cavern and drains their udders, dwell a hundred more of the accursed Cyclopian kind, scattered here and there by this sinuous beach or roaming the mountain-tops. The third crescent of the moon is already filling with radi-ance, and I still drag out my days in the forests amid forlorn lairs and dwellings of wild beasts, scanning from a cliff the towering Cyclops, and trembling at their voice and the sound of their feet. The boughs yield me a sorry sustenance of berries, and stony cornels and uprooted herbs are my food. Though I watched all, not till now I beheld this fleet drawing to the shore, and to this – prove what it might! – I devoted myself. Enough to have fled that godless race! Destroy ye this life – better so! – by what death soever ye will!"

'Scarce had he spoken, when we saw, on the mountain-summit, shepherd Polyphemus himself, moving in huge bulk and tending to the familiar strand, – a monster fearful and hideous, vast and eyeless. A pine-trunk governed his hand and strength-ened his step, and with him his fleecy ewes, – sole joy and solace they of his ill! So soon as he touched the deep waves and was come to ocean, he laved therein the blood streaming from his gouged eye, and strode through the flood, now at mid tide; nor yet had the billows wetted his giant flanks. With the eager-ness of fear, we hastened our flight far thence, received the sup-pliant who had merited so, and in silence severed the cable; then, prone, swept the main with emulous oar. He heard, and turned his foot toward the sound of the signal. But when power was denied him to lay hand on us, and his pursuit availed not to cope with the Ionian rollers, he lifted his voice in a mighty cry, at which the deep and all its waves shook, and Italy trembled to the heart, and Aetna moaned in her winding caverns. But the Cyclopian brood rushed at his summons from the woods and tall hills down to the haven, and thronged the shores. There we saw the Aetnean brotherhood – with eyes glaring and heads aloft to the skies – standing in vain, a conclave of fear: – even so stand heaven-challenging oaks on some mountain peak, or cone-bear-ing cypresses – a towering forest to Jove, or a grove to Dian. The spurs of dread urged my comrades headlong to fling the sheets loose for any course soever, and to fill their canvass with the ear-liest breeze that offered. On the other hand, the command of Helenus warned them that they should hold not their way betwixt Scylla and Charybdis – where the passage betwixt either lay a hand's breadth removed from death. Thus our resolve was taken to set sail back once more, when, lo, the North came blow-ing from the straits of Pelorus! Past Pantagia's mouth and its living rock, past the Megarian gulf and lowly Thapsus, I voyaged, while Achaemenides, hench-man of Ulysses the evil-starred, pointed each coast, as returning he skirted again the region of his wanderings.

'Stretched before the Sicanian bay lies an island, fronting wave-beat Plemmyrium, – Ortygia styled by an earlier race. Thither, as Fame witnesses, Alpheus, Elis' stream, won his secret way under the foam, and now at the lips, Arethusa, of thy fountain, mingles with the Sicilian wave. So commanded, we paid our homage to the high powers of the place, and thence I passed the bountiful soil of stagnant Helorus. Anon we grazed the tall cliffs and beetling rocks of Pachynus, and far away Camarina – by behest of Fate, unstirred for ever – rose before our eyes, with the plains of Gela, and great Gela herself, named with the name of her stream. Soon the steep of Acragas – sire of gallant steeds in the years to come! – revealed its stately walls in the distance. And thee, palm-crowned Selinus, I left with a heaven-sent breeze, and skirted the Lilybaean shallows and the perils of their ambushed reefs; till the haven and joyless strand of Drepanum received me. There, buffeted by so many a tempest of ocean, I lost, alas, my father Anchises, my stay in all sorrow and calamity. There, kindliest of parents, didst thou abandon my weariness, saved in vain – ay me! – from dangers so stern! Nor did prophet Helenus, when he rehearsed his tale of horrors, nor dire Celaeno foreshow this agony. This was the crown of my sorrows, this the goal of my long pilgrimage, and thence, when I parted, a god drave me on your shores.'

Thus, sole amid listening ears, father Aeneas told his tale, unfolded the decrees of Heaven, and his voyagings: then at length was mute, and, here ending, ceased.

BOOK IV

BUT THE QUEEN, stricken long ere this by the pangs of love, fostered the wound in her veins and pined under the secret flame. Full often the hero's worth, full often the glories of his line, came coursing back on her soul: deep-fixed in her breast clung his lineaments and words, and longing withheld the peace of sleep from her limbs.

The morrow's dawn had removed the weeping shades from the firmament, and was revisiting earth with Phoebus' torch, when thus, as the madness wrought on her brain, she spoke to the sister who was heart of her heart: 'Sister Anna, what visions of the night bewilder and appal me! Who is this stranger guest that is come under our roof? With what gallant mien he bears him! How stout of spirit and arms! For me, I believe – nor believe in vain – that he springs of celestial lineage. Fear argues the base-born soul. Ay me, through what storms of fate he has struggled! What wars he recounted, endured to the end! Were not the resolve rooted in my soul, steadfast and motionless, never more to ally me with any man in the nuptial bond, since my earliest love proved traitor and deceived me with death, – were I not utterly weary of bridal chamber and bridal-torch, perchance I might have yielded to this one frailty! Anna, – for avow it I will, – since the day when my hapless consort Sychaeus died, and our hearth was bedewed with the blood that a brother spilt, he alone has swayed my sense and assailed my purpose till it totters. I feel again a spark of that ancient flame: but I would pray that rather Earth yawning to her base may engulf me or the almighty Father smite me to the shades with his thunderbolt – to the pallid shades of Erebus and the nether midnight – ere, Chastity, I violate thee or annul thy laws! He who first bound me to himself is departed with all my love: let him keep it with himself and cherish it in his tomb!' Thus she said, and the starting tears laved her bosom.

Anna made response: 'O dearer than the light to thy sister, wilt thou mourn in solitude and wither away through all the days of thy youth, and know not the sweetness of children nor the guerdons of love? Thinkest thou that dust and the sepulchred dead reck of constancy? What though no suitor have yet touched thy wasted heart – not in Libya, nor, before Libya, in Tyre? What though Iarbas be scorned, and those princes else that the Afric soil, victory-fraught, doth nurture? Wilt thou combat love, even when love pleases? And comes not the thought to thy mind, in whose realms thou art settled? On this hand the Gaetulian cities with their unconquered peoples hem thee round: on that, a region parched and forlorn, and Barcaeans raging far and near. Why speak of the wars that impend from Tyre, or the menace of our brother? For me, I believe that under the authority of Heaven and the grace of Juno these Ilian barques have held their course hither before the breeze. How fair, my sister, shalt thou behold this city arise, and this empire, by such alliance! With the swords of Troy at our call, to what pinnacle of power shall the glory of Carthage ascend! Do thou but implore the favour of Heaven, and, when the gracious rites are paid, give scope to thy

welcome and weave plea upon plea for delay, while the tempest
and watery Orion rave their fill upon the main – while his fleet *is*
shaken and the sky may not yet be braved!'

Her words fired the queen's soul with the flame of a great
desire, gave hope to her doubting mind, and broke the restraints
of shame. First they approached the shrine, and from altar to
altar sought peace. They offered ewes, duly chosen, to Ceres the
Giver of Law, to Phoebus and father Lyaeus, and before all to
Juno, mistress of the marriage-tie. Herself, in radiant loveliness,
goblet in hand, Dido poured the wine fairly betwixt the horns of
a shining steer, or paced by the laden altars before the presence
of deity, hallowed the day with sacrifice, and – her eager gaze
fixed on some victim's opened breast – sought counsel of the
quivering heart. Alas for the blind soul of the seer! What availed
vows and fanes to her frenzy? All that while the subtle flame was
devouring her marrow, and the unspoken wound lurking and
living deep in her breast!

Fire-consumed, the unhappy Dido roved brain-sick through
all the town, like a doe when the arrow has found its goal, – a
doe, whom, careless amid her Cretan glades, some shepherd in
weaponed pursuit has pierced from afar, and left, unknowing, the
winged steel in her flank: she, in fugitive course, ranges Dicte's
forests and lawns, but the mortal reed clings fast in her flank. –
Now she would lead Aeneas at her side through the city's heart,
and show him the wealth of Sidon and the walls built to his hand,
then begin to speak and in mid utterance grow mute. Now, with
declining day, she would seek the self-same banquet, pray once
more in her folly to hear the travail of Troy, and once more hang
on his moving lips. Then, when the guests were parted, when the
dim moon was shrouding her light in turn, and the setting stars
advised to sleep, she mourned forlorn in the solitary hall and
clung to the couch he had left – hearing him and seeing him,
though he was afar and she was afar. Or, enthralled by the sire
imaged in the child, she would hold Ascanius to her breast, in
hope to beguile the love that she might not utter. The towers
begun rose no more, the youth resigned the practice of arms, and
built neither haven nor sure rampart for the day of battle: the
disused works hung idle, and the giant menace of the walls, and
the fabric evened with the skies!

So soon as Jove's loved consort was ware that the queen was
possessed by thus dire a malady, and that thought of her womanly fame could no more retard her passion, so speaking the

child of Saturn accosted Venus: 'Fair, in all truth, the renown, and ample the spoils that ye win, thou and thy boy, – that great and glorious deity! – when one woman falls under the wiles of two gods! Nor deem that it escapes me, how, in dread of my city, thou hast held in mistrust the hospitable hearths of stately Carthage. But what shall be the term? or what skills now this bitterness of strife? Were it not better done to establish an eternal peace and a marriage-pact? What thou soughtest with all thy soul, that thou hast: Dido loves and burns, and has caught the madness in her blood! Then let us rule this people in common with joint sovereignty: be it hers to serve a Phrygian lord, and, in lieu of dowry, to commit her Tyrians to thy right hand!'

To her – aware that she had spoken with feigned intent, seeking to draw the empire of Italy to her Libyan coasts – thus Venus, answering, began: 'What folly could spurn such offer, or choose rather to battle against thee? – if only, as thou sayest, Fortune shall attend our deed! But I wander uncertain of Fate's decree, whether it be the will of Jove that a single city should enfold the Tyrians and them that have sailed from Troy, – whether he would see the nations mingled and alliance joined between them. Thou art his spouse: for thee it is meet to assay his mind by prayer. Advance, and I will follow!' Then imperial Juno took the word: 'That task rest with me! Now lend ear, while, in brief, I expound the mode by which we may achieve our pressing purpose. Aeneas and with him the stricken Dido prepare to follow the woodland chase, so soon as the morrow's Sun shall display his orient flames and his rays uncurtain earth. On them, while the bustling riders spread their toils round the forest lawns, I will pour from heaven a darkening rain-cloud with hail commingled, and rouse the startled skies with thunder. Their train shall scatter and flee, and be lost to view in the gathering gloom; and Dido and her Trojan prince shall come to the self-same cave. There I will be, and – thy compliance assured – I will join them in stable wedlock and consign her to him for ever. Such shall be their bridal!' Unresisting, Cythera's queen yielded assent to her suit, and smiled at the discovered ruse.

Meanwhile Dawn rose and abandoned Ocean. Under the nascent beam, the chosen chivalry streamed through the gates: nets of wide mesh, snares, and broad-pointed hunting spears were there; Massylian horsemen came spurring forth, and hounds keen-scented and strong. At the palace-door the Punic lords awaited their queen, who lingered in her chamber; while

her palfrey stood resplendent in purple and gold, and proudly
champed the foaming bit. At last she came in the midst of her
thronging retinue, clothed in a mantle of Sidon with embroidered hem, – of gold her quiver, gold-bound her tresses, and
golden the buckle that clasped her purple robe! Nor less the
Phrygian squires and joyous Iulus advanced in her train. Himself,
fair beyond all the rest, Aeneas entered the troop by her side, and
joined his company to hers. Such as Apollo is when he deserts his
wintry Lycian and the streams of Xanthus to visit his mother's
Delos, and there renews the dance, while Cretan and Dryop and
painted Agathyrsian revel banded about his altars; but himself he
walks the peaks of Cynthus, confining with plastic hand his
streaming locks in delicate leaves and entwining gold, and the
quiver rattles upon his shoulder: – so, with tread light as his,
moved Aeneas, and beauty as glorious shone on his peerless
countenance!

When they had reached the high hills and trackless brakes, lo,
wild goats, ousted from their rocky eminence, came running
down the slope; while elsewhere stags were speeding apace over
the open plain, rallying in flight their dusty squadrons, and aban-
doning their mountains. But, in the heart of the valleys, young
Ascanius, exultant on mettled steed, passed at full speed now
these and now those, and prayed that among those craven herds
some foam-covered boar might be granted to his vow, or a tawny
lion descend from his hill.

Meantime a sullen murmuring confounded the skies, and there
followed a flood of rain with hail commingled. The Tyrian
squires, the Trojan chivalry, and the Dardan child of Venus' son,
scattered in terror and sought diverse refuge throughout the
fields; and the torrents rushed from the heights. Dido and her
Trojan prince came to the self-same cave. Primeval Earth and
presiding Juno gave the sign. The lightnings and conscious ether
flashed on their bridal, and the Nymphs cried acclaim from the
mountain-summits. That day was the first source of death, the
first of disaster! For now Dido was moved by no censure of eye
or tongue, and she dreamed no more of a furtive love: but marriage she styled it, and the name was cloak to her frailty!

Incontinent Fame sped through the great cities of Libya –
Fame, swiftest created of evil things. Nurtured by motion, at
every step she gathers strength, – timorous and small at birth;
but soon she towers to the stars, and hides her head within the
clouds. Her, as men tell, her parent Earth, stung with ire against

Heaven, brought forth, latest sister to Coeus and Enceladus, fleet of foot and rapid pinion, a monster huge and horrible: and for every plume that bedecks her frame – hear and wonder! – an eye holds vigil beneath, a tongue and a mouth give voice, and an ear starts up to listen. By night she flits shrieking through the dusk betwixt sky and earth, nor declines her eyes in gentle sleep: by day she sits sentinel on the summit of a roof or stately tower, and affrights great cities, – lover of the false and evil no less than herald of truth! In those days she began exultant to fill the nations with motley rumour and to blazon alike the done and the undone: – how Aeneas was come, a scion of Trojan line, with whom as consort the lovely Dido disdained not to mate, and now they were whiling the livelong winter away in mutual dalliance, oblivious of their realms and captive to shameful passion. This news the loathly goddess scattered abroad in the mouths of men; then straight turned her course to king Iarbas, incensed his soul with her word, and added rage to rage.

He, offspring of Ammon by a ravished Garamantid Nymph, had reared a hundred vast temples, a hundred altars, to Jove in his broad domains: there he had hallowed the Fire, watcher eternal of the gods, – had hallowed the soil fattened by the blood of oxen, and the portals blossoming with garlands of thousand hues. Distraught in soul, and fired by that bitter rumour, they tell, he stood before the altars full in the presence of Heaven, and, suppliant with lifted palms, much entreated Jove: 'Almighty Jupiter, in whose honour the Maurusian people, feasting on broidered couches, now pour libation of the grape, beholdest thou these deeds? O my father, when thou hurlest thy bolts do we tremble in vain? Are thy cloud-fires, that terrify our hearts, blind, and vain their promiscuous roar? This woman – this wanderer in our territory – who founded her little town at a price, to whom we assigned a strip of our coast to plough, and gave her sovereignty over its soil, has spurned our alliance and taken Aeneas to her throne·– her lord and paramour! And now this second Paris with his eunuch retinue, his chin and essenced love-locks bound with turban of Lydia, joys in his conquest, while we, forsooth, bear gifts to thy altars and foster thy bootless glory!'

As so speaking he prayed, hand upon altar, the Omnipotent heard, and inclined his gaze to the royal walls and the lovers dead to thought of their fairer fame; then spoke to Mercury, and gave him such mandate: 'Hasten, my son, and go! Call the Zephyrs and wing thee earthward: accost the Dardan prince

who now dallies in Tyrian Carthage nor regards the city of
Fate's gift; and bear down my charge through the fleet airs. Not
such his fairest mother promised him to us, nor to such end
twice rescued him from the Grecian sword; but she deemed that
in him was one who should rule Italy, fraught with empire and
fierce in battle, – who should perpetuate a line from the proud
blood of Teucer, and bring the wide world under his sway. If all
the glory of that destiny avails not to fire him, and he assumes
not the burden himself for his own renown, does the father
begrudge Ascanius the towers of Rome? What devising, or what
hoping, tarries he in a hostile nation, nor regards his Ausonian
progeny and the Lavinian fields? Let him sail! This is the sum!
Herein be thou herald of ourself!'

He ceased: the son prepared to obey the command of his
mighty sire. And first he bound on his feet the sandals of gold
that bear him in aery flight, whether over ocean or over earth,
swift as the rushing blast, then took his wand – that wand wherewith he summons the pale spirits from Orcus, banishes others to
the gloom of Tartarus, gives slumber and withholds, and unseals
the death-glazed eye. On this reliant he drove the gales before
him, and floated through the troubled clouds. And now, onward
flying, he beheld the peak and towering flanks of stout Atlas, –
Atlas, whose pine-crowned head, encircled by sable clouds, the
winds and rains lash eternally, – whose shoulders the drifted
snow mantles, while torrents fall sheer from his aged cheeks, and
his shaggy beard is stark with ice. There first, poised upon equal
wing, he of Cyllene halted: thence headlong he shot with all his
force to the flood; like that bird which wings its lowly flight
round shores and fish-haunted cliffs hard above the water-level.
Even so the Cyllenian-born, as he fared from his mother's sire,
sped through the disparting air, betwixt earth and sky, to the
sand-strewn shore of Libya!

So soon as, with plumed foot, he touched the outskirting
cabins of Carthage, he descried Aeneas founding towers and
building dwellings anew. A blade was at his side, starred with
yellow jasper, and a mantle, blazing with Tyrian grain, hung
from his shoulders – a gift that Dido had given from her treasures, and shot the warp with threaded gold. Straight he assailed
him: 'Is it thou who now layest the foundations of proud
Carthage, rearing, wife-enslaved, a city of beauty? Alas for thy
forgetfulness of kingship and fortune! Himself the sovereign of
Heaven, who guides by his deity sky and earth, sends me down to

thee from the light of Olympus. Himself he enjoins me to bear this his mandate through the fleet airs: What devising, what hoping, laggest thou indolent on Libyan soil? If all the glory of thy great destiny avails not to move thee, yet regard thy rising Ascanius – the hope of Iulus thine heir – to whom thou owest the empire of Italy and the Roman realm!'

With such utterance the Cyllenian spoke, and, speaking, fled from mortal vision and vanished into thin air, far from ken.

But Aeneas stood dumb and distraught at the sight: his hair rose with horror, and his voice clove to his throat. Aghast at the solemn warning and the imperious voice of Heaven, he burned to flee away and desert that pleasant land. But, alas, what could he do? With what address dare he now solicit the frenzied queen? What prelude should he choose? And as this way and that he divided the swift mind and swept it ubiquitous over all the range of thought, in his hesitance this seemed the better counsel: he summoned Mnestheus, and Sergestus, and gallant Serestus, and bade them mutely equip the fleet, muster their crews to the strand, and hold their tackle in readiness, – but dissemble the cause of their changed design! Himself meanwhile – since Dido, in her singleness of heart, knew naught, nor mistrusted that so strong a love might be severed – would assay to find access and watch what hour might be the smoothest for his tale, what course the fairest to his goal. With joyful speed one and all obeyed his word and discharged his command.

But the queen – who shall deceive a lover's thought – divined his plot, and first presaged the tempest to come: for even in safety she feared the worst. To her the same godless Fame brought the tidings of madness – that they armed the fleet and prepared for voyage. Sense-bereft and infuriate, she raved aflame through the breadth of the city, like some Thyiad in triennial orgy, when, at motion of the holy symbols, the cry of *Bacchus* goads her awaking heart, and Cithaeron calls with midnight clamour. At length she took the word, and assailed Aeneas: 'Traitor! and didst thou think to disguise such iniquity, and, soft-footed, to steal from my land? Can our love not hold thee, nor the hand thou gavest me once, nor Dido who shall die as it is bitter to die? More, must thou labour at thy fleet under a wintry sky, and hasten – ruthless that thou art – to plough the main while the North is at his height? What! were thy bourne no alien fields, no dwellings unknown, did thine ancient Troy remain thee, would thy barques seek Troy through mountainous seas? Is it Dido thou fleest? By these tears and that hand of thine, – since my own deed has left me nothing more in my day of sorrow, – by our union and by our bridal begun, if in any wise I have deserved well of thee, if aught of mine has been sweet to thee, pity this sinking house, and (if prayer still have place!) I pray thee put away thy purpose! For thy sake I have won the hatred of Libyan tribes and Nomad kings, and my Tyrians are estranged: for thy sake, yet again, my honour is dead, and that fair fame of other days – my sole title to the stars! To whose mercy wilt thou leave me at the point of death, guest of mine? – since this is the one relic of the name of husband! For why should I linger on? That I may see Pygmalion raze his sister's city, or Gaetulian Iarbas lead me captive away? At least if some child had been granted me by thee ere thy departure, if some baby Aeneas were playing in my halls, whose face in despite of all might image thine, then would I seem not utterly undone and desolate!'

She ceased: he by warning of Jove stood with fixed eye, sternly prisoning his grief deep in his heart. Then briefly at last he replied: 'Never, O queen, will I deny that all the merits thy tongue can number have been thine: nor ever shall the thought of Elissa be bitter to me, while yet I have remembrance of myself and the breath governs these limbs. Few words, as the hour demands, I will speak. I hoped not in stealth to dissemble my departure – deem not so! I held not out the bridegroom's torch at any time; and I came not to such alliance. Did the fates suffer me to be captain of my own life, and at my own will to order my troubles, before all I would dwell in the city of Troy amid the loved relics of my kindred; the lofty halls of Priam should yet stand; and this hand should have founded for the vanquished a resurgent Pergamus. But now to broad Italy Grynean Apollo bids me fare, and to Italy the Lycian oracles. There is my love, there my country! If the towers of Carthage and the vision of a Libyan city can stay thee, Phoenician as thou art, say, what sin is there that the Teucrians should settle on Ausonian soil? To us, also, is forgiveness if we seek alien realms! Often as Night invests the earth in her weeping shades, often as the starry fires arise, the troubled phantom of Anchises my sire admonishes me in slumber and terrifies me. And I grieve for Ascanius my child, and the injustice that falls on his dear head, while thus I amerce him of his Hesperian crown and the fated plains. And now the herald of Heaven, at Jove's own behest – one and both be witness! – has borne his mandate down through the fleet airs. These eyes beheld the god in full light of day entering thy walls, and these ears drank his words. Cease to fire thyself and me with lamentation: not of free will do I follow Italy!'

For long she viewed him askance as he thus spoke: hither and thither she rolled her eyes, and her mute gaze roved over all his frame; then she kindled and flashed into speech: 'Traitor that thou art! no goddess bare thee, no Dardanus began thy line; but Caucasus, horrent with rugged cliffs, begat thee, and Hyrcanian tigresses gave thee suck! For why should I wear the mask? What heavier blow do I still await? Did he sigh when he saw me weep? Did that stony glance once flinch? Was he softened to a single tear? Or had he one thought of pity for her who loved him? What first, or what last? No more, no more, does imperial Juno, or Saturn's son our father, bend an eye of justice earthward! In the world is neither faith nor trust! Flung, a beggar, on my shores, I took him, and – brain-sick fool! – bade him share my realm. I drew his shattered armada and its crews from the jaws of death. – Woe is me! I am whirled away by the Furies, all aflame. Now must Apollo turn augur; now must the Lycian oracles speak; now, at Jove's own behest, comes the herald of Heaven through the skies, bearing his cruel mandate! These, forsooth, are the tasks that exercise the gods above – these the cares that break their calm! As for thee, I keep not thy person, I refute not thy pleas. Go thy way: seek thy Italy with the winds, hunt thy empire through the waves! Yet I trust, if Justice still have a voice in Heaven, that thou wilt drain the cup of retribution on some mid-ocean rock, there to call, and call again, on the name of *Dido*! From far away will I follow thee with gloomy fires, and when chill death shall have sundered spirit and clay, wheresoever thy place, there my ghost shall be at thy side. For, villain, thou shalt be requited! I shall hear thy cries, and the tale will reach me in the depths of hell!' Thus far she said, then curbed herself in mid speech, and fled sickening from the light, turned from his gaze, tore herself away, and left him hesitant and timorous with many a half-framed word on his lips. Her handmaidens raised her, bore her fainting limbs away to her marble chamber, and laid them on her couch.

But good Aeneas, though he longed to soothe and assuage her agony and to speak comfort to her sorrow, with many a sigh and resolution tottering under the weight of his great love, yet fulfilled the commands of Heaven and repaired to the fleet again. Then, indeed, his Teucrians bent to their toil, and, all along the strand, launched the tall barques. The anointed hulls were set afloat: zealous for departure, the sailors bore down from the forests oars still clothed in leaves and timbers unwrought. From all the city they might be seen flocking in act to go: – even as when ants, in forethought of winter, ravage a great pile of corn and store it in their granaries; their dusky line marches the plain, bearing the spoils through the grass along narrow highway; part, with labouring shoulders, push the big grains; part marshal the column and chastise the malingerer, and all the path is a ferment of toil. What then, Dido, was thy thought, as thou sawest that deed? What sighs didst thou utter, gazing from thy skyey turret on the shores alive far and wide, and surveying before thy gaze the whole main, tumultuous with their loud clamourings? Felon Love, to what constrainest thou not mortal hearts! Again she must stoop to tears, again solicit him with prayer, and bow her spirit to love, lest she should leave aught untried and die in vain!

'Anna, thou seest what speed they make upon all the shore around. From every hand they are mustered: even now their canvass invites the breeze, and the merry sailors have crowned the poops with garlands. If I have availed to look for such bitterness of grief, sister, I shall avail to endure it also. Yet, Anna, in my misery, do me this single office: for thee alone that traitor regarded, and to thee would entrust even the secrets of his breast; and alone thou knewest the mode and hour whereat he would soften to access. Go, my sister, and, suppliant, entreat our haughty foe: – I swore not with the Danaans at Aulis to uproot the people of Troy; I sent no fleet to Pergamus, nor unsepulchred dust or spirit of Anchises his sire. Why forbids he my pleas to enter his obdurate ear? Whither will he rush? Let him grant this last boon to one who loved him to her sorrow: – that he await an easy flight and a fair wind. I sue not now for the whilom marriage which he forswore, nor that he resign his beauteous Latium and desert his empire. I ask but a vain respite – a breathing-space to my frenzy, till the fortune that has overcome me shall teach me how to mourn. This last grace I entreat of thee – pity thou thy sister! – and when thou hast rendered it my death shall find thee requited in full!'

Such were her prayers and such the laments that her sister carried, and carried again, heart-broken. But him no laments could move, and inflexible he heard her every word. Fate stood in his path, and Heaven sealed his unmoved ear. Even as, when the Alpine winds, sweeping with emulous blast now hence and now thence, strive to uproot some oak, strong in the strength of his many years, a moaning rises, the stem quivers, and the deepening leaves strew the soil; but the tree clings to his cliff, and stretches his roots as far toward Tartarus as he lifts his head to the heavenly realms: – so the storm of entreaty broke from this hand and that incessantly upon the hero, and his mighty heart was pierced with sorrow; yet unmoved his purpose remained and idly the tears fell!

Then, at last, the unhappy Dido, Fate-tortured, prayed to die: for weariness it was to behold the vaulted heavens. And, the more that she might fulfil her intent and abandon the day, often as she laid her gifts on the incense-burning altars, she saw – word of horror! – the holy streams darken and the outpoured wine change into foul and boding gore. This sight she revealed to none – no, not to her sister.

More, there stood in the palace a marble shrine to her earlier lord, which she held in wondrous honour, crowning it with snowy fillets and festal boughs. Thence she seemed to hear the voice of her husband speaking and calling when night hung grey over earth; and oft on the roof the owl wailed forlorn with his sepulchral dirge and long-drawn note of melancholy; while many a prophecy, withal, of the old-world seers affrighted her with warning of dread. As she slept, the form of very Aeneas hounded her, pitiless of her frenzy, and ever she seemed abandoned to her sole self, – ever journeying uncompanioned on an endless way, and seeking her Tyrians in a lorn land: – even as when raving Pentheus sees the Eumenids banded, and a double sun and a twofold Thebes dawn on his gaze; or as Agamemnonian Orestes, tragic fugitive, when he flees his mother armed with brands and venomous snakes, and the avenging fiends sit by his door.

Thus, when, overborne by sorrow, she had taken the frenzy to her heart and resolved to die, self-communing she debated the hour and fashion, and accosted her mournful sister, with mien belying her thought and hope serene on her brow: 'Sister, I have found a way – sister, rejoice with me! – that shall restore him to myself or unchain my love from him. Hard by the limit of Ocean and the sunset lies the farthest Ethiop clime, where mighty Atlas holds, revolving on his shoulder, the pole, gemmed with burning stars. Thence has been revealed to me a priestess of Massylian race, guardian of the Hesperids' fane, wont erstwhile to preserve the holy boughs on their tree, and to give the dragon his feast, sprinkling dewy honey and slumber-laden poppies. With spells she claims to release such minds as she will, but on others to bring the pangs of desire – to stay the running water and to turn the stars in their courses. She calls forth the spirits that walk by night, and thou mayest see earth moaning under the foot, and ashes descending the hills. Heaven be witness, dear my sister, and thou, and thy sweet life, that unwilling I invoke the sorcerer's art! Raise silently a funeral-pile to the skies in the inner court of my palace, and let them lay on it that villain's sword, which he left pendent in the chamber, and all his relics, and the bridal couch that saw my fall. Some comfort it will be, as the priestess commands, to blot out every memorial of his accursed self!' This said, she was mute, and instant her cheeks paled; yet Anna deemed not that these strange rites were a curtain for her sister's death: her mind conceived not such height of madness, and she feared no worse than when Sychaeus bled. Therefore she prepared to do the deed.

But the queen, when the death-pyre had risen skyward in the heart of her home, huge with brands and cloven oak, hung the place with garlands and crowned it with funereal leaves. Above she set on the couch his vesture, his masterless sword, and his image, – well knowing what should be. Around stood the altars, and the priestess, with locks unloosed, thundered from her lips the names of thrice a hundred gods – Erebus, and Chaos, and threefold Hecate, and maiden Diana of the triple countenance. Waters she had sprinkled, that welled (she feigned) - from Avernus' fount: rank herbs were sought, cut by brazen sickle under the moon, and filled with black and milky venom; and sought was the love-charm, torn from the brow of a new-born foal and reft ere the dam could seize it. Herself, the meal in her pure hands, the queen stood by the altars in flowing robe, one foot unsandalled, and called on the gods and fate-conscious stars to be witness ere she died; then implored what deity soever holds just and mindful ward over them that love as they are not loved.

It was night, and throughout the earth weary frames were reaping the peace of sleep: the woods and the savage seas were still, and the hour was come when the circling stars roll midway in their course, when silent is every field, and the cattle, and the painted birds, – both they that tenant the broad breast of the silvery lake and they that dwell in the thorny thickets of the country, – all laid in slumber beneath the dumb midnight. But not so the soul-racked Phoenician queen; nor ever did she sink to sleep, or welcome the night to eye or heart. Her cares redoubled; Love rose again remorseless, and she tossed on the mighty tide of anger. Then thus she began, and so she debated within her heart: 'Think, how is it with me? A laughing-stock, shall I make trial again of my suitors of yore, and, suppliant, entreat a Nomad bridal from those whose hand I have scorned so often ere this? Shall I, then, follow the Ilian fleet and stoop to the Teucrians' utmost behest? Because, methinks, they warm at thought of the aid I lent before, and the grace of my old-time kindness stands firm in their remembrance! But grant that I would, and who shall permit? or who receive me, the loathed woman, on those proud decks? Alas, lost one, thou knowest naught, nor yet hast fathomed the forsworn heart of Laomedon's seed! What then? Shall I flee alone, companion to his exultant seamen? Or, begirt with my Tyrians and all the array of my people, shall I fall upon them? – to urge once more over the main, and bid spread sail to the winds, them whom hardly I availed to tear from their city of Sidon! Nay, die as thou hast merited, and let the steel annul thy sorrow. Thou it was, sister, – thou, who, conquered by my tears, didst lay on my madness this burden of calamity and cast me a prey to the enemy! It has not been mine to live my life guiltless of wedlock and reproachless as the creatures of the field, tampering not with such care: I have kept not my faith – faith pledged to the ashes of Sychaeus!'

Such the lamentation that broke from her heart. But Aeneas, now that he was steeled to go, now that all was duly ordered, slept on his high poop. And, as he slept, a vision of the god, returning in the same aspect, visited his dreams, and seemed thus again to admonish him, – in all things like to Mercury, voice and colour, yellow locks, and the graceful limbs of youth: 'Goddess-born, and canst thou, with this peril above thee, slumber and sleep? Madman, seest not the after-dangers that beset thee? Hearest not the Zephyrs breathing fair? Resolved on death, she is pondering in her heart fell villany and treachery, and rousing the swirling tide of passion. Fleest not hence hot-footed, while hot-footed thou mayest? Anon thou wilt see the brine a turmoil of shattered timbers, see torches flashing fierce and the strand fervent with fire, if the rays of dawn discover thee tarrying in this land. Up and go! – truce to delay. A fickle thing and changeful is woman always!' Thus he said, and mingled with the shadows of night.

On the instant, Aeneas, appalled by the sudden phantom, tore himself from sleep and roused his comrades: 'Hasten, friends!

awake, and seat you by the thwarts! Linger not, but unfurl the sails. Lo, once more a god, sent from high Heaven, urges to make speed and flee, and to sever the twisted cables! O holy one above, whosoever thou art, we follow thee and again obey thy mandate with gladness! O be thou with us, graciously prosper us, and light the sky with kindly stars!' He said; snatched his sword lightning-like from the scabbard, and smote on the hawser with naked steel. Incontinent one and all caught the fire: with eager hand and foot they quitted the beach, and their galleys hid the face of ocean, as zealously they tossed the spray and swept the blue.

And now the early Dawn, rising from Tithonus' couch of saffron, was gilding earth with her new-tricked beams. – So soon as the queen from her turret saw the first whitening glimmer of light, and the fleet standing to sea with even sails, and knew that the strand was vacant and the harbours tenantless, thrice and four times she struck her fair breast and tore her yellow hair: 'King of Heaven,' she cried, 'shall he go? Shall this alien have mocked our realm? And will they not take sword? Will the pursuers not issue from all my city, and men fling out the ships from my docks? Away! bring flames with instant speed, get me weapons, ply your oars! – What say I? Where am I? What madness works on my brain? Unhappy Dido, now do thy godless deeds touch thee? *Then* was the time, when thou gavest him thy sceptre! Behold the hand and faith of him who, they tell, bears always with him his ancestral gods – of him who bowed his neck to receive his time-worn sire! Could I not tear him away, rend him limb from limb, and scatter him over the waves? Could I not slay with the sword his comrades – nay, Ascanius himself, and set him a cate at his father's feast? – But the fortune of battle had been doubtful! What though it had? Whom feared I, doomed to die? I had assailed his encampment with fire: I had filled his gangways with flame: I had blotted out sire and son and all their race; then crowned the hecatomb with myself. Thou Sun, whose rays survey every work of earth, and thou, Juno, mediatress and witness of this my agony, and Hecate, whose name wails nightly through the cross-ways of cities, and ye Sisters of vengeance, and ye gods of dying Elissa – hear me now, bend your wrath on the sins that challenge it, and give ear to my prayer! If that miscreant must touch haven and float to earth – if so the fates of Jove require, and thus the decree is fixed – yet harassed by the weaponed battle of a fearless people, homeless and landless, and

rent from the embrace of Iulus, let him sue for aid and behold his
countrymen shamefully dead! Nor yet, when he shall submit him
to the terms of a partial peace, may he enjoy his kingship or the
day of prosperity, but let him fall before his hour, tombless on
the surrounding sand! Thus I pray: thus ebbs voice with blood.
And ye, my Tyrians – let your hate persecute his stock, with all
the line that shall be, and send this guerdon down to my dust!
Let there be no love betwixt the nations and no league! Arise,
thou avenger to come, out of my ashes, and follow the Dardan
settlers with fire and with sword, both now and hereafter, and
whensoever strength shall be given! May shore be set against
shore, wave against wave, and spear against spear! May they fight
– both they and their children's children! Such is my malison.'

So she said, and swept her mind over all the range of thought,
seeking how soonest to break from the light she loathed; then
briefly spoke to Barce, Sychaeus' nurse – her own was laid in her
ancient country, a handful of blackened ashes: 'Dear my nurse,
bring me hither sister Anna. Bid her hasten to sprinkle her limbs
with river-water, and bring with her the victims ordained for
expiation. This done, let her come; and shade thou thy brows
with the sacred garland. My purpose runs to fulfil those rites that
duly I prepared and began, that I may set the seal to my sorrow,
and the flames may devour the Dardan's pyre.' She ended: zealously the aged feet went on their errand. But Dido, unnerved and
unsexed by her ghastly purpose, with blood-shot eyes rolling and
hectic fires burning on her quivering cheeks, burst, pale at the
death to come, through the inner door of the palace, mounted in
frenzy the towering pile, and bared the Dardan sword, – gift
asked not to such end! There, as her eye lit on his Ilian garb and
the familiar couch, she paused awhile for weeping and thought,
flung herself on the pillow, and spoke her last words: 'Ye relics,
sweet while God and Fate willed, receive this breath and release
me from this agony! I have lived, and the course, that Fortune
allowed, I have run; and now I shall descend a queenly spectre
beneath the earth. I have built a stately city; I have seen my ramparts; I have avenged my lord, and exacted the penalty from my
brother and foe: – happy, alas, and more than happy, if but the
Dardan keels had touched not our strand!' She said; and, with
lips pressed to the pillow: 'Unvenged we shall die, but die we!'
she cried – 'thus, ah thus, is it pleasant to journey to the shadows!
Let the Dardan, with stony gaze, feast on this fire from the main
and bear with him my death for omen!' She ceased; and, with the

words yet on her lips, her retinue saw her fallen on the sword, the blade reeking with gore, and her hands incarnadined. To the summit of the halls the cry ascended, and Fame raved through the stricken city. The palace moaned with lamentation and sobbing and the wail of women, and the sky echoed to their dirge: – as though all Carthage or ancient Tyre were falling, with the foemen streaming in and the infuriate flames rolling their tide over the domes of man and god! Swooning the sister heard, and with hasty foot ran, fear-smitten, through the throng, tearing her cheeks and beating her breast, and called on the dying by her name: 'Sister, and was it this? Didst thou seek to deceive me? This did thy death-pile – this thy fires and altars purpose? Forlorn that I am, what shall be my earliest plaint? Didst thou disdain thy sister's companionship in death? Thou shouldst have called me to the selfsame doom! One pang of the steel – one hour – would have taken both! Did these hands build thy pyre, this voice call on our country's gods, that, with thee so laid, I, the pitiless, should be far away? Thou hast undone thyself and me, sister, and the people and elders of Sidon and all thy city! – Let me lave her wounds in water, and catch on my lips the last errant breath that may yet linger!' Scarce had she said, ere she had mounted the high steps, and, with bitter sobs, was clasping and caressing her dying sister on her bosom, as she strove to stem the red streams of blood with her robe. She, assaying to lift her heavy eyes, swooned again; and the wound, deep fixed, grated in her breast. Thrice, leaning on her elbow, she uplifted herself: thrice she rolled back on the pillow, and with wandering eyes sought the light in high heaven, and moaned to find it.

Then all-puissant Juno, in pity for her long agony and the travail of her passing, sent Iris down from Olympus to release the reluctant spirit from its intermingled clay. For, since neither by Fate she perished nor by merited death, but, hapless, before her day in the fire of sudden frenzy, not yet had Proserpine reft the yellow lock from her crown and consigned her to the Stygian shades. Therefore Iris, dew-glancing and saffron-winged, flew through the heavens, trailing a thousand diverse hues in the fronting sun, and halted overhead: 'This I take by command, an offering to Dis, and free thee from the body.' She said; and, with her right hand, severed the lock: and instant all warmth fled away, and life vanished into the winds.

BOOK V

MEANWHILE AENEAS, under full sail, held unswerving on his mid-ocean course, cleaving the billows as they gloomed beneath the North, with many a backward glance at the city, which now glared to the death-fires of hapless Elissa. What cause had kindled so vast a flame they knew not: but the bitter pang of a great love outraged, and the knowledge what a woman's frenzy may achieve, led their Teucrian hearts through paths of dismal augury.

Their barques had made the high seas, and no land more met the view, but everywhere the sky and everywhere the main, when a gloomy cloud halted overhead, fraught with night and tempest, and ocean was ruffled by the dark. Even Palinurus at the helm called from his high poop: 'Alas, why have these giant clouds girt the pole? Neptune, father, what wouldst thou do?' He said; then commanded to gather the tackle and bend to the toiling oar, turned the canvass aslant to the breeze, and so pursued: 'Great-souled Aeneas, not though Jove's word were my warrant could I hope to make Italy under this sky! The changing gales roar across our track, risen from the sable West: the air thickens to mist, and we avail neither to struggle onward nor barely to maintain our ground. Since the day is with Fortune, let us follow, and turn our way whither she beckons! Nor far distant, I ween, are the faithful coasts of thy brother Eryx and the havens of Sicily, if only with unforgetful mind I retrace the stars that I watched erewhile.' Then good Aeneas: 'Myself I have long seen that so the winds will, and in vain thou battlest against them. Veer sail and course! Could there be any soil sweeter to me – any bourne more welcome to our weary ships – than that which holds me Dardan Acestes and guards on her bosom the dust of Anchises my sire?' So said, they sailed for the harbour: the fair-blowing Zephyrs swelled their canvass and the fleet sped bounding over the flood, till joyously at last they touched the familiar strand.

But Acestes, far away on a lofty mountain-summit, admired the approach of his compatriot barques, and ran to meet them, roughly accoutred with hunting-spears and the fell of a Libyan bear – Acestes, whom a Trojan mother bore to Crimisus' stream. Not heedless of his old-time ancestry, he gave them joy of their return, gladly welcomed them to his country treasures, and solaced their weariness from friendly store.

When, with the renascent sun, the bright Morn had driven the stars in flight, Aeneas summoned his men to conclave off all the beach, and spoke from a mounded eminence: 'Ye great sons of Dardanus, race sprung from the gods' high lineage, the months are sped and one circling year sees its fulfilment since we committed to earth those bones, the relics of my divine sire, and hallowed the mourning altars. And now the day, if I err not, is come, which ever I shall keep in sorrow and ever in honour: – such, O Heaven, thy will! Did I spend this day an exile on Gaetulian quicksands, or storm-tossed on the Grecian main, or in Mycene town, yet would I perform my annual vows and the solemn ordered festival – yet would I load the altars with due offering! But now – not, methinks, without celestial counsel and will – we stand, far otherwise, even by the dust and ashes of my father, and the winds have borne us into a friendly haven. Then, come: one and all let us render this glad homage! Entreat we the gales; and may *his* will be that, when my city is raised, I shall pay these rites year by year in fanes holy to his name! Acestes, the son of Troy, grants you two heads of cattle according to the tale of your ships. Bid to the banquet the gods of your fathers' hearths and them whom your host adores. More, if the ninth dawn shall display the kindly light to mortal eyes and her rays uncurtain earth, I will appoint contests for my Teucrians: – of fleet vessels the first: then let them whose feet are swift for the race, and them who walk in hardihood and strength, skilled to speed the javelin and light arrow, or bold to join battle with raw gauntlet, be present all, and look for the guerdon that victory merited shall earn. – Set a seal upon your lips, and circle your brows with leaves!'

So saying, he veiled his temples in the myrtle of his mother. Thus did Helymus; thus Acestes, the ripe in years; thus child Ascanius; and all their company followed. From the assemblage he moved to the sepulchre with retinue of many thousands, midmost in the vast attendant troop. There, in due libation, he poured on the soil two goblets of pure wine, two of fresh milk, and two of sacrificial blood; then scattered bright-hued flowers, and so spoke: 'Hail, holy father! hail once more ye ashes that I rescued in vain! hail soul and shade of my sire! It was not given, with thee at my side, to seek the borders of Italy and her fated fields, nor yet Ausonian Tiber – wherever his streams flow!' He said; and ceased, when a serpent rolled forth from the holy base, smooth and huge with seven folds and seven coils, peacefully encircling the tomb and gliding between the altars, his back streaked with blue, his lucent scales flaming with shot gold: – even as the rainbow amid the clouds flashes a myriad changing hues in the adverse sun. While Aeneas gazed and wondered, with long train he wound slowly among the bowls and polished goblets, tasted the feast, and again vanished innocent beneath the mound, leaving the altars that had fed him. Thus spurred, the prince resumed his filial worship, uncertain whether he should hold that vision the Genius of the place or his sire's Familiar. He slew, as the ritual ordains, two ewes, two swine, and as many black-bodied steers, poured wine from the vessels, and invoked the spirit of great Anchises and the shade unprisoned from Acheron. Nor less his men brought glad offerings, each of his abundance. They piled the altars, slew the steers, arrayed the cauldrons, and, couched on the sward, placed embers below the spits and broiled the flesh.

At length the awaited day was come, and the steeds of Phaëthon swept up the ninth dawn in cloudless radiance. Fame and the renown of honoured Acestes had roused the neighbouring peoples, and their festal assemblage thronged the strand, – some to gaze on the men of Aeneas, some prepared for the contest also. First the rewards were laid to view in the midst of the course: – hallowed tripods and verdant wreaths; palms, the victors' guerdon, and weapons of war; robes stained in purple, and a talent's weight of silver and gold. Then, from a central mound, the trumpet sounded the opening fray.

First came to the contest four galleys, the flower of all the fleet, evenly matched and heavy-oared. Mnestheus and his bold rowers urged on their swift Leviathan – Mnestheus, in after days, of Italy, from whose name is the Memmian line. Gyas captained the Chimaera, vast of length and of bulk as vast, a floating city, driven by his Dardan seamen in triple tier with oars rising in threefold rank. Sergestus – from whom the Sergian house holds her style – sailed in his great Centaur; and Cloanthus (Roman Cluentius, know thy race!) in his sea-blue Scylla.

Far out in the main is a rock, fronting the spray-washed shore, which at seasons lies sunken and lashed by the swelling billows when wintry Corus hides the stars, but, under a tranquil sky, rises silent amid the waves, a plain-like surface, loved haunt of the basking cormorant. There father Aeneas set his goal – a green bough of leafy holm – for signal to the sailors, that they might know whence to return and where to reverse the long circuit of their course. This done, they chose their place by lot. On the poops stood the captains, far-refulgent in splendour of purple and gold: for the rest, their manly brows were shaded by wreaths of poplar, and their bare shoulders shone with the anointing oil. They set themselves to the thwarts: their arms strained to the oars; and, straining themselves, they awaited the signal, while pulsing fear and the wakening lust of glory tugged at their throbbing hearts.

Then, when the trumpet tone sang clear, on the instant all leapt from their stations: the cry of the seamen struck on the heavens, and the brine foamed, upheaved by their swinging arms. Side by side they cleft their furrows, and all the sea yawned under the rending oars and triple-beaked prows. Not with such dizzy speed, when the paired coursers race, do the chariots pour from the barriers, and, rushing, devour the plain! Not so do the charioteers shake their streaming reins over the restraintless team and hang prone for the blow! Then every grove rang to the cheers and shouting of men and to the partisans' zeal: the pent shores rolled back the cry, and the smitten hills shook responsive to the clamour. Amid the loud confusion Gyas passed his peers, and shot out on the waves ahead: him Cloanthus followed, better-oared, but clogged by his labouring bulk of pine. Next, at equal distance, the Leviathan and the Centaur contended to win pride of place: and now the Leviathan gained; now the huge Centaur passed her victorious; now one and both sped together, front by front, their long keels ploughing the salt flood!

At length they approached the rock and were hard upon the goal, when Gyas – still foremost and victor over half the watery course – called loudly on Menoetes, the helmsman of his barque: 'Whither so far on the right? Bend thy course hitherward; cling to the beach, and let the oar graze the left-lying cliff! The rest may hold the deep!' He said; but Menoetes, in fear of the ambushed reef, turned his prow to the flowing main. 'What dost from thy track? To the rocks again, Menoetes!' cried Gyas in recall, and, lo, he descried Cloanthus imminent in his rear, and holding the nigher course. Between the ships of Gyas and the reverberant crags he shot inward on the left, and incontinent out, passed his leader, left the goal, and found the sure seas. And now resentment kindled to flame in Gyas' young heart: the tears coursed down his cheeks, and, oblivious alike of his own honour and his crew's safety, he hurled the timorous Menoetes from the tall poop sheer into the flood; took the helm, steersman and captain in one, and, cheering his men, swung the rudder to the rock.

But Menoetes, laden with years and dripping in drenched raiment, rose hardly at last from the depths below, and, scaling the
summit of the crag, sat him down on the dry stone. The Teucrians laughed as he fell, laughed as he swam, and laughed again as
he vomited the brine from off his chest. And now a glad hope
fired the rearmost pair, Sergestus and Mnestheus, to outrun the
laggard Gyas. First Sergestus took the lead and neared the rock –
the lead, yet not by his keel's full length: with part he led, part
the Leviathan pressed with rival stem! But, pacing the mid-decks
among his men, Mnestheus spurred them on: 'Now, o now, rise
to your oars, ye that fought with Hector – ye whom I chose for
my company when Troy fell! Now put forth that might, now that
spirit, which ye shewed on the Gaetulian sands, on the Ionian
main, and on Malea's pursuant billows! No more Mnestheus
seeks the palm, no more strives to conquer! Though, o – yet be
the victory, Neptune, to whom victory thou hast given! But think
it shame to return the last! Men of my country, achieve thus
much, and avert dishonour!' With giant effort they flung themselves forward; the brazen barque quivered to their mighty
strokes, and the ground fled from under them. Then, while the
quick-taken breath shook their limbs and parching lips, and the
sweat flowed in streams over all their limbs, bare chance brought
them the meed they hoped. For, as wildly Sergestus urged his
prow inward to the rocks, and came up in over-straitened passage, he lodged – unhappy! – on the projecting rocks. The crags
shook; the oars dashed griding upon the dented coral, and the
shattered prow hung impotent. The seamen sprang up, and, with
loud clamour, stayed the galley, seized iron-shod stakes and
keen-pointed poles, and gathered their broken oars from the
flood. But Mnestheus, rejoicing, his zeal but fired by success,
with sweeping oars and winds blowing to his call, made the
unimpeded seas and ran his course on the open main. Even as a
dove, startled from the cavern in whose rocky coverts lie her
home and loved nestlings, bends her flight to the fields, and, with
loud-beating wings, flutters in terror through her dwelling; till
anon, floating in the tranquil air, she skims her liquid way, nor
stirs her rapid pinions: – so Mnestheus, so his fleeting Leviathan,
clove the last waters, and so her own speed lent her wings! And
first he left Sergestus struggling on the tall rock amid the shallows, while he called in vain for help, and assayed to run with
shivered oars. Next he caught Gyas and his vast Chimaera. Bereft
of her helmsman, she gave way; and now Cloanthus alone was

left, hard at the very goal! For him he made, and, with force strained to the utmost, pressed hard upon him. Then, in truth, the shouting redoubled, and the plaudits of every lip urged the pursuer on, till the skies flung back the din. These thought it shame, did they not maintain the glory that was theirs and the honour they had won, and would barter life for renown: to those success was food, and the semblance of power gave power indeed! And perchance, with levelled stems, they had parted the prize, had not Cloanthus, his either palm stretched over the wave, broken into prayer and called Heaven to hear his vows: 'Ye gods whose sovereignty Ocean obeys, whose seas I sail, on this strand will I set glad-hearted a snowy bull before your altars, to discharge my vow, and cast his entrails far into the salt waves, and pour out the liquid wine!' He said; and all the quire of Nereids, and of Phorcus, and maiden Panopea, heard him in the nether flood; and Father Portunus himself impelled him on his course with mighty hand. Fleeter than southern gale or winged arrow, his galley fled to land and vanished in the deep haven! Then he of Anchises born, when all were duly summoned, declared, by the herald's clear tones, Cloanthus the victor, and draped his temples in green laurel; then, for bounty to the crews, gave three steers to each at their choice, and wine, and a great talent of silver to bear away. For the captains he added especial guerdons: to the conqueror a gold-wrought scarf, round which strayed, in double stream, a deep bordering of Meliboean purple; woven wherein was the princely boy, as with spear and racing foot he pursued the swift stags to weariness on leafy Ida – bold, and as one that pants for breath. But soon from Ida the swooping bird, Jove's armour-bearer, had borne him in crooked talons aloft and away; and alone stood his grey-haired guards, stretching their availless hands to the stars, while fiercely the hounds bayed to heaven. But on him whose prowess had achieved second place he bestowed a corslet of linked and polished mail, with triple texture of gold, which, under Troy-towers, his own conquering hand had stripped from Demoleus by the marge of swirling Simoïs – a sight of beauty, and, in battle a sure defence. Scarce could his henchmen, Phegeus and Sagaris, sustain its massy folds on their labouring shoulders: yet once Demoleus, clad therein, would pursue amain the wavering of Troy! Two cauldrons of bronze he made the third prize, and two bowls, wrought in silver and rough with chasing.

And now all had received their meeds, and were departing in

pride of possession, their brows bound in crimson ribands, when – hardly, by dint of toilsome effort, unlodged from that cruel rock – with oars lost and a single crippled tier, Sergestus brought up his barque, jeered and unhonoured. As oft a serpent, surprised on the highway, whom a brazen wheel has crossed athwart, or some wayfarer with heavy blow left half-slain and mangled under a stone, vainly assays to flee, and writhes his long spires – one half defiant with glaring eye and hissing throat reared skyward: one, wounded and maimed still retarding him, as he twines knot upon knot and coils himself upon himself: – so the ship rowed on her tardy course; yet made sail, and under full canvass entered the port! Rejoiced to find the vessel safe and her crew returned, Aeneas assigned his promised meed to Sergestus, and a handmaid fell to his lot, – not unversed she in Minerva's toils, – Crete-born Pholoë, with twin sons at her breast.

This contest sped, good Aeneas took his way to a grassy plain, surrounded on all sides by woods and winding hills. In the centre of the vale ran the circuit of a theatre; and thither, with thousands in his train, the hero moved in the heart of the assemblage, and took his seat on a rising mound. There, for all who might wish to contend with racing foot, he had rewards to wake ambition and guerdons to propound. From every hand the Teucrians came with Sicanians at their side: and foremost of all came Nisus and Euryalus, – Euryalus graced by youth's fair bloom, Nisus by reverent love for his tender years. On their steps followed princely Diores of Priam's generous line; then Salius and Patron with him, Acarnanian the one, the other of Tegean house and Arcadian blood; next two of Sicily's manhood, Helymus and Panopes, both woodland-trained and attendants of old Acestes; with many else, whom twilit fame has left obscure. Then, amid their throng, Aeneas spoke: 'List to my words, and give heed with joyful heart! From all your number there is none who shall depart without gift of mine. To each I will award twin Cretan shafts, refulgent with polished steel, and a silver-chased axe for him to bear. This meed shall be one for all: but the three foremost shall receive the rewards, and the green olive shall wreathe their brows. To the first be assigned for his victory a gaily caparisoned steed: to the second, an Amazonian quiver charged with Thracian arrows, embraced by a belt of ample gold and clasped by a smooth-jewelled buckle: for the third, let him depart requited with this helmet of Argos!'

So said, they took their place, and suddenly, the signal heard, swept over the course and left the barrier behind, streaming forth like rain from the cloud and looking to the end. Nisus was first away, and flashed out far in the van of all the rest, swifter than the breeze or the wings of the thunderbolt! Next to him – but at long interval the next! – followed Salius; then, a space behind, Euryalus ranked the third, and, after Euryalus, Helymus; in whose rear behold Diores flying, heel grazing heel, and shoulder close upon shoulder! And, had more of the course remained, he had passed him, darting in advance, or left the issue in doubt! And now, hard by the last stage, exhausted they were verging to the goal, when Nisus luckless wight! – tripped in the treacherous pools, where the gore of the slaughtered steers had been spilt upon earth and soaked the green sward below. There, triumphant at thought of victory already won, he held not his foot, as it tottered on the ground he trod, but fell prone, full in the unclean ordure and sacrificial blood; – yet forgot not Euryalus, forgot not his love! For, rising amid the slippery foulness, he threw himself in Salius' path; and, as Salius lay rolling on the dense sand, Euryalus shot past, and, conqueror by grace of his friend, won the leader's place and flew onward amid applauding hands and lips. Behind came Helymus, and Diores, now third for the palm. But now Salius filled with his outcry the whole assemblage of that vast theatre and the presence of the elders in the forefront, clamouring that his honours, so foully lost, should be restored. For Euryalus stood the vulgar favour, his decent tears, and worth that shines the brighter in a fair frame. Nor less Diores lent loud support – Diores, who succeeded to the palm, and attained the last prize in vain, should Salius regain prime honour! Then father Aeneas: 'Your meeds remain to you assured, and this boy's guerdon none moves from its rank! Suffer me, then, to shew compassion to a guiltless friend unfortunate!' So saying, he bestowed on Salius the ample fell of an Afric lion, ponderous with shaggy mane and claws of gold. Then Nisus: 'If such rewards pertain to the vanquished, and such pity to the fallen, what meet recompense shall be given to Nisus, whose prowess had merited the highest crown, had not he, like Salius, succumbed to Fortune's malice?' And, with the word, he displayed his countenance and limbs marred by the slime and ordure. Smiling, the kindly prince bade a buckler be brought, the work of Didymaon's art, that, on Grecian soil, he had torn from the hallowed portals of Neptune's fane. With this fair gift he contented the gallant youth.

Then, when the race was run and the award discharged: 'Come now,' he said, 'in whose stout heart dwells a ready spirit, and with gauntleted hand let him lift his arms for battle!' So speaking, he assigned a double prize for the fray: to the victor a steer decked in gold and garlands; a sword and noble helm for solace to the vanquished. Delay was none: for straight the face of Dares was seen, as in all his vast strength he rose amid the loud-murmuring throng, – Dares who alone was wont to brave the conflict with Paris, – Dares who, by the tomb where great Hector sleeps, struck down conquering Butes in his giant bulk (scion, he vaunted, of Amycus' Bebrycian race), and laid him in death on the yellow sands. Such was he who upreared his towering head for the first conflict, his outstretched arms swinging from side to side, his blows scourging the air! Another they sought for him: but not one out of all that array found heart to approach the champion and indue the gauntlets. Exultant, then, and thinking that all resigned the palm, he stood before the feet of Aeneas, and, no more delaying, laid his left on the bull's horn, and spoke: 'Goddess-born, if no man dares to hazard the encounter, what end shall there be to my standing' How long beseems it that I linger? Bid me take thy boon away!' With a single voice the Dardans shouted assent, and urged that the promised meed be paid him.

On this, Acestes assailed Entellus with keen rebuke, as, couched on the green turf, he sat beside him: 'Entellus, bravest of heroes once, but bravest in vain! will thy patience suffer such high guerdon to be won disputeless? Where have we now Eryx the divine, bootlessly famed thy master? where that glory, broad as Sicily, and the spoils pendent in thy halls?' To this he: 'No cowardice has banished love of honour or thought of renown! But my blood is chill and dull with the slow-footed years, and my feeble strength is frozen within me. Had I – as once I had – the trust of that idle boaster – had I my youth of old, unbribed by the meed of yon fair steer I had taken the lists; nor reck I of gifts!' He said; and flung into the midst two gauntlets of giant weight, wherein bold Eryx was wont to lift his hand for battle, and to bind his arms in their stubborn hide. All minds were amazed: so huge the seven vast folds of oxhide stark with insewn lead and iron! Chief, Dares stood aghast, and, shrinking, refused the issue; while Anchises' great-hearted son turned this way and that their ponderous mass and the huge volume of their thongs. Then from the old man's breast came such utterance: 'What if any had

beheld the gauntlets that armed Hercules' self, and the fatal fray
on this very strand? This harness thy brother Eryx once wore:
stained even now thou seest it with his blood and spattered brain!
With this he stood against great Alcides; and in this was I
trained, while a more generous blood nurtured my strength, and
jealous age lay not yet strewn hoar over either temple. But if
Trojan Dares brooks not our arms, – if such the resolve of good
Aeneas, and so Acestes, author of this combat, approves, – then
make we the battle even! A truce to thy tremblings! I forgo thee
the gloves of Eryx; and doff thou thy gauntlets of Troy!' He said;
and flung back from his shoulders the doubly-folded robe, bared
the great joints of his limbs, his great bones and thews, and stood
gigantic on the mid sands.

Then Anchises' princely child brought gauntlets of equal
weight, and bound the hands of each in impartial weapons.
Straight either combatant took his stand, rose on tiptoe, and,
undaunted, lifted his arms in the air aloft. With heads erect and
drawn back from the reach of blows, they mingled hand with
hand and challenged encounter: – better, the one, in nimbleness
of foot, and reliant on his youth: the other strong in might of
limb; but his tardy knees trembled and tottered, and a sick panting shook his vast frame. Many a fruitless blow they showered
each on the other, and with stroke upon stroke their hollow
flanks and chests echoed long and loud; while about ear and brow
the quick hands flashed, and their jawbones rang under the hard-
smiting gloves. Entellus stood firm, and, motionless in unchang-
ing posture, baffled the onslaught with body and vigilant eye
alone. His foe, as one who with engines of war assaults a stately
city or sits in embattled leaguer against a mountain fortalice,
assayed now this approach, now that, and with guileful intent
ranged all the lists, pressing him with many a vain attack. At
length Entellus, rising, shewed his right uplifted on high.
Quickly the other foresaw the descending stroke, and, with
nimble body, darted aside from its path! Entellus' strength was
spent in air, and, self-undone, he fell to earth in his titan bulk, a
mighty man mightily fallen: – as often on Erymanthus or towering Ida falls a hollow pine, uptorn from the roots! Teucrians and
men of Sicily – all rose in their zeal. The clamour mounted to
the skies; and foremost Acestes ran to his help, and pityingly
raised his lifelong friend from the ground. But, nothing downcast
nor dismayed by his mischance, more keenly the hero re-entered
the fray, with anger waking fury, and shame and conscious worth

kindling his might. Like fire he drove Dares precipitate through the lists, raining his blows now with the right and now with the left. Delay there was none, nor respite: thickly as the hail rattles on the roof from the bursting cloud, so sped the hero's recurrent blows, as, with either hand fast-plied, he buffeted and battered Dares.

Then father Aeneas suffered not their passion to rise higher, nor Entellus to rage with exasperate soul, but set a term to the conflict and rescued the fainting Dares, thus speaking with words of solace: 'Unhappy man! What dire frenzy has possessed thy mind? Perceivest not a strength other than thine, and the gods now ranged against thee? Then yield thou to Heaven!' He said; and his word annulled the conflict. But Dares his faithful friends led thence, with feeble knees trailing and head swaying from side to side, as he spat from his mouth clotted blood and teeth commingled in the blood! To the ships they took him; then, at summons, received the casque and the sword, and resigned palm and bull to Entellus. And now the conqueror, flown in spirit and exulting in his meed: 'Goddess-born,' he cried, 'and ye Teucrians learn what might dwelt in my youthful frame, and from what a death ye have recalled your rescued Dares!' He said; and planted himself in face of the fronting steer, as it stood the battle's reward; drew back his hand and levelled the stubborn gauntlets fairly betwixt its horns, rising for the blow; then dashed them against the bone and shattered the brain. Prone the creature fell, and, quivering, lay lifeless on the sod! He, from above, thus broke into speech: 'A better life, Eryx, I pay thee in lieu of Dares' death, and here – victor to the end – resign glove and art!'

Straight Aeneas invited all, who so desired, to contend with the fleet shaft, and proclaimed the rewards. With his own mighty hand he upreared the mast from Serestus' galley, and, from its high summit, hung, in a cord passed through, a fluttering dove – mark for their levelled steel. The archers gathered; the lots were flung, and a brazen helm received them. First before all, amid favouring cheers, issued the place of Hippocoon, Hyrtacus' son; whom Mnestheus followed, conqueror but now in the naval strife – Mnestheus in his green olive-crown. Third came Eurytion – thy brother, far-famed Pandarus, who in other days, commanded to undo the truce, didst wing the first weapon into the hosts of Argos! Last, and lowest sunk in the casque, was Acestes, ready even yet with heart and hand to assay the toils of youth.

Then, with stalwart arms, the archers bent their curving bows, each for himself, and drew shaft from quiver. And first, from the strident sinew, the arrow of Hyrtacus' youthful son fled through the sky, parting the fleet airs, attained the mark, and struck full in the mast's adverse timber. The bole shook; the bird fluttered her timorous wings, and all around rang again with cheers. Next gallant Mnestheus took his stand with drawn bow, aiming to the height, and levelled eye and shaft alike. But, alas, his steel availed not to touch the bird herself, but severed the knots and flaxen bonds, which chained her foot as she hung from the mast: and soaring she fled to the winds and clouds of heaven! Then quickly Eurytion, who, with ready bow, had long held his arrow on the string, called his brother to his prayer, marked the dove, – triumphant now in the open skies, – and pierced her, as, on beating pinion, she flew under a sable cloud. Breathless she fell, leaving her life in the ethereal stars, and descending brought back the shaft in her breast.

And now, the palm lost and won, Acestes remained alone: yet he sped his arrow into the air aloft, displaying – reverend sire! – his art and loud-singing bow. On this a sudden portent, fraught with solemn presage, broke on their view: – its truth the high issue shewed anon; and too late the dread-inspiring seers declared its boding import! For, flying, the reed caught fire in the humid clouds, writ its course in flame, and vanished, utterly consumed, into unsubstantial air: – as often stars, unsphered from the firmament, shoot athwart the night with streaming tresses! Trinacrians and Teucrians alike stood helpless with bewildered souls and praying lips. Nor did great Aeneas spurn the omen; but, embracing the glad Acestes, loaded him with noble gifts, and so spoke: 'Take them, sire: for Heaven's sovereign Lord has willed by this sign that, exempt from the lot, thou shouldst receive peculiar honour! This guerdon shall be thine, as once it was old Anchises', – a bowl embossed with figures, which, in other years, Thracian Cisseus gave to my father's keeping, a princely gift, memorial of himself and pledge of his love!' So saying, he crowned his temples with green laurel, and styled Acestes victor, sole above all: nor did good Eurytion grudge him his honour preferred, though himself alone had struck down the dove from her aery heights. Next in order of reward came he who had severed the bonds: last, he whose winged reed had lodged in the mast.

But father Aeneas, ere yet the contest was sped, summoned Epytus' son to his side, – guardian and guide of Iulus' childish years, – and thus spoke to his faithful ear: 'Away, and charge Ascanius, if he now holds his boyish troop in readiness and has marshalled his cavalcade, to lead in his squadrons to his grandsire's honour and display himself in arms.' He said; and himself commanded the instreaming throng to depart from the length of the course and to leave the lists clear. The boys rode in, and, with even ranks, passed shining on bridled steeds before their parents' gaze; while, admiring as they went, all Sicily and Troy cried acclaim. The locks of all were duly confined in diadems of shorn leaves and each bore two steel-tipped cornel-shafts: on the shoulder of some were polished quivers, and on the upper breast a flexile circlet of gold passed round the neck. Three in number were the mounted squadrons, and three the captains that rode to and fro, each followed by twice six boys glittering in tripartite array under companion chiefs. One youthful band rode gaily behind a little Priam, his grandsire living in his name, – famed scion, Polites, of thine, and destined to Italy's increase! Now he reined a Thracian courser, dappled with flakes of white, white his fetlocks' forefront, and white the forehead which proudly he reared. Next came Atys, whence the Latin Atii draw their race, – little Atys, the boyish love of boy Iulus. Last, and in beauty fairest of all, came Iulus on a Sidonian steed, which radiant Dido had given in remembrance of herself and pledge of her love. All their company else rode horses of Sicily, the boon of old Acestes.

With applauding hands the Dardans welcomed their anxious train, and joyed, as they gazed, to trace in the sons their fathers' lineaments of old. – When they had ridden merrily round all the concourse in view of their kindred, the son of Epytus, as they stood expectant, cried the signal from far and sounded his whip. In equal troops they galloped apart and dissolved their array, three by three, into disjunct bands; and again, at summons, wheeled back and bore down with lances couched. Then they entered on other charges and other retreats, in encountering lines; wound circle on alternate circle, and under arms evoked the semblance of battle, now wheeling in unguarded flight, now turning their spears in menace, and again riding abreast in all peace. As once, men tell, in high Crete, the labyrinth held a path threaded betwixt sunless walls, – a traitorous device perplexed by a thousand ways, wherein the maze, undiscovered and irretrievable, baffled the signs set for guidance: – even so the sons of Troy rode in their tangled course, weaving a sportive web of conflict and flight, like dolphins, who, skimming the watery expanse, cleave the Carpathian or Libyan main.

This mode of horsemanship and these games Ascanius first restored, what time he girdled Alba the Long with walls, and taught the early Latins to celebrate them, even as did he, in his boyhood, and, with him, the youth of Troy. They of Alba taught their children; and from Alba mighty Rome received the heritage, and preserved the ancestral wont: and *Troy* now are the boys styled and *Trojan* their company!

Thus far the ritual was paid to Anchises the blest: but now Fortune began to turn and bely her faith. For while, in interchange of sports, they rendered their homage to the tomb, Juno, Saturn's child, sent Iris down from Heaven to the Ilian fleet, and breathed gales to waft her on her way, revolving many a thought, and with her ancient anger yet unsated. She, hasting her journey along the arch of myriad hues, hied swiftly down on her virgin path, unseen by man. She saw the vast concourse; she traversed the beach, and scanned the forsaken harbour and warderless fleet. But, remote on the lorn strand, the women of Troy wept their lost Anchises, and, weeping, gazed all on the unplumbed deep. 'Alas, and do seas so many, and tracts of foam so wide, await yet our weariness?' they cried with a single voice, and prayed for an abiding city, heart-sick of enduring ocean's travail. Into their midst, then, she flung herself, no tyro in the arts of harm, and resigned her celestial countenance and garb. Beroë she became, – Beroë, the aged wife of Tmarian Doryclus, once blest with race and fame and children, – and, in such semblance, mingled with the Dardan matrons: 'O hapless we, whom the Achaean's conquering hand dragged not to death under the walls of our fathers! O ill-starred race, to what fatal doom does Fortune reserve thee? The seventh summer now wanes since Troy was cut down; and we wander still, though we have travelled every sea and every land, past many a churlish rock and under many a star, pursuing the while, wave-tost, a fugitive Italy over the great deep! Here are the borders of Eryx our brother, and Acestes proffers welcome. Who shall gainsay that we raise our ramparts and give a city to our citizens? O my country, and thy gods reft from the enemy's hand in vain! shall there no more be a Troy-town in the mouths of men? shall these eyes never see the rivers of Hector, Xanthus and Simoïs? Nay, up and burn with me these accursed barques! For in dreams I have seen the phantom of Cassandra the prophetess, and she gave me lighted brands. *Here seek ye your Troy*, she said, *here your home is!* And now the hour calls for the deed; nor can portents so high brook delay. Lo, four altars to Neptune! Flame and resolve the god himself ministers!'

She said; and incontinent seized fiercely the felon torch; brandished it with forceful hand far uplifted, then flung it forth. The women of Ilium gazed with awakening mind and astonied heart. Then one of their throng, – eldest-born of all, – Pyrgo, the royal nurse of Priam's many sons: 'Matrons, here is no Beroë! Not this Doryclus' Rhoeteian spouse! Note ye the tokens of divine beauty and the lightning of her eyes, her breath and her lineaments, the sound of her voice, and the walk of her feet! Not long ago myself I parted from Beroë, leaving her sick and rebellious that she alone must be portionless in this festival, nor might pay to Anchises the honours that are his due!'

She spoke; but the matrons, wavering and dubious at first, scanned the vessels with malign gaze, hesitant betwixt their wistful love for the country at their hand and the fated realms that beckoned them; when the goddess on even wing soared to the skies tracing her great arch beneath the clouds. Then, at last, dazed by the portent and stung by madness, they cried aloud and snatched fire from the hearths within, – part despoiling the altars, – then flung on the fleet leaves and boughs and brands. Unleashed, the Fire-god swept raging over thwarts and oars and the painted poops of fir.

To the tomb of Anchises and the seated theatre Eumelus plied, herald of the burning vessels: and, looking back, their own eyes discerned the dark ashes eddying in clouds. Foremost of all Ascanius, as gaily he led the galloping troop, spurred instantly to the turmoiled camp, nor could his breathless guardians stay him. 'What strange frenzy is here?' he cried. 'Alas my hapless countrywomen, whither now, whither would ye go? No foe – no hostile encampment of Argos – ye burn, but your own hopes! Behold me – your own Ascanius!' And he flung before their feet the empty casque, accoutred in which he portrayed the mimic war. Aeneas and his Trojan bands came hastening together: but the matrons, in dismay, fled scattered here and there over the strand, and stole to the woods or the chance shelter of rocky caverns. Loathing the deed and the light, they were changed and knew their friends; and Juno was banished from their hearts. Yet none the more did the flames and fire resign their unvanquished strength! Under the moist timber the tow lived, disgorging slow wreaths of smoke; the clinging heat fed on the hulls, and the plague spread downward through all: nor could the heroes' might, nor the floods they poured, avail.

Then good Aeneas tore the vesture from his shoulders, and with outstretched palms called Heaven to aid: 'Almighty Jove, if thou loathest not yet the Trojans to a man, if thy mercy of old aught regards our human sorrow, grant now, O Father, that the fleet may escape the flame and snatch from destruction the slender fortunes of Troy! Or, if so I have merited, fill thou full the cup, and with hostile thunderbolt send me down to death and whelm me here under thy right hand!' Scarce had the words left his lips, when the rains streamed forth and a gloomy tempest raved restraintless: and the high places of earth and her plains quaked to the thunder. The tumultuous flood came rushing from all the sky, pitch-black amid the serried gales of the South. The hulls were filled to overflowing, and the smouldering oak was drenched, till all the fire died, and all the barques, save four, were delivered from destruction.

But father Aeneas, deep-wounded by this cruel hap, revolved in swift change, now this way and now that, his mighty burden of care: – whether to rest in the Sicilian fields, careless of Destiny, or to assay the coasts of Italy. Then aged Nautes, whom Pallas, Tritonian maid, had schooled beyond all mortals else, and given him the glory of perfect art, inspiring him to answer what the dread wrath of Heaven foreshowed or what the order of fate required: – he, then, began, and so spoke comfort to Aeneas: 'Goddess-born, as Fate urges – whether onward or backward – let us follow! Whatever shall fall, Fortune is conquered always by endurance! Here thou hast Dardan Acestes, sprung of celestial line: take him to share thy councils, and claim his willing alliance! Commit to him all for whom there is no space, now that these ships are lost, and all that are weary of thy great emprize and of thy fortunes. And choose the stricken in years, and the wave-worn matrons, and whatsoever sails with thee that is weak and timorous of peril; and grant their weariness to possess a city in this land. They shall call their town Acesta, and no man forbid the name!'

Then, kindling to these words of his aged friend, he swept his distracted mind over all the range of care: and sable Night, throned on her chariot, rode up the sky. In a little while the form of his sire Anchises seemed to descend from heaven and break into sudden utterance: 'My son, dearer than life, in the days when life remained me, my son, who hast wrestled so long with Ilium's destiny, I come to thee by mandate of Jove, who has driven the fire from thy fleet and pitied thee at last from the empyreal height! Obey the sage counsel that now white-haired Nautes gives thee: convey into Italy the flower of thy chivalry and the stoutest hearts! A hardy race, and of rugged life, must thou war down in Latium. Yet first approach thou the nether halls of Dis, and through the deeps of Avernus hasten, son, to meet me! For godless Tartarus holds me not, nor the shades of sorrow; but I dwell in the pleasant synods of the just, and in Elysium. Thither the chaste Sibyl will escort thee when many dusk kine have bled: and then shalt thou learn all thy race and the city prepared for thee. And now fare thee well! Dewy Night rolls on her midmost course, and the remorseless Day-star has breathed on me with the panting breath of his orient steeds!' He ceased; and fled as smoke into the unsubstantial air. 'Whither now wilt thou speed?' cried Aeneas. 'Whither thus amain? Whom fleest thou? Or who withholds thee from our embrace?' So speaking, he quickened the ashes and slumbering flames, and, with holy meal and laden censer, paid his suppliant homage to the Lar of Pergamus and the secret hearth of hoary Vesta.

Straight he called his friends – Acestes first – and expounded the command of Jove, the counsel of his loved sire, and the resolve now settled in his breast. Not long their debate; nor did Acestes gainsay the behest. They enrolled the matrons in a city, and planted there such of the company as willed – souls that hungered not for glory. Themselves they renewed the thwarts, restored the charred timbers of the vessels, and fashioned oars and cordage – few in numbers, but with valour that fainted not in battle. Meanwhile Aeneas traced the walls with the plough, and allotted dwellings: this he bade be *Ilium*, and these places *Troy*. Trojan Acestes rejoiced in his novel realm, appointed a forum, and gave laws to an assembled senate. Then, on the summit of Eryx, they founded a star-pointing fane to Idalian Venus, and assigned a priest and a grove of ample sanctity to Anchises' sepulchre.

And now, when all the people had feasted for nine days, and sacrifice had been rendered on the altars, placid breezes lulled the seas, and the recurrent South called whispering once more to the main. Along the winding shores rose a great lamentation, and, friend embracing friend, they lingered a day and a night. And now the very matrons, – the very men, – to whom erstwhile the sight of the sea seemed bitterness, and intolerable its tyranny, would fain sail and endure to the end the journey in all its weariness. Them good Aeneas solaced with kindly words and, weeping, commended to his kinsman Acestes. Next he bade slay three steers to Eryx, and a ewe-lamb to the Tempests, and duly fling loose the hawser. Himself, meanwhile, crowned in shorn leaves of olive, stood at distance on the prow, and, goblet in hand, cast the entrails into the briny waves and poured the streaming wine. A wind, rising from the stern, followed them on their way, and zealously the seamen smote the foam and swept the watery levels.

But Venus, meantime, care-harrassed, addressed her suit to Neptune and thus unbosomed her plaint: 'The heavy anger and insatiate heart of Juno constrain me, Neptune, to stoop.to all entreaty: for neither length of days nor any piety may soften her; and the dictates of Jove, and Destiny's self, leave her unbroken and unbowed. It suffices not that with dire hatred she has eaten out their city from the heart of Phrygia's people, and dragged the relics of Troy through all extremity of vengeance: she persecutes the ashes and dust of the slain! The source of such fury may herself know! Even thou wert my witness of late in the Afric waves, what sudden turmoil she engendered, mingling, in vain reliance on Aeolus' storms, all ocean with heaven, and daring the deed in thy mid empire. And now, behold, driving the matrons of Troy through paths of crime, foully she has burned their ships, and compelled them – their fleet destroyed – to abandon their crews to an unknown soil! For the remnant of their course, I pray thee, grant them without peril to sail thy waves: grant them to reach Laurentine Tiber – if my suit is lawful, if there the Sisters vouchsafe them a city!'

Then spoke Saturn's son, lord of the fathomless deep: 'All right hast thou, Cythera's queen, to trust in my realms – those realms whence thou drawest birth! And I have merited so! Often have I quelled the madness and dread fury of sky and sea: nor less upon earth – Xanthus and Simoïs bear witness! – has been my care of thy Aeneas! When Achilles in pursuit was hurling Troy's breathless hosts against their ramparts, and consigning his thousands to death – when the choking rivers groaned, and Xanthus availed not to find a passage nor to roll himself to ocean – on that day I plucked Aeneas from the slayer in sheltering cloud, as he fronted Peleus' great son with less puissant arm and less puissant gods; though I desired to uproot from their foundations those walls of forsworn Troy that mine own hands had built! And

changeless my purpose still abides: dispel thy fears! Scatheless he
shall approach the haven of Avernus, as thou prayest. One alone
there shall be, whom, lost on the flood, he shall seek and find
not: – one life shall be given for many!'

When his words had soothed her heavenly heart to gladness,
the great Sire yoked his steeds in gold, curbed their fierceness
with foaming bit, and loosely shook forth from his hand the
many reins. In azure car he sped skimming the plains of ocean;
the waves sank, the heaving main grew smooth under his thundering axle, and the clouds fled from all the expanse of heaven.
Straight appeared the manifold shapes of his attendant train, –
huge whales, Glaucus, with his greybeard quire, Palaemon (Ino's
child), and the fleet Tritons, and all the array of Phorcus – while
on the left were banded Thetis and Melite and maiden Panopea,
Nesaeë and Spio, Thalia and Cymodoce.

On this joy's soft vicissitude thrilled the anxious soul of father
Aeneas; and he commanded every mast to be reared with instant
speed, and every sail to be stretched on its yard. Together all set
their sheets, and, at one time and the same, loosed the canvass,
now on the left, now on the right: together they turned, and
turned again, the peaked sail-yards aloft; and favouring gales
bore on the fleet! In the van, before them all, Palinurus led the
serried line; and by him the others shaped their course, obedient
to command.

And now dewy Night had almost reached her goal in the central heavens, and, stretched by the oars along the hard benches,
the seamen had surrendered their limbs to slumber's quiet influence; when Sleep, lightly gliding from the ethereal stars, parted
the dusk air and clove the shades, in quest, Palinurus, of thee,
and laden with fatal dreams for thy guiltless eyes! On the tall
poop the god alighted in semblance of Phorbas, and opened his
lips to such intent: 'Palinurus, Iasus' son, the seas themselves
convoy the fleet; the winds breathe steadily: it is slumber's hour.
Pillow thy head, and steal those weary eyes from their toil!
Myself for a space will assay thy charge.' To whom Palinurus,
scarce lifting his gaze: 'Wouldst thou have me blind to the face of
the tranquil flood and the quiet waves? Wouldst thou have me
put faith in that monster of unfaith? Say, shall I trust Aeneas to
the forsworn gales? – I who have been cozened so oft by the
treachery of an unruffled sky!' Such reply he vouchsafed; and,
rooted to his grasp, withdrew no whit his hand from the rudder
nor his eye from the stars. But, lo, the god, – waving over either

temple a bough, steeped in Lethe's dew and charmed to slumber by Stygian spell, – constrained his swimming eyes to resign the struggle. And hardly had the sudden sleep touched his nerveless limbs, ere bending above he flung him sheer into the flowing waves, rending away, as he fell, part of the poop and the rudder, and calling vainly and oft to his comrades. Himself, on rapid pinion, soared into the substanceless air. – Yet no less the fleet rode securely over the deep, and sped onward, dauntless in the promise of Father Neptune.

And now, advancing, it neared the cliffs of the Sirens, ; perilous of yore, and white with the bones of many men, though then the raucous cliffs but echoed afar to the incessant waves, when the sire grew ware that the errant barque floated void of her master, and with his own hand guided her over the mighty flood, much sighing and stricken to the heart by his friend's doom: 'O trustful over-much in the calm of sky and deep, thou shalt lie, Palinurus, naked on the alien strand!'

BOOK VI

THUS, WEEPING, he spoke and gave rein to the fleet, and at length rode by Cumae and her Euboean shores. They turned the prows to sea; the anchor with biting tooth gripped the barks, and the crooked keels lined the beach. All ardent, the banded youth leaped out on the Hesperian strand. Part sought the seeds of flame lurking in veins of flint: part despoiled the woods – dense covert of the wild beast – and shewed the discovered streams. But good Aeneas repaired to the heights, whereover Apollo holds ward aloft, and to the cavern, vast and remote, that guards the secrecy of the dread Sibyl, on whom the seer of Delos breathes his great mind and soul, and unfolds the days to be. And now they drew to the groves of Trivia and the golden fane.

Daedalus, – so fame tells, – when he fled from the realms of Minos, adventuring on rapid pinion to commit himself to the skies, floated along his unwonted path to the icy North, then hovered and alighted on the Chalcidian hill. There first restored to earth, he consecrated, Phoebus, to thee the oarage of his wings, and reared a mighty temple. On the doors was seen Androgeos dead; and, nigh to him, the children of Cecrops, doomed – ah woe! – to the yearly penalty of seven lives of their sons. – There stood the urn, and they drew the lots! – Fronting

these, the Gnosian land rose in counterpart from the main.
There was portrayed that cruel passion for the bull, the device of
Pasiphae's lust, and the mingled birth of two-fold kind, the
Minotaur – pledge of a nameless love. There was that laboured
pile and its maze, – inextricable for ever, had not Daedalus, in
compassion for the queen's great love, himself resolved the traitorous riddle of the palace, guiding with a clue the lover's viewless footsteps. And thou, also, Icarus, – a great part had been
thine in the great work, had grief allowed. Twice he assayed to
depict thy fate in gold: twice the father's hands sank impotent.

All this their gaze would have perused in order, had not
Achates returned from his errand in their van, and, with him, the
priestess of Phoebus and Trivia, Deiphobe, Glaucus' child, who
thus addressed the king: 'Not such the sights that this hour
demands! Now were it meeter to slay seven steers from the
unyoked herd, and as many ewes duly chosen.' Aeneas thus
admonished, – and his men delayed not to do her sacred bidding
– the priestess summoned the Teucrians into the lofty shrine.

Of the Euboean rock, one vast side is hewn into a cavern,
whither lead a hundred broad avenues and a hundred gateways,
whence issue voices as many, charged with the Sibyl's response.
The threshold was barely gained, when the maiden cried: 'It is
the hour to inquire your fates! The god, – behold the god!' And
as she stood by the doors and spoke, suddenly her countenance
and her hue changed, and her tresses fell disordered: her bosom
panted, her wild heart swelled with fury, and she grew taller to
the view, and her voice rang not of mortality, now that the god
breathed on her in nigher presence. 'Art thou slothful,' she cried,
'in vow and prayer? Slothful, Aeneas of Troy? For only so shall
be unsealed the mighty portals of this awe-stricken fane.' She
said, and was mute. A chill trembling thrilled through their stout
Teucrian breasts, and the king broke into prayer from his heart
of hearts: 'Phoebus, who hast pitied always the sore agony of
Troy, – Phoebus, who didst wing the Dardan shaft from Paris'
hand to the frame of Aeacus' son, – under thy guidance have I
entered these many seas, that circle their great continents, and
Massylia's farthest tribes, and the fields that the Syrtes fringe.
And now, at length, we clutch at the borders of a receding Italy!
Then grant that thus far – nor farther – the star of Troy shall
have followed us! Ye, too, at this hour, may meetly spare the
people of Pergamus, gods and goddesses all, who brooked not
Ilium nor the high renown of our Dardan realm! And thou,

prophetess most holy, who foreknowest the days to come, vouchsafe (for I ask but the kingdom due to my destiny) a home for the Teucrians in Latium, – a home for their way-worn gods and the storm-tost deities of Troy! Then will I raise to Phoebus and Trivia a fane of solid marble, and in Phoebus' name ordain days of festival. Thee also a solemn shrine awaits in our realm: for there I will set thine oracles and the mysteries of fate that thou shalt reveal to my people; and I will consecrate chosen men to thy service, gracious maid! Only commit not thy songs to the leaves, lest, disordered, they flit abroad, the sport of boisterous winds. Let thine own lips prophesy, I entreat thee.' He said, and his lips were still.

But in her cavern the prophetess, intolerant yet of Phoebus' will, raved in limitless frenzy, straining to exorcize the mighty god from her soul: but all the more he curbed her foaming lips to weariness, subdued her fierce heart, and moulded her to his constraint. And now the hundred vast doorways of the shrine swung open of their own accord, and the response of the priestess came wafted through the air: 'O thou that at length hast outworn the great perils of the deep – though others, and heavier, await thee upon earth – the children of Dardanus shall come to the realm of Lavinium (trouble not thy soul for this), but they shall joy not at their coming. War – grim war – I descry, and Tiber foaming with torrents of blood! Thou shalt lack not a Simoïs, nor a Xanthus, nor a Dorian camp. Even now, another Achilles is prepared for thee in Latium, – goddess-born no less than thou! Nor anywhere shall Juno forbear to dog thy Teucrians: while thou, suppliant in the day of need, – what people of Italy, what city shall have heard not thy prayer! And the source of all this woe to Troy shall again be a foreign bridal, – again an alien bed. But yield not thou to any woes: but with bolder front fare forth to meet them in the path that thy fortune shall allow! The earliest step to salvation, – little though thou deem it, – shall be taken from a Grecian town!'

In such words the Cumaean Sibyl chanted her mysteries of fear from her shrine, and moaned from out the cavern, shrouding truth in darkness: – so potent the rein that Apollo shook above her frenzy, and the iron that he planted in her soul! So soon as the madness ceased and her raving lips were hushed, the hero began: 'Maiden, affliction can display no lineament that is new or strange to these eyes. All this I have foreknown and debated erewhile in my spirit. One boon I entreat! Since here, men say, is the portal of the infernal king and the sunless pool of brimming Acheron, be it granted me to pass to the sight and presence of my dear sire! Teach me the way, and unlock the hallowed gates! Him, through a ring of flames and a thousand pursuant spears, I bare into safety on these shoulders and rescued from the enemy's midst: his feeble frame accompanied my wanderings, and endured at my side every sea, every menace of ocean and sky, beyond the strength and desert of age. Nay, he it was who charged me, alike by prayer and command, that, suppliant, I should repair to thy presence and draw nigh to thy door! If Orpheus, reliant on his Thracian lyre and tuneful strings, could summon again the spirit of his bride – if Pollux redeemed his brother by interchange of death and treads and retreads the path so oft – of thy grace, I entreat thee, have compassion on son and sire; for thou hast all power, nor in vain hath Hecate set thee over the groves of Avernus! – What skills it to speak of Theseus? What, of great Alcides? In my veins, also, flows the blood of sovereign Jove!'

So prayed he, hand on altar, when thus the prophetess took the word: 'Seed of lineage celestial, Troy-born son of Anchises, light is the descent to Avernus! Night and day the portals of gloomy Dis stand wide: but to recall thy step and issue to the upper air – there is the toil and there the task! Few only have had the power – sons of the gods, whom a gracious Jove hath loved, or the flame of virtue exalted to the stars! The tract between is shrouded in forest and round it slide the black encircling folds of Cocytus! But if such yearning possess thy soul – if so deep thy desire, twice to float on the Stygian lake, twice to behold the gloom of Hell – and thy pleasure be to indulge this frenzied emprize, then hearken what must first be done! In a shady tree, a bough lies hidden, golden of leaf and pliant stem, and dedicated to Juno below. This all the grove conceals; and the shadows in the dusky glens enfold it. Yet to none is it given to enter the viewless places of earth, ere he have plucked from the tree its golden-tressed fruit; for such is the tribute that beauteous Proserpine hath ordained shall be brought for her proper meed. When the first is rent away a second, golden no less, succeeds, and the bough blossoms with ore as precious. Therefore let thine eye be piercing in the quest, and thine hand pluck it when duly found. For, if thou art called of Fate, lightly and freely it will obey: else, the strong hand shall avail thee not to subdue it, nor the tempered steel to sunder it. More, – though, alas, thou knowest it not, – the breathless clay of thy friend lies, defiling all the fleet with the presence of death, while thou seekest our response and lingerest on our threshold. Him lay thou first in his own place, and shelter him in the tomb. Lead black cattle to the altar: be that thy first peace-offering! So shalt thou behold, at the last, the Stygian groves and the realms untravelled by the living!' – She said, and locked her lips in silence.

With eyes downcast and countenance sorrow-clouded, Aeneas left the cavern and pursued his way, revolving in spirit the darkened future. By his side went loyal Achates, pacing under like weight of care; and much they communed with one another in changing discourse – what lifeless comrade the prophetess boded, what corpse for the burial! And, lo, when they came, they descried Misenus on the dry beach reft by an untimely death – Misenus, son of Aeolus, whom none surpassed in waking the heart of man by his clarion and kindling the battle by his note. Henchman once of great Hector, in Hector's train he braved the fray, glorious alike by trump and spear. Soon, when Achilles' victorious hand had despoiled his lord of life, the dauntless hero stooped not to lower service, but followed the banner of Dardan Aeneas. But on that day, while haply he thrilled the seas with hollow shell and, infatuate, challenged Heaven to dispute the palm, jealous Triton – if credence be meet – seized his mortal frame and plunged him amid the rocks into the foaming flood. So all made their loud moan about him; good Aeneas above the rest. Then, unlingering, they discharged in tears the command of the Sibyl, and with emulous zeal piled the altar of sepulture with trees and exalted it heaven-high. Forth they went into the immemorial forest, where the wild beasts dwelt in lofty covert. The pines tottered and fell, and the smitten holm rang under the axe; ashen beams and fissile oak they cleft with the wedge, and from the hills rolled down the great mountain-ashes.

Nor less, amid their toil, Aeneas was foremost to cheer his men and to gird him with weapons even as theirs. And as, communing himself with his own sad heart, he gazed on the measureless forest, so, haply, he shaped his prayer: 'O that now, in this great forest, the golden bough might gleam upon our eyes from its tree! For over-truly – alas! – the prophetess told of thee, Misenus!' Scarce had he spoken, when it so fell that two doves came flying from heaven before the very visage of the hero, and alighted on the green sward. Straight the heroic prince knew them for his mother's birds, and joyously sent up his prayer: 'If any way there be, O guide ye our feet! and bend your course through the skies to those groves where the precious bough shadows the fertile earth! And thou, goddess and mother, desert not our dubious fortunes!' So saying, he stayed his steps and watched what signs they brought, and whither their flight would tend. Feeding the while, they advanced on the wing so far as the eye of the travellers might discern them: then, when they drew to the gorge of noisome Avernus, incontinent they soared aloft, and, gliding through the unclouded blue, lit side by side on their chosen goal – a tree, through whose branches flashed the contrasting glimmer of gold. As, in the snows of winter, the mistletoe – sown of no parent tree – blossoms in unfamiliar leaves and encircles the tapering boles with shoots of saffron, so seemed the aureate foliage on the dark holm, so tinkled the foil to the gentle breeze. – Straight Aeneas seized it, overbore its reluctance with eager hand, and brought it to the Sibyl's prophetic roof.

Nor less, meanwhile, on the strand, the Teucrians wept Misenus and tendered the last meed to his ingrate dust. And first they built a pyre, unctuous with brands and high-piled with oaken beams. They wreathed the sides in sober leaves, planted funereal cypresses in the front, and decked the summit in the dead man's shining panoply. Part prepared the heated water, in cauldrons bubbling over the flames, and, moaning, washed and anointed the chill clay; then laid the tear-dewed limbs on their couch, and cast above them purple robes – the wonted pall. Part – sad ministry! – stooped beneath the giant bier, and, as their fathers used, held the torch beneath with averted eyes. Offerings of frankincense, viands, and bowls of streaming oil, were flung upon the fire and consumed. Then, when the embers were sunken and the flames burned low, they slaked the relics and thirsty ashes with wine, and Corynaeus gathered the bones again and enshrined them in a casquet of bronze. Thrice, moreover, he bore pure water round the circuit of his comrades, sprinkling them with light spray from a bough of fruitful olive, and purified them all, and pronounced the last farewell. But good Aeneas raised over the dead a massy sepulchre, with the arms of the hero's calling, his oar and his trumpet, under a skyey hill, that now from him is called *Misenus*, and preserves his name eternal throughout the ages. – This done, he hastened to fulfil the Sibyl's mandate.

A cavern there was, that yawned abysmal and vast – jagged, and guarded by its sunless lake and the midnight of its groves – wherever no winged creature could fly on its way unscathed: so pestilent the breath steaming from its dark gorge to the cope of heaven! Here the priestess first set four steers, black of body, and poured wine upon their brows; then, plucking the topmost tufts from betwixt the horns, laid them on the holy flames for earliest offering, calling the while on Hecate, queen alike in Heaven and Hell. Others set the knife to the throat and caught the warm blood in vessels. Himself, Aeneas smote with the sword a ewe-lamb of sable fleece to the mother of the Furies and her mighty sister, and to thee, Proserpine, a barren heifer. Then to the Sty-gian king he reared altars by night, and placed on the flames whole carcases of bulls, pouring rich oil over the burning flesh. But, lo, about the first rays of the orient sun, earth began to moan under foot, and the ridges of forest to tremble, and hounds seemed to bay through the twilight, as the goddess drew nigh. 'Hence, O hence,' cried the prophetess, 'ye that are uninitiate! Withdraw ye from all the grove! And thou – get thee on thy way and unsheathe thy brand! Now is the hour, Aeneas, for the dauntless spirit – now for the stout heart!' So far she spoke; then, frenzied, cast herself into the cavern; while he, with no timorous step, held pace with his guide.

Ye Gods, who bear sceptre over souls, ye mute phantoms, and ye, Chaos and Phlegethon, realms far-silent beneath the night, – suffer me to speak as I have heard – suffer me by your will to reveal that which is hidden in the abysms of earth and darkness!

Dim under the lone night, they journeyed through the shad-ows, through the vacant halls of Dis and his unsubstantial king-dom: – even as one who journeys in a forest under the niggard light of the faltering moon, when Jove has curtained the sky in shade, and the blackness of night bereaves Nature of her hue. Hard before the portal, in the opening jaws of Hell, Grief and avenging Cares have made their couch; and with them dwell wan Disease and sorrowful Age, and Fear, and Hunger, temptress to Sin, and loathly Want – shapes of ghastly mien – and Death, and Toil; and Sleep, Death's brother, and the guilty Joys of the Soul, and doom-fraught War, full in the gateway, and the iron cham-bers of the Furies, and raving Discord with viperous locks bound in sanguine fillets.

In the midst is an elm, shadowy and vast, with boughs and age-worn arms spread wide; and in it, men say, dwell vain Dreams, adherent to every leaf. And many a shape else is there of beasts monstrous and manifold – Centaurs couchant by the doors, Scyl-las double-formed, Briareus with his hundred hands, and the creature of Lerna hissing fearfully; the Chimaera, weaponed with flame, the Gorgons, and the Harpies, and the semblance of the tricorporate shade. Thereon Aeneas, unnerved by sudden alarm, snatched at his sword and offered the naked edge to their approach: and had not his sage companion admonished him that these were but lives, substanceless and bodiless, flitting under a hollow phantasm of form, he had rushed upon them, cleaving the shadows asunder with idle steel.

Hence parts the way which leads to the billows of Tartarean Acheron; whose turbid stream seethes with mud and giant eddies, and disgorges into Cocytus all its sands. Water and river are guarded by a grim ferryman, ghastly and foul, – Charon, his chin an unkempt mass of hoariness, his glaring eyes flame-shot, his squalid, knotted garb pendent from his shoulders. Pole in hand, himself he drives his bark, trims the sails, and convoys the dead in sable galley: for, old though he be, the age of a god is hale and green. To him the whole throng rushed, streaming to the bank, – matrons, and men and great-souled heroes who had lived their lives; boys and maidens unwed, and youths laid on the pyre before their parents' eyes. In legions they came, many as the leaves that fall in the forest at the first chill breath of Autumn, – many as the birds that flock from the unplumbed flood to earth, when the season of snows drives them fugitive across the waves, and consigns them to a sunnier clime. There they stood, all pleading that first they might make the passage, their hands out-stretched in yearning for the farther shore. But the grisly ferry-man received now these and now those, while others he thrust away and banished afar from the strand. Wondering, and moved by the turmoil: 'Speak, maiden,' Aeneas cried, 'and say, what imports this concourse to the river? What seek the souls? Or what judgement dooms these to quit the brink, – those to row sweeping through the livid waters?' To him the aged priestess made brief response: 'Seed of Anchises, offspring most sure of Heaven, thou seest the deep pools of Cocytus and the morass of Styx, by whose power the gods fear to swear and swear the false. All this throng that thou viewest is helpless and tombless. The ferryman is Charon, and they that sail the flood are the buried. Nor may he bear them away from those awful banks, across the hoarse waters, ere their bones have found a resting-place. For a hundred years they wander and flit round these shores: then, nor before, they are received and review the pool of their desire.' The child of Anchises paused, and, much pondering, stayed his steps, pitying at heart their cruel doom. There he beheld, all mournful and guerdonless of death's last tribute, Leucaspis and Orontes, captain of the Lycian fleet, who together had sailed from Troy over the windy deep, and together were whelmed by the South, vessel and men alike engulfed.

And lo, his helmsman Palinurus drew nigh – Palinurus, who but now, as he voyaged from Libya, with gaze riveted to the stars, had fallen precipitate from the poop into mid ocean. So soon as with straining eye he traced his sad features in the great gloom, he took the word and thus spoke: 'What god, Palinurus, reft thee from us and sank thee under the ocean-floor? Speak and say! For in this sole response Apollo – never erst proved faithless – deluded my soul, in that he prophesied, thou shouldst be scatheless from the deep and shouldst come to the borders of Ausonia! And is this his plighted faith?' But he: – 'Anchises' son, my liege, neither did the tripod of Phoebus beguile thee, nor any god whelm me in the deep! For, as I kept my appointed ward, and governed our course, I fell, and haply by sheer force rent away the rudder, to which I clung, and dragged it down with me. Be witness the cruel seas, that for myself I conceived no such fear as for thy ship – lest, despoiled of her helm and bereft of her master's hand, she might fail amid the mountainous billows that arose! For three wintry nights, the boisterous South flung me through the brine, over the infinite main. Hardly, on the fourth dawn, uplifted on a crested wave, I descried Italy, and, little by little, swam to earth. And now safety was in my grasp; but while, cumbered in my dank weeds, I clutched with bended fingers at the jagged points of a mountain crag, a barbarous race assaulted me with the sword, and in their ignorance deemed me a prize. Now the wave possesses me; and the winds toss me on the shore. Therefore, I beseech thee, by the pleasant light of heaven and the air, by thy sire, and by the hope of thy rising Iulus, rescue me, unvanquished that thou art, from these woes! Either cast earth upon me – the power is thine – and seek again the Veline port; or, if any way there be – if any thy goddess mother reveal (for not, methinks, without celestial warrant thou preparest to sail these dread streams and the Stygian pool) – vouchsafe thy hand to my misery and take me with thee across the flood, that in death at least I may find a haven of calm!' So had he spoken, when thus the prophetess began: 'Whence, Palinurus, this unhallowed yearning of thine? Is it thou, the tombless, who wouldst look on the waters of Styx and the Furies' relentless stream, and tread the brink unbidden? Abandon hope that the decrees of heaven may bend to prayer! Yet hear, and forget not my word, that shall solace the hardship of thy lot: for, far and wide throughout their cities, the peoples upon that border shall be driven by portents from Heaven to propitiate thy dust, to rear thee a sepulchre, and to render yearly offerings thereto; and the place shall bear for ever the name of Palinurus.' His sorrows assuaged by her word, for a little space grief fled from his anguished heart, and he rejoiced in the land to bear his name.

So they pursued their journey begun, and drew to the river. But, on the instant, so soon as the rower descried them from the Stygian wave, wending through the voiceless grove and turning their steps to the bank, unchallenged he accosted them, and assailed them with rebuke: 'Whosoever thou art, that in harness of war tendest to our streams, haste thee; speak thine errand whence thou standest, and stay thy step! Here is the world of Shadows, of Sleep, and of slumberous Night: no body of the living my Stygian barque may receive! Nor to my joy, in sooth, did I yield Alcides passage over the lake, nor Theseus and Pirithous – though they were the seed of Heaven, and of strength unvanquished. The one stretched forth his hand to enchain the warder of Hell, and dragged him trembling from the King's very throne: the twain assayed to ravish our queen from the chamber of Dis!' To this the Amphrysian priestess in brief: 'Shrink not away! Here no such treachery harbours; no violence our weapons import! In peace the huge watcher of the gate may bay for ever in his cavern, affrighting the bloodless shades: in peace and honour Proserpine may dwell in her uncle's hall! Trojan Aeneas, for piety famed and arms, descends to seek his sire in the nethermost gloom of Erebus. If the vision of duty so signal moves thee not, yet know this bough!' – and she discovered the bough that lay unseen in her vesture. At once the surging ire of his heart was lulled, and they held no further parle; but surveying in wonder that awful gift of the fateful rod, seen now after so many days, he turned his sable barque and approached the shore; then discharged the rout of other spirits, who sate by the long thwarts, cleared the gangways, and, with the act, received the giant frame of Aeneas in his hull. Groaning under his weight, the sewn craft drank in the ooze through its bursting seams; till at length prophetess and hero were landed scatheless across the wave, on the dreary slime and grey sedge.

These realms echo to the triple-throated bark of huge

Cerberus, whose enormous bulk reposes in a cavern that fronts the stream. To him the priestess, who saw that the serpents of his neck began to bristle, flung a cake drowsy with honey and medicated corn. He, opening his triple jaws in rabid hunger, snatched it as it came, and, his monstrous frame relaxed, sank to earth, and lay with vast limbs covering all the den. The warder's vigilance entombed, Aeneas gained the approach, and passed swiftly from the bank of that stream whence none return.

Straight, voices broke on their ears, and sore wailing, – the souls of infants weeping, whom, on life's earliest threshold, portionless of its bliss and torn from their mothers' breast, the black day swept from sight and merged in the bitter wave of death. By these stood they who were doomed to die on lying charge. Yet not without the lot, not without judgement, these seats are assigned! Minos sits president and shakes the urn: he summons his conclave of the silent, and he notes their lives and sins. The regions, that succeed, a mournful people tenants; – they, the innocent, who raised their hands in self-slaughter, and, for loathing of the sunlight, flung life away. Alas, how gladly now would they endure, in the upper air, both penury and all duresse of toil! The laws of Heaven forbid; the unlovely pool with its weary waves enchains them, and Styx, nine times interfused, debars them.

No great way hence, spread wide upon every hand, the Mourning Plains, that men so style, encounter the view. Here, unseen in secret walks and embowered in groves of myrtle, dwell they whom relentless Love consumed with wasting pain: even in death, the pang abandons them not. In this region he discerned Phaedra, and Procris, and sad Eriphyle, pointing to the wounds of her pitiless son, and Evadne, and Pasiphaë. At their side went Laodamia, and Caeneus, once youth, now woman, and restored by revolving Fate to her ancient semblance. Among these, Phoenician Dido, fresh from her death-stroke, wandered in the great forest. So soon as the hero of Troy stood nigh to her, and knew her dim form through the shadows – as one that, when the month is new, sees, or thinks he sees, the moon rising amid the clouds – the tears began to fall, and he spoke to her in loving tenderness: 'Unhappy Dido! and did the messenger, then, speak sooth, who told that thou wert undone, and that the steel had wrought thy doom? Alas, was I the cause of death to thee? By the stars I swear – by the gods in Heaven, and by all that is sacred in these abysms of earth – reluctantly, O queen, I sailed from thy shore! But the divine command, which now constrains me to journey through these shades, through realms rugged and blighted, and midnight profound, drove me thence, obedient to the behest: nor could I deem that, departing, I would bring upon thee this agony of sorrow. O stay thy step, nor withdraw thee from our view! Whom wilt thou flee! The last word that Fate allows is upon my lips!' So Aeneas spoke, with welling tears, striving to soothe the burning soul, mirrored in her grim eyes. She, with averted face, held her gaze fixed on earth; and her countenance was no more stirred by his faltered speech, than had she stood a pillar of stubborn flint or a cliff of Marpesian rock. At length she tore herself away, and, unreconciled, fled again to the shady grove, where her old-time lord responded to her sorrow, and Sychaeus gave love for love. – Yet, none the less, stricken to the heart by her unjust fate, Aeneas followed her afar with tears, and pitied her as she went.

Thence he assayed his appointed journey. – And now they walked those farthest fields, where sequestered dwell the renowned in war. Here Tydeus met his gaze; here Parthenopaeus, battle-famed; and the phantom of pale Adrastus. Here were princes of Dardan line, sore wept on the upper earth, and fallen in fight; and he sighed to behold them all in their long array: – Glaucus, and Medon, and Thersilochus, the three sons of Antenor, with Polyboetes, Ceres' priest, and Idaeus, still charioted, still weaponed. To right and to left, the clustering ghosts thronged round him; and it sufficed them not, once to have seen him; but they would fain linger still, and pace by his side, and learn the cause of his coming. But the Danaan chieftains and the legions of Agamemnon, so soon as they discerned the hero, and his harness refulgent through the dusk, wavered in panic fear. Part turned to flee, as erewhile when they sought the ships: part lifted a feeble voice, but the cry they assayed left them frustrate with gaping throat.

And here he descried Deiphobus, the son of Priam, his whole frame mangled, his visage cruelly marred – his visage and either hand – his temples shorn of the reft ears, and his nostrils maimed by hideous butchery. Scarce, indeed, he knew him, as, trembling, he sought to cover the traces of that nameless vengeance: then, in the once familiar tones, ungreeted he addressed him: 'Deiphobus – hero of battle, scion of Teucer's exalted line – what heart hath willed to exact such ruthless penalty? What hand hath been permitted to do this deed on thee? On that last fatal night, fame brought me tidings that, wearied by slaying thy thousands, thou wert sunk above a formless pile of Pelasgian dead. Then, with these hands, I upraised to thee, on the Rhoetean shore, a tenant-less sepulchre, and thrice with loud voice called upon thy spirit. Thy name and arms stand ward over the place; thyself, friend, I could not see nor lay in the natal soil that I left!' To which the son of Priam: 'Naught, friend of mine, didst thou leave undone! Thou hast paid in full to Deiphobus and to the shade of the slain! But me my destiny, and the deathly guilt of the Spartan woman, whelmed in this flood of calamity; behold these, the tokens that she left of her love! For how we whiled away that last night in deluding joys thou knowest: and over clear must remembrance start! When the fate-fraught horse came at a bound over the summit of Troy-towers, and brought, in impregnate womb, an armed infantry, she feigned a solemn dance and led our Phrygian dames around, clamorous in Bacchic frenzy, herself, in their midst, waving the broad flames and summoning her Danaans from the citadel-height. In that hour, I lay care-worn and heavy-eyed in our accursed bridal chamber: and, as I lay, a deep and pleasant sleep, calm as death, weighed upon me. Meantime, my matchless consort emptied the palace of every weapon: – even my faithful sword she had purloined from under my head! – then, flinging wide the door, called Menelaüs beneath my roof, hoping, I doubt not, that the guerdon would be precious in a lover's esteem, and that so she might cancel her ancient tale of ill! What boots it to linger? They burst into my chamber – they and, leagued with them, the scion of Aeolus, that counsellor of sin. Ye gods, repay the like to Greece, if with pious lips I call for vengeance! But thou, speak in thy turn, and say what chance hath brought the quick to the dead. Comest thou driven a pilgrim over ocean? Or what pursuit of fate constrains thee to tread these joyless, sunless abodes, these realms of turmoil?'

In this interchange of converse, the Dawn, on roseate car, had already crossed the mid cope of heaven in her empyreal course. And perchance they had so consumed their allotted space, but the Sibyl at their side admonished them with brief address:

'Night falls, Aeneas; we weep, but the hours pass. Here is the place, where the road parts in twain. To the right, it runs under the palace-walls of sovereign Dis; and thereby our way to Ely-sium lies. But the left-hand path is the path of vengeance, and guides the sinner to godless Tartarus.' Thereto Deiphobus: 'Be not angered, mighty priestess! I will go my way, – I will fill full the tale and restore me to my darkness. Go thou, our glory, – go, and a kindlier fate be with thee!' Thus far he said, and, on the word, turned and went.

Suddenly Aeneas glanced back, and, under a leftward cliff, descried a broad fastness sheathed in a triple wall. About it shot a circling river of torrent flame, Tartarean Phlegethon, swirling with thunderous rocks. In the van rose a giant gate and pillars of solid adamant, that no strength of man – nay, not the denizens of an embattled Heaven – may overthrow: star-challenging stands the iron tower, and Tisiphone, her gory pall girt high, sits sleepless night and day, holding guard at the portal. Thence issued a sound of moaning, and the strident, pitiless scourge; anon, the clank of iron and trailing fetters. Aeneas halted, and, paling, drank in the tumult. 'What features here hath sin to shew? Speak, maiden, and say! What burden of vengeance is thus imposed? What din so loudly assails our ear?' Then began the prophetess: 'Famed captain of Troy, none that is innocent may plant foot on that guilt-stained threshold. But, when Hecate set me over the groves of Avernus, her own lips taught me Heaven's penalties, and she guided me through all. Over these realms Gnosian Rhadamanthus holds iron sway, and chastises secret guilt, and hears its tale, and exacts confession of every crime, that man hath committed among men, and, exultant in the vain deceit, delayed atonement till the latest hour of death. Forthwith avenging Tisiphone, girt with the lash, scourges the cowering sinner, scorn in her mien, and, with grim serpents brandished in her left, summons her pitiless sisterhood. Then at last the infernal gates dispart, grating on horrid hinge. Seest thou the sentry that sits by the portal – the shape that guards the threshold? With fifty throats yawning black, the Hydra, yet fiercer, habits within: while Tartarus' self gapes with abrupt descent, and stretches twice as far, down through the shades, as the heavenward gazing eye looks up to Olympus and the firmament. Here the antique brood of Earth – the Titan strain – hurled down by the bolted thunder, welter in the nethermost abyss. Here, too, I saw the twin sons of Aloeus, giant-statured, who set their hand to pluck down the height of Heaven, and to banish Jove from his ethereal throne. And Salmoneus I saw, acquitting the remorseless penalty, that fell on him as he mimicked Jove's fire and the thunder that speaks from Olympus. Charioted behind four coursers, a torch shaken in his hand, he fared in triumph through the peoples of Greece and the heart of Elis' city, demanding the homage due to deity; – madman, who would counterfeit the storm-cloud and the levin inimitable, by the clang of bronze and the trampling of horn-footed steeds! But the almighty Sire, amid serried clouds, flung his bolt – no firebrands he, nor torches of pitchy glare! – and smote him headlong below in the raving whirlwind. Tityos, moreover, was there to see – foster-child of Earth's universal motherhood. Over nine full acres his body lies stretched, while a monstrous vulture tears with crooked beak at his imperishable heart and the flesh impregnate with pains: deep lodged beneath his breast, it delves for the banquet, and the renascent filaments know no respite. What boots it to rehearse the Lapiths, Ixion or Pirithous? (What boots it to tell of Tantalus), over whose head pends the gloomy rock, ever in act to fall, ever in seeming descent? The banqueting couches gleam high on golden pillars, and the feast is set before his face in kingly luxury: but, couched at his side, the eldest of the Furies forbids him to lay hand upon the board, and starts erect with torch uplifted and thunder on her lips. Here dwell they who, while life endured had hatred for their brethren, a blow for a parent, or the toils of fraud for a client; who found wealth and brooded thereover alone, nor shared it with their kin (the greatest number this); who were slain for adultery; or who followed unrighteous war, nor feared to break the allegiance plighted to their lords – all prisoned, all awaiting their doom. That doom, seek not thou to learn; nor yet the guise of fortune wherein they are whelmed! Some roll huge rocks unceasingly, or hang bound on the spokes of wheels: Theseus, unblest, sits where he shall sit for ever, and Phlegyas in agony cries warning to all, and, loud-voiced, proclaims through the gloom: *Behold, and learn to do justice and contemn not the gods!* This bartered his country for gold and set upon her the tyrant's yoke; laws he made for a price, and for a price unmade. This assailed his daughter's bed and forced a nameless bridal. All dared unutterable sin, and succeeded where they dared. – Not though a hundred tongues were mine – a hundred mouths and a voice of iron – could I number all those forms of crime, or rehearse the tale of vengeance.'

So said, the aged priestess of Phoebus pursued: 'But come thou now, resume thy way, and fulfil the service thou hast assayed. I descry those battlements, reared by the Cyclopian forge, and the gates with fronting arch, where our commandments received enjoin us to lay these offerings.' She ceased; and, advancing side by side through the twilight of the ways, they abridged the intervening space and drew to the doors; where, gaining the entry, Aeneas sprinkled himself with living water and planted the bough full on the threshold.

This at length performed and the service of the goddess discharged, they came to the realms of joy – the pleasant lawns of the Happy Groves, and the seats of the Blest. Here an ampler ether invests the plains in radiance, and they know their own sun and their own stars. Part ply their limbs in the verdant lists and, in sportive conflict, wrestle on the yellow sand: part tread the dance, and sing. Amid these the priest of Thrace sits in flowing cincture, and, with sevenfold note, makes music to their measure, sweeping his lyre, now with the hand, anon with quill of ivory. Here is Teucer's immemorial race, a fairest line – great-hearted heroes, that were born in better years – Ilus and Assaracus, and Dardanus, parent of Troy. – Distant, he marvelled at their arms and shadowy cars. Their spears stood planted in earth, and their yokeless steeds browsed over the champaign at large. For all the delight in chariot and armour, that was theirs among the living – all their care in pasturing their sleek coursers – follows them, changeless, when they are laid beneath the soil. And, lo, others he descried, to right and left, feasting on the green-sward and singing in quire a joyful paean, all in a scented grove of laurel, whence the waters of Eridanus roll upward, broad-brimming through the forest. Here was the company of them, who battled and bled for their fatherland; here they who were priests and holy, while life knew them still; they who were loyal bards and sang meetly for Phoebus' ear, or ennobled life by arts discovered; with all whose service to their kind won them remembrance among men – each brow cinctured with snowy fillet. Whose circumfluent throng the Sibyl accosted: – Musaeus before the rest; for he stood the centre of the multitude, that gazed upward to his face, as head and shoulders he towered above them: 'Say, ye happy souls, and thou, best of bards, what region – what haunt – owns Anchises? For his sake have we journeyed hither and sailed the great rivers of Erebus.' To her the hero, in brief reply: 'To none is there a fixed abiding-place. We tenant the shady groves, and dwell pillowed on the velvet banks, or in meadows fresh with running brooks. But ye – if such be the desire of your heart – ascend this ridge, and instant I will set your feet on an easy path.' He said, and, stepping in their van, showed them the lustrous plains below. These seen, they descended the mountain-crest.

But, deep in a green valley, father Anchises stood lost in

thought, surveying the prisoned spirits, destined hereafter to the sunlight, and reviewing, as it fell, the full tale of his people – his loved posterity, and their fates and fortunes, their manners and deeds. He, soon as he saw Aeneas advancing to meet him over the sward, extended either eager palm, while the tears streamed down his cheeks and a cry escaped his lips: 'And hast thou come at length? Has the love that failed not thy father's hope vanquished that perilous path? Is it mine, my son, to look on thy face, and to hear and answer thy familiar tones? Thus, in truth, my musing heart deemed that the issue would be, as I pondered thy times; nor hath my care belied me! How many the lands, how wide the seas, whereover thou hast travelled to my arms! What storms of peril, my son, have tost thee! How I feared the Afric realms might harm thee!' But he: 'Thy shade, my father, thy troubled shade, that ever and again rose before me, constrained me to wend to these portals! My fleet rides the Tyrrhene brine. Suffer me to clasp thy hand – suffer me, father of mine – nor withdraw thee from our embrace!' So he said, while the tears rained down his cheeks. Thrice, where he stood, he assayed to throw his arms round his neck: thrice the phantom fled through the hands that clutched in vain, light as the winds and fleet as the pinions of sleep!

Meanwhile, in a retired vale, Aeneas discerned a sequestered grove and whispering forest brakes, with the river of Lethe floating past those homes of peace. About it hovered peoples and nations unnumbered: – as when, in the cloudless summer, bees alight on the thousand-hued flowerets and stream round the snowy lilies, while all the plain murmurs to their busy hum. Starting at the sudden vision, Aeneas, unknowing, inquired the cause – what were yon distant streams, who the men that in serried array beset the banks? Then father Anchises: 'Spirits they are, to whom Fate owes a second body, and by the wave of Lethe river they drink the careless waters and deep oblivion. Long, in truth, I have desired to tell thee of these and reveal them before thine eyes – long, to rehearse this generation of my children, that so the more thou mayest rejoice with me in Italy discovered.' – 'O father, shall we deem that any spirits travel hence, aloft to our earthly sky, and return again to the sluggish clay? What unblest yearning for the light possesses their blind hearts?' – 'I will speak, my son, nor hold thee in doubt,' rejoined Anchises; and unfolded all in order.

'First, know that heaven and earth, and the watery plain, and the Moon's lucent sphere, and Titan's star, an indwelling spirit sustains, and a mind, fused throughout the limbs sways the whole mass and mingles with the giant frame. Thence the race of man and of beast, and the life of every winged thing, and the monsters that Ocean bears under his marble floor. To these seeds a flame-like vigour pertains and an origin celestial, so far as the noxious body fetters them not, nor terrene limbs dull them, and members born but to die. Hence they fear and desire, and grieve and joy, nor discern the sky from their midnight fastness and viewless dungeon. Nor yet, alas, when life's latest gleam is fled, are they utterly freed from all ill and all the pests of the body; and it needs must be that many a taint, long ingrained, should be rooted wondrous deep in their being. Therefore they are amerced by punishment and pay the price of ancient evil. Some are hung outspread to the substanceless winds: from others the stain of guilt is washed clean under the waste of waters, or burnt away by fire. We suffer, each in his proper spirit; then are sent to the spacious plains of Elysium, where some few abide in the blissful fields; till at length the hoary ages, when time's cycle is run, purge the incarnate stain, and leave but the purified ethereal sense and the unsullied essential flame. All these, that thou seest, when they have turned the wheel through a thousand years, God summons in their legions to the river of Lethe, that, with memory disenthroned, they may review the vaulted heavens and conceive desire once more to tenant the flesh.'

Pausing, Anchises drew his son, and, with him, the Sibyl, into the midmost assemblage and the heart of the murmuring throng; then mounted a hillock, whence, in full view, he might scan all their long array, and note the lineaments of them that came:

'Come now and hearken to thy destiny, while my lips rehearse the glory that hereafter shall follow the Dardan line, and thy children's children, who shall be born of Italian race – illustrious souls and heritors of our name. He whom there thou seest – a youth leaning on maiden spear – holds the next allotted place in light, and first shall rise into the realms of day, Italian blood mingling in his veins – Silvius, Alban name. Him – thy latest child – thy spouse Lavinia shall bear to thee in the evening of life, a silvan king and the father of kings; and from him shall our line bear sceptre in Alba the Long. He that stands next is Procas, glory of the Trojan race; and, with him, Capys and Numitor, and he who shall renew thy name, Silvius Aeneas – peerless alike in piety and battle, if ever he shall mount the throne of Alba. What

men they be! Mark the might their port displays, and the civic
oak that shades their brows! These are they who shall rear for
thee Nomentum, and Gabii, and Fidenae city: – these, who shall
set on the hills Collatia's towers, and Pometii and Inuus' fort,
and Bola and Cora, that now are nameless lands, but shall then
be names. Romulus, withal, the child of Mavors, shall come at his
grandsire's side – Romulus, whom his mother Ilia shall bear of
the blood of Assaracus. Seest not, how the twin plumes rise from
his crest – how his father's own cognizance even now marks him
for the world above! Look, my son, and know that under his auspices shall glorious Rome bound her empire by earth, her pride
by Olympus, and, one in self, circle with her battlements the
seven hills, blest in a warrior race: even as the Berecyntian
Mother rides, chariot-borne, tower-crowned, through the Phrygian cities, rejoicing in her celestial offspring and clasping a hundred of her children's children – all dwellers in Heaven, all
tenants of the upper skies. Hither now turn thine either eye, and
behold this people, Rome's and thine. Here is Caesar and all
Iulus' strain, destined to ascend the great cope of heaven. Here,
yea here, is he of the promise that so often thou hast heard –
Caesar Augustus, child of deity, who shall establish again the age
of gold in Latium, through the fields where Saturn erewhile was
king, and shall enlarge his sway past the Garamant and Indian, to
the land that lies beyond the stars, beyond the path of year and
sun, where heaven-sustaining Atlas upholds on his shoulder the
fiery star-gemmed sphere. Even now, at dread of his coming, the
Caspian realms and Maeotian land tremble to the divine
response, and wavering and confusion reign by the mouths of
sevenfold Nile. Nor, in truth, did Alcides traverse such space of
earth, though he pierced the stag of brazen foot, though he
stilled the woods of Erymanthus, and taught Lerna to quake
before his bow; nor he who guides his car by reins of the vine-
leaf, all-conquering Liber, driving his tigers down from the tall
peak of Nysa. And doubt we yet to enlarge valour by exploit? Or
doth fear forbid to set foot on Ausonian earth? – But who is he
apart, conspicuous with olive-boughs, and in act of sacrifice? I
know the locks and hoary beard of that Roman king, who, called
from lowly Cures and a penurious earth to high dominion, shall
base the infant city securely on his laws. Next shall succeed one
fated to break his country's ease, and *Tullus* shall rouse to battle
his peace-worn warriors and the hosts that have forgot to triumph. On whom follows Ancus, the over-vaunting – even now

too eager for the breath of vulgar favour. Wouldst thou see the Tarquin kings, and the proud soul of avenging Brutus, and the fasces he regained? He shall be first to receive the consul's power and the axes of dread; and, when his sons would wake the sleeping war, their father shall summon them to penalty, for freedom's fair sake. Unhappy he, howsoever the after-world may judge of that deed! Yet shall the patriot's love prevail, and the unquenched thirst of renown! – And now survey the Decii and Drusi yonder, and Torquatus with pitiless axe, and Camillus bringing the standards again! But they whom thou seest refulgent in equal arms, souls at concord, now and so long as they are prisoned in night – alas, what mutual war, what battled legions and carnage shall they rouse, if ever they mount to the vital air! For the father shall descend from the Alpine heights and Monoecus' citadel, and his daughter's spouse shall confront him with the weaponed East! O my children, steel not your hearts to such dire conflict, nor turn your mighty hands against the breast of your motherland! And thou, who drawest thy lineage from Olympus – be thou first to shew mercy! Cast the sword from thy grasp, thou blood of my blood! – There stands he who shall drive his car in victory to the Capitol heights – triumphant over Corinth, glorious from slaughtered Achaea. Argos he shall uproot, and Agamemnonian Mycenae, and the heir of Aeacus' line, seed of Achilles armipotent, avenging his fathers of Troy and Minerva's polluted fane! Who could quit thee in silence, great Cato – or, Cossus, thee? Who the Gracchan race, or the twain of Scipio's line – two thunderbolts of war, the bale of Libya? or Fabricius great in poverty? or thee, Serranus, as thou sowest in thy furrowed fields? Ye Fabii, whither whirl ye my toiling steps? Thou art he, the Greatest, who singly restorest our state by delay! – Others, I ween, shall labour the breathing bronze to softer mould; they shall charm the features of life forth from the marble; they shall plead the cause with apter tongue; their wand shall trace the courses of heaven; and they shall tell the renascent stars! Roman, be this thy care – these thine arts – to bear dominion over the nations and to impose the law of peace, to spare the humbled and to war down the proud!'

Thus father Anchises; then, while they admired, pursued: 'Behold, how Marcellus advances, graced in the spoils of his own good sword – his victorious brow towering over all. This is he shall stay the Roman realm, when it totters beneath the shock of armed confusion: his horse's hooves shall trample on Carthaginian and rebel Gaul, and his hand, that reft it, shall hang before Father Quirinus the third suit of steel.' And now Aeneas – for he saw walking by his side a youth of comely form, shining in arms, but with downcast eyes and little joy on his visage: 'Who is he, my father, that thus attends the warrior's path? A son, or one of the heroic strain of his children's children? How the retinue about him murmurs praise! What majesty is in his port! Yet sable Night hovers round his head with mournful shade.' Then father Anchises began, while his tears welled: 'O my son, seek not to know the great agony of thy people! Him the fates shall but shew to earth, nor suffer longer to be. Too great in thy sight, O Heaven, the power of Rome's children, had this thy guerdon endured! What moaning of men shall echo from that famed Field to Mavors' queenly city! What obsequies, O Tiber, shalt thou see, when thou flowest by his new-raised grave! No child of Ilian blood shall raise his Latin ancestry so high in hope, nor ever again shall Romulus' land so vaunt her in any that she fosters. Alas for piety, alas for old-world faith, and the hand unvanquished in war! None scatheless had met his blade, whether on foot he marched against the foeman, or buried the spur in the flank of his reeking steed! Ay me, thou child of tears, if haply thou mayest burst the cruel barriers of fate, thou shalt be *Marcellus!* Give me lilies from laden hands; let me scatter purple blossoms, and shower these gifts – if no more – on the spirit of my child, till the barren service be so discharged.' Thus, through all that region, they wandered at large in the wide plains of mist, surveying all. And when Anchises had escorted his son throughout, and fired his soul with love of the glory to be, anon he rehearsed the wars that forthwith he must wage, and told of the Laurentine peoples, and the city of Latinus, and how pursuing he might flee or face each toil.

There are two gates of Sleep: – of horn, fame tells, the one, through which the spirits of truth find an easy passage; the other, wrought smooth-gleaming with sheen of ivory, but false the visions that the nether powers speed therefrom to the heaven above. There, with these words on his lips, Anchises parted from son and Sibyl, and dismissed them by the ivory gate.

Plying his way to the fleet, Aeneas joined his company; then sailed unswerving along the shore to Caieta's haven.

BOOK VII

THOU, TOO, Caieta, nurse of Aeneas, dying hast bequeathed an eternal fame to our shores; and still thine honour keeps thy resting-place, and in great Hesperia – if that be glory! – thy name marks thy dust!

But good Aeneas, when the last rites were duly rendered – when the mounded tomb was raised, and the deep seas were still, sailed forth on his way and left the haven. The breezes were blowing into the night; and, with beams dancing on the lustrous main, the bright moon smiled on their voyage. First they skirted the coast of Circe's realm; where, amid her treasures, the daughter of the Sun thrills her untrodden groves with incessant song, and in her queenly halls burns sweet-scented cedar-wood to illume the night, the while with shrill comb she sweeps the delicate warp. Thence they heard the ireful cry of lions, recusant of their bonds and roaring in the late nocturnal hour, and the raging of bristled boars and pent bears, and the howling of vast phantasmal wolves; creatures all, that Circe – fell deity! – had transformed, by potent herbs, from human semblance to bestial visage and frame! But lest the pious of Troy should approach that unholy strand, and, entering the haven, suffer the same unblest spell, Neptune filled their sails with a fair wind, and winged their flight, and bore them past the fervid waters. –

And now the sea mirrored the orient red, and from her ethereal height the yellow Dawn shone in rosy chariot; when the winds were hushed and every breath suddenly fell, and the oars toiled slowly through sluggish waves. And now Aeneas, gazing forth from the flood, descried a mighty forest; and, in the midst, Tiber's pleasant stream, leaping to the main with racing eddies and yellow burden of sand. About and above were gay-plumed birds, familiars of bank and channel, charming the heavens with song and flitting amid the woods. Bidding his crews change course and turn their prows to land, glad-hearted he entered the shaded river. –

Now come thou, Erato, and I will unfold what kings, what times, what modes of circumstance, – reigned in ancient Latium, when first the alien host ranged its barques on Ausonia's strand; and the prelude of opening battle I will recall! Heavenly maid, be thou my monitress! I will sing grim wars, and embattled lines, and princes whom valour urged to doom, – sing Etruria's bands

and all Hesperia mustered in arms! A nobler cycle of deeds
dawns on my view: a nobler task I assay!

King Latinus, grey-headed now, ruled over field and town in
the calm of a long peace. He, fame tells, was sprung of Faunus
and Marica, Laurentine nymph. To Faunus Picus was sire; and
Picus vaunts him thy seed, O Saturn: thou art the prime author
of their line. To him, by Heaven's doom, was no son, nor male
descent; for the flower that budded was plucked in youth. One
daughter remained – sole stay of the house, sole mistress in the
ample palace-halls – already ripe for wedlock, already of womanly years. From broad Latium and all Ausonia came many a
wooer: but fairest of all came Turnus, the mighty heir of a far-
descended line; whom to call son the queen strove with wondrous yearning; but celestial portents with manifold terrors
forbade. In the heart of the palace, deep-bowered in the inmost
courts, stood a laurel, sacred of leaf and preserved in awe through
many years. Men told how old Latinus himself found it there,
when he built his earliest towers, and hallowed it to Phoebus,
and named his people *Laurentine* by its name. Now on its summit
– hear and wonder! – clustering bees, floating with loud murmur
athwart the limpid air, sate leaguered, and, foot linked to foot,
hung in sudden swarm from the verdant bough. Instant the
prophet spoke: 'Behold an alien's advent! From the self-same
region marches his host to the self-same goal, and commands our
topmost towers!' More, while Lavinia stood maiden-like by her
father's side, with holy brand kindling the altar, they saw a sight
of dread. For she caught the fire in flowing tresses, and all her
head-gear burned in the bickering flames, – her queenly hair
blazing, blazing her jewelled coronet, – till, enwrapped in smoke
and yellow light, she scattered fire throughout the palace. Fearful
and wondrous Fame reported that vision. For the voice of the
seers declared, that to herself she boded glory of fame and fate,
but to her people a mighty war.

But the king, troubled by the omen, sought the oracle of
Faunus, his prophet-sire, and questioned the groves beneath
deep Albunea, where the queen of forests sounds to her sacred
rill and her dim glades exhale in pestilential vapour. Hence the
peoples of Italy and all the Oenotrian land seek answer in the day
of doubt; hither when the priestess brings her offering and lays
her down to sleep under the silent night, couched on skins of
slaughtered ewes, she sees a myriad phantoms flitting in marvellous mode, and hearkens to voices manifold – holds communion

with Heaven and speaks with Acheron in the abysm of Hell. Here then, also, King Latinus, himself in quest of answer, duly slew a hundred fleecy sheep and lay pillowed on their hides and outspread wool; when suddenly a voice spoke from the deep grove: 'Seek not, my child, to ally thy daughter in wedlock with the Latin, nor rest thy faith in the bridal chamber that is prepared! From afar shall come thy sons, whose blood shall exalt our name to the stars – whose children's children shall view the subject globe spinning beneath their feet, where the recurrent sun looks upon either ocean!' This, the response of Father Faunus and the counsel he gave in the silent grove, Latinus confined not within his lips; but Fame's wide-circling flight already had borne the tidings to Ausonia's cities, when the children of Laomedon moored their barques to the river's grassy bank.

Aeneas, and his captains, and fair Iulus, couched their limbs under the boughs of a lofty tree, and there set forth the banquet, spreading wheaten cakes along the sward to sustain their viands – for Jove himself inspired the thought – and crowning the Cereal base with fruits of the field. Here, then, it chanced that the poverty of their meal constrained them – all else consumed – to assail their scant store of bread, to profane with hand and venturous tooth the cake's fateful round, nor to spare the broad squares. 'What! we devour our tables too!' quoth Iulus, jesting; then ceased. Instant that utterance revealed the bourne of their travail; instant the sire caught it from the lips of his son, and stilled his speech, admiring the celestial sign. Then straight he cried: 'Hail, land of destiny, promised to me! And hail, ye faithful divinities of Troy! Behold our home; behold our country! For now remembrance comes that Anchises bequeathed me this mystic decree of fate: *My son, when borne to an unknown shore, hunger shall compel thee – all viands spent – to consume thy boards, then hope thou a home to thy weariness, and there remember to rear thine earliest dwellings and to gird them with a wall!* This was that hunger: this the supreme trial reserved, that shall set an end to death! Then up, and, glad with the sun's prime ray, let us walk abroad from the haven, and explore what be these regions, who their habitants, and where the city of the nation! Now pour your goblets to Jove, invoke with prayer Anchises our father, and restore the wine to the board.'

So said, he wreathed his brows in a leafy spray, and implored the Genius of the place, and Earth – eldest of gods – and the Nymphs, and the rivers yet unknown; then Night, and Night's orient signs, and Jove of Ida, and the great Phrygian Mother, each in order, with the twain that gave him life – in Heaven the one, in Erebus the other. On this, the Father omnipotent thrice thundered loud from the firmament on high, and, with his own hand, shook forth to view a cloud blazing with golden shafts of light. Incontinent the bruit was noised through the Trojan ranks, that the day had come to found their promised city: emulously all renewed the banquet and, cheered by the high presage, set on the bowls and crowned the wine.

On the morrow, when the nascent Day was gilding earth with her earliest torch, disparting they explored the city and bounds and coasts of the nation. Here, men told, were, the waters of Numicius' fount; here Tiber's stream; and there the stout Latins dwelt. – Then he of Anchises born commanded a hundred envoys, the chosen of every order, to bend their steps to the king's august town, shaded all by the boughs of Pallas – there to place gifts in his hand and entreat peace for Troy. Delay was none: they hastened with zealous step to do their mandate; while the prince with shallow trench traced his city-walls, labouring the ground, and circling, after the semblance of a camp, this his first settlement on the strand with battlements and mounds. And now, their journey outworn, the embassage discerned the towers and stately roofs of Latium, and drew to the ramparts. Before the city, boys and youths in the first flower of age schooled them in horsemanship, and tamed their harnessed steeds on the dusty plain; or bent the elastic bow, or hurled the tough javelin amain, or vied in strife of foot or hand – when a messenger spurred past with tidings for the ear of his grey-haired king, that men were come of gigantic port and attire unknown. Bidding them be called within the palace, he seated him in the midst on the throne of his fathers.

Royal and vast, sublime on a hundred columns, rose his halls above the city height, erst the palace of Laurentine Picus, clothed in reverend forest and the awe of generations. Here, obedient to sacred ordinance, the kings received their sceptres and first uplifted the insignia of power: this temple was their senate-house, the scene of their sacrificial feasts; and here, when the ram was slain, the elders sat ever along the tables' unbroken line. More, there stood in the portal the images of their forefathers of yore, all wrought in sequence from ancient cedar, – Italus and father Sabinus, planter of the vine, the pruning-hook still in his carven hand, and aged Saturn, and the semblance of Janus,

double-visaged, and all their kings else from the beginning, and
they who felt the mortal steel in battle for their fatherland. And
many arms, moreover, hung on the sacred doors, – captive cars
and crooked axes, helmet-plumes and massy bars of city-gates,
and spears, and shields, and beaks wrenched from ships of war.
Picus himself sat there, bearing Quirinus' wand and girt in short-
ened robe, on his left the holy shield, – Picus, the tamer of
steeds, whom, in the frenzy of desire, Circe smote with her
golden rod, and by poisons changed to a bird with scattered hues
upon his wing.

Such was that temple of the Gods, wherein Latinus, seated on
his ancestral throne, summoned the Teucrians to his hall and
presence, and, as they entered, greeted them with placid mien:
'Say, ye sons of Dardanus, – for your race and city we know, nor
unheralded hath been your course over ocean, – what seek ye?
What cause, or what necessity, hath borne you to our Ausonian
shore through so many an azure sea? But, whether strayed from
your way or tempest-driven, chances that full often betide the
sailor on the main, – howsoever ye have entered the banks of our
river and ride in our haven, – mistrust not our welcome, but
know in our Latin race the people of Saturn, just by no rigour of
law, but established in righteousness by untrammelled will and
the custom of ancient deity. And in truth I remember, though
years have dimmed the tale, that Auruncan elders told how Dardanus was sprung from this soil of ours, and hence won his way
to Phrygia's Idaean cities and Thracian Samos that now men
style Samothrace. From Corythus' Tuscan home he fared; and
now the golden courts of starry Olympus receive him to his
throne, and yet an altar is added to the altars of the gods!'

He ceased, and Ilioneus pursued: 'O king, illustrious seed of
Faunus, no murky tempest hath driven us, wave-tost, to land
upon your shores; no star nor strand misread hath beguiled us
from the course we held! Of fixed purpose and free intent we
draw, one and all, to this thy city – exiles from an empire, the
greatest once that the Sun beheld as he journeyed from the uttermost heavens. From Jove is the beginning of our race; in Jove
their sire glory the children of Dardanus; and of Jove's sovereign
line is Trojan Aeneas, our king, that hath sent us to thy doors.
How fierce the storm that burst from fell Mycenae, to pass over
the plains of Ida, – how, driven by fate, the twin worlds of
Europe and of Asia met in the shock of arms, – even he hath
heard, whom the ends of earth hold sequestered, by Ocean's

refluent stream; and he whom the zone of the tyrant Sun, mid-most extended of the four, estranges from mankind! From out that cataclysm we have fled over many a waste of waters; and now we ask a little space for our country's gods, a harmless footing on thy coast, and the air and water open to all. We shall bring no shame upon the realm, nor light shall be the report of your glory or dim the grace of this your deed, nor ever shall Ausonia repent that she received the Trojans to her breast! By the star of Aeneas I swear, and his right hand, puissant in trial of friendship or weaponed battle: many a people and many a nation – scorn us not, that we come to thee with fillets in our hands and prayers on our lips! – have courted our alliance and desired our union; but Heaven's imperious decree drove us in quest of your soil. Hence Dardanus was sprung; hither Apollo calls our returning feet, and, with instant mandate, urges us to Tuscan Tiber and the hallowed waters of Numicius' spring. More, these lowly guerdons from the days of our prosperity – relics snatched from a flaming Troy – our prince bestows upon thee. This the gold, where from his sire Anchises poured libation by the altars: this the apparel of Priam, when he gave, as his fathers gave, their laws to the assembled nations – his sceptre, his sacred diadem, and his robes that the dames of Ilium wrought.'

While thus Ilioneus spoke, Latinus sate motionless, with downcast gaze rooted to earth and eyes intently rolling. And much though the embroidered purple and sceptre of Priam touched his kingly soul, yet more his daughter's bridal and mar-riage-chamber gave him pause, as he revolved in spirit the oracle of ancient Faunus. 'This,' he mused, 'is he, the pilgrim from an alien home, foreshown my son and called to sovereignty co-equal with my sceptre; sire of a brave and peerless race, whose might shall gain the world!' Gladly, at last, he spoke: 'Heaven prosper our emprize, and the presage itself hath given! Trojan, thy wish shall be granted! Nor scorn I your gifts: long as Latinus shall reign, ye shall lack not the bounty of a generous soil nor the opu-lence of Troy! Let but Aeneas come in presence, if so he yearn for us, if so he covet the bond of our amity and the style of our alliance – let him come, nor shrink from friendly faces! To me it shall be a moiety of peace, to have touched your sovereign's hand! And now, in return, bear back to the king this my charge: I have a daughter, whom the voice of my father's fane and many a celestial sign forbid me to unite with any bridegroom of our people: for sons shall come from a foreign shore – such, say the prophets, is Latium's fate – whose blood shall exalt our name to the stars. Him, I deem, Fate calls; and him, if my soul augurs aught of truth, I choose.'

So said, the old king made choice from all the number of his steeds: – three hundred stood sleek in their lofty stalls. Straight he commanded that to each Teucrian, from first to last, one should be brought, fleet of foot and caparisoned in broidered housings of purple. Golden were the chains that hung pendent from every breast, of gold their trappings, and yellow gold foamed under their champing teeth; but to Aeneas, the absent, he assigned a chariot and twin coursers of ethereal seed, with nostrils expiring flame, sprung of that furtive issue which subtile Circe raised to her father from the womb of a spurious dam. – So, with Latinus' gifts and message, high-mounted on their steeds, the children of Aeneas returned, and peace went with them.

But, lo, Jove's fierce consort, heavenward-bound from Inachian Argos, was sailing through the air, and, above Pachynus, looked forth from the far Sicilian sky, and discerned Aeneas, light-hearted, and his Dardan fleet. She saw his roofs arising – saw the land his friend, and the barques deserted; then, pierced with bitter anger, halted, and, shaking her head, broke into speech: 'Ay me, that loathed stock! That Phrygian doom, which crosses our doom! Fallen, did they bleed on the Sigean plains? Captured, were they led captive away? When Troy burned, were they consumed with fire? Through walls of steel and walls of flame they have found their way! But, methinks, my deity is weary at last, and sleeps! My hatred is sated, and I am still! Nay, when they were hurled from their country's breast, still my vengeance was bold to follow them through the waves, and I fronted the exiles over all the main! I have spent against Troy the powers of sky and sea. And what have the Syrtes and Scylla – what drear Charybdis – availed me? They have reached their bourne: they are hid in Tiber's channel, careless of ocean and me! And Mars could destroy the Lapiths and their giant race: the sire of gods himself yielded time-honoured Calydon to Dian's choler – though what sin in Lapith or in Calydon had merited such penalty? But I, Jove's imperial spouse, who have endured – alack! – to leave naught undared, who have stooped to every device – I am vanquished by Aeneas! But if my godhead be over feeble, surely I shall not shrink to implore aid, where aid may be found; and if Heaven be inflexible, Hell shall be unleashed! It shall not be mine

– I grant it – to debar him from the Latian crown; and Lavinia remains his bride irrevocably by the doom of Fate: yet mine it is to defer the issue and admit impediment to his high emprize, – mine to blot out the peoples of either king. At this price of their lieges' lives, be father and son united! Trojan and Rutulian blood shall flow for thy dowry, maiden, and Bellona shall lead thee to the bed! Not sole the daughter of Cisseus bare a fire-brand in her womb and was delivered of nuptial flames! In her own child Venus hath borne the like – a second Paris, a second deathly torch for resurgent Troy!'

So said, she descended to earth, clothed in terror, and summoned baleful Allecto from the seat of the vengeful goddesses and the infernal dusk; Allecto, to whom tearful wars, and strife, and treachery, and noxious crimes, are a wellspring of delight: – a fiendish shape, loathed even by her Plutonian sire, and loathed by her hellish sisterhood; – so manifold her changing forms, so dire the aspect of each, so frequent the vipers that breed from her sable head! Whose fury Juno inflamed with such utterance: 'Grant me, maiden daughter of Night this task – thine own – this service, that our honour and glory may abide unshaken and unremoved, nor the children of Aeneas avail to ensnare Latinus in their alliance or to beset the borders of Italy! Thou canst arm brethren, single-souled, to strife, and kindle discord on the hearth; thou canst win entry for the scourge and funeral torch under the quiet roof: thou hast a thousand names, a thousand arts of mischief. Rouse thy prolific breast, smite asunder the pact of peace, and sow the seed of war in guilt! In one self-same moment, let the youth desire, demand, and seize the sword!'

Straight Allecto, dank from Gorgonian poisons, sped first to Latium and the lofty halls of Laurentum's king, and sat before the silent door of Amata, who, with fervent heart tortured by woman's distress and woman's anger, brooded on the Teucrians' advent and Turnus' hymeneal. On her the fiend cast a serpent from out her livid tresses, and thrust it into her bosom, to her very heart of hearts, that, maddened by its unholy power, she might embroil all the house. Gliding between her robe and smooth breasts, it rolled untouching and inspired with viperous breath the frenzied heart of the unwitting queen. To the twisted gold on her neck it turned in all its snakish bulk – turned to the riband of her long fillet, enwreathed her locks, and strayed, softsliding, over her limbs. And while the nascent plague, stealing onward in fluent venom, began to thrill her sense and pervade her frame with fire, nor yet her soul had caught the spark throughout all her breast, softly, and as mothers use, she spoke, much weeping for her daughter's and the Phrygian's wedlock: 'Father, and shall Lavinia's hand be given to exiled Troy? nor pitiest thou thy child and thee? Pitiest not her mother, whom – soon as the North shall blow – false-hearted he will desert – a pirate that hastes to ocean, when the damsel is reft? Was it not thus, that the Phrygian shepherd won to Lacedaemon, and bore Helen from Leda's arms to his Trojan towns? Where is thy plighted faith? Where thine old-time care for thy people, and the hand so oft outstretched to Turnus, thy kin? If a Latian maid must seek an alien alliance – if so thy resolve be fixed, and the command of Faunus, thy father, bind thee – yet I hold it truth that all lands, which freedom disjoins from our sway, are alien; and that so the gods import! Even Turnus, wouldst thou trace his line to the fount, is sprung of Inachus and Acrisius and mid Mycenae!'

When, after such vain trial of words, she saw that Latinus stood firm against her, – when the serpent's maddening venom was pulsing in every vein and coursing through all her being, – then, in truth, the unhappy queen, stung by ineffable torment, raved in ungoverned frenzy through the great city. As oft a top, spinning under the fast-plied scourge, which boys in gamesome mood urge circumvolant round some forlorn court, wheels in dizzy career beneath the driving thong, while the beardless throng gazes down, in untaught wonder, on the whirling wood to which their blows lend life – so, with course as furious, she was swept through the heart of cities and fierce peoples. Nay, more, she feigned the Bacchic call, adventured a greater sin, and embarked on greater madness – flew to the forests and hid her child on the leafy hills, thinking to bereave the Teucrians of their bridal and retard the nuptial torch. 'Evoe Bacchus!' her cry rang loud, 'thou alone art worthy of the maid! For to thee she assumes the supple wand, for thee she leads the dance, and vows to thy service her lengthening tresses!' Fame winged her flight abroad, and the matrons, with flaming souls infuriate, hastened all with a single zeal to seek abodes, they knew not where! From their vacant homes they came, and bared neck and hair to the winds; while with vibrant cries others thrilled the heaven, and, in cincture of fawn-skins, bore spears of the vine. Central in their throng, the fiery queen lifted high a blazing pine-brand, and sang the marriage-song of her daughter and Turnus; then rolling her sanguine eye-balls, cried sudden and fierce: 'Hearken, O matrons of Latium, wheresoever ye be! If in your faithful hearts there be any kindness left for hapless Amata – if ye are still stung by care for a mother's right – unbind the fillets from your hair, and enter the orgies with me!' Such was the queen, as, from this hand and that, Allecto drove her with Bacchic goad amid the woods – amid the wild-beasts' solitary coverts!

So soon as she deemed that the first shafts of frenzy were edged enough, and Latinus' purpose overthrown with all his household, incontinent the woeful fiend soared on dusk wing to the walls of the bold Rutulian – that city which, men tell, Danae, thither borne by the headlong South, founded and peopled from Acrisius' kingdom. Ardea our grandsires styled the place; and still Ardea stands, an august name; but her sun is set. Here, in his stately towers, Turnus slumbered and slept at dead of midnight; when Allecto resigned her grim lineaments and hellish limbs, and assumed the face of an aged dame, – furrowed her loathly brow with wrinkles, indued silver tresses, fillet-bound, and enwreathed a spray of olive; – then, in semblance of ancient Calybe, priestess of Juno and her shrine, offered her to the prince's view, and thus spoke:

'Turnus, and wilt thou brook all thy toils outpoured in vain, and thy sceptre passed to Dardan strangers? The king denies thee thy bride, thy blood-bought dowry, and they seek an alien to inherit thy crown! Go now, front the thankless peril, and be laughed to scorn! Go, hew down the Tyrrhene lines, and shield Latium with thy peace! Thus, in very presence, Saturn's almighty daughter bade me speak to thee, when thou shouldst lie in the calm of night. Then up, and, with glad heart, make ready to arm thy powers, and issue from the gates to battle! Burn the captains of Phrygia, who are anchored in thy fair stream, and consume their painted barques! The imperious might of heaven commands! Let King Latinus himself – if he consent not to yield thy bride and observe his word – feel thine arm, and approve at last the might of Turnus and Turnus' sword!'

Then, with mocking lips, the prince responded: 'Their fleets ride on Tiber's wave. I know; nor, as thou deemest, has the news escaped my ear: raise no such terrors before me! Nor yet is queenly Juno forgetful of us. But thou, O mother – thine age is outworn and rusts, and, effete to conceive the truth, vexes thee with profitless care, and, among warring kings, deludes thy presaging soul with idle alarm. Thy watch is over images and fanes. War and peace men shall administer, whose charge war is!'

At his words Allecto flashed into anger: and, as he yet spoke, a sudden trembling assailed his limbs, and his eyes were set in horror; so manifold the serpents that hissed from the Fiend, so vast the shape that dawned on his view! There, rolling her flaming eyes, she flung him backward, hesitant and seeking further speech; reared twin snakes from her tresses, brandished her resonant scourge, and pursued from rabid lips: 'Behold me, who am outworn and rust, – whom age, effete to conceive the truth, deludes among warring kings with idle alarm! Look well and see! I am come from the seat of the dread Sisters, and war and death are in my hand!'

So saying, she hurled a torch full upon him, and deep in his breast fixed the brand, fuming with pitchy glare. A horror of fear broke his slumbers, and the sweat, bursting from all his frame, laved bone and limb alike. Insane, he shrieked for arms – sought arms in chamber and hall, while within him raged the lust of the steel and the guilty frenzy of war, with resentment crowning all: – even as when flaming twigs are piled, loud roaring, under the sides of a bubbling caldron, and the heated waters leap up; the pent flood steams and chafes, high surging in foam, till no longer the wave contains itself and the black vapour mounts skyward. Thus the word went forth to the captains of his chivalry, that they march upon king Latinus; for peace was sullied. 'Sharpen the sword,' was his command, 'defend Italy, expel the foe from her bounds: for I come, and, coming, will suffice for both Teucrians and Latins!' When so he had said and called Heaven to witness his vow, emulously the Rutulians spurred each the other to arms – one, moved by the peerless grace of his youth and beauty; one, by his ancestral kings; and yet a third, by the glorious deeds of his hand!

While Turnus filled his Rutulians with the spirit of valour, Allecto, on Stygian wing, sped to the Teucrians. With new guile she marked the place, where, along the shore, fair Iulus was hunting with net and horse. Here the maid from Hell's stream flung before his hounds a sudden lure to madness, touched their nostrils with the familiar scent, and urged them hot-footed in chase of the stag. This was the source of disaster to be: thence the rustic spirit was kindled to war! There was a stag of faultless form, stately-antlered, torn erewhile from its mother's breast, and nurtured by Tyrrhus' sons and by Tyrrhus – ranger he of the royal herds, and warder of the plain far and wide. Their sister Silvia had trained him obsequious to her command, and with ceaseless care she adorned him – wreathing his antlers in soft garlands, combing his wild coat, and laving him in the crystal spring. He, patient of her hand and accustomed to his master's board, roved the woods and, late though the night, returned freely to his home and its welcome door.

But now, as he wandered afar, the ravening hounds of huntsman Iulus roused him, while haply he floated down the stream or allayed his heat on the verdant bank. Ascanius, too, burning with desire of the prime honour, sped a shaft from his bended bow: nor did Heaven desert his errant hand; for, sharp-singing, the reed came driven through belly and flank. But the wounded creature fled for refuge under the familiar roof, and moaning, entered his stall, where, bleeding and suppliant-like, he filled all the house with his plaint. First Sister Silvia, with open hands beating on her arms, cried for aid, and summoned the stout countrymen. They, for the cruel fiend lurked in the still woods, came ere she thought – armed, one with a charred stake, one with ponderous knotted club: for whatsoever lay ready to their quest, anger made a weapon. Breathing great wrath, an axe in his hasty hand, Tyrrhus summoned his array – in such guise as when the tidings chanced to find him, cleaving an oak in four with inward driven wedges.

But, from her watch-tower, the unpitying goddess, seizing the moment of ill, mounted the stall's lofty roof, and from the summit blew the shepherds' signal, straining her hellish voice on the writhen horn, till every grove trembled and the deep forests echoed again. Even Trivia's distant lake heard the sound: Nar river heard, in his white and sulphurous waters: the springs of Velinus heard, and startled matrons clasped their babes to their breasts. Then swift to the voice wherewith the dread clarion sang to arms, the stubborn husbandmen, snatching their weapons, ran mustered from all hands: nor less the opening camp disgorged the warriors of Troy, to succour Ascanius. The edge of battle was set. No more they contended in rustic quarrel with heavy clubs and fire-pointed stakes, but with double-edged steel they tried the issue. Far and near bristled the black harvest of naked swords, while brass shone to the challenging sun, and flung its light to the clouds: – as, when a wave begins to whiten under the wind's earliest breath, little by little the sea swells, and higher its waves rise, till from the uttermost deeps it surges to heaven! And now young Almo, once eldest of Tyrrhus' sons, as he fought in the foremost line, fell beneath the hurtling shaft: for the wound lodged in his throat and cut short in blood the passage of the liquid voice and the slender life. About him lay many dead, and among them old Galaesus, slain while, in the cause of peace, he flung himself between the hosts – justest then, and wealthiest, of all in Ausonia's fields. For him five flocks bleated, five herds lowed their return, and a hundred ploughs turned his soil.

While thus they battled with wavering issue along the plain, the goddess, her promise achieved, now that the war had tasted blood, and the first encounter joined in carnage, fled from Hesperia, and, mounting the cope of heaven, addressed Juno in the haughty tone of victory:

'Lo, for thee discord is made perfect in grim war! Bid them now unite in amity and conclude alliance! Since I have sprinkled the Teucrians with Ausonian blood, thus will I crown my task, if thy will be assured: I will bring by my rumours the bordering cities to battle; I will kindle their spirit with the lust of infuriate war, that from this hand and that their succour may stream; and their fields shall be strewn with arms!' Then Juno, in answer: 'Of terror and treachery is no dearth! The seed of battle is sown; sword against sword the combat is waged; and the weapons, that chance first supplied, new blood stains! Such union, such bridal, be solemnized by Venus' illustrious son, – yea, and by King Latinus! But he our Sire, sovereign in high Olympus, would not, that, licentious, thou shouldst thus wing the upper air. Hie thee away! Whatsoever may yet betide in this struggle, myself shall order it!' Thus Saturn's daughter: she, upraising her strident pinions, serpent plumed, sought her home by Cocytus' flood and abandoned the heights above. There is a place in the heart of Italy, on which the tall hills look down, renowned and fabled on many shores – the vale of Amsanctus. Obscure with myriad leaves, it lies pent between two walls of forest; and in its midst a roaring torrent crashes in dizzy eddies over the rocks. Here men show an awful cavern, the vent of cruel Dis; where a fathomless gulf, through which Acheron breaks, yawns with pestilential jaws. There the Fury plunged her fell deity, and unburdened earth and sky.

Nor less, meanwhile, Saturn's imperial daughter set the last touch to war. One and all, the shepherds rushed from the stricken field to the city, and bore back their slain, – Almo's boyish limbs, and old Galaesus' mangled visage, – imploring Heaven and adjuring Latinus. Turnus was there, and, amid the fever and the cry of blood for blood, harped their fear again:

'Troy was bidden to Latium's realm, the Phrygian stock tainted Latium's blood, and he was spurned from the door of Latium's king.' Then the kindred of those dames, who, in Bacchic frenzy, revelled dancing through the trackless forests, – for not lightly weighed Amata's name, – came mustering from every hand, and importuned war. For war they clamoured incontinent with one voice, blinded by jealous deity – for an unblest war, thwarting omens and oracles celestial. Emulous, they surged round Latinus' palace: he, like a rock of ocean unmoved, stood resistent – like a rock of ocean, that, while the seas break in thunder, fronts, broad-based, the many barking waves; and the cliffs and foaming boulders roar round it in vain, and the seaweed, dashed upon its side, falls frustrate back. But when no power was vouchsafed him to overcome their purblind counsel, and all things moved to the nod of pitiless Juno, with reiterate appeal to Heaven and the dumb skies, the old king spoke: 'We are broken, alas, by Fate, and whirled by the storm! O my hapless people, with your own impious blood shall ye acquit this penalty! Thee, Turnus, thy crime – thee, the dire vengeance – shall await, and with belated vows thou shalt cry on the gods. For my peace was won; and now, full in the haven's mouth, I am despoiled of a tearless passing!' Nor farther he pursued, but shut him in his chamber and dropped the reins of kingship.

A custom ruled in Hesperian Latium, held sacred, in unbroken line, by the Alban cities, and sacred held still by Rome, when they wake the War-god to thought of battle – whether their hands prepare to carry bloodshed and lamentation to Getan or Hyrcanian or Arab, or whether they march on Ind and follow the Morn to her rising, and reclaim their eagles from the Parthian. There are twin Gates of War – so men style them – hallowed by religious fear and the awe of cruel Mars. They are shut by a hundred brazen bolts and the iron's immortal strength, and Janus quits not his ward on the threshold. There, when the Fathers' sentence stands immutable for battle, the consul, stately in Quirinal robe and Gabine cincture, unbars with his own hand the grating portals, and with his own lips invokes the sword: then the rest take up the cry, and the brazen horns ring conspiring in harsh assent. Such the mode, in which, then also, they urged Latinus to proclaim war against the people of Aeneas, and to unclose the fatal gates. But the grey-headed king refrained his hand, recoiled averse from the loathed ministry, and hid himself in the obscure dark. Then the queen of Heaven, down-shooting from the empyrean, smote with her Saturnian hand on the reluctant portals, and upon revolving hinge burst open the iron-clamped doors of War. – Unstirred, erewhile, and inert, Ausonia flashed into flame. Here, on foot they assayed to march the plains; there, high-mounted on stately coursers, men spurred infuriate through the dust: and every tongue cried for arms. Part, with unctuous lard, burnished their smooth shields and lucent spears, and on whetstones edged the battle-axe: and joyfully they saw the standard upreared, and joyfully heard the trumpet call. With anvils set, five great cities renewed their armament – Atina's might, Tibur's pride, Ardea and Crustumeri, and Antemnae, tower-crowned. These forged hollow helms for the guarded head, and plaited willow frames for the buckler: those hammered breast-plates of bronze, and polished greaves from the ductile silver. – Thus ended the honour of share and scythe, thus all their love of the plough; as they tempered again their fathers' swords in the furnace! And now the bugle sang, and the watchword for war passed on. Hastily one seized the casque from his chambers; one compelled his snorting steeds to the yoke, accoutred him in shield and triple hauberk of gold, and girt his constant blade to his thigh!

Now from opened Helicon, ye Muses, wake your strains, – what kings arose to battle; what legions, by whom captained, thronged the champaign; what harvest of men, what blaze of steel, even then graced Italy's kindly earth! For, heavenly Sisters, ye remember and ye can tell: but to us scarce the low whisper of Fame is wafted!

Fierce from the Tyrrhene strand, Mezentius, scorner of the gods, came foremost to war, and armed his array. At whose side went Lausus, his son, unmatched in fairness of frame save by Laurentine Turnus – Lausus, tamer of steeds and scourge of wild beasts, who from Agylla's city led a thousand men, that followed him in vain – Lausus, whose filial obedience merited a happier lord – a sire other than Mezentius!

After these, Aventinus, beauteous seed of beauteous Hercules, vaunted on the sward his palm-crowned chariot and victorious coursers, and on his shield bore his father's cognizance – the hundred snakes of the serpent-cinctured Hydra. Him, the fruit of her furtive travail, Rhea the priestess bore into the regions of day – a woman mingled with deity – after the conquering Tirynthian, fresh from the blood of Geryon, had touched the Laurentine fields, and laved his Iberian open in the Tuscan stream. In their hands his men bore javelins and grim pikes to battle, and fought with tapering falchions and the Sabellian dart. Himself he marched on foot, swinging a huge lion's skin, that bristled shaggy and terrible, the white teeth grinning above his head; and thus he entered the royal halls in his grim attire, with the Herculean garb clasped on his shoulders.

Next twin brethren left the walls of Tibur, and the people styled by their brother Tiburtus' name – Catillus and gallant Coras, youths of Argos. In the van of battle they rode through the thick-volleyed spears, as when two cloud-born Centaurs descend from a mountain's tall crest, while with racing feet they leave Homole or snowy Othrys, and the vast forest yields place to their course, and loud-crashing the thickets give way.

Nor was the founder of Praeneste's city found wanting, – that king, who, as consenting ages witness, was born to Vulcan among the rural herds, and found on the hearth, – Caeculus. Him a rustic legion followed, wide-spread – both they who dwell in high Praeneste and the fields of Gabine Juno – by the cool Anio and the Hernican rocks with their dewy streams, – and they who are nurtured by rich Anagnia, or, father Amasenus, by thee! Not all of them had armour, nor shields and rattling chariots: the most hailed bullets of livid lead; in the hands of part were two javelins; and caps of tawny wolfhide were the covering of their heads. The left foot was bare as they stepped; a boot of raw skin enclosed the right.

But Messapus, the tamer of steeds, offspring of Neptune, whose life was proof against fire and against steel, with sudden call summoned to arms his peoples, lapt in ease so long, and his hosts disused to battle; and once more he loosened his blade. Here marched the Fescennine powers and they of the Falerian plains: here the men of Soracte's crags and the Flavinian fields, of Ciminus' mountain and lake and the groves of Capena. They marched in even measure and sang of their king: – as often snowy swans in the moist clouds, when full-fed they return, and from their long throats the clear strains issue, till Cayster and the reverberant Asian fen echo far away. Nor would any deem that these mingled multitudes were brass-clad legions: but rather that, high in air, a raucous cloud of birds urged their flight from the deep to the shore.

And now Clausus came, captaining his great array – great the captain as his array – Clausus, of the ancient Sabine blood, from whom the Claudian tribe and house are now spread abroad in

Latium, since the day when Rome was portioned with the Sabine. With him went Amiternum's vast battalion and the Elder Quirites, Eretum's mustered powers and olive-bearing Mutusca, they who dwell in Nomentum's city, in Velinus' Rosean lands, on Tetrica's rugged crags and Severus' mount, in Casperia and Foruli, and by the waters of Himella – they who drink of Tiber and Fabaris, they whom cold Nursia sent, the Hortine orders, the Latin peoples, and they betwixt whom Allia, name of woe, flows with estranging flood: – many as the billows that roll on the floor of the Libyan main, when fierce Orion sinks in the wintry wave; dense as the ears that parch under the new-risen sun, on the plain of Hermus or the yellow fields of Lycia! Their bucklers rang, and the fearful earth quaked under their trampling feet.

Next, Agamemnonian Halaesus – sworn foe of the Trojan name – yoked his steeds to the car, and, in Turnus' cause, swept a thousand warlike nations to battle: those who delve the Massic hills and their smiling vineyards; those whom the Auruncan sires sent down from their mountain-tops, or who fared from the bordering Sidicine plains; those who marched from Cales; those that tenant the banks of Volturnus' shallow stream; and, by their side, the rough Saticulan and the Oscan bands. Polished javelins were their weapons, but these it was their use to fit with a pliant thong. A targe protected their left, and they wielded crooked scimitars for the close encounter.

Nor, Oebalus, shalt thou pass unheralded by my strains – thou, who, men tell, wast borne by the Nymph of Sebethus' stream to Telon, what time he reigned over Teleboan Capreae, stricken already in years. But the paternal fields sufficed not his son; and even then, broad-realmed, he ruled over the Sarrastian peoples and the plains that Sarnus waters – over all that dwell in Rufrae and Batulum, and on Celemna's soil, and over them on whom Abella's towers look down through the apple-blossom! In Teuton fashion they hurled the lance; their helms were bark reft from the cork-tree; and brass glittered on their crescent shields, glittered from their brands.

Thee, too, Ufens, Nersae sent to battle from her mountains, illustrious in the fame of thy prospering sword – whose clan, rugged among the rugged and bred to the woodland chase, walks the harsh Aequiculan glebe. Armed they till the earth, and exultant they drive the new-won spoils and live by the pillaging hand.

More, from the Marruvian race, his helm featly decked with

leaves of the fruitful olive, came stout-hearted Umbro, the priest, sent by Archippus the king – Umbro, who, by the spell of his song and hand, would sprinkle the dews of sleep on the viperous brood and on the foul-breathing snakes of the water, soothing their ire and healing their bite by his skill. But the bite of the Dardan point he availed not to heal, and against that stroke he found no charm in his slumber-laden songs, nor in the herbs that he culled on the Marsian hills! Umbro – thee the groves of Angitia wept, thee Fucinus' crystalline wave, thee thy limpid lakes!

Nor less Hippolytus' fairest son marched to war – Virbius, whom his mother Aricia sent, all-glorious. In the groves of Egeria he was nursed round the moist shores, where Diana's altar stands blessing and blest. For the tale is told, how that Hippolytus – when he fell by his stepdame's art and slaked his father's vengeance in blood, rent asunder by his panic-smitten coursers – was restored by the Healer's herbs and the love of Dian, and once more beheld the starry firmament and respired the upper air. Then the Sire omnipotent, in anger that any mortal should rise from the nether shades to the vital light, with his bolted thunder himself hurled down to the Stygian flood that child of Phoebus, discoverer of such daring leechcraft. But Trivia, gracious Queen, hid Hippolytus from the view of man, and sent him far away to the keeping of Egeria, the Nymph, and her grove, that there, alone in the Italian woods, he might live out his days unknown and, *Vitbius* named, be no more Hippolytus. And thence it comes that no hooves of horses may tread her fane and holy forest, since, in terror of the ocean monsters, they wrecked the chariot and flung her charioteer forth upon the shore. None the less, his son schooled his ardent steeds on the level plain, and, charioted, sped precipitate to battle!

In radiant beauty, with weaponed hand, and head towering sheer above all, Turnus himself moved in the van. On his lofty helm, triple-plumed, rose the Chimaera, with throat breathing Aetnean fires; raging the more and wild with dire flames, as the blood flows faster and the fray waxes fiercer. But, on his spotless shield, Io – memorable theme! – was blazoned in gold, a heifer now with bristled hide and uplifted horns, while Argus stood ward over the maid, and, from embossed urn, father Inachus poured his stream. There followed a sable cloud of infantry, and on all the plain the bucklered squadrons gathered thick – the Argive hosts and the Auruncan bands, the Rutules and the old Sicani, the Sacranian lines and the Labicians with painted targe;

they, O Tiber, who till thy glades and Numicius' sacred shore, whose ploughshare cleaves the Rutulian hills and Circeii's headland, whose fields are watched by Jove of Anxur and Feronia smiling in her verdant grove; where the black marsh of Satura lies, and cold Ufens threads his way through the lowly vales and sinks into ocean.

To crown the tale, Volscian Camilla, warrior-maid, came leading her mounted host and her squadrons resplendent in brazen mail. No distaff, no weaving basket, claimed those womanly hands: but her girlish frame was stubborn to endure the battle, and her feet were swift to outstrip the winds. She might have flown over the topmost blades of the untouched corn, nor, flying, have scathed the tender ears. She might have sped over the mid seas, poised above the swelling wave, nor dipped her glancing feet in the flood.

The youth came streaming from house and field, and matrons stood in admiring throng, viewing her, as she rode, with rapt astonishment – how the purple's regal splendour draped her shoulders of marble; how the clasp entwined her tresses with gold; how her own hands bore the Lycian quiver and the pastoral myrtle tipped with steel!

BOOK VIII

WHEN HIGH ON LAURENTUM'S TOWER Turnus upreared the ensign of war, and the horns rang in harsh concert – when he spurred his fiery steeds, and clashed his weapons – straight men's souls were troubled; eagerly all Latium conspired in rude rebellion, and her warriors raged exasperate. Messapus and Ufens, chief of the captains, with Mezentius, scorner of Heaven, levied succours from every hand, and far and near bared the wide fields of husbandmen. More, Venulus was sent to the city of great Diomede, there to entreat aid, and announce that the Teucrians planted foot in Latium; that Aeneas was come with his fleet, bearing his vanquished gods into Italy, and proclaiming himself the fate-crowned king; that many tribes flocked to the Dardan standard, and the Dardan name was heard through the breadth of Latium: – what structure this foundation augured, what issue of battle he desired, should Fortune attend him, was clearer to himself than to King Turnus or King Latinus.

Thus it went with Latium. But the hero of Laomedon's line

watched all, tossing on the troubled tides of care; and now hither, now thither, swiftly he transferred his divided mind, and swept it over all the range of thought: as when a gleam of water, tremulous in the brimming bronze, is flung back from the sun or the lustre of the mirrored moon; then glances abroad over all, till mounting skyward it strikes the fretted roof high above. It was night, and, through all the earth, weary creatures, bird and beast alike, lay wrapped in deep slumber; when father Aeneas, with heart wrung by that lamentable strife, flung him down by the river's brim, under the chill cope of heaven, and allowed sleep to steal, belated, over his frame. Before him the deity of the place, Tiber of the pleasant stream, seemed, in very presence, to uplift his white head through the poplar leaves. Thin lawn draped him in mantle of grey, and shady reeds crowned his hair. Then thus he addressed the prince, and, speaking, assuaged his sorrow:

'O child of celestial race, who, from the foeman's midst, dost bring to us again the city of Troy and preservest Troy-towers immortal, thyself long awaited by Laurentine soil and Latin fields – here thy home is sure, and sure the gods of thy home! Shrink not, nor dread the menace of war: the ire and malice of Heaven are spent! Even now, lest thou deem this the idle figment of sleep, thou shalt discover beneath the holms on my bank a huge sow with a litter of thirty heads, white as she reclines on earth, and white the young about her teats: a sign, that when thirty years have rolled, Ascanius shall found the White Town – Alba, illustrious name. Doubt clouds not my prophecy! Now lend ear, and I will show thee in brief how thou mayest surmount in triumph the task that confronts thee. In these coasts an Arcadian people, sprung from Pallas, who have followed Evander the king and his banners, have chosen a site and set their city on the hills – from Pallas their forefather styled Pallanteum. These wage ceaseless war with the Latin race: these unite to thy camp in alliance, and league thee with them. Myself I will guide thee betwixt my banks, unswerving along the stream, that thy climbing oars may overcome the adverse current. Then rise, goddess-born, and, as the first star fades, meetly prefer thy prayers to Juno, and vanquish with suppliant vows her anger and her menace. When thine is the victory, mine shall be thy worship. I am he whom thou seest, as I lave the banks with my welling flood, and wind through the furrowed fields of plenty – azure Tiber, dearest of rivers to Heaven! Here is my stately home: my fount flows from towering cities.'

Thus the River said; then plunged into the nethermost depths of his pool, while night and sleep fled from Aeneas. He rose, and, with eyes turned to the orient light of the ethereal orb, held, as use ordains, water from the stream in his hollow palms, and poured this utterance to Heaven:

'Nymphs, Laurentine Nymphs, from whom is the generation of rivers, and thou, O father Tiber, with thy sacred wave – receive Aeneas, and, in this late hour, guard him from peril. In what spring soever thy pools contain thee, as thou pitiest our travails, – whatsoever the soil whence thou issuest in thy beauty – ever my worship, ever my gifts shall grace thee, horn-crowned River, monarch of the Western streams! Only be thou present, and more nearly confirm thy will!'

So he prayed, and, choosing two galleys from his fleet, manned them with oarsmen and accoutred the crew in arms.

But, lo, the omen broke sudden on their wondering gaze: for on the green marge, recumbent along the sward, they descried a spotless sow, one in hue with her milk-white brood: whom good Aeneas offered in sacrifice to thee – even to thee – imperial Juno, and set mother and young before thine altar. All that livelong night Tiber calmed his swelling flood, and, refluent, halted his silent wave, smoothing the face of the waters to the semblance of a gentle lake or unruffled pool, that naught might impede their labouring oars. Thus, swiftly they abridged the voyage begun. With cheerful murmur the pine slid careened along the stream, while the waves and the unwonted wood admired the heroes' far-flashing shields, and the painted hulls that breasted the river. Through the night and the outworn day they rowed and ascended the spacious reaches, overshadowed by motley trees and glancing betwixt verdant woods over the tranquil tide. – The flaming sun already had scaled the mid arch of heaven, when they discerned in the distance city-walls, and a tower, and scattered roofs – now exalted to the stars by Rome's empery, then Evander's scant domain! Quickly they swung the prows to land, and drew to the town.

It fell that on that day the Arcadian king paid his annual homage to Amphitryon's great child and his kindred of Heaven, in a grove before the city. With him Pallas his son, with him the flower of his realm and his needy senate, offered incense, and the warm blood reeked by the altars. At sight of the high-masted ships, gliding through the twilit forest and plying the noiseless oar, alarmed by the sudden vision they started, one and all, from

their abandoned boards. But Pallas, undaunted, bade them forbear not the rite, and, seizing his spear, flew himself to front the
strangers, and called from a mound afar: 'Warriors, what cause
hath constrained you to adventure on an unknown path?
Whither bend ye? What race claims you? what home, where left?
And bring ye hither peace or the sword?' Then father Aeneas
spoke from the tall stern, a branch of peaceful olive outstretched
in his hand: 'Men of Troy thou seest, and arms inimical to
Latium, whose haughty battle hath driven us fugitive. We seek
Evander. Bear this message, and say that chosen captains of Dardania are come, suing for his allied spears.' Pallas stood, awe-
struck at the mighty name; then: 'Come forth,' he cried,
'whosoever thou art; speak before my father's face, and prove the
welcome of our hearth!' And with kindly grasp he greeted him,
and seized and clung to his hand. Thus, advancing, they forsook
the stream and entered the grove; where with courteous speech
Aeneas accosted the king:

'Best of the sons of Greece, to whom Fortune has willed that I
address my prayer and proffer the fillet-wreathed bough, I feared
not because thou wert a Danaan chief – an Arcadian and linked
to the twin sons of Atreus by blood. But conscious worth and
Heaven's holy oracles, the kindred of our sires, and thy fame that
pervades the earth, allied me with thee, and urged me willingly
on the pathway of Fate. Dardanus, first father and founder of
Ilium's city, born – as Greece relates – of Atlantean Electra,
sailed to our Teucrian realm. Electra was sprung of mightiest
Atlas, whose shoulder sustains the celestial spheres. Ye have Mercury for sire, whom fair Maia conceived and bore on the snowy
peaks of Cyllene. But Maia, if we credit the tale that our ears
have heard, was the seed of that self-same Atlas who uplifts the
starry firmament: and thus the lineage of both disparts from a
single stock. Reliant on this, I sent no envoys, nor assayed my
overtures by rule: myself and my life are in thy hands, and, suppliant, I stand at thy gates! The pitiless sword of Daunus' race is
drawn against us, as thee: and they deem that, if we be cast forth,
nothing lets but their yoke shall be set over Hesperia's uttermost
bounds, and themselves shall hold the sea that laves her above
and the sea that laves her below. Then give friendship, and
receive! With us are hearts stout in battle, high souls, and a
people approved by deeds!'

Aeneas ceaséd. While he spoke, Evander's gaze had long roved
over his face, and eyes, and all his frame: then in brief he

returned: 'Bravest of the Teucrians, with what joy do I receive and acknowledge thee! How memory strays to the words, the voice, and the visage, of great Anchises thy sire! For I call to mind, how Priam, Laomedon's child, when he journeyed to Salamis to view the kingdom of his sister Hesione, prolonged his way and visited our cold Arcadian borders. In those days the springtide of youth bloomed on my cheeks, and I wondered at the princes of Troy, and wondered at Laomedon's son; but state-lier than all Anchises moved. My heart burned with youthful ardour to accost the hero and feel his hand in mine; till I approached him, and eagerly led him under the battlements of Pheneus. And as we parted, he gave me a lordly quiver, furnished with Lycian shafts, a scarf inwoven with gold, and two golden bridles that now my Pallas possesses. Therefore, this hand that ye seek is already plighted to you in league, and, so soon as the morrow's light shall dawn once more on the world, I will send you hence cheered by my succour and aided by my powers. Meanwhile – since in amity ye are come hither – with minds attuned, solemnize with us this yearly festival, which it were sin to defer, and be strangers no more to your allies' board!'

This said, he commanded that they replace the viands and the goblets removed, and himself ranged his guests on the grassy seat, with especial honour welcoming Aeneas to the cushion of a lion's shaggy hide and gracing him with a throne of maple. Then youths, chosen for the service, and the priest of the altar, brought, in emulous haste, roasted carcasses of bulls, piled on the baskets Ceres' corn, wrought by the hand of man, and ministered the juice of Bacchus' grape; while Aeneas, and, with him, his war-riors of Troy regaled them on the chine of an ox entire and on the flesh of sacrifice.

When hunger was appeased and the desire of food assuaged, King Evander spoke: 'No vain superstition, ignorant of the gods of old, has burdened us with this solemn rite, with this ordinance of festival, and this altar of reverend sanctity. Preserved, O Trojan guest, from the bitterness of peril, we render sacrifice, and, year after year, pay honour where honour is due. First mark yonder rock-hung cliff, – how the massy crags are flung shattered afar, how the mountain home stands desolate, and the boulders are fallen in giant ruin. Here, receding to fathomless depth, pierced never by the solar ray, yawned a cavern, tenanted by the dire shape of half-bestial Cacus. The ground steamed incessant with new-spilt blood, and, nailed to the proud doors, pale faces of men hung grim and gory. This monster was sprung of Vulcan; and Vulcan's black fires he belched from his mouth, as he stalked in titanic bulk. But to our longing also there was an end, and Time brought succour in the advent of a god. For the great avenger came, and Alcides, triumphant in the slaughter and spoils of triple Geryon, drove this way the huge bulls in victory, and his oxen thronged vale and stream. But Cacus, with his robber's soul infuriate, resolved to leave naught undared or untried in crime or in craft, ravished from the stalls four goodly bulls and as many beauteous heifers. And these – to annul the true course of their footprints – he dragged by the tail to his cave, and, when the track gave perverse testimony, hid his booty in the sunless rock; and he that searched saw no signs leading to the cavern. Meanwhile, when, in act to depart, Amphitryon's son was already moving the full-fed herds from their stalls, the oxen began to low farewell, and all the woodland was filled with their plaint, as clamorously they left the hills. But one of the kine returned the cry, bellowing in the dreary cave, and from her dungeon baffled the hopes of Cacus. Instant at this Alcides' wrath flashed out in black choler, and, snatching his arms and his oaken club, all knotted and ponderous, he raced to the crest of the skyey hill. Then, as never before, our eyes saw Cacus in fear and trembling: for swifter than the East he fled on the moment, and sought his cavern with feet winged by dread.

'Scarce had he shut him within, and, from severed chains, lowered the vast boulder hung in iron by his father's art, and fortified his doorway by support of such barrier, when, lo, he of Tiryns came in the fury of his heart, and, surveying every access, turned his face this way and that, and gnashed his teeth. Thrice in hot anger he traversed all Mount Aventine: thrice he assailed the craggy portals in vain, and thrice sank wearied in the valley. There stood a pointed column of flint, with the rock on all sides cut sheer away, rising from the ridge of the cavern in dizzy eminence – fit site for the nests of unclean birds. This – as, sloping from the ridge, it inclined to the river on the left – he shook, urging it full from the right, till he tore it loose from the nethermost base; then, with sudden shock, hurled it down. To that shock the infinite heavens thundered, the banks leapt apart, and the shuddering stream recoiled. But the den of Cacus, and his vast palace, lay naked to the view, and the gloomy pit stood plain: even as though earth, rent asunder by some resistless force, were to unlock Hell-gates and disclose the pallid realms abhorrent to

Heaven, and from above were descried the unbottomed abyss, and phantoms dazed by the invading light. On him, then, – as he bellowed in unearthly sort, surprised by the unhoped day and pent in the hollow rock, – Alcides rained missiles from aloft, and called every weapon to his aid, pressing him with boughs and great millstones. But he, for now no other escape from peril was left, belched from his jaws huge volumes of smoke – hear and wonder! – and involved his lair in viewless obscurity, till the eye was impotent to see, and, in the depths of his cave, rolled a smoke-wrapt midnight of darkness commingled with fire. The high heart of Alcides brooked not this, and headlong he flung himself at a bound through the flames, where the eddying smoke whirled thickest, and the vast cave surged black and vaporous. Here, where amid the gloom Cacus disgorged his idle fires, he seized him, limb entwined with limb, and, in unremitting grasp, stifled him till the eyes burst forth and his throat was drained of blood. Straight the doors were torn open and the dark den bared to sight: the purloined oxen and the rapine, abjured erewhile, were displayed to the sun, and the hideous carcass dragged out by the heels. Men could not sate their hearts, gazing on those terrible eyes, – on the visage of the brutish monster, on his shaggy bristled breast, and the flames quenched in his throat. From that time has this worship been paid, and a joyous posterity keeps the day – Potitius foremost, founder of this observance, and the Pinarian house, guardian of Hercules' rite. This altar himself set in the grove – this altar, that by us shall ever be named the Greatest, and ever greatest shall be. Then come, sirs, and, in homage to merit so glorious, wreathe your hair with leaves and stretch forth the cup in your hand; call on our common deity, and with willing hearts make offering of wine.' He ceased: and the double-hued poplar, pendent in twining foliage, invested his locks with the shade of Hercules' love; and a goblet charged his right. Unlingering, all poured glad libation on the board, and prayed to the gods.

Meanwhile the star of evening drew nigher along the slope of heaven. And now the priests, clad in hides, as custom ordained, moved in procession – Potitius at the head – with torches flaming in their hands. Renewing the festival, they brought welcome offerings for a second repast, and piled the altars with laden platters. Then came the Salii to sing round the fires of sacrifice, their temples crowned with poplar sprays, – of youths the one quire, white-haired the other, – and with chanting lips they extolled the glories and deeds of Hercules: – how his infant hand strangled the twin serpents, earliest of his stepdame's terrors; how the sword in that selfsame hand shivered mighty cities, Troy with Oechalia; how he endured to the end a thousand perilous toils under King Eurystheus, by the bitter doom of Juno. 'Thou, O hero unvanquished – thou it was who didst slay the cloud-born people, double-bodied, Hylaeus and Pholus, and the monsters of Crete, and the great lion under Nemea's crag. Before thee the Stygian waters trembled: before thee, the warder of Hell, as he lay in his bloody cave upon half-gnawn bones. Not any shape could affright thee, – not Typhoeus himself when he towered in arms, – and counsel forsook thee not, when with multitudinous heads the snake of Lerna encircled thee. Hail, seed indubitable of Jove, thou new-won glory of Heaven, and with auspicious foot visit us and our worship of thee!' Such was the burden of their song; and they crowned the tale with Cacus' cavern, and its lord of the fiery breath, till all the forest and every reverberant hill echoed to their clamour.

Then, the rite discharged, the concourse repaired to the city. The time-worn king kept his son and Aeneas by his side to attend his steps, and, walking, lightened their way with changing discourse. Admiring, Aeneas turned his swift glance over all, and, spell-bound by the scene, inquired gladly and gladly heard, each by each, the memorials of an earlier world. Then King Evander, founder of Rome's citadel: 'Once these woods were tenanted by Fauns and Nymphs, native born, and by a generation of men, sprung from boles of trees and the obdurate oak. They had neither rule of life nor culture, nor knowledge to yoke the ox, nor to lay up stores, nor to husband their gains; but forest boughs and the huntsman's rude trade yielded their sustenance. And no help came till Saturn descended from skyey Olympus, fleeing before the arms of Jove and exiled from his ravished throne. He it was gathered into a state that ungentle race, scattered over mountain peaks, and gave them laws, and chose that their land be called Latium, since within those borders he had lain latent and secure. Under his sway passed those ages that men style golden: in such serenity of peace he ruled the nations; till with stealthy step there succeeded a degenerate time of a baser hue, and, in its train, the frenzy of war and the lust of possession. Then came the Ausonian host and the Sicanian tribes, and time and again the land of Saturn resigned her title. And kings came, and Thybris, gigantic and fierce, from whom in later days we of Italy have called

Tiber's stream, while ancient Albula has lost her authentic name. Myself – as, outcast from the land of my fathers, I voyaged to the extremity of ocean – the inevitable doom of Fate, and Fortune's omnipotence, planted on this soil, spurred onward by the awful warnings of Carmentis, Nymph and mother, and Apollo, who inspired her lips.

Scarce had he ceased; when, advancing, he showed the altar and the gate that Rome styles Carmental, in immemorial tribute to Carmentis the Nymph, prophetess of fate, who first foretold the greatness that should dawn on the sons of Aeneas, and the renown of Pallanteum. Next he displayed a spacious grove, where bold Romulus made his Asylum, and the Lupercal, shrouded by the cool rock, and hallowed, in Arcadian wont, to the name of Lycaean Pan. He showed, moreover, the forest of sacred Argiletum, and called the place to witness, as he rehearsed the slaying of Argus, his guest. Thence he led them to the Tarpeian height, and the Capitol – golden now, erst an unkempt mass of thickets. Yet even then the dread sanctity of that region appalled the fearful rustics: even then they quailed before the forest and the crag. 'This grove,' he said, 'this hill with its leafy crown, a god inhabits: – what god, we know not! My Arcadians hold that full oft they have looked on Jove himself, when his right hand shook the darkening aegis and summoned the storm-clouds. More, in these twin towns of the shattered walls, thou seest the relics and memorials of men of an elder day. This tower father Janus built, this Saturn; and Janiculum one was styled, and Saturnia the other.'

In such interchange of converse they neared the palace of Evander's poverty, and saw scattered herds lowing in the Roman forum and amid the splendours of Carinae. When they stood before the dwelling: 'These doors,' he pursued, 'victorious Alcides stooped to enter, and these halls contained his might. Dare, O guest of mine, to contemn riches; like him, mould thy soul till it be worthy of deity; and bring not disdain to our scanty estate.' Thus saying, he led Aeneas' heroic frame under the roof of his lowly dwelling, and couched him on strewn leaves and the fell of a Libyan bear. – And Night came down, and her sable wings enfolded earth.

But Venus – for not idle the maternal care that dismayed her soul! – moved by the Laurentine menace and the grim call to arms, had recourse to Vulcan, and thus began in her golden nuptial chamber, with words breathing celestial love: 'While the

embattled Grecian kings harried the fated citadel of Troy, and
her towers, doomed to fall by the hostile flame, I asked no succour to their misery, no weapons of thy resource and art; nor,
dearest consort, would I task thee and thy toils to no avail – deep
though my debt to the children of Priam, many though my tears
for the bitter agony of Aeneas. Now, by Jove's mandate, his foot
is on the Rutulian borders; and suppliant I come to thee, as I
came not before, and ask arms from the deity I revere – a mother
for her son. Thou didst bend to the tears of Nereus' daughter, to
the tears of Tithonus' spouse! Behold the mustering nations –
the cities that with closed gates sharpen the sword against me
and the lives of my people.'

The goddess ceased, and, as he delayed, flung her snowy arms
about him and fondled him in soft embrace. Sudden he caught
the wonted spark; the familiar glow entered his being, and
coursed through his melting frame: – even as when, bursting
from the thunderclap, the glittering streak of fire runs fringing
the storm-clouds with blinding light. His consort felt, and, smiling at her ruse, knew that she was fair. – Then the old god spoke,
bound in love's eternal chain:

'Why delvest so deep for pleas? Whither, goddess, is vanished
thy trust in me? Had such been thy care of old, of old I had
armed the Teucrians, and deemed it not sin: for neither the all-
puissant Sire nor Fate forbade Troy to stand, and Priam to wear
the crown, for ten years more. And now, if thou preparest war,
and this is thy sentence, whatever diligence I may avouch to my
craft, whatever iron and molten electrum may achieve, whatever
fire and air avail – cease to mistrust thy power by this humility of
prayer!' So saying, he bestowed the embrace desired; then sank
on the bosom of his queen, and wooed calm slumber to his limbs.

Then, so soon as sleep was fled, banished by the rest it gave,
and retiring Night wheeled in mid career – at the hour when a
woman, whom need constrains to support life by her distaff and
the pittance of the loom, wakes the embers and slumbering
flames, and, adding night to her laborious day, holds her maidens
to the long lamp-lit task, that she may keep her husband's bed
without stain and nurture his infant sons: – even thus, nor at
more slothful hour, the Lord of Fire rose from his soft couch to
the labours of the smith. – Fast by the Sicilian coast and Aeolian
Lipara rises an island, sublime with smoking cliffs. Beneath it
thunders a cavern, and the vaults of Aetna, hollowed by Cyclopian forges; mighty blows are heard re-echoing from the anvil,

bars of Chalyb steel hiss through the depths, and the fire pants in the furnace: for here is Vulcan's home, and the soil owns Vulcan's name. – Hither, on that day, the Lord of Fire descended from high Heaven.

In the dreary cave his Cyclops were labouring iron – Brontes and Steropes and Pyracmon with naked limbs. In their hands a thunderbolt was assuming shape, such as those that the Father hurls down unnumbered from all heaven; part already was polished, part remained imperfect. Three shafts of writhen rain, three of watery cloud, they had wrought therein – three of ruddy fire and the winged southern blast: and now they were blending in their work glittering terrors, and sound, and fear, and the anger of pursuant flames. Elsewhere they urged on for Mars the chariot and flying wheels, wherewith he rouses men and cities to battle; and with golden scales of serpents emulously burnished the horrid aegis – accoutrement of ireful Pallas – and her knotted snakes, and the Gorgon's self on her divine breast, with neck severed and eyes revolving. 'Away with all,' he cried, 'remove your labours begun, O Cyclops of Aetna, and give ear to me! Arms ye shall make for a fearless warrior. Now is need of strength, now of the quick hand, now of the lessons of our art. Banish delay!' No farther he said: but incontinent all bent to their equally portioned toil. Brass and golden ore flowed in streams, and the wounding steel was molten in the vast furnace. They formed a mighty shield, that, sole, might withstand every Latin spear, and plated it with seven folds, circle on circle. Some with panting bellows drew in and expelled the blast: others plunged the hissing bronze in the trough; and the cave moaned under its load of anvils. In measured rhythm, one by one they lifted their giant arms, and with gripping tongs turned the metal.

While the lord of Lemnos made such dispatch on his Aeolian shores, the gracious dawn and the matin songs of birds under his eaves roused Evander from his humble home. The old king arose, drew on his tunic, and bound his feet in Tyrrhene sandals; then buckled to shoulder and side his blade of Tegea, flinging round him a leopard's skin pendent from his left. Nor lacked he guard; for two dogs went before him from his high-raised threshold, attendant on their master's steps. Thus the hero, mindful of his words and the service promised, sought the dwelling of his guest and the privacy of Aeneas. Nor less the Trojan was abroad with the morn. With his father Pallas walked; with his comrade,

Achates; till meeting they clasped hands, and, seated in the inmost chamber, at length enjoyed full freedom of converse. And first the king:

'Mightiest captain of the Teucrians – whose life enduring, this tongue shall never confess the star of Troy set, nor her empire vanquished! – our name is great, but our strength is small to give succour in war. On this hand we are prisoned by the Tuscan stream: on that, the Rutulian presses hard, and his weapons clash about our wall. None the less, my purpose is to unite with thee broad peoples and hosts that flourish under many a king. An unhoped chance reveals thy salvation, and the call of fate hath led thee hither. No great way hence, established on immemorial rock, stands Agylla's peopled city, where of old the war-famed Lydian race settled on the Etruscan peaks. For many years it prospered, till Mezentius the king governed it with iron sceptre and bloody sword. What profits it to recount the nameless murders, the pitiless deeds, of that tyrant? Heaven visit them on him and his! Nay, he would link the quick to the dead, joining – fell discovery of torment! – hand to hand and face to face, and, in the streaming gore and corruption of that woeful union, so slay them by a lingering doom. But the day came when his citizens, outworn by such impious frenzy, besieged him and his palace in arms, hewed down his henchmen, and hurled fire to his roof. He, amid the slaughter, fled for refuge to Rutulian soil, and found defence among the friendly spears of Turnus. Therefore all Etruria has risen in righteous fury, and at the point of the sword they demand their king for punishment. – Of these thousands, Aeneas, I will make thee captain! For their chafing barques throng all the shore, and they bid the banners advance; but the aged soothsayer restrains them with fateful presage: *O ye chosen of Maeonia's land, flower and strength of your fathers' realm, – ye, whom just resentment spurs against the enemy, and Mezentius kindles with the anger himself hath earned, – none of Italy born may sway thus mighty a people! Choose ye an alien leader!* Therefore the Etruscan array is encamped on this plain, awed by the warning of Heaven; and Tarcho himself has sent envoys to me, with the crown and sceptre of the kingdom, and offers the ensigns of royalty, will I but enter their camp and mount the Tyrrhene throne. But the frosts of sluggish eld, the feebleness of many years, and strength that is past the day of deeds, deny me dominion. My son I would fain urge to the task, did not the blood of his Sabine mother, mingled with mine, make this in part his fatherland. Thou, on whose years and descent alike Fate smiles – whom deity summons – enter thou on this office, the fearless captain of Troy and Italy! More, I will give thee this my Pallas, our hope and comfort. Under thy guidance let him learn to endure warfare and the grim toils of battle; let him view thy prowess, and revere thee from his early years. To him I will consign twice a hundred Arcadian horsemen, the choice of our chivalry; and Pallas shall bring thee as many else by his proper gift.'

Scarce had he spoken; and Aeneas – Anchises' child – and faithful Achates stood with downcast eyes, revolving each in his own sad heart many a troubled thought, had not Cythera's queen granted a sign from the cloudless sky. For, unforeseen, a flash came quivering from the empyrean, thunder-heralded, and suddenly all nature seemed to totter, while the trumpet's Tyrrhene note rang through the firmament. They looked up: again, and yet again, the mighty peal crashed, and in the serene expanse of heaven they saw arms, cloud-enwrapped, gleaming red through the translucent air and clashing in thunder. The rest were aghast: but Troy's hero knew that in the sound spoke the promise of his goddess-mother. Then:

'Ask not, my friend, ask not,' he cried, 'what issue these portents bode to our journey! It is I who am called! This sign the goddess who bore me foretold she would send from Olympus' height, did war assail, and would bring through the skies Vulcanian arms to my succour! Alas, what carnage awaits the hapless of Laurentum! What vengeance, Turnus, thou shalt yield me! How many a buckler and helm, how many a warrior's stalwart frame, shalt thou roll, O father Tiber, under thy wave! Now let them clamour for battle, and dishonour treaty!'

This said, he rose from his lofty seat, and, first quickening the oblivious altars with the fire of their divinity, approached in gladness the Lar of yesterday and the household's lowly gods; while Evander alike and the men of Troy offered chosen ewes in wonted sacrifice. Next he plied to the ships and revisited his men, from whose number he chose the stoutest hearts to follow himself to battle: the residue sailed down the waters and floated idly along the descending stream, messengers to Ascanius of his sire and his fortunes. Steeds were assigned to the Teucrians who sought the Tuscan borders; and one they led to Aeneas for especial guerdon, all caparisoned in a tawny lion's fell that glittered with claws of gold.

With sudden flight Rumour sped blazoned through the little

town – that the horsemen rode with speed to the doors of the
Tyrrhene king. Trembling matrons redoubled their vows; fear
trod closer on peril, and the War-god's semblance rose larger on
their view. Then Evander, clasping the hand of his departing
son, clung to him with insatiable tears, and so spoke:

'O, would Jupiter restore me the years that are fled, and make
me as I was when, hard beneath Praeneste, I smote down their
vanward lines and, victor, burned their high-piled shields! With
this right hand I sent King Erulus down to hell, though at birth –
a tale of dread! – Feronia gave to her child three lives and threefold weapons to wield. Thrice must he be laid low in death; yet
on that day this hand bereft him of all his lives and as oft stripped
him of his arms. Never, my son, would I now be torn from thy
sweet embrace; never should Mezentius have loaded his neighbour's grey head with scorn, nor slain his thousands with ruthless
sword, nor widowed my city of so many a citizen! But ye, O
powers above, and thou, Jupiter, king and lord of gods, pity, I
implore, the Arcadian king, and list to a father's prayer! If destiny
and your will ordain the safety of my Pallas, if, living, I shall see
and meet him again, then I pray to live – I am patient to endure
whatsoever trial ye will! But, Fortune, if thou threatenest some
nameless disaster, now, oh, now be it granted me to break the
bond of this cruel life, – while my care is ambiguous still, while
my presage is unproved, while thou, dearest boy, my sole and
latest delight, art still in mine arms; nor let a message more bitter
wound these ears!' Such the words that the father uttered at their
last parting; then swooned, and his servants bore him within the
palace.

And now the horsemen had issued from the open gates, Aeneas
and loyal Achates in the van, then the princes else of Troy; while
in the midmost line rode Pallas himself, conspicuous in broidered scarf and emblazoned arms: such as the star of morn, that
Venus most loves of all the sidereal fires, when, laved in the
ocean flood, he uplifts his sacred head in heaven and the darkness
melts away. On the walls stood trembling matrons, with eyes
pursuing the dusty cloud and the squadrons that glittered in
brass. They, by the path that led soonest to their journey's goal,
moved in panoply through the brakes. A shout arose, a column
was formed, and the sound of galloping hooves shook the crumbling plain. There stands a vast grove by Caere's cool stream,
that the reverence of an earlier day has endowed with sanctity far
and near: on all sides sheltering hills enclose it and surround the

woodland with sombre pines. Fame tells that the Pelasgians of yore, pristine habitants of Latium's borders, dedicated grove and festal day to Silvanus, the god of field and flock. Not far thence Tarcho and his Tyrrhene bands lay encamped in sure position; and now from the hill-top all their host could be discerned, and their pavilions wide-spreading over the champaign. Hither came father Aeneas and his chosen warriors, and refreshed their steeds and weary limbs.

But Venus was come in celestial beauty, bearing her gifts through the clouds of heaven; and when she descried her son in a secluded vale, in the chill stream's distant privacy, offered herself to his view, and thus accosted him:

'Behold this guerdon that my lord hath perfected by his promised art! Then, shun not, my child, in the coming days to defy the haughty Laurentines and their fiery Turnus to battle!' So saying, Cythera's queen sought the embrace of her son, and placed the arms all radiant under an oak that fronted his view. He, exulting in the divine gift, and in honour thus signal, could not sate his eyes with the vision, as he swept them from point to point, and, admiring, turned in hand and arm the helmet, plumed with terror and shooting flame, the fate-fraught sword, and the stark corselet of brass, huge and blood-red, – as a sable cloud, when it kindles to the sunbeams and glitters far, – then the burnished greaves of electrum and doubly-refined gold, the spear, and the shield's ineffable fabric. There the Lord of Fire – no stranger he to prophecy nor witless of the ages to dawn – had wrought the fortunes of Italy and the triumphs of Rome; there, every generation of the stock that should spring from Ascanius, and the ordered line of their stricken fields. And the mother-wolf he had fashioned, couched in the green cave of Mars. About her teats the twin boys hung playing, and, unfearing, licked their dam; she, her shapely neck bent back, caressed each in turn and moulded their limbs with her tongue. Hard by this he had added Rome and the Sabine maidens, lawlessly reft in full concourse of the theatre, what time the Great Games were solemnized, and a new war suddenly arising betwixt the children of Romulus and aged Tatius with his stern Cures. Soon the selfsame kings, their mutual conflict resigned, stood armed before the altar of Jove, goblet in hand, and with sacrifice of swine concluded their league. No great way thence chariots driven apart had torn Mettus asunder (but, Alban, it behoved thee to abide by thy word!), and Tullus whirled the liar's corpse through the forest, and the briars dripped with a ghastly dew. Nor lacked there Porsenna, commanding that they receive the exiled Tarquin again, and hemming the city with mighty leaguer; while the sons of Aeneas rushed upon the sword for freedom's sake. On his brow might be seen anger and menace portrayed, that Cocles should dare to lay the bridge low and Cloelia should break her fetters and swim the river. In the topmost shield, Manlius, warder of the Tarpeian height, stood before the temple and held the lofty Capitol; and the rough thatch lay fresh on Romulus' palace. And here the silver goose, flitting through gilded arcades, cried that the Gauls were on the threshold. The Gauls were come through the thickets and their feet were on the summit; for they were shielded by the darkness and the dusk guerdon of night. Their locks were golden, and golden their vesture; the stripes of their cloaks shone bright, and their snowy necks were encircled with gold; each brandished two Alpine javelins, and long shields guarded their limbs. Here his hammers had wrought the bounding Salii and the naked Luperci, the wool-bound crests and the sacred bucklers that fell from heaven; and in cushioned cars chaste matrons moved in solemn train through the city. Away from these he added, withal, the abodes of Hell, the towering portals of Dis, the penalties of sin, and thee, Catiline, hung from a frowning cliff and trembling before the face of the Furies; and the privacy of the just, and Cato giving laws to them. Betwixt all the semblance of the swelling sea flowed wide-streaming in gold, though the blue foamed with whitening waves; and about it wheeled dolphins of lustrous silver, lashing the waters with their tails, and cleaving the tide. In the midst the brazen-beaked fleets of Actium's battle met the view; and the eye might see all Leucate aswarm with the array of war, and the waves ablaze with gold. Here on the tall poop stood Caesar Augustus, leading his Italy to the fray, with senate and people and gods of home and of heaven, while from his auspicious brows twin flames shot, and his father's star beamed over his crest. Elsewhere Agrippa, under the favour of wind and deity, high-towering led his column – his temples refulgent with the prows of the naval crown, that glorious cognizance of battle. There Antonius, with his barbarous powers and motley arms, victor from the peoples of the Dawn and the strand of the ruddy sea, bare with him Egypt, and the might of the East, and utmost Bactria; and by his side went – O vision of shame! – his Memphian paramour. At once all closed, and the whole main foamed convulsed by the sweeping oars and triple-toothed prows. To the deep they sped. A man might deem that the Cyclades floated, uptorn, on ocean, or that mountain-height clashed with mountain: – so mightily the seamen urged onward their turreted ships. Flaming tow and winged steel flew volleyed from their hands, and the plains of Neptune were crimsoned with unfamiliar carnage. In the midst, the queen called upon her hosts with their native cymbal, nor as yet cast back her glance on the twin serpents behind her. Gods monstrous and manifold, and barking Anubis, stood with lifted weapons against Neptune and Venus, and against Minerva. In the heart of the conflict Mavors raged, graven in iron, with the fell Sister-fiends descending from heaven; and in rent robes Discord walked exultant, while Bellona followed her with bloody scourge. Actian Apollo saw the sight, and drew his bow from on high; in terror whereof all Egypt and Ind, and all of Arabia and Saba, turned to flee. The queen herself seemed to spread her sails to the responsive winds, and even now to fling loose the slackened sheets. Her, amid the slaughter, the Lord of Fire had shown pale at the coming death, convoyed by the waves and the western gale; while over against her was Nile, his mighty frame in the throes of grief, opening wide his folds, and with all the expanse of his raiment inviting the vanquished to his azure bosom and sheltering streams. But Caesar, entering the walls of Rome in threefold triumph, consecrated to the gods of Italy the immortal tribute he had vowed – thrice a hundred stately shrines throughout all the city. The ways rang with mirth and games and applause. – In every fane was a quire of matrons; in every fane an altar stood, and before the altar slain steers strewed the ground. Himself, seated in the snowy portal of shining Phoebus, reviewed the offerings of the peoples and affixed them to the haughty doors, while the conquered nations defiled in long procession, diverse in tongue, diverse in fashion of attire and in arms. Here Mulciber had portrayed the Nomad race and the ungirt African, here the Lelex and the Carian and the quivered Gelonian. Euphrates now passed with gentler wave, and the Morini, uttermost of men, and the double-horned Rhine and the untamed Dahans, and Araxes fretting at his bridge.

Such sight the hero surveyed, admiring, on Vulcan's shield, that his mother gave, and, though he knew not of the deeds, yet rejoiced in their pictured semblance, as he upraised on his shoulder the fame and fate of his children's children.

BOOK IX

WHILE IN THE FAR DISTANCE such deeds were wrought, Saturnian Juno sent Iris from heaven down to the gallant Turnus, – Turnus, who then, as it fell, sate in his sire Pilumnus' grove and the hallowed vale. To whom, with roseate lips, spoke the child of Thaumas:

'Turnus, that which thou mightest have prayed, and no god promised, – behold, the circling hours have brought it thee unsought! Aeneas has left town, and crews, and fleet, to seek the kingdom of the Palatine and the habitation of Evander. Nor suffices this! He has won his way to Corythus' utmost cities and the Lydian host, and he arms the mustered countrymen. Why art thou hesitant? Now is the season to call for thy steeds – the season to summon thy chariots! Away with all delay, and fall on the turmoiled camp!' She said, and on even wing soared skyward, tracing, as she fled beneath the clouds, the mighty arch of her bow. The prince knew his monitress, and, lifting either hand to heaven, with such utterance pursued her flight: 'Iris, glory of the sky, who hath sent thee, shot from the clouds, down to me upon earth? Whence is this sudden serenity of the air? I see the firmament parting in twain, and the stars wandering about the pole! Whosoever thou art that callest to arms, I bow to thy powerful sign!' And so saying he went onward to the river and took up water from the brimming wave, with reiterate prayer entreating the gods and burdening heaven with vows.

And now all the army was advancing over the open plains, splendid on gallant chargers, splendid in broidered raiment and gold, with Messapus marshalling the van, the sons of Tyrrheus the rear, and Turnus their captain in the midmost column: – even as Ganges, when through the silence he rises high with his seven tranquil streams, or Nile, when his bountiful flood ebbs from the champaign and at length he is sunk in his channel. The Teucrians looked forth and saw a sudden cloud gathering black in dust, and darkness arising over the plains. First Caicus called from the ramparts opposite: 'What mass, my countrymen, rolls hitherward in misty gloom? Get ye steel, and linger not! Serve weapons; ascend the walls! The enemy is on us, ho!' Loud clamouring, the Teucrians streamed in through every gateway and manned the bulwarks. For such had been the charge of Aeneas, the wise in war, when he went upon his way: – that, were aught to chance in the meanwhile, they should neither adventure to order their array for battle nor to put faith in the open field, but should keep only to the camp and their walls' protecting mounds. Therefore, though shame and anger advised them to the conflict, yet they barred the gates and discharged his behest, awaiting the foe under arms in the shelter of their towers.

Turnus, who had spurred onward in the van of his tardy column, with retinue of twenty chosen horsemen, rode suddenly to the gates, borne on a white-dappled courser of Thrace and helmed in a red-plumed casque of gold. 'Is there one, ye gallants, who at my side will lead the way to the enemy! Behold!' he said; and, whirling his javelin, flung it heavenward – the prelude of war – and galloped towering on the plain. His band took up the cry, and followed with dread and dissonant clamour, wondering at the craven hearts of Troy – that no man was found to brave the impartial field and the encountering lance, but all nursed the camp! Hither and thither he rode in fury round the walls, seeking entry where entry was none. Even as a wolf that lies in ambush against the full fold, when, beaten by the winds and rains, he ravens round the pens at dead of night, and safe beneath their mothers the lambs bleat unceasingly; he, exasperate and reckless, rages in anger against the absent prey, wearied by the long-gathering lust of food and his dry, bloodless jaws: – not otherwise kindled the Rutulian's ire, as he surveyed walls and camp; and resentment blazed in his iron frame. By what mode should he assay his approach? What path pursued might dislodge the imprisoned Teucrians from their rampart, and drive them streaming into the plain? Fast by the side of the camp lay the fleet, hedged by earthen mounds and by the flowing river: the fleet he assailed, calling to his exultant train for fire, and, with heart as hot, clutched the flaming pine in his hand. Then in truth they bent to the toil, spurred by Turnus' presence, and all the band armed them with murky torches. Instant they stripped the hearths: smoking brands flung a pitchy glare, and Vulcan rolled to the stars a cloud of glowing ashes.

What god, ye Muses, repelled those fierce flames from Troy? Who warded from the ships that perilous fire? Speak and say! Ancient the warrant of that deed, but everlasting the fame! – In those earliest days, when, on Phrygian Ida, Aeneas began to shape his fleet and prepared to sail the deep seas, the tale is told how she of Berecyntus, the great Mother of gods, addressed sovereign Jove, and said: 'Grant, O son, to thy mother's prayer the boon that she asks thee for Olympus subdued! A grove I had on the mountain crest, whither men brought me sacrifice, dim with the shade of many a pine and with boles of the maple. These gladly I bestowed on the Dardan prince, when he lacked a fleet; but now anxious fear racks my doubting soul. Resolve thou my dread, and vouchsafe that thy parent's entreaty may thus much avail – that they be overborne neither by stress of voyage nor by the whirling wind. Be it counted to them for good, that their roots were in my hill!'

Whom answering, her son who sways the stars in the firmament: 'O mother, whither wouldst thou wrest the fates? Or what seekest thou for thine own? Shall barques fashioned by mortal hand possess the immortal privilege? Secure, shall Aeneas traverse perils insecure? To what god is such power permitted? Not so: but hereafter when their service is done and they have attained their bourne in Ausonia's havens, from each that hath escaped the waves, and borne the Dardan prince to the fields of Laurentum, I will take away the shape of mortality and bid them be goddesses of the great sea, like to Doto, Nereus' child, and Galatea, when they breast the foaming main!' – He ended; and by the waters of his Stygian brother, by those banks where the torrent pitch eddies in black abysm, he nodded confirmation, and, nodding, shook all Olympus.

Thus the promised day was come and the Sisters had fulfilled their appointed times, when Turnus' injurious deed admonished the Mother of Heaven to avert the brands from her sacred ships. First now a strange light flashed before their eyes, and a great radiance was seen speeding from the Dawn athwart the sky, and in it the quires of Ida. Then a voice of terror fell through the air, filling the hosts of Troy and Rutulia: 'Take not thought, ye Teucrians, to defend my ships, nor lay your hands upon your swords. Sooner shall Turnus fire the seas, than these holy pines! Go ye in freedom; go, goddesses of ocean: the Mother commands!' And incontinent each vessel severed her bonds from the shore; and, like dolphins, all plunged with submerged prow into the depths, whence – strange and portentous sight! – as many maiden faces appeared, glancing amid the waves.

Aghast was every Rutulian heart: behind his affrighted steeds even Messapus trembled; and, with hoarse murmur, Tiber river paused and recalled his waters from the brine. But his trust failed not Turnus' unfearing soul! Nay, he spoke in encouragement and rebuke: 'On the Trojans these portents fall! Jove himself has stripped them of their wonted succour. They await not our Rutulian steel and flame! Thus the ways of ocean are shut against Troy, and hope of flight there is none. The moiety of nature is lost to them, and the earth is in our hands: for in all their thousands the nations of Italy bear the sword. The fateful responses of Heaven – whatsoever they be – that these Phrygians vaunt, dismay me not. Fate and Venus are paid in full, now that their Trojans have attained the fruitful fields of Ausonia. I, too, have my fate to encounter theirs, – to hew down with the sword the accursed race that has stolen my bride! That pain stings not the sons of Atreus alone, nor alone is Mycenae licensed to rise in arms. *But once to have perished is enough!* Nay, enough it should have been once to sin, then loathe utterly all but the whole of woman's kind! These are they who trust in their intervening rampart, – whose courage is fired by the hindrance of their trenches, that petty pale betwixt them and death! Yet saw they not their Trojan battlements, that the hand of Neptune built, sinking in the flames? But ye, my chosen, – who of you is ready, sword in hand, to tear down their bulwarks? Who assaults the bewildered camp at my side? I need not arms from Vulcan, nor a thousand ships, to do battle against Troy! Let all Etruria join their alliance forthwith! They need fear neither the hour of night nor the coward's theft; nor shall they find us ambushed from the view in a horse's belly! My resolve is fixed: in the broad light of day we will circle their walls with fire. By proof they shall learn that they are matched not with Danaans, nor with those Pelasgic legions that, till the tenth year, Hector held at bay! Now since the fairer portion of day is done – for what remains, gallants, refresh your limbs in gladness after this prosperous issue, and be assured that battle prepares!'

Meanwhile Messapus received charge to beset the gates with posted sentries, and ring the battlements with fires. Twice seven Rutulians were chosen to guard the walls with soldiery, and on each followed a hundred warriors, purple-plumed and glittering in gold. Disparting they varied the watch, and, couched on the sward, drank their fill, uptilting great bowls of bronze. The fires shone all, and the warders passed the slumberless night in play.

All this the Trojans viewed from their rampart above, as they held the height in arms. Weapons in hand, they explored the gates with fearful haste, and threw gangways from bulwark to bulwark. Foremost laboured Mnestheus and bold Serestus, whom father Aeneas had ordained to be captains of his warriors and pilots of the state, should adversity call; while along the walls, dividing the peril, the whole host kept changing vigil over their allotted charges.

Nisus was warder of the gate, – Hyrtacus' warrior-son, whom huntress Ida had sent attendant on Aeneas, swift to hurl the javelin and speed the light shaft. At his side was Euryalus – none fairer among Aeneas' people ever wore the harness of Troy! – a boy whose unshaven cheek showed the earliest bloom of youth. They were bound by a single love; side by side they charged in the fray; and in that hour also they kept the gate in community of guard. First Nisus spoke: 'Is it the gods, Euryalus, who kindle this ardour in our souls? Or does the unblest yearning of each become his god? Long time has my heart burned to adventure battle or some great deed; and peace and rest content it not. Thou seest the Rutulians – what faith in their star possesses them. Their lights gleam few and scattered; they lie unmanned by wine and sleep; and far and wide silence reigns. Then learn my wavering thought; the purpose that now rises in my mind. People and senate, – all demand that Aeneas be summoned and messengers sent with certain tidings. If they promise the boon that I ask for thee – for enough the glory to me – methinks I might find a path beneath yonder mound to the city-walls of Pallanteum!' Thrilled by high love of honour, Euryalus stood astounded, and instant he addressed his hot-souled friend: 'Nisus, and dost thou shun my alliance in this great emprize? Shall I send thee alone into the midst of peril? Not so did Opheltes my sire, grown grey in battle, breed and nurture me amid the terrors of Argos and the travails of Troy! Not such the part I have played at thy side, since I followed noble Aeneas and the utmost hazards of his fate! In this breast – even in this – dwells a soul that contemns the light, and counts that honour for which thou strivest well bought at the cost of life.' To which, Nisus: 'Deem not that I had such fear of thee; nay, the thought had been crime! As I speak truth, so may great Jupiter, or whosoever beholds us with righteous eyes, restore me in triumph to thee! But if aught – as oft thou mayest see betide in like desperate perils – if aught, whether chance or deity, sweep me to a disastrous goal, I were fain that thou shouldst live; for thy years more merit life. Let there be one to commit me to earth, rescued from battle or redeemed at a price; or – if this Fortune's wonted malice deny – to render the last rites to the absent and pay the tribute of a grave. Nor, child, would I be the cause of such agony to thy unhappy mother, who, of many mothers, alone has followed her son, nor regards the city-walls of great Acestes.' But he: 'Vainly thy pretexts are spun; my purpose changes not nor falters so soon! Haste we'; he said, and, with the word, roused the guards. They, succeeding, observed their watch: he, quitting his ward, walked by Nisus' side in quest of the prince.

All creatures else throughout all lands lay in slumber, with cares assuaged and hearts oblivious of their sorrows: but the chief captains of Troy, flower of the host, held momentous council on the fortunes of the state, – how it behoved to act, or who now should be their messengers to Aeneas. Leaning on long spears they stood, shield upon arm, in the mid-space betwixt camp and plain. It was then that Nisus and Euryalus together prayed with urgency for instant audience: for the matter was great and would requite delay. First Iulus welcomed the impatient pair, and bade Nisus speak his errand. Then thus the son of Hyrtacus: 'Listen, ye people of Aeneas, with impartial mind, nor measure our offer by our years! Relaxed by sleep and wine, the Rutulians lie in silence. Our own eyes have seen where stratagem may be assayed – the open ground in the forked way from that gate which lies nighest the sea. There the circle of fire is broken, – the smoke rolls black to the stars. If ye permit us to use occasion, and seek Aeneas and the walls of Pallanteum, soon shall ye see us returned, laden with spoils and fresh from a mighty slaughter. Nor can the path deceive us as we journey. By dint of incessant hunting we have descried the outskirts of the city in the dim vales, and all the river is known to us.' Then Aletes, bowed with years and ripe in wisdom: 'Gods of our fathers, under whose shadow Troy ever rests, not yet, in despite of all, do ye purpose utterly to blot out Teucer's race, when ye have brought us such valour in our youth and hearts thus steadfast.' And as he said, he held the shoulders and hands of each, while the tears rained down his cheeks and face. 'Sirs, what guerdon – what worthy guerdon – shall I deem may be paid you for this high deed? First and fairest shall be the reward of Heaven and the knowledge of duty done. The remnant ye shall speedily receive from good Aeneas, and from Ascanius, the young in years, who never shall forget your glorious deserts.' 'Nay,' and Ascanius took the word, 'I whose sole salvation lies in the return of my sire – Nisus, I adjure you both by the great gods of our home, by the Lar of Assaracus, and by white-headed Vesta's shrine – all my fortune

and all my trust I lay upon your knees; recall my father, restore
him to sight; with his recovery sorrow vanishes! Two goblets
shall be my gift – wrought of silver and rough with chasing – that
he took when Arisba fell, two tripods, two great talents of gold,
and the immemorial bowl that Dido of Sidon gave. But if victory
be mine, if ever I grasp the sceptre of captured Italy and assign
her spoils, thou hast seen the charger of Turnus and the arms
wherein he moved all golden: steed, shield, and crimson plumes
will I except from the lot – thy guerdon, my Nisus, from this
hour. More, my sire shall bestow on thee twice six matrons of
choicest beauty, and captive warriors, his harness with each; and
– to crown his boon – all that domain whereof King Latinus himself now is lord. But thee, whose years mine follow at nigher
interval, thee, noble boy, I now take to my heart and embrace
thee, my comrade in every chance. Without thee will I seek no
glory to gild my fortunes: come peace, or come war, in deed or in
word thou shalt be the staff of my trust!'

To whom Euryalus, in reply: 'Time shall not prove me degenerate from the promise of this bold emprize: let but Fortune's
first cast aid us, not thwart! But, above all thy gifts, there is one
that I would entreat from thee. I have a mother, of Priam's
ancient line, who laid not her careworn head in our Ilian soil, nor
in King Acestes' city, but went forth with me. Her I now leave in
ignorance of this peril, be it great or small, and without word of
farewell, because – Night and thy right hand be witness – I might
not endure that she who bare me should weep. But thou, I pray,
comfort the helpless, succour the deserted! Let me carry with me
this hope in thee, and with bolder front I will encounter whatsoever shall befall.'

Moved to the heart the children of Dardanus broke into tears –
chief of all the fair Iulus, as the image of his own filial love struck
upon his soul. Then thus he spoke: 'Assure thyself that all shall
be done that is due to thy mighty enterprise: for thy mother shall
be my mother – Creusa, save for Creusa's name. Not slight our
debt to one that has borne such a son! Whatever fortune attend
thy deed, I swear by my life, as my father was wont to swear: – all
that I promise to thee, if thou return in prosperity, shall remain
unforfeited to thy mother and thy house!' So, weeping, he spoke;
and, with the word, undid from his shoulder the gilded blade
fashioned with wondrous art by Gnosian Lycaon, and featly
cased in scabbard of ivory. To Nisus Mnestheus gave the fell,
stripped from a shaggy lion, and loyal Aletes changed helm for

helm. Once armed, they advanced without delay; and, as they went, all the throng of nobles, young and old, escorted them to the gate with vows. Nor lacked there fair Iulus, dowered beyond his years with manly spirit and thought, burdening them with many messages to his sire. But the winds scattered all, and flung them, frustrate, to the clouds!

Issuing, they crossed the trenches, and through the shadows of night sought the fatal camp – doomed, yet charged with the doom of many. Everywhere they saw senseless frames stretched along the sward in drunken slumber, chariots uptilted on the shore, men lying amid wheels and harness, and piles of weapons and pools of wine. First Hyrtacus' son broke silence: 'Euryalus, here is need of the unflinching hand: now occasion calls! By this path our journey lies. Keep thou watch and far-reaching ward, that no hand may be lifted against us from behind. Here I will wreak destruction till a broad highway be made for thy feet.' So said, he was mute: and instant his blade assailed proud Rhamnes, who, pillowed on high-piled coverlets, lay, with broad chest heaving to the deep breath of sleep – a kingly augur, best-beloved of Turnus his brother king: but not all his augury availed to thwart his doom. Three of his henchmen he slew by his side, where careless they slumbered amid their arms. Remus' armour-bearer he slew, and the charioteer, found at his horses' feet. He severed their drooping necks with the steel; then reft their lord of his head, and left the trunk spurting blood, while earth and couch streamed with black gore. Nor less Lamyrus and Lamus fell; and Serranus, the young, the beautiful, who had played long and deep that night, and lay with the Wine-god heavy on his limbs – happy he, had his play outworn the livelong night and endured to the dawn! Even so, goaded by hunger's maddening pang, an unfed lion riots through the full folds, gnashing his bloody teeth, and mangling and tearing the feeble flock that is dumb with fear! Nor less the carnage of Euryalus! He caught his partner's flame, and, in his infuriate course, invaded the nameless multitude that lay in his path: Fadus and Herbesus, Rhoetus and Abaris – unwitting these; save Rhoetus, who with wakeful eyes beheld all, but cowered behind a great bowl in fear. Thence as he arose, hard at hand he plunged his sword to the hilt full in his breast, and drew it back incarnadined with streaming death. Dying, the Rutulian gasped out his soul, and wine commingled with blood: the foe pursued his stealthy massacre. And now he drew near Messapus' powers. He saw the last fire failing, and

horses, tethered duly, cropping the grass; when Nisus in brief –
for he saw him swept away by the reckless lust of blood: – 'Forbear we: for the unfriendly dawn is nigh! Of vengeance we have
drunken enough; and a way is cut through the foe!' Many a warrior's accoutrement, wrought in solid silver, they left behind –
with many a bowl, and many a fair coverlet. Euryalus descried
the trappings of Rhamnes and his baldrick, gold-embossed – gifts
that erewhile, in pledge of amity from the absent, richest Caedicus sent to Tiburtine Remulus, and Remulus, as he lay dying,
consigned to his grandchild for his own. These he rent away, and
flung them – vain defence! – over his stout limbs; then donned
Messapus' shapely helm with its glancing plumes. This done they
issued from the camp and sought less perilous ground.

Meanwhile a vanguard of horse, dispatched from Latinus'
town, while the remnant of their host halted on the plains in
battle array, came riding with messages to Turnus the king.
Three hundred they numbered – all shielded men, Volcens at
their head. And now they approached the camp and drew to the
walls; when at distance they descried the two turning aside by the
leftward path, and, in the glimmering shadow of night, his helm
betrayed the unthinking Euryalus, flashing as it met the lunar
ray. Nor did the sight fall on heedless eyes! From his column
Volcens called loudly:

'Stand, warriors! What imports your journey? Who are ye that
travel in arms? Or whither wend ye?' No answer they made, but
quickened their flight to the wood, and rested their hope on the
night. On this hand and that, the horsemen barred the familiar
crossways, and the circle of their sentinels beset every passage. –
The forest stood wide-spreading with horrent thickets and shady
holms: serried briars thronged it on every hand, and through the
hidden tracks the path gleamed fitfully. Hampered by the
gloomy boughs and the burden of his spoil, Euryalus, in fear,
strayed from the line that marked his way. Nisus sped thence;
and now, oblivious, he had outpassed the enemy, and those
regions – *Alban* styled thereafter from Alba's name – where in
those days stood the lofty stalls of King Latinus. When, halting,
he looked back in vain for his lost friend: 'Unhappy Euryalus,' he
cried, 'where have I left thee? Or by what path shall I seek thee?'
Unravelling once more the tangled maze of that treacherous
wood, he scanned, the while, and retraced his steps, as he wandered in the silent brakes. He heard the horses, heard the din and
the signals of pursuit. Yet a little while and a cry broke on his

ears, and on the instant he saw Euryalus, in the hands of all their band, betrayed by the ground and the gloom, bewildered by the sudden onslaught, and dragged helpless away, despite all his frustrate struggles. – What could he do? With what force – what arms – might he adventure the rescue? Or should he cast himself amid their swords to his doom, and, bleeding, find a swift death and glorious? – Hastily he drew back his arm with poised lance, looked up to the moon on high, and so prayed: 'O goddess, Latona's child, be with us and succour our evil case – thou the glory of the stars, the guardian of the greenwood! If ever my father Hyrtacus brought tribute to thy altars for me, – if ever I swelled the meed from my hunting with offerings hung to thy dome or affixed to thy hallowed roof, – grant me to confound this mass, and guide my javelin through the airs!' He ceased, and with all the strength of his frame flung the steel. The flying spear flashed through the shadows of night, struck the back of Sulmo as he stood averted, then broke, and with splintered shaft pierced the midriff. Chill in death he rolled, while the warm tide gushed from his breast, and long-drawn sobs shook his sides. This way and that they gazed round. He, thus emboldened, already poised a second dart from the tip of his ear. Ere their confusion abated, the whistling spear passed through Tagus' either temple and lodged warm in his cloven brain. Volcens raged infuriate, yet nowhere descried the author of the wound, nor where to wreak his flaming vengeance. 'Yet thou, meanwhile, with thy hot blood shalt pay me the penalty for both,' he cried; and with naked brand rushed on Euryalus. Then in truth terror-stricken, sensebereft, Nisus called aloud; for no longer could he hide himself in darkness – no longer endure that bitter agony: 'On me, – here I stand who did the deed, – on me turn your steel, Rutulians! Mine is all the guilt. He dared not, nor, daring, could have achieved! – Heaven and the conscious stars be witnesses! He loved but his hapless friend too well!' So he pleaded: but the sword, driven by that strong arm, had passed sheer through the ribs and was rending the snowy breast. Euryalus rolled over in death: along his fair limbs blood streamed, and his drooping neck sank on his shoulder – as a purple flower, that the plough has severed, languishes and dies, or as poppies, weighted by random showers, bow laden heads on weary necks. But Nisus rushed into their midst, and sole among all sought Volcens – in Volcens his only care! Around him the clustering foemen closed, and assailed him on every side. Natheless he pressed on, whirling the lightning of his blade, till full in the mouth of the shrieking Rutule he plunged it, and, dying, bereft his enemy of life; then flung his pierced frame on the clay that was his friend, and there at length, in the peace of death, slept well.

Happy pair! if aught of power resides in my verse, the years may roll, but shall never efface you from the memory of time, so long as the house of Aeneas shall dwell by the Capitol's unmoved rock and the Father of Rome bear sceptre!

Their spoils and booty secured, weeping the victor Rutulians bore Volcens dead to the camp. Nor in that camp was their sorrow less when Rhamnes was found with his life-blood spilt, and Serranus, and Numa, and those many princes fallen in one red burial. To the corpses and the warriors stricken to death – to the ground reeking fresh with carnage and the full-foaming streams of gore – they ran in their multitudes; and there, each communing with each, they recognized the spoils – Messapus' shining helm and the trappings so hardly regained by the sweat of their brow.

And now the early Dawn, rising from Tithonus' couch of saffron, was bespanglng earth with her new-tricked beams: the sunlight was streaming in, and day had revealed the world, when Turnus, himself in arms, to arms summoned his warriors. Each captain marshalled his brass-mailed lines, and with motley rumours edged their anger. More, on lifted spears they affixed – O vision of woe! – the heads of Nisus and Euryalus, and followed loud clamouring. On the left portion of the walls – the right was girt by the river – the stout hearts of Troy opposed their battle array, held the broad trenches, and stood on the turret-heights, plunged in gloom and moved by the sight of those upreared heads, that their weeping eyes knew too well, though now they streamed with black and corrupted gore.

Meanwhile, on disaster-laden pinions, Fame flew through the trembling town, and sped to the ears of Euryalus' mother. Instant the warmth abandoned her careworn frame: the shuttle dropped from her hands, and the threads were unrolled. Forth she rushed in her misery, and with a woman's cry of anguish, ran frenzied – her tresses rent – to the walls and the vanward lines, heedless she of the eyes of men, heedless of the peril and hurtling spears; then filled the sky with her plaint: 'Is it thus, Euryalus, that I see thee again? Couldst thou, the late solace of my years – couldst thou leave me desolate so cruelly? And was permission to speak the last farewell denied to thy hapless mother, when they sent thee into jeopardy? Ay me, on alien soil thou liest, flung forth for the Latin dogs and fowls to tear! Nor might I, who bare thee, give thee burial! I laid thee not out; I closed not thine eyes; I washed not thy wounds; nor shrouded thee in that robe which night and day I hastened to achieve for thee, beguiling with the loom the sorrows of age and womanhood. Whither shall I follow thee? What land now possesses thy mangled limbs, thy dismembered body? Is this all, my child, that returns to me of thyself? Was it this that I followed over earth and ocean? Pierce me, ye Rutulians, if ye know aught of a mother's love; on me hurl your every spear; here let your steel first drink blood! Or thou, great Father of Heaven – be thou pitiful, and with thy bolt smite this hated life down to hell, since in no wise else can I sever the cruel bonds of being!' At that wailing cry their spirits faltered; a groan of sorrow ran through their lines, and their broken strength was palsied for battle. Then, as her fire of grief burned fiercer, Idaeus and Actor, at command of Ilioneus and tearful Iulus, seized her and bore her in their arms within.

But on the shrill-tongued brass the distant trumpet rang loud and terrible; a shouting followed and heaven re-echoed. On came the ordered Volscian lines under their driven roof of shields, intent to fill the moat and tear down the palisade. Part, in quest of entrance, assayed to scale the walls with ladders where the beleaguered array was thinnest and light shone through rifts in the serried ring of foemen. In answer, the Teucrians, whom year-long war had inured to defend their battlements, showered omnifarious weapons, and with strong pikes thrust down the assailants. Rocks of fatal weight, moreover, they rolled below, in hope to break the armoured ranks; yet under the firm-locked penthouse the enemy still laughed at peril – but no longer availed! Where the great throng surged imminent, the Teucrians rolled and overthrew a mountainous mass, that laid low the Rutulians far and wide and shattered their encasing steel. And now the stout Rutulians had no more zest to contend in that blind mellay; but with missiles they strove to unman the ramparts. Elsewhere, Mezentius – dread sight! – was brandishing his Etruscan pine and hurling smoky flames; while Messapus, the Neptune-born, tamer of steeds, breached the palisade and called for ladders to the battlements.

Thou and thy Sister Nine, Calliope, list to my prayer! Inspire my song – what slaughter, what deaths the brand of Turnus wrought on that day, what warriors each hero consigned to doom – and with me unfold the great scroll of war!

Posted on ground of vantage, a tower with lofty gangways loomed high above the view; which all the Italians, with utmost strength, strove to storm, and, with utmost force of their powers, laboured for its overthrow: while the Trojans, responsive, hurled stones in defence, and rained missiles through the hollow loopholes. First Turnus cast a burning brand that lodged flaming in the side, then, fanned by the wind, assailed the planking and fastened with consuming fang on the gateways. Within were confusion and turmoil, and men seeking in vain to escape calamity. For, while huddling they shrank backward to the part where destruction was not, under the sudden weight the tower fell, and all the empyrean thundered to the crash. Half-dead they came to the ground, pierced by their own spears or with breasts impaled on the stubborn wood. Scarce Helenor and Lycus escaped alone – Helenor in the flower of youth, whom, in furtive commerce, a Licymnian slave bore to Lydia's king and dispatched to Troy in forbidden arms, lightly accoutred with sheathless sword and shield unblazoned and unrenowned. He, when he saw himself in the midst of Turnus' thousands with Latium's embattled lines arrayed on this hand and that, like a wild beast that, beset by the serried ring of huntsmen, rages against the steel, flings herself to foreseen death, and is borne at a bound above their spears – so the youth rushed to his doom amid the foe, and, where he saw their lances thickest, thither took his way. But Lycus, far swifter of foot, wound betwixt hostile lines and brands, and, gaining the wall, strove to grasp the lofty battlements and reach the hands of his friends. Whom Turnus, pursuing alike with foot and javelin, thus taunted in triumph: 'Fool, didst thou hope to escape our hand?' And with the word, he clutched him as he hung, and tore him down with a great fragment of the wall: even as Jove's armour-bearing bird soars to the height, bearing aloft, in his crooked talons a hare or a snow-white swan; or as the wolf of Mars snatches from the fold a lamb whose loud-bleating mother recalls it in vain! On all hands the battle-cry ascended. Charging, they filled the trenches with earth, while their comrades flung lighted brands to the pinnacles. With a massy rock, huge fragment of some hill, Ilioneus whelmed Lucetius as, flame in hand, he pressed to the gate. Liger slew Emathion, Asilas Corynaeus – skilled, one with the javelin, one with the distant arrow's elusive flight. Before Caeneus Ortygius fell: before Turnus victorious Caeneus. Itys and Clonius, Dioxippus and Promolus bled by Turnus' hand,

and Sagaris, and Idas, as he stood advanced on the turret-height. Privernus Capys struck down: Themilla's spear had first lightly grazed him; he – fond fool – flung away his shield and clapped his hand to the wound. So the feathered shaft came fleeting, pinned the hand to his left side, and, buried within, broke through the lung with mortal stroke. – In resplendent arms stood the son of Arcens, lustrous in Spanish purple, with needle-broidered scarf – a youth of fairest presence, whom Arcens his sire had sent from his mother's fostering grove by the waters of Symaethus, where Palicus' altar stands blessing and blest. But, casting aside his lances, Mezentius, with tightened thong, thrice whirled the whistling sling round his head; and the molten lead cleft his temples in twain, where he stood adverse, and stretched him in all his length on the wide tract of sand.

Then, Fame tells, Ascanius first levelled his winged arrow in war, wont ere then to pursue the timorous creatures of the chase, and laid low the gallant Numanus – Remulus surnamed – whom the bridal bed had but now allied to Turnus' younger sister. He, with heart puffed at thought of his nascent royalty, strode before the vanward lines, loud-tongued and gigantic, clamouring taunts meet and unmeet to record:

'Blush ye not, twice-captured Phrygians, again to be pent within leaguered ramparts, and again to oppose your walls to death? These are they who would wed our maidens at point of sword! What god – what madness – drove you to Italy? Here are no sons of Atreus, no false-mouthed Ulysses! The stubborn race of a stubborn stock, we bear our new-born infants down to the river and harden them in the pitiless, ice-cold wave. Our boys pass sleepless nights in hunting and outweary the forest – their only sport to rein the steed and dispatch the shaft from the bow: but, patient of toil and inured to want, our youth tames earth with the hoe or shakes cities in battle. All our life is spent in the service of the steel; with lance reversed we smite the flanks of our oxen, and tardy age impairs not the strength of our spirit nor quells our vigour. On white hairs we press the helm; and our delight is ever to drive the new-reft booty and to live by the despoiling hand. But ye – ye are clothed in broidered saffron and shining purple: your heart is set on sloth, your love on the restrainless dance; and your tunics are sleeved and your turbans beribboned! Phrygian maids, in sooth! – for Phrygian men ye are not! – get ye over Dindymus' heights where the twin-mouthed pipe makes music to your familiar ears! The cymbals of Ida's queen are calling – calling, the Berecyntian flute! Away! leave arms to men, and resign the steel!'

As so in ominous strain he vaunted, Ascanius brooked him not, but, turning, levelled his shaft from the horse-hair string and took his stand with arms drawn apart, yet stayed to entreat Jove with suppliant vow: 'Jove omnipotent, deign to smile on my bold assay! Year after year this hand shall bear offerings to thy fane, and before thine altar shall stand a steer with gilded brow, white as the snow, with head borne high as his dam's, his horn already meet for the fray, his hooves already spurning the sand!' The Father heard, and, from an unclouded space of sky, thundered on the left; while at the same moment rang the fatal bow.

From the drawn string the arrow fled with her song of death and clove the head of Remulus, so that the steel pierced either hollow temple. 'Go now, and mock valour with insult! Thus twice-captured Phrygia answers Rutulia!' This, and no more, Ascanius. The Teucrians cheered responsive, and, shouting for joy, rose heaven-high in courage.

In that hour, it chanced, fair-tressed Apollo, cloud-throned, looked down from the ethereal tract on the Ausonian lines and the leaguered camp, and thus bespoke the triumphant prince: 'Good speed to thy youthful valour, child! So shalt thou scale the stars, thou scion of gods, sire of gods that shall be! Justly shall all wars fated to come sink to peace under Assaracus' race, nor can the bounds of Troy confine thee!' So saying he shot from the heights of ether, parted the breathing gales, and repaired to Ascanius; then changed the lineaments of his visage and became ancient Butes – Butes, the armour-bearer of Dardan Anchises erewhile, and the loyal warder of his gate, till a father's care made him Ascanius' henchman. Like to the greybeard in all Apollo moved, – in voice and in hue, in white locks and dread-clanging arms, – and so addressed the hot-souled Iulus: 'Be it enough, O seed of Aeneas, that unscathed thou hast seen Numanus bleed by thy shaft! This earliest meed of glory great Apollo vouchsafes to thee, nor envies thy bow, unerring, as his! For the rest, my child, refrain from the combat!' Thus Apollo began, and, with the words yet on his lips, fled from mortal vision and faded from view in the substanceless air.

The Dardan princes knew the god, and his celestial arms, and heard his quiver clash as he went. Therefore, by the word and will of Phoebus, they quelled Ascanius' zeal for battle, themselves resumed the fray, and flung their lives into manifest jeopardy.

Along the walls the shout ran from battlement to battlement, and men drew their resilient bows or twisted their javelin thongs. The ground was all strewn with spears; shields and hollow helms rang conflicting, and the battle rose fierce and high: – wild as the showers, that, when the Kids set in rain, travel from the West and scourge the earth – dense as the hail that the storm-clouds volley on the main, when Jove, glooming amid the southern blasts, hurls the watery tempest and bursts the hollow mists in heaven!

Pandarus and Bitias, sprung from Idaean Alcanor's loins, whom silvan Iaera nurtured in the grove of Jupiter – warriors tall as their native pines and hills – flung open the gate, entrusted to them by their captain's charge, and, reliant on their own good swords, invited the foe to enter the walls. Themselves within stood before the towers to right and left, cased in steel, the plumes waving above their stately heads: – even as by the crystalline stream, whether on the banks of Po or nigh to pleasant Athesis, twin oaks rise star-pointing, lifting their unicorn crowns to heaven and nodding with aery crests. In surged the Rutulians, when they saw the entrance clear. On the instant Quercens and Aquiculus, all beautiful in arms, Tmarus of the reckless heart, and Haemon, seed of Mars, turned and fled with all their array, or, turning not, resigned their lives on the threshold's verge. At this, passion flamed higher in their exasperate souls, and now the Trojans mustered their rallied powers, and ventured on closer conflict and longer sallies.

While far away Turnus swept raging against the routed columns, news came that the foe, flushed by new bloodshed, had flung his gates wide. Stung with ineffable anger, he abandoned his emprize, and rushed to the Dardan gate and the haughty brethren. And first Antiphates – for first Antiphates came – he slew with hurled javelin, bastard son of great Sarpedon by a mother of Thebê. Through the yielding air flew the Italian cornel, and, lodging in his throat, pierced deep into the breast: the black and cavernous wound disgorged a foaming tide, and the iron grew warm in the cloven lung. Then Meropes and Erymas, then Aphidnus bled by his hand; then Bitias fell, flame in his eyes, fury in his soul, but not before the javelin – not to the javelin had he rendered his life! Loud-screaming came the whirled falaric, driven like the thunderbolt; whose stroke not two bull hides, not the staunch corselet with its twin scales of gold, availed to withstand. The giant limbs tottered and fell; earth groaned, and his massy shield dropped thundering above the dead. So may the rocky pile fall on Baiae's Euboic shore, compact of mountainous blocks, then flung into the main; so, prone, it descends in ruin, and, dashed into the waves, sinks deep to the appointed place, while the seas are turmoiled and the black sands seethe up – while at the sound the deeps of Prochyta quail, and Inarime's rugged bed, laid by behest of Jove on Typhoeus.

And now Mars armipotent gave new strength and courage to the Latins, and plied his keen goad deep in their hearts, but on the Teucrians sent Flight and sable Fear. From every hand the assailants thronged, now that the battle had ample verge, and the warrior-god possessed each soul. Pandarus, when he saw his brother fallen – saw how fortune stood, and the chance that governed the day – with desperate effort opposed his broad shoulders and swung the gate on the turning hinge, leaving many a comrade shut out from the walls in that fatal fray, but enclosing others with himself as they streamed to shelter. Madman! who saw not the Rutulian king bursting through in the columns' midst, but with his own hands pent him within the camp, like a grisly tiger amid the helpless cattle! Incontinent a strange light flashed from his eyes, and his arms clanged fearfully; on his crest the plumes quivered blood-red, and lightnings shot flickering from his shield. With sudden terror Troy knew that hated face and titanic frame. Then great Pandarus leapt forth, and, blazing with rage for his brother dead, cried: 'Not this Amata's bridal palace! Not Ardea's ancestral walls encircle their Turnus! Thine eyes are on the foeman's camp, and thy feet shall find no egress!' To whom Turnus, smiling with heart unruffled: 'Begin, if aught of valour reside in thy spirit, and join encounter! Thou shalt tell to Priam how here also was found an Achilles!' He ceased. The other, with might strained to the uttermost, flung his spear, rugged and knotted with unpeeled bark. The winds received the blow, Saturnian Juno turned aside the coming wound, and the javelin lodged in the gate. 'But not from this blade, that my strong arm wields, shalt thou escape: for not such is he that bestows weapon and wound!' So saying, he rose high to speed his uplifted steel, clove the forehead midway betwixt either temple, and with ghastly stroke sundered the unbearded cheeks. Loud-crashing, Pandarus fell; and earth shuddered beneath the monstrous weight. His sunken limbs, his arms spattered with the gory brain, rolled to the ground in death, and, to left and right on either shoulder drooped half a head!

In panic haste the Trojans fled routed; and, if instant thought had come to the conqueror to burst the barriers and admit his allies through the gates, that day had been the last both of battle and of Troy! But rage and the mad lust of slaughter drove him infuriate against the confronting foe. First Phaleris he overtook; then hamstrung Gyges; and, seizing their spears, hurled them against the backs of the fugitive mass, while Juno ministered might and courage. Halys he sent to rejoin them below, and Phegeus, his shield transfixed; then Alcander and Halius, Noëmon and Prytanis, as on the ramparts unwitting they roused the fray. Calling on his comrades, Lynceus advanced athwart his way. From the rampart on the right he swept his vibrant sword and caught him. Severed by that single close-dealt blow, head and helmet lay far away! Next Amycus bled, the mighty hunter, whom no man surpassed in skill to anoint the dart and arm the steel with venom; then Clytius, of Aeolus' line; and Cretheus, whom the Muses loved – Cretheus, the Muses' friend, whose delight was ever in song and lyre and numbers strung upon the chord, whose strains were ever of steeds, and battles, and weaponed heroes!

At last, hearing of the slaughter of their men, the captains of Troy, Mnestheus and bold Serestus, hastened together to the scene, and beheld their comrades wavering and the foe within their gates. Then Mnestheus: 'Whither now, whither,' he cried, 'do ye bend your flight? What other walls, what farther city, have ye yet in prospect? Shall it be told, my countrymen, how a single man – and he compassed on every side by your ramparts! – shed torrents of your blood, hurled so many a hero to hell, and paid not the penalty? Recreants, have ye neither pity nor shame for your calamitous motherland, for your ancient gods, and great Aeneas?' His words were flame to their hearts: they rallied and halted in serried array; while, step by step, Turnus receded from the battle towards the river and the part which the waters laved. Emboldened thereby, loud-clamouring the Teucrians pressed on, massing their band – as when a troop of huntsmen assails an angry lion with menacing spears: he, alarmed, retreats exasperate and fierce-eyed; for wrath and courage forbid him to turn and flee, nor yet, despite of his desire, can he charge through the line of lances and men. So Turnus, in doubt, drew back with unhastened step and soul boiling with rage; yet even then twice dashed amid the enemy, twice drove their routed columns fleeing along the walls. But from the camp the whole host mustered with speed, and no longer Saturnian Juno dared to supply him with strength in counterpoise: for Jove had sent Iris, airborne, from Heaven, charged with no gentle hest to his sister, did not Turnus withdraw from the Teucrian towers. Therefore, by bare dint of shield and arm, the hero could no longer avail; so dense the steely rain that whelmed him. Round his hollow temples the casque rang with incessant clash; the solid brass cracked under the hail of stones; the horse-hair crest was shorn away; and the buckler sufficed not to ward the blows from his head. The Trojans and Mnestheus himself, thundering in arms, showered volley on volley of spears. Then from all his body the sweat poured in clammy stream – for breathing-space there was none – and sickly gasps racked his weary limbs. Then at length, in full panoply, he cast himself at a bound sheer into the river. Tiber with his yellow flood received him as he came, uplifted him on gentle wave, and, purging the stains of death, restored him in joy to his hosts.

BOOK X

MEANWHILE WAS OPENED the palace of all-puissant Olympus, and the Sire of gods and King of men summoned a council to the starry halls, from whose height he surveyed the expanse of earth, and the Dardan camp, and the Latin peoples. In the twin-doored chambers they sate, while their lord began: 'Great sons of Heaven, wherefore is your sentence reversed, and whence this bitterness of strife in your discordant souls? My nod forbade that Italy should close with Troy in the shock of war. What conflict is this that thwarts my mandate? What terror hath beguiled either these or those to rush to arms and brave the steel? The rightful day of battle shall dawn – prevent it not! – when, in years to be, fierce Carthage shall unbar the Alps and hurl fell destruction upon the towers of Rome. Then shall be scope for rapine, for hatred and for strife! Now let be, and in cheerfulness assent to the league that I ordain!'

Thus Jupiter in brief; but not brief the answer of golden Venus:

'O Father, sovereign eternal of men and things – for what power else may we yet entreat? – seest thou how the Rutulians triumph, while Turnus, behind his stately steeds, sweeps through the midmost ranks and rides on the partial tide of war? Their stony barriers no longer protect my Teucrians: nay, within the gates – amid the very ramparts – they join encounter and flood the trenches with gore! And Aeneas, unknowing, is far away! Wilt thou never grant that the leaguer be raised? Again an enemy threats the walls of our infant Troy: a second host is mustered; and once more, from his Aetolian Arpi, Tydeus' son arises against Teucer's race! For me, I doubt not, – in a little while my wounds shall bleed, and she, who calls thee father, too long delays the mortal spear! If without thy leave and in despite of thy deity the Trojans have voyaged to Italy, let them atone their sins, nor aid thou them with thy succour! But if they are come obedient to so many an oracle uttered by gods above and spirits below, why now can any reverse thy commandment and order the fates anew? What boots it to rehearse the fleet fired on Eryx' strand, the storm-king and his raving gales summoned from Aeolia, and Iris sped from the clouds? Now even Hell she rouses – sole portion of Nature yet untried! – and Allecto, unleashed on the upper air, raves through the Italian towns. The thought of empire moves me not; that hope is faded with our fortunes: let victory fall where victory thou sendest! If there be no region of earth that thy stony-hearted consort will allow to my Teucrians, yet, Sire, I beseech thee by the smoke of fallen Troy: – let me dismiss Ascanius unhurt from arms – let the son of my son still live! Aeneas, indeed, may be tossed over unknown seas, and follow where Fortune allows him way: *him* let me avail to shield and withdraw from the fatal fray! Amathus is mine, and lofty Paphus, Cythera and Idalia's fane: there, the sword resigned, let him live his inglorious days! Command, if thou wilt, that the sceptred hand of Carthage lie heavy on Ausonia: in him thy Tyrian towns shall encounter no stumbling-block! What hath it profited him, that he escaped the doom of war, that he broke through the ring of Argive fires, and drained to the lees so many a peril of the main and the desolate earth, while his Teucrians sought Latium and a resurgent Pergamus? Were it not better done, to have set him down by the last ashes of his country, and the ground where Troy stood – and fell? Sire, I entreat thee, restore to my disastrous people their Xanthus and their Simois: let Teucer's race turn once more the wheel of Ilium's fate!'

Then imperial Juno, shot with fierce passion: 'Why constrainest thou me to break my deep silence and to publish my hidden grief? Did man or god compel thine Aeneas to assume the sword and march in enmity on King Latinus? Fate-prompted, I grant thee, he sailed to Italy, – overborne by Cassandra's frenzy!

Yet did we urge him to quit his camp? to commit his life to the winds? to entrust his battlements and the sum of war to a child? to tamper with Tyrrhene faith and embroil the quiet peoples? What god – what harsh tyranny of ourself? – drove him to his harm? Where shalt thou find Juno herein, or Iris sped from the skies? It is sin to thy sight, that Italy circles thine infant Troy with flames, and that Turnus treads the land of his fathers, – Turnus, whose grandsire is Pilumnus, whose mother divine Venilia! How thinkest thou, when with murky brands thy Trojans assail the Latins? when their yoke is set on another's fields – and they drive the spoil? when they choose whose children they will wed, and tear the betrothed from her lover's bosom? when their hands proffer peace and their galleys bristle with spears? Thou hast power to steal Aeneas from Grecian hands and to offer them mist and substanceless air for the dastard they seek, – power to translate his barques into as many nymphs: – is it utter crime that *we* lend our feeble aid to Rutulia? *Aeneas, unwitting, is far away.* Away and unwitting let him remain! *Paphus is thine Idalium and high Cythera.* Why meddlest thou with these rough hearts, this city that teems with war? Is it we that assay to overthrow from their foundation the tottering fortunes of thy Phrygia? We? – or he who cast the hapless Trojans to the teeth of Achaea? What cause drove Europe and Asia to rise to battle? What pilfering hand shattered their league? Was it I led the Dardan leman to breach Sparta's walls? Was it I put weapons in his hand, or woke the war with Cupid's bow? Then was the hour to fear for thy beloved! Now thou arisest over-late with unjust plaint, and thine insults are bandied in vain!'

Thus Juno pleaded, and all the immortals murmured assent to one or other: – even as the rising winds murmur, when caught in the forest, and the obscure sounds roll on, betraying to the seaman the approaching gale. Then the all-puissant Sire, prime force of the universe, began: and, as he spoke, the high house of heaven grew still and earth trembled to her base; silent was the empyrean above; the Zephyrs were hushed, and Ocean calmed his submissive waves: 'Then take these my words to your hearts, and implant them there! Since it may not be that Ausonia join alliance with Troy, and your discord admits no term, whatever the fortune of each on this day, whatever hope he pursue, be he Trojan or be he Rutulian, – all shall be even in my sight, whether by Fate's will the Italian leaguer hems the camp, or whether by Troy's blindness and the sinister admonishment of prophecy!

Nor do I exempt Rutulia. As each hath sown, so shall he reap, in toil or in triumph! Jove's sovereignty is one for all. Destiny shall find her way!' By the waters of his Stygian brother, by the banks where the torrent pitch eddies in black abysm, he nodded confirmation, and, nodding, shook all Olympus. Thus ended their parle. Then from his golden throne Jove arose, and the circle of immortals escorted him to the threshold.

Meantime about every gate the Rutules pressed hard, intent to slaughter the defenders and engirth the ramparts with flame. But the legion of Troy was pent within the beleaguered walls, and hope of escape was none. Sorrowful and powerless they stood on the turret-heights, and their thin ring lined the battlements. Asius, Imbrasus' son, and Thymoetes, Hicetaon's child; the two Assaraci, and Castor, with greyheaded Thymbris: – such was the foremost rank, while at their side were Clarus and Thaemon, who fared from the Lycian hills, brothers both of Sarpedon. And there – great as Clytius, his sire, or Menestheus, his brother – was Lyrnesian Acmon, his whole frame astrain, bearing a giant rock scarce less than its native hill. Here with javelins, there with stones, they assayed the defence, launching the firebrand or fitting the shaft to the string. And lo! in their midst, his fair head unhelmed, was the Dardan boy, Venus' most rightful care, – shining as a solitary gem shines amid the yellow gold bedecking some fair throat or brow; or as ivory gleams, set by the artist hand in boxwood or Orician terebinth, – while his loose locks, gathered in a circlet of ductile gold, streamed down his neck of snow. Thee, too, Ismarus, the proud nations saw dealing thine unerring wounds and arming the reed with venom – Ismarus, noble scion of a Maeonian house, in that land where men till their generous fields and Pactolus waters them with gold. Nor lacked there Mnestheus, whom Turnus, driven erewhile from the rampart, exalted heaven-high in glory; nor Capys, whose name yet lives in the name of Campania's city!

So all day long each had coped with other in the close encounter of grim war: and now Aeneas was sailing the midnight seas. For when – Evander left – he entered the Etruscan camp, seeking the king, he announced his name and his race, the boon that he desired and the recompense that he brought; instructed him of the powers that Mezentius mustered to his cause, and the violence of Turnus' heart; then recalled how frail is the hope of our mortal estate, and mingled entreaty with his pleas. Delay was none: on the instant Tarchon united forces and struck alliance.

Then, the ban of Fate removed, the Lydian race embarked – committed by Heaven's mandate to the charge of an alien captain. In the van rode Aeneas' galley; under whose prow Phrygian lions bore the yoke, while, above, Ida reared her head – fairest of visions to exiled Troy. There the hero sat pondering the changeful issue of arms; and fast by his left was Pallas – now asking of the stars, their guidance in the midnight gloom, anon of all his travails on flood and field.

Now, Muses, open Helicon! Awake your strains, and sing what powers escorted Aeneas the while from the Tuscan strand, sailing the seas in vessels armed for war!

First Massicus came cleaving the blue in his brazen Tiger – Massicus, whom a thousand banded warriors followed from Clusium's walls and Cosae city; armed all with arrows, their light quivers and fatal bows slung athwart the shoulder. With him went grim Abas, all his train in dazzling arms, while Apollo shone on his poop in gold. To him Populonia had given six hundred of her sons, all versed in war; three hundred Ilva sent from her generous isle, where the Chalyb mines yield their undiminished treasure. Third sailed great Asilas, interpreter betwixt gods and men, whom the filaments of sacrifice obeyed, and the stars of heaven, and the tongue of birds, and the thunderbolt's presaging fires. A thousand men he swept to war in serried array of horrent spears, whom Pisa – Alphean town on Etruscan soil – bade follow his banners. Next Astyr came, the fair of face – Astyr, whose trust was in his steed and armour of myriad hues. Three hundred, one in loyalty, swelled his ranks from them whose hearths are in Caere and Minio's plains, in ancient Pyrgi or feverous Graviscae.

And thou, bravest captain of the Ligurians, Cupavo of the poor estate and scanty retinue – unsung I would not leave thee, with thy swan-plumes, – emblem of a father's form – rising from thy crest in token of Love's cruelty. For the tale is told how Cycnus, mourning for his beloved Phaëthon, strove to solace his breaking heart by the Muse's aid, and sang amid the poplar-shades and the leaves of the whilom sisterhood, till, clothed in downy plumage, his form grew white as eld, and he left the earth, and, singing, soared to the stars. And now his son, sailing with a warrior-band of like years, with straining oars urged onward the giant Centaur, that, looming above the flood, high towering menaced the waves with mighty rock and ploughed the deep with enormous keel.

Nor less from his natal shores, the child of prophetic Manto and the Tuscan river, summoned his host – Ocnus, who gave thee, Mantua, thy battlements and his mother's name; Mantua, of ancestors many, though diverse their blood! Three races there are, and in every race four peoples; while she, the queen of all, draws her strength from Tuscan blood. Hence, also, the hated name of Mezentius armed five hundred men; whom, on hostile pine, Mincius, Benacus' son, crowned with grey flags, led into the main. – Onward, in ponderous course, came Aulestes, his hundred oars lashing the wave, while the waters foamed with surface upchurned. Him the huge Triton conveyed, with shell defying the azure flood: down to the flanks, as he swam, his hispid front announced the man; below, a monstrous fish succeeded, and the whitening billows murmured under the brutish breast.

So many the chosen princes who sailed to the succour of Troy in thrice ten ships, ploughing the briny expanse with brazen stems!

And now day had deserted the sky, and gracious Phoebe was spurning the central heaven on her night-wandering car: Aeneas the while – for care denied slumber to his limbs – sat at his post, with his own hand governing the tiller and administering the sails. And lo, midway in his course, a company, that shared his wanderings erewhile, confronted him: for the Nymphs, whom Cybele's grace had endowed with deity of the sea and bidden be ships no more, came swimming in even line through the disparting waves – a goddess in lieu of every brass-bound prow that once stood ranged by the strand. From afar they knew their king, and, dancing, encircled him. Then Cymodocea, whose speech was fairest, followed behind, and, grasping the poop with her right, raised her breast; while with the left she parted the silent flood. And now she accosted the wondering prince: 'Wakest thou, Aeneas, scion of gods? Wake, and fling loose the sheets of thy sails! It is we, – the pines of Ida, from her sacred crown, – now Nymphs of ocean, once thy fleet! When the traitorous Rutulian urged us precipitate with fire and with sword, reluctant we broke thy bonds and are come through the deep in quest of thee. This transmuted form the Great Mother gave us in compassion, and granted us to be goddesses and to live our days beneath the foam. But Ascanius, thy child, is immured within moat and wall, amid the flying spears and Latium's fiery battle! Even now the Arcadian horse, united with brave Etruria, holds the appointed place; and Turnus' resolve stands firm – to throw his squadrons between, and disjoin them from the camp. Up, then, and, with the first glimmer of dawn, bid thy allies be summoned to arms, and take that shield which the Lord of Flame himself wrought for thy conquering arm and rimmed the borders with gold! The morrow's light – if thou deem not my message idly spoken – shall break on mountainous piles of Rutulian dead!'

She ceased; and, departing, impelled the tall ship with her right – yet not over great the impulse. Fleeter than javelin or wind-swift arrow it fled through the waves, and the rest in order quickened their course. Lost in amazement, Troy's hero and Anchises' son knew not how to think, yet high his heart swelled at the omen. Then, looking to the vault above, he prayed briefly:

'Gracious Mother of Heaven, Ida's queen, whose delight is in Dindymus, in tower-crowned cities and lions harnessed for thy bridle – stand thou at my hand in the van of battle, bring this presage to the appointed issue, and with propitious foot come, O goddess, to thy Phrygians!'

Thus far he said: and meantime the returning day was rushing on in fullness of light, and the dark was fled.

First he commanded the host to follow his signals, to attune their spirit to arms, and prepare for the fray. And now, as he stood on the towering poop, he could discern the Teucrians and his camp; when, on the instant, he upreared the blazing shield on his left. From their battlements the Dardans shouted to heaven; rekindling hope woke their ire, and the javelins flew from their hands: – as, when under the sable clouds cranes of Strymon cry their signal, while clamorously they stem the air, and, with loud note and joyful, flee before the Southern gales. But to the Rutulian king and the captains of Ausonia all was strange, till, turning, they descried the galleys bearing to the strand and all the sea afloat with ships. On the prince's helm the cone burned red, flame shot from his crest on high, and torrent fire streamed from the golden boss: as oft, through the cloudless night, ensanguined comets glare ruddy and baleful; or as the splendour of Sirius – herald of drought and disease to suffering mortality – springs to birth and saddens heaven with malefic beams.

Yet Turnus' unfearing heart abated not in confidence to prevent them on the shore and repel the advancing foe from land. 'Ye have prayed and the hour is come: ye may break them with the sword! Comrades, the god of battles is in your hand! Now let every man bethink him of wife and home: now recall the high deeds that won glory to our sires! Let us front them, ere they call us, by the wave, while confusion yet reigns and their feet falter still from the deck! Fortune is ally to the brave.' He said, and pondered with himself whom to lead to the assault, whom to leave in siege of the beleaguered ramparts.

Meanwhile Aeneas landed his crews from the tall ships by gangways. Many there were observed the ebb of the failing sea, and, leaping, braved the shallows: others betook them to the oars. Tarchon, marking a tract on the beach, where no shoals seemed to be and no breakers roared, but with advancing tide the ocean came washing without shock, incontinent turned his prow thither and conjured his men: 'Now, ye chosen, bend to the stout oar! Up and on with your galleys; cleave this land of the foeman with your beaks, and let the keel plough herself a furrow! In such a roadstead I would brook even shipwreck, could I but once gain the land!' Thus, and to such purpose, Tarchon; and his men rose to their oars and urged the foam-dripping barques to the Latin fields, till the prows attained the dry land and every hull came hurtless to rest. But not thy vessel, Tarchon! For, dashed upon a shoal, she long hung in doubtful balance, buffeting the waves, on the fatal ridge; then broke and lodged her crew full amid the billows, there to contend with shattered oars and floating thwarts, while the refluent wave sucked back their feet!

No chains of delay held Turnus. Like flame he swept his full array against the Teucrians, and ranged it on the strand in face of the foe. The trumpets sang. And foremost Aeneas, in presage of the issue, assailed the yeoman ranks of Latium and drove them in confusion as Theron bled – a giant among men, who, unchallenged, sought encounter. But through the quilted brass, through the tunic all stark with gold, the sword drank from his naked side. Then Lichas he smote, who was cut from the womb of a lifeless mother, and consecrated, Phoebus, to thee – though what did it profit him that his infant life escaped the perils of the steel? At brief distance he struck down in death stubborn Cisseus and towering Gyas, whose clubs felled squadrons at once. Vain the arms of Hercules to succour them, vain their mighty hands and Melampus their sire – Melampus who stood by Alcides so long as ever the painful earth yielded him toil and travail! Lo, as Pharus flung his deedless vaunts, he launched his javelin and fixed it full in the clamorous mouth! And thou Cydon, in thy disastrous quest of Clytius, his cheeks scarce touched by the springtide of youth – thou hadst fallen under the Dardan hand and lain in piteous sort, oblivious of all thy loves, had not the serried band of thy brethren advanced to the rescue – all sons of Phorcus, seven their number, seven the spears that they flung! But, of the seven, part glanced defeated from helmet and shield: part, as they grazed the body, gentle Venus turned aside. Instant Aeneas called to loyal Achates: – 'Ply me with weapons; of all that have tasted Grecian flesh on the plains of Ilium, not one shall this hand hurl in vain against Rutulia!' Then he caught and flung a mighty javelin, that, flying, tore through the brass of Maeon's shield and shattered breastplate and breast. To his aid ran Alcanor, and with his right upheld his falling brother: piercing the arm, the spear flew onward and held its bloody tenour, while the dying hand hung by the sinews from the shoulder. Then Numitor, tearing the lance from his brother's corpse, threw at Aeneas; but availed not to transfix the confronting foe, and grazed the thigh of great Achates.

Now Clausus of Cures came reliant on the strength of youth, and at distance struck Dryopes under the chin with heavy thrust of his stark spear, that, while he assayed to speak, pierced the throat and bereft him of voice and life together: but he, his forehead striking on earth, fell with clotted blood gushing from his lips. Three, too, of Thrace, sprung from Boreas' high lineage, and three whom their father Idas and their native Ismarus sent, he slew as the chances of battle willed. To the rescue Halaesus ran with his Auruncan bands; nor less Messapus, Neptune's child, came behind his fiery steeds. Now these, now those, struggled to unlodge the enemy, and the encounter raged amain on the very threshold of Ausonia. – As oft in the ample heavens conflicting winds rise to battle with equal fury and equal might; not they, not the clouds, not the seas give ground; the war hangs long in even scale, and element fronts element at bay: – even so clashed the ranks of Troy and the ranks of Latium, foot locked to foot and man pitted with man.

But in other quarter, where a torrent had driven abroad rolling rocks and bushes uptorn from the bank, Pallas beheld his Arcadians – unused to charge in dismounted line – breaking to flight before pursuant Latium: for the rugged ground had constrained them to resign their steeds. One hope was left in the hour of need; and entreating, upbraiding, he fired their valour: 'Friends, whither flee you? By your gallant deeds, – by the name of Evander your king – by the fields where ye fought and conquered – and by my hopes, that now rise aspirant to my father's glory – trust not to the fugitive foot! It is the steel that must hew our path through the foe. Where yon living mass drives thickest, there lies the way, whereby our peerless motherland calls you – and Pallas in your van – back to herself! The hand of deity weighs not on us: mortals, we are pushed by a mortal foe, and our lives and our hands are many as his! Lo, Ocean imprisons us with his great salt barrier; already earth fails our flight: shall we seek the main – or Troy?' He said, and burst into the heart of the serried foe.

First Lagus met him, drawn to his death by unkind fate. For, while he tore at a ponderous stone, the Arcadian, with flung spear, transfixed him where the central spine ran parting the ribs; then withdrew the steel as it quivered amid the bones. Nor could Hisbo – though such his hope – descend upon him unawares: for as he came, infuriate and reckless for his comrade done to death, Pallas prevented his onset and buried the sword in the swelling lung. Now Sthenius he assailed and – scion of Rhoetus' ancient line – Anchemolus, who dared to profane his stepdame's bed. Ye, too, the brother twins, fell on Rutulia's plains – Larides and Thymber, children of Daucus, one in semblance, to your kindred indistinguishable, to your parents a sweet perplexity. But between you now Pallas made grim distinction! For thy head, Thymber, the sword of Evander swept away; and thy severed hand, Larides, sought, forlorn, for its lord, while the dying fingers twitched and closed once more on the brand!

Fired by his rebuke and the sight of his glorious deeds, Arcadia rushed to the fray, while anger and shame unsheathed each sword.

Then Pallas pierced Rhoeteus as, charioted, he came fleeing past. This moment of respite – and no more – Ilus gained: for at Ilus he had flung from distance the stout spear, which Rhoeteus, intervening, caught, as he fled from thee, best Teuthras, and from Tyres thy brother. In death he rolled from the car, with heels drumming the Rutulian plain! And as, on a day in summer, when the winds have risen to his wish, a swain launches his scattered fires among the woods, and on the instant all between is caught and an unbroken line of red stretches with horrid front over the broad fields; he, from his seat, gazes down victorious on the triumphant flames: – even so, Pallas, all that was noble in thy host rallied from every hand to succour thee! But Halaesus – grim warrior – advanced on their hostile ranks, crouching for the spring behind his arms. Ladon he slew, and Pheres with Demodocus; shore away Strymonius' right with glittering blade, as he raised it against his throat; smote Thoas on the face with a rock, and shivered the bones, commingled with brain and blood. Halaesus his prophet-sire had hidden from Fate in the forest; but when, in the fullness of years, his age-worn eyes closed in death, the Sisters laid hand upon their victim and doomed him to Evander's arms. Him Pallas assailed, first praying: 'Grant, O father Tiber, to this steel that I poise for the cast, a prosperous issue and a path through Halaesus' iron breast! Thine oak shall wear his weapons and spoils.' The god heard; and Halaesus, while he shielded Imaon, offered – unhappy! – his breast defenceless to the Arcadian lance!

But Lausus – giant of the war – left not his columns in terror at that great death. First, front to front, he slew Abas, who stayed the tide of their battle as an oaken knot the axe! The youth of Arcadia fell; fell Etruria, and ye, Teucer's sons, whom the Grecian sword destroyed not! Equal in captaincy and equal in power, the armies met. The rearmost closed up the ranks, till the throng was such that neither arm nor blade had play. Here Pallas drove urgent on; there Lausus opposed. Nor they differed in years, nor in radiance of beauty; but to both Fortune had denied return to their fatherland. Yet He who reigns in high Olympus suffered them not to meet face to face; no distant doom awaited them at the hand of a greater foe!

Meantime his gracious sister warned Turnus to come to Lausus' aid, and on fleet chariot he came, cleaving the ranks between. Then, seeing his allies: 'It is time to desist from battle. Alone I encounter Pallas; alone will I exact my proper due! Would but that his father were here to see!' He said, and his men gave back from the forbidden space. But, as the Rutulians retired, the warrior-youth – surprised by the haughty mandate – gazed in astonishment on Turnus, swept his glance over that giant bulk, and grim-eyed scanned all at distance; then answered the king, word against word: 'Glory shall soon be mine – whether from a captain slain or an illustrious death! My sire will smile on either event: then forbear thy threats!' So said, he advanced into the mid lists; while the blood gathered, cold as ice, about every Arcadian heart. Down from his car Turnus leapt, in act to join encounter on foot. And as a lion, observant from above, descries a bull standing on some distant plain intent on battle, then flies to the fray – so seemed the coming of Turnus. But Pallas, when he deemed him within range of a spear-cast, advanced the first, in hope that chance would assist where he dared with unequal arm – and thus called on the majestic heavens: 'By my father's welcome, and the board where thou satest a stranger-guest, I entreat thee, Alcides – be with me in my great emprize! Let Turnus watch me strip the bloody arms from his expiring limbs, and let his glazing eyes brook the sight of a conqueror!' Alcides heard and, stifling a deep sob in his heart of hearts, broke into ineffectual tears. At this with mild accent the Father bespoke his son: 'Each hath his proper day: brief and irreparable is the span of life to all: but to enlarge his fame by prowess – this is the brave man's task! How many a son of the gods fell under Troy-towers! Nay, did not Sarpedon, our own child, bleed at their side? On Turnus also his destiny calls, and he nears the goal of his allotted years!' He said, and averted his gaze from the Rutulian fields.

But Pallas flung his spear with forceful arm, and plucked the flashing sword from its containing scabbard. Where the summit of the mail rises to guard the shoulder, the flying steel alighted, and, rending a way through the buckler's marge, at last grazed in very deed the mighty frame of Turnus.

Then Turnus, long poising the steel-tipped shaft on Pallas, hurled it and cried: 'See thou whether our weapon pierce not deeper!' He ceased: with vibrant shock the point tore through the centre of his shield, through so many a plate of brass and iron, through so many a swathe of encircling bull-hide; then broke the corselet's resistance and gored the heroic breast within! In vain he wrenched the warm weapon from the wound: by the selfsame passage blood and sense came ebbing away! Prone he fell on the wound; the armour clashed above him, and, dying, he bit with ensanguined mouth at the hostile earth! Then Turnus, standing above the dead: 'Arcadians,' he cried, 'give heed, and bear this my word back to Evander: as the sire hath merited, such I restore the son! Whatever honour resides in a tomb, whatever solace in a bier, this freely I give. Full high shall mount the price of Aeneas welcomed!' And, so saying, he planted his left foot on the corpse, and tore the ponderous belt away with its figured scene of sin: that youthful band foully slain on one nuptial night, and the chambers red with blood—which Clonus, son of Eurytus, had graven in ample gold. Now Turnus triumphed in the prize and exulted in possession! Alas, for the spirit of man, blind to Fate and the doom to be, impotent to observe the mean on the wave of prosperity! An hour shall come for Turnus, when he were fain to have bought Pallas' safety at a great price – when he shall loathe those spoils and that day! – But with many moans and tears, his comrades laid their hero on his

shield and bore him away in dense procession. O source of
sorrow and greater glory, that returnest to thy sire! This one day
gave thee to war, this one day takes thee hence; yet vast the piles
thou leavest of Rutulian slain!

And now no random fame of that dread calamity, but a surer
messenger, plied to Aeneas, and told that his troops were wavering a hair's breadth removed from death, and that the moment
was come to succour the routed Teucrians. Instant his sword
reaped down all that stood to hand, and infuriate he hacked a
path through the broad column, while, Turnus, he sought for
thee, yet glorying in the new-spilt blood! Pallas – Evander – all
rose before his eyes: the board which on that day first welcomed
his errant steps, and the hands outstretched in kindness! Then
four youths, the sons of Sulmo, and as many whom Ufens nurtured, he took alive, to slay in sacrifice to the dead and bedew the
funeral flames with their captive blood. Next, from distance, he
levelled the hostile lance at Magus: he, while the shuddering steel
flew over, ran warily beneath, and, clasping the hero's knee,
poured his suppliant accents: 'By the spirit of thy father, by the
nascent promise of Iulus, preserve – I beseech thee – this life to
my son and my sire! A princely home is mine, with talents of figured silver buried from day in its vaults, and mine are massy
ingots of gold, wrought and unwrought! Not on me hinges the
victory of Troy, nor can a single life make difference so great!'
He paused, and Aeneas returned: 'Those many talents of silver
and gold that thou vauntest spare thou for thy sons! At that hour
when Pallas bled, Turnus – not I – abolished this thy traffic of
war! So deems the ghost of my sire, Anchises, so Iulus!' He said;
then, grasping the helmet with his left, bent back the suppliant's
neck and buried the sword hilt-deep within him. Nor far thence
moved Haemon's son, priest of Phoebus and Trivia, his temples
wreathed in the fillet's holy riband, himself all shining in snowy
robe and vestments. Him he met and pursued athwart the plain;
then, bestriding the fallen, slaughtered him and wrapped him in
dreadful night; while Serestus stripped his arms and bore them
on his shoulder, a trophy to thee, O King Gradivus!

Caeculus, born of Vulcan's line, and Umbro, descending from
his Marsian hills, repaired the ranks. In fury the Dardan drove
against them. His brand had shorn away Anxur's left, with all the
circle of his shield – Anxur, who had uttered some brave vaunt in
thought that his hand would avouch his word, and, with spirit
uplifted heaven-high, had promised himself, I ween, white age

and venerable years! – when Tarquitus, whom Dryope the
Nymph had borne to silvan Faunus, fronted his flame-like
course, proud in refulgent arms. He, with back-swung lance,
fixed his massy buckler to the encumbered corselet; then, amid
his idle prayers and the thousand pleas that trembled upon his
lips, struck his head to the sod, and, spurning the warm trunk
beneath, thus called from unpitying heart: 'Lie, now, where thy
terrors lie! No kindest mother shall commit thee to earth, nor
shroud those limbs with the tomb of thy sires! To the vultures
shalt thou be left; or, sunk beneath the flood, the wave shall whirl
thee and hungry fishes mouth thy wounds!' Unresting, he sped in
chase of Antaeus and Lucas – who fought in Turnus' van – of
gallant Numa and yellow-haired Camers, scion of noble Volcens,
who was richest in land of Ausonia's sons and reigned in mute
Amyclae. And as Aegaeon was – who, the tale is told, was lord of
a hundred arms and a hundred hands, and flashed fire from fifty
mouths and fifty breasts, what time he fronted the bolts of Jove,
thundering on fifty levelled shields and waving fifty naked blades
– such was Aeneas, as over all the plain he glutted his rage with
victory when once his steel grew warm! And now, lo, he swept
against the four steeds of Niphaeus' car and their opposing
breasts! At sight of his giant stride and the dread menace of his
ire, trembling they turned, and, rushing backward, flung forth
their charioteer and dashed his chariot to the strand.

Meanwhile, behind twin-yoked coursers of snow, Lucagus and
Liger, his brother, broke into the midst – fierce Lucagus brandishing his sheathless sword, his brother reining the wheeling
steeds! Aeneas brooked not the hot fury of their onslaught, but
made in and loomed enormous on their view, with adverse spear.
To whom Liger: 'Not Diomedes' horses dost thou behold, nor
Achilles' car, nor Phrygia's plains! This day shall thy battles and
thy life end upon Italian earth!' Thus flew the words of insensate
Liger: but not in words Troy's hero couched his response, for he
flung his javelin against the foes! And as Lucagus, hanging prone
to the stroke, admonished his steeds with the spear, and, advancing his left foot, prepared for the fray, the lance made entry
through the lower marge of his shining shield, then gored the
leftward groin. Hurled from the chariot, he rolled dying on the
field, while good Aeneas greeted him, bitter tongued: 'Lucagus,
no coward flight of thy coursers hath betrayed thy car; no vain
shadow from the enemy hath turned them: springing from the
wheels, thyself thou desertest both!' So saying, he caught their

heads. But, sliding from the selfsame car, the unhappy brother outstretched his helpless hands: 'By thyself – by the parents who gave being to such a child – spare this life, O mighty one of Troy, and have mercy on my prayer!' Farther he had pleaded; but Aeneas: 'Not such thy words but now! Die, and let brother forsake not brother!' And with the steel he pierced the breast and unbared the vital seat. – Such the carnage that the Dardan chief wrought along the plains, fierce as the torrent flood or the gloomy whirlwind; till at length his young Ascanius, and the warriors beleaguered in vain, burst forth and left the camp.

Meantime Jove unlocked his lips and accosted Juno: 'Sister and sweetest wife in one, thy thought was truth – thy sentence errs not! It is Venus upholds the Trojan powers – not, methinks, the living valour of their hands, nor their bold spirits unbowed by peril!' To whom Juno meekly: 'Why, fairest consort, wilt thou torture this sick heart, that trembles at thy stern accent? Had my love that spell which once it had – and meetly had – not now had thine omnipotence denied me this boon: power to withdraw Turnus from battle, power to preserve him scathless for his father Daunus! Now let him perish and slake the vengeance of Troy with guiltless blood! And yet his name is drawn from our lineage – Pilumnus his sire in the fourth degree – and with generous hand and unstinted gifts full oft has he heaped thy fane!'

To her, in brief response, the king of skyey Olympus: 'If thy prayer import but a delay of present death, – a respite from thy warrior's fall, – and so thou apprehend my will, bear Turnus away in flight, and snatch him from the jaws of fate! Thus far indulgence hath room. But if thought of a deeper favour lurks under thy prayer, and thou weenest that the sum of war may be moved or altered, thou nursest a barren hope!'

And Juno, with falling tears: 'What if thy heart should yield where thy tongue denies, and Turnus' span remain him assured? Now a heavy doom awaits his innocent life, or my errant mind is void of truth. Yet, O that rather I were mocked by lying fears, and that thou – who canst – wouldst turn thy beginnings to a better end!'

So said, she shot incontinent from high heaven, cloud-girt and driving storm before her through the air, and sought the Ilian lines and the camp of Laurentum. Next from a hollow cloud (strange vision and miraculous!) the goddess wrought a phantom, substanceless and powerless, in likeness of Aeneas; adorned it with Dardan arms, mimicked the great shield and the plumes on his godlike head; then dowered it with vacant speech and sense-less utterance, and bade it move with the hero's tread: – such, Fame tells, the shapes that flit when death is past, or the dreams that mock the slumbering brain! But exultant the spectre leapt before the vanward ranks, provoking the foe with weaponed hand and taunting lips. Turnus pressed on, and from distance hurled his strident spear; the shadow wheeled round with retreating step! Then the Rutulian, when he deemed that Aeneas turned and fled, and his storm-tossed soul drank in the fallacious hope: 'Whither away, Aeneas? Forsake not the plighted nuptial couch: at this hand shalt thou receive, the soil thou hast sought across the flood!' So clamouring he pursued, brandishing his naked blade, nor saw his joy vanishing with the winds!

Moored, as it chanced, to the ledge of a frowning rock, with ladders flung forth and gangway ready, stood the ship, wherein king Osinius had sailed from the coasts of Clusium. Here, in hot haste, the semblance of fugitive Aeneas flung itself to hiding: nor with less of speed Turnus followed, overbore all hindrance, and sprang across the lofty bridge. Scarce had he touched the prow, when Saturn's child sundered the cable and swept the dissevered barque over the refluent tide. On this the form of shadow sought no farther refuge, but soared sublime and faded in gloom and mist. And while Aeneas was calling his absent foe to battle, and sending down to death warrior on warrior that fronted his path, the winds meantime were whirling Turnus far out to sea!

Witless of the event, thankless for his salvation, he gazed back, with suppliant voice and either hand uplifted to heaven: 'Almighty Sire! and didst thou hold me to have merited such foul reproach? Is this the penalty thou hast willed me to pay? Whither am I borne? Whence am I come? What flight conveys me home? – in what guise conveys me? What of that heroic band, who followed my banner and me? Have I not left them all – accursed thought! – in the jaws of a fearful death? Do I not see them wavering and hear the moans of the fallen? What may I do? How shall earth yawn deep enough for me? Nay, be pitiful, ye winds! Drive this galley on reef or on rock – from Turnus' heart the prayer is uttered! Hurl it upon the quicksand's cruel shoals, where neither Rutulian may follow, nor Rumour blazon my shame!'

So saying, he veered in spirit this way and that. Frenzied for the black dishonour, should he fall upon the sword and drive the bitter steel through his side? – or plunge amid the brine, swim to the winding beach, and hurl himself again on the Teucrian spears? Thrice he assayed either way: thrice imperial Juno stayed his hand, and – compassion in her soul – restrained her warrior. Over the parting deep he sped, convoyed by wave and tide, and was borne at length to his father Daunus' ancient city.

But meanwhile, at behest of Jove, Mezentius, like fire, took up the fray and assailed triumphant Troy. About him swarmed the Tyrrhene lines – all their hatred, all their frequent spears, bent against one solitary foe! As a cliff that juts into the infinite sea, exposed to the raving winds and fronting the main, endures all the shock and menace of sky and wave, itself unmoved – so he, unterrified, hurled Hebrus, Dolichaon's child, to earth, and with him Latagus and fleeing Palmus: Latagus he caught full in mouth and face with a huge boulder, rent from some hill; Palmus, the dastard, he hamstrung and left to roll; then gave the armour to be worn on Lausus' shoulders, the plumes to adorn his crest. Nor less Evanthes, the Phrygian, bled, and Mimas, compeer of Paris from the birth: for on one same night Theano bore him to Amycus his sire, and Cisseus' royal daughter gave Paris – that firebrand in her womb – to the day. In his father's city Paris sleeps; on the Laurentine shore Mimas lies unknown! And as a mighty boar, driven by snarling hounds from his mountain-top, – whom pine-crowned Vesulus has sheltered through many a year, and Laurentum's fen pastured in silvan reeds, – when once he is come amid the toils, turns to bay, fierce-snorting, with bristled shoulders, and no man's courage mounts to resentment or approach, but all assail him at distance with darts and riskless clamour, – even so, among all that hated Mezentius, and hated justly, not one found heart to close with unscabbarded steel, but from far they plied him with missiles and wide echoing din. But he, unfearing and deliberate, moved hither and thither, gnashing his teeth and shaking the javelins from his shield.

From Corythus' ancient bounds Acron of Greece had come, fleeing his country and an unwed wife. Him when Mezentius saw afar, gay in crimson plumes and the purple of his plighted bride, dealing havoc amid the ranks, – as oft a fasting lion, ranging the deep coverts under hunger's maddening impulse, if he chance to descry a timorous roe or stately-antlered stag, opens his cavernous jaws in delight, uprears his mane, and clings couchant above the flesh while foul gore bathes his insatiate lips, – so the Tuscan leapt, all eagerness, against the serried foes. Acron, the ill-fated, fell spurning the blackened ground in his last agony, and encrimsoning the shivered spear. The same arm deigned not to smite Orodes down as he fled, nor to inflict an unseen wound with the flung lance. Face to face and front to front he met him and, man against man, joined encounter, conqueror not by guile but by the steel in a brave man's hand! Then, planting his foot on the prostrate form, and leaning on the spear: 'Warriors,' he cried, 'here lies the great Orodes – no mean pillar of the war!' Shouting, his men took up the exultant paean. But he, with his latest breath: 'Whosoever thou art, not long shall the victim be unvenged, nor long shall the victor triumph! Thee, also, a like doom marks, and soon thou shalt lie on the selfsame field.' Then Mezentius, anger struggling with his smile: 'Die thou meantime! With me the Sire of gods and King of men may deal.' So saying, he drew his weapon out from the flesh; ungentle rest and iron sleep fell heavy on the glazing eyes, and their lids closed on eternal night.

Now Caedicus slew Alcathous, Sacrator Hydaspes, Rapo Parthenius and Orses in his stubborn strength. By Messapus Clonius bled, and Erichaetes, Lycaon's child – one prone on earth, through the stumbling of his unreined steed, the other on foot. On foot, no less, had Lycian Agis advancèd; yet him Valerus, heritor of his grandsire's arm and heart, struck down. Before Salius Thronius fell, and Salius before Nealces, master of the javelin's cast and the distant shaft's elusive flight.

And now with stern hand Mars meted out impartial woe and mutual death. Victors and vanquished – alike they slew and alike they fell, and neither these nor those knew thought of flight. In the halls of Jove immortal eyes looked pityingly down on the vain fury of either host, and wept for the bitter agony of man. Here Venus, there Saturnian Juno, sate opposite and gazed; while pale Tisiphone below raged amid the thousands.

But Mezentius, shaking his huge spear, moved tempestuous athwart the plain. – Great as Orion, when, with shoulder overtopping the waves, he marches on foot through the heart of Nereus' realm, cleaving his path through the mighty waters, or when, bearing from the mountain-crest some time-honoured ash, he walks the earth and hides his head among the clouds, – so strode Mezentius towering in steel!

On the other side Aeneas, descrying him in the long column, prepared for encounter. He, undaunted, held his ground, awaiting his high-hearted foe, steadfast in massive strength; then, with eye measuring the distance that might suffice his spear: 'Now speed me my right hand – sole deity to me – and this lance that I poise for the cast! Clad in spoils reft from yon pirate's carcass, thou shalt stand, my Lausus – such my vow – a living trophy of Aeneas.' He said, and from far hurled the whistling steel. Flying, it leapt from the shield and struck peerless Antores betwixt side and flank – Antores, Alcides' friend; who, sent from Argos, had cloven to Evander's side and found his home in an Italian town. Hapless he fell under an alien wound, and, with gaze turned heavenward, thought in death on his well-loved Argos. Then good Aeneas flung his spear: through the sheltering orb of triple brass, through the linen folds and fabric woven of three bull-hides, it sped and lodged in the nether groin – yet bore not its strength to the goal. Exultant at sight of the Tyrrhene blood, Aeneas snatched his sword incontinent from the thigh, and drove like flame on his bewildered foe. – Deeply Lausus groaned for love of his dear sire, when he saw that sight, and the tears rolled down his face. And here – if that old-world day may win credence for thy generous deed – these strains, at least, shall not pass unsung thy harsh and disastrous doom, nor thy noble prowess, nor thyself, the young and glorious! Useless and encumbered, his foeman's lance trailing from his shield, the sire withdrew his retreating step; when forward the son shot, and closed amid the conflicting swords. And even as Aeneas rose with right hand in act to smite, he struck up the blade and gave the slayer pause. Loud-clamouring his comrades followed, showering spears, and with missiles confounding the enemy from far, till the father might retire under shelter of the filial shield. Aeneas raged at bay in his sheath of steel. And as oft when the storm-clouds descend in volleyed hail, every ploughman, every husbandman, has fled from the plain, and the traveller lies hid in safe fortalice – either the river's bank or the arch of some beetling rock – while the rains descend on earth; that so, when the sun returns, they may assay the laborious day again: even so Aeneas, whelmed from this hand and that under the storm of spears, endured the cloud of war, till its thunderous fury should be utterly spent, assailing Lausus with rebuke, Lausus with menace: 'Whither hastenest to death, adventurous beyond thy strength? Infatuate! love hath made thy valour blind!' Yet no whit less he charged madly on; and now the tide of fury surged higher in the Dardan captain's heart, and the Sisters gathered the latest threads of Lausus' span. For Aeneas drove his stout blade sheer through the youth and buried it to the hilt within. Through the buckler –

frail armour to second his menace! – through the tunic that his mother wove with flexile gold, the point passed on; blood filled his breast, and through air the life fled sorrowing, nor knew the body more. But when Anchises' seed beheld the look on that dying face – that face so marvellously pale – heavily he groaned in pity, and stretched forth his hand, while before his soul rose the semblance of his own filial love: 'What now, unhappy boy – what shall good Aeneas give thee for these thy glories? what guerdon worthy of thy great soul? The arms that were thy delight, keep thou for thine own; and – if that be aught to thee – I restore thee to the spirits and ashes of thy sires. Yet, ill-fated that thou art, one thought shall solace thee for thy piteous doom: thou fallest by great Aeneas' hand!' Then, chiding his laggard comrades, he raised their captain from earth, where he lay with his fair-decked tresses blood-befouled.

Meantime, by the wave of Tiber river, the father stanched his wounds with water, and rested his reclining frame against a tree-bole. At distance his brazen helm drooped from the boughs and his heavy arms lay in peace upon the sward. About him stood chosen warriors; he, sick and panting, eased his neck, while the unshorn beard strayed over his breast. And much he asked of Lausus, and full many a man, he sent to recall him and convey the mandate of his sad sire. But Lausus his weeping comrades bore lifeless upon a shield – a mighty man, and slain by a mighty stroke. Far off the disaster-boding soul knew their lamentation. With dust on dust he defiled his white hairs, extended either palm to heaven, and clung to the dead: 'My child, and was I so chained to love of life, that I suffered thee, blood of my blood, to front the enemy's hand for me? Am I, thy father, preserved by these wounds of thine? Art thou dead, that I may live? Ay me! now at last the bitterness of death is come: now is the iron within my soul! It was I, my son, who sullied thy name with guilt – I, whom they drove in loathing from sceptre and ancestral throne! Vengeance I owed to my mother-land and the hatred of my people: would but that I had surrendered this sin-stained life by every form of death! And now I live, nor as yet depart from the sight of man and day – but depart I will!' And, with the word, he raised himself on his stricken thigh, and, though the deep wound crippled his might, yet, with spirit unbowed, bade his charger be brought. This was his glory, this his solace; on this he rode unconquered from every field. – Then, so speaking, he began to the sorrowing creature: 'Rhaebus, long have we lived, if any

thing soever be long to mortal man! This day shalt thou bear
away in triumph yon bloody spoils with the head of Aeneas slain,
and avenge with me the pangs of Lausus; or, if our strength avail
not to find a path, side by side thou shalt bleed with me! For,
brave heart, I trow thou wilt not stoop to endure a stranger's bidding, nor to serve a Teucrian lord!' So said, he mounted and
once more disposed his limbs on their familiar seat, and charged
either hand with sharpened javelins, his head resplendent in brass
and shaggy with horse-hair plume. So, wind-swift, he galloped
into the midst, while in his heart surged the mighty tides of
shame and madness wedded to agony.

And now thrice he called in trumpet-tones on Aeneas. And
Aeneas knew the call, and prayed with exultant heart: 'So may
the great Father of Heaven ordain, so Apollo on high! Begin, and
join encounter.' Thus far he said, and advanced to meet him with
menacing spear. But he: 'Fiercest foe, why seekest thou to terrify
me, when thou hast robbed me of my son? There lay the sole
path whereby to achieve my ruin: I fear not death: I spare not for
thy gods. Cease; I am riding to my end, yet first I bring thee
these gifts!' He said, and hurled a javelin at his enemy; then
planted another and yet another, flying in vast circle: but the
golden shield sustained them all. Thrice he rode, wheeling to the
left, round the foe that fronted him on foot, flinging weapons
from his hand: thrice Troy's hero turned, carrying the great
forest of steel on his protecting brass. Then, weary of the long-
spun delays, weary of plucking forth so many a spear-head, and
hard-pressed in the unequal fray, much debating at length he
sprang out and cast his lance full between the hollow temples of
the war-horse. The steed reared himself upright, with heels lashing the air, flung his rider, came down above him and encumbered him; then, falling headlong, lay with shoulder oppressing
his prostrate form, while Trojans and Latins fired heaven with
their cries. Up flew Aeneas, and snatched his sword from the
scabbard; then, standing above: 'Where now is the fierce Mezentius and that wild savagery of soul?' To whom the Tuscan, as
with upturned gaze he drank in the air of heaven and regained
his sense: 'Thou bitter foe, why railest thou and threatenest
death? Slay! It is no crime to slay. I came not to battle in quest of
mercy; nor such the pact that my Lausus hath made betwixt thee
and me! One sole boon I ask of thee, by whatever grace is due to
the vanquished: grant my clay to be laid in earth. I know that the
keen edged anger of my people surrounds me. Shelter me, I pray,

from this their fury, and vouchsafe to my son and me the union of a grave!' He said, and, unblenched, received the expected steel in his throat, while the vital stream spread flooding over his armour.

BOOK XI

MEANTIME THE GODDESS of morn rose out of Ocean. Aeneas, though duty urged him to allow a space for the burial of his friends, and the fatal field still clouded his soul, yet, with the orient beams, began to pay the conqueror's vows to Heaven. On a mound he reared a giant oak, stripped of its encircling boughs, and clothed it in the lucent arms reft from Mezentius' kingly frame – a trophy to thee, great god of battles. Thereto he affixed the plumes, yet wet with a bloody dew, the warrior's shattered spears, and his corselet stricken and pierced in twice six places; to the left arm he bound the brazen buckler, and from the neck hung the sword of ivory; then, with such prelude, exhorted his triumphant bands – for all the serried throng of his captains girt him round: – 'Heroes, the greatest deed is done: for what remains, let fear be unknown! These are the spoils – the first-fruits won from yon proud tyrant – and here is Mezentius as my hands have made him! Now our march lies to Latium's king and Latium's battlements. Prepare your arms, forestall the battle in spirit and hope, that no delay may impede your ignorance, nor any craven thought retard your timorous steps, so soon as high Heaven shall grant us to uplift our banners and lead forth our chivalry from the camp! Meanwhile commit we our friends and their tombless bodies to earth – sole tribute that can reach the deeps of Acheron! Go,' he said, 'grace with the last rites those glorious souls, whose blood hath bought us this second father-land: and first to Evander's mourning city let Pallas be sent, whose heart sank not when the black day swept him hence and plunged him in all-unripe death.'

So, weeping, he said, and turned his steps to the threshold where grey Acoetes held ward over Pallas' breathless limbs, com-posed already for the burial: – Acoetes, that bore erewhile Evan-der's Parrhasian arms; but now, under less happy star, went forth the appointed guardian to his much-loved foster child. Around stood all the menial train, and thronging Trojans, and women of Ilium – their mourning tresses unloosed in wonted mode. But when Aeneas entered the lofty portal, they smote upon their breasts and raised the loud wail to the stars; and the dwelling of the king re-echoed to their ecstasy of woe. He, when he saw the pillowed head of Pallas, and his face white as the snow, and the gash of the Ausonian point wide-yawning in his marble breast, so spoke, while the tears welled up: 'Unhappy boy, and did Fortune, in her radiant coming, grudge thee to me, that thou mightest not behold our kingdom nor ride victorious to the city of thy father? Not such the parting promise that I gave to Evander thy sire, when he kissed me as I went and sent me with his benison to high sovereignty, yet warned me in fear that fierce were the men and stubborn the race that should front my sword! And now *he*, perchance, doubly blinded by idle hope, bribes Heaven and piles his altar with gifts: *we*, with the vain tribute of our tears, escort his son's clay that now owes naught to any power soever above us! Unhappy! who shalt see thy child thus cruelly done to death! And is this our return – our much-hoped triumph? So ends my unfaltering pledge? Yet shall thine eyes, Evander, behold no dastard driven routed with shameful wounds; nor shall the father pray for that bitterest of deaths – when the son lives, and lives dishonoured! Ay me, how stout an arm is lost to thee, Ausonia, and lost, Iulus, to thee!'

His lament so made, he bade them raise the piteous corpse, and sent a thousand men, the chosen of all his host, to attend the last rite and weep with the weeping father – scant solace of that great sorrow, but due to the unhappy sire! Others, unlingering, plaited the wicker-work of a soft bier from shoots of arbute and oaken twigs, and shadowed the high-piled couch under leafy canopy. Here they laid the youth aloft on his rustic litter – fair as some blossom culled by a girlish hand from tender violet or languid hyacinth, whose radiance and native beauty are not yet fled, though the breast of Earth no longer ministers food and strength! Then Aeneas brought two robes, stiff-rustling with gold and purple, which, in other days, Sidonian Dido wrought for him with her (own) queenly hands – a labour of love – and shot the warp with threading gold. Mournfully he placed the one over the boyish dead for his latest tribute, and shrouded those locks doomed to the fire; heaped high the prizes of the Laurentine fray, and bade the spoils be carried in long-drawn procession; then added those steeds and arms of which he had despoiled the foe. The victims' hands he had already bound behind their backs, ere he would send them as offerings to the nether shade and sprinkle the flame with their sacrificial blood. And now he commanded his captains to bear with their own hands tree-boles accoutred in armour of the foe, with hostile names affixed. Worn by the load of disastrous years, Acoetes came led along – now marring his breast with clenched hand, now rending his cheeks, and anon flinging his whole frame prostrate to earth. His chariot, too, they led forth, all flecked with Rutulian blood. Behind marched Aethon, the battle-steed, weeping, while great gouts bathed his face. Others bore his spear and helm; for the rest was held by conquering Turnus. Then followed a melancholy band – Troy, and all Tuscany, and Arcadia, with arms reversed. Soon, when all the long retinue was past, Aeneas halted, and, with deep sigh, thus resumed: 'Us the same fell destiny of war summons hence to other tears. Hail for ever, noble Pallas, and for ever farewell!' Nor farther he said, but turned toward the frowning walls, and bent his steps to the camp.

And now an embassage was come from the Latin city, all shrouded with olive-boughs and imploring a boon: – that he would restore the dead, that lay where the sword had strewn them along the plains, and suffer them to enter their earthen tomb. No war, they pleaded, is waged against the vanquished and them that have left the light: let him show mercy to those who were once called his friends and the kindred of his bride! Whom good Aeneas – for not despicable their prayer! – crowned with his grace, and so pursued: 'Men of Latium, what malice of Fortune hath enmeshed you in such bitterness of strife, that ye eschew our amity? Ye ask me peace for the dead, whom the War-god's lot hath taken? Full willingly would I grant it to the living! I had not come, save Destiny had assigned me a place and habitation here; nor war I with your people: your king forsook our alliance, and deemed it better to entrust him to Turnus' spears! Yet had it been juster that Turnus should face this hazard of death. If he prepares to end the struggle by the strong hand, his part had been to encounter me with this steel; and he had lived, whom God or his own right arm had given to live! Now go, kindle the fire beneath your ill-starred countrymen.' Aeneas ceased: they stood in mute wonder, with eye and countenance turned on each other.

Then Drances, the elder-born, whose hatred and injurious tongue held him ever at enmity with young Turnus, unlocked his lips and thus returned: 'O great in glory, greater in arms – hero of Troy, how may my praises equal thee with the stars? Shall I first marvel at thy righteousness, or at thy labours in battle? For us it remains to carry thy response with grateful hearts to our native city, and – if any turn of Fortune shall point a way – to unite thee with Latinus our king. Let Turnus seek him alliance where he will! Nay, it shall be our delight to raise the massy walls of thy destiny, and bear the rocks of Troy on our Latian shoulders!' With this he ceased, and all murmured assent with a single voice. For twelve days the pact was made, and – Peace their mediatress – Teucrians and intermingled Latins roamed woodland and hill, unharming and unharmed. The tall ash rang under the two-edged steel; they laid low the pines that challenged heaven, and unceasingly their wedges clove the oak and fragrant cedar, and their groaning wains transported the mountain-ash.

And now winged Fame, herald of that dire sorrow, filled Evander's ears, and Evander's palace and city-walls, with her tidings – Fame, that but now proclaimed Pallas victor in Latium! The Arcadians came streaming to the gates, and, after their immemorial wont, seized upon funeral torches, till, parting the dim tract of fields, the road shone with a great line of flame. To meet them came the Phrygian train, and united their lamenting bands. Soon as the matrons saw them entering their streets, with cries they fired the mourning city. But no constraint could withhold Evander! Into the midst he rushed, and, when they laid down the bier, fell above Pallas, and clung to him weeping and moaning, till hardly at long last grief allowed passage to his voice: 'Not such the promise, my Pallas, thou gavest to thy sire! Ah, how gladly now wouldst thou entrust thee with more of caution to the cruel War-god's hand! – I knew what potent charm lies in glory won by a maiden sword – how sweet the laurels of the first field! Alas for the unhappy firstfruits of my child, and the harsh prelude that heralds the coming war! Alas for my vows and prayers to which no god hearkened! And thou, my pure-souled wife – happy thou in the death that spared thee not for this agony! But I have lived and defied my fate, only to linger here – a father without a son! Would that I had followed Troy's allied arms, and fallen whelmed under the Rutulian spears! Would that I had given mine own life, and this procession were bringing me – not Pallas – home! Nor yet, men of Troy, would I censure you, nor our treaty, nor the hands we clasped in friendship: this lot was foredoomed to fall on my white head. But if death, ere his prime, awaited my child, yet will there be comfort in the thought that he fell after slaying his Volscian thousands, and fell while leading the Teucrians into Latium! And, Pallas, I could not grace thee with worthier, funeral than this which good Aeneas accords, and the princes of his Phrygia, and the Tyrrhene captains, and all the Tyrrhenian host. Great trophies they bring of those that thine arm consigned to death. And thou, Turnus – thou, also, hadst now been standing, a giant trunk encased in steel, were thine age as his, and the strength of thy years the same! But why, unhappy, withhold I the Teucrians from the sword? Go, and forget not to bear this my message to your king: *If I linger out this hated life now that Pallas is slain, the cause is thy right hand, which – as thine eyes have seen – owes Turnus to sire and to son! This sole room is left for thy merits and fortune to fill. I ask not for joy in life: in me joy were crime: I ask but to bear this tidings to my son beneath the nether shades.'*

Meantime Aurora had lifted her gracious light on high for weary mortality, and returned with the round of task and toil. Already father Aeneas, already Tarchon, had reared the pyres on the winding strand. Hither, as his fathers used, each man brought the bodies of his kindred, and, as the fires were lit beneath, darkness enshrouded the high heavens in gloom. Thrice, girt in resplendent arms, they ran their course round the burning piles; thrice circled the sad funeral-flame on their steeds, and cried from wailing lips. Their tears rained on earth, rained on their armour, and the shout of men and clang of trumpets surged to the stars. And now part flung on the fires spoils torn from Latian dead, helms and fair-wrought swords, bridles and glowing wheels; part, the familiar offerings – their friends' own shields and the blades that prospered not. Around, full many a stout ox was slain in sacrifice to Death; while bristled boars, and cattle harried from every field, were butchered above the flames. Then, over all the strand, they watched their comrades burning, and stood guard above the blackening pyres; nor could be torn away till dewy Night rolled round the cope of heaven, now gemmed with glittering stars.

Nor less, elsewhere, the stricken Latins built piles innumerable. Part of their many slain they buried beneath the sod; part they raised and carried to the bordering fields, then sent them homeward to their city: the residue, a great mound of undistinguished carnage, they burned unnumbered and unhonoured; till on every hand the broad plains shone emulous with frequent fires. The third morn had withdrawn the chill curtain of shade from heaven, and sadly men were levelling the mounds of ashes, sweeping the mingled bones from the embers, and heaping

hillocks of warm soil above them. But in the homes of rich Latinus' city the voice of sorrow was loudest, and greatest the share
of that long agony. Here were mothers, and their sons' unhappy
brides, and tender-hearted sisters weeping, and boys orphaned of
their sires – all cursing the unhallowed war and Turnus' hymeneal: he, they cried, he himself should decide the issue by arms
and the naked steel, who claimed for himself the empery of Italy
and her chiefest honours! Fierce Drances edged their anger,
attesting that Turnus alone was called, Turnus alone defied to
the fray. Yet, in other sort, many a sentence, the while, was cast
for Turnus in varying phrase; the shadow of the Queen's great
name sheltered him; and his high fame, broad-based on hard-
won trophies, lent him support.

Amid this turmoil, while the flames of faction were hottest, lo!
– to fill full the cup – the envoys from Diomedes' great city
returned despondent with his message: all their toil had been idly
spent; their gifts, their gold, and their solemn pleas, had nothing
availed; Latium must seek another sword, or sue for peace from
the Trojan king! Even Latinus' royal soul fainted under the
burden of sorrow. The celestial anger, and the fresh-made graves
before his eyes, warned him that Aeneas was called by Fate and
upborne by the manifest will of Heaven. Therefore, by his kingly
word, he summoned a high conclave of the princes of his people,
and gathered them within his stately portals: and streaming they
came to the royal halls through the crowded streets. Eldest in
years and first in dominion, Latinus sat in their midst, but with
little joy on his brow. And now he enjoined the embassage,
returned from the Aetolian city, to speak and say what message
they brought, and bade them rehearse their answer in order and
completeness. Then, silence imposed on each tongue, Venulus
began, obedient to his word:

'Citizens, we have looked upon Diomedes and the Argive
camp: our journey is achieved, its perils overcome, and we have
touched that hand whereby the kingdom of Ilium fell! He, the
victory won, was founding his city of Argyripa, named by the
name of his father's race, in the fields of Iapygian Garganus. So
soon as we gained ingress, and liberty was accorded to speak
before his face, we preferred our gifts and revealed our name and
country – who our invaders, what cause had drawn us to Arpi. He
lent ear, then so returned with unruffled mien: "O happy races,
Saturnian realms, children of time-honoured Ausonia! what spite
of Fortune disturbs your peace and lures you to challenge an

unknown fray. All we, whose swords profaned Ilium's holy soil –
I pass in silence the lees of war that we drained under those towering walls, the brave whom yon fatal Simois whelms! – all of us
throughout all the world, have paid the penalty of our guilt in
nameless torment, a band that even Priam might weep to see!
Minerva's fell star be my witness, and the Euboic cliffs, and
avenging Caphereus! Driven from that warfare to distant strands,
Menelaus, Atreus' seed, roams exiled to the very columns of Pro-
teus; and Ulysses has looked on the Cyclops of Aetna! Shall I
rehearse Neoptolemus' shattered realm, Idomeneus' ruined
hearth, or the Locrians dwelling on Libya's shore? He of
Mycene, himself, lord of our Argive powers, bled on his threshold's verge by the hand of his felon spouse: Asia had fallen, the
adulterer took up the fray! Shall I tell how an envious Heaven
denied that I should return to my ancestral altars, and see the
wife of my yearning, and my fair Calydon? Even now grim-vis-
aged portents pursue me: my lost friends have fled into the sky
on wings, and flit as birds about the rivers (oh, the dire punishment of my people!), while the crags ring to their tearful cries.
This – and no less – had I to hope, even from that day when with
frenzied steel I assailed the flesh of deity, and wounded the hand
of Venus with impious stroke! Nay, urge me not – urge me not
to such combat! I have no feud with Teucer's race since Troy-
towers fell; I have no remembrance and no joy in those ancient
ills. The gifts that ye bring to me from your native coasts, give ye
to Aeneas in my stead. We have fronted his angry blade; our
hand hath encountered his: then credit one who has proved how
vast his form when he rises to the shield, how fierce the whirlwind of his flung lance! If Ida's earth had but borne two others
like to him, Dardanus, unassailed, had come to the cities of
Inachus, and Greece were mourning the fates reversed. Long as
we lingered round the battlements of obdurate Troy, it was
Hector's and Aeneas' hand that halted the victory of Greece and
turned back her feet till the tenth year was come. Both stood
high in courage, and both were glorious in arms: Aeneas was first
in piety. Join hand to hand in alliance, as best ye may: but beware
your swords clash not with his!" So, noble king, thou hast heard
both the answer of thy brother-king, and his sentence on our
great war.'

Scarce had the envoys concluded, when a various murmur ran
along the trembling lips of Ausonia's children: even as, when
impeding rocks check some racing river, the pent flood begins to

murmur and the neighbouring banks echo to the plashing waters. Soon as their minds were calmed, and the confusion of tongues allayed, the king began from his throne aloft, first invoking Heaven:

'Latians, I could have wished (and it had been better so!) to have determined ere this on our estate – not summon our conclave at such an hour, when the foe is seated at the walls. We wage an ill-omened war, my countrymen, with a heaven-descended race and men unconquered, whom the battle never wearies nor defeat constrains to sheathe the sword. If ye have rested any hope in borrowed aid of Aetolian spears, resign it. Himself is each man's hope: but ye see how slender it is. What universal ruin has stricken the remnant of our prostrate fortunes, is plain to your eyes and the touch of your hands. Yet I censure no man: what the height of valour could do, is done; we have fought with every sinew of our kingdom. Now I will unfold the judgement, formed in my wavering mind, and expound it in brief if ye lend me heed. An ancient domain is mine, that borders on the Tuscan stream, stretching far toward the set of sun, up to and beyond the Sicanian confines: there Auruncan and Rutulian sow the seed, subdue its stubborn hills with the share, and pasture their roughest slopes. Let the whole of this region, with the pine-clad belt of its high hill, be ceded to the Teucrians' friendship; propound we just terms of treaty, and call them to share our realm. If so strong their desire, let them settle and build their city. But if they incline to win another country, another nation, and are free to quit our soil, let us build twice ten ships of Italian oak: or, if they can fill more, all the timber lies by the water-edge. Let their part be to prescribe the number and fashion of their vessels, our to accord the brass, and labouring hands, and docks. More, to convey our word and confirm the treaty, I would that a hundred Latin envoys, sprung from our best blood, should go with hands proffering the bough of peace, carrying in gift talents of gold and ivory, and the chair and robe, ensigns of our sovereignty. – Give counsel for the good of all, and succour our fainting fortunes!'

Then Drances, bitter as ever, whom Turnus' renown goaded with the poignant stings of backbiting envy, – lavish of his wealth and ready of tongue, though his hand was cold to battle, deemed no mean counsellor in debate, and powerful in faction: his mother's high birth ennobled a lineage, which, on the father's side, he professed uncertain: – Drances arose, and piled the fuel of his words on their rising anger:

'Gracious king, the theme whereon thou takest our counsel is dark to no man, and needs no word of mine! All confess that they know whither the star of our people tends; but their timorous lips are mute! Let him give liberty of speech and abate his tempestuous pride, through whose disastrous leadership and sinister soul – for speak I will, though he menace me with arms and death! – so many a sun of battle is set, and we behold our city plunged in grief, while he, his trust in flight, assails the encampment of Troy and affrights the skies with his clashing steel. Add one gift more to that wealth of treasure thou bidst us send and promise to the Dardans, – but one, O best of kings! – nor let any man's violence avail to withhold thy paternal hand from yielding thy daughter to a noble consort, a worthy hymeneal, and confirming this peace by covenant eternal! But if such extremity of terror possess our minds and hearts, *him* let us entreat, and from *him* implore his gracious assent – that he would deign to give way and restore their just rights to king and country! Why fling thine unhappy countrymen so often into the jaws of peril, O fountain-head of Latium's ills? In war is no salvation: peace we all ask of thee, Turnus – peace and the one inviolate sanction of peace! Lo, foremost of all, I, whom thou deemest thy foe, – and I reck not though I be! – come suppliant to thy feet. Pity thy kindred; resign thy pride; and, defeated, withdraw! Routed, we have seen enough of death, enough of desolation in our broad fields. Or, if Fame spurs thee, if such valiance musters in thy breast, if the dowry of a palace touches thee so nearly, – be bold and bear an unshrinking heart against the expectant foe! What! shall we, unvalued lives, – a crowd unburied and unwept! – fall bleeding upon the plains, that Turnus may wed a royal spouse? Do thou also bear thy burden, and – if any might be in thee – if thou hast aught of thy fathers' prowess – dare to look on the face of him who calls thee!'

At these words Turnus' vehemence flamed out; he groaned, and thus the deep-drawn accents broke upon his heart: 'Truly, Drances, thy large utterance is never stinted at the moment when battle calls for hands; and when the senate is summoned thou art first in the fray! But our conclave needs not to be filled with words – great though they be, as they fly securely from thy lips, while the mounded walls hold back the foe and the moats are not yet running blood. Then thunder glibly on – as glibly thou art wont to thunder – and let Drances' tongue impeach me of fear, since Drances' hand has piled those unnumbered heaps of Teu-

crian slain, and studded the frequent fields with the trophies of
Drances' sword! What living valour may achieve thou mayest try
if thou wilt. Nor, in truth, are enemies far to seek; to left and
right they encircle our walls! March we to the encounter? Why
lingerest? Will thy prowess reside for ever in thy braggart tongue
and those recreant feet of thine? – *Defeated?* I? And who, foulest
liar, may justly uphold me defeated, that shall see swollen Tiber
surging high with Ilian blood, and Evander's house and Evander's Ilian fallen in one ruin, and his Arcadians stripped of their
arms? Not so did Bitias and giant Pandarus experience me, nor
those thousand men that in one day this victorious arm hurled to
Hell, pent though I was within their walls and girt by hostile battlements. *In war is no salvation*, Madman, let thy presage fall on
the Dardan's head, and on thine own fortunes! Go on: cease not
to confound all by thy fears, – to extol the might of a twice-con-
quered people, and, in counterpoise, to slight the sword of Latinus! Now the Myrmidon princes quail before Phrygia's arms,
and Aufidus' refluent flood flees from the Adriatic wave! Or
when this artist in sin feigns terror for my feud, and edges his
calumny with fear. . . ! Never shalt thou lose such a life as thine –
nay, never blench – by this right hand: let it dwell with thee, and
inhabit that familiar breast! – Now, sire, I return to thee and the
grave theme of thy thought. If thou restest no farther hope on
our swords – if our desolation is thus complete – if, our lines
once broken, we are fallen for ever, and Fortune, once fled, can
never return – let us sue for peace and outstretch our craven
hands in entreaty! Yet, oh, did some spark of our old-time valour
remain! Blest beyond others in his labours, and heroic of soul,
would I esteem the man who – rather than brook that sight – fell
dying and bit the earth once and for all! But if we still have
means, if all our youth be not taken yet, if Italy still hold cities
and peoples to aid us, if their glory has come to the Trojans
through rivers of blood (for they, too, have their deaths, and the
same tempest swept over all!) – why faint we ignobly upon the
threshold? Why do tremors assail our limbs ere the trumpet has
sung? Oft Time, and the fickle act of the capricious years, have
changed man's lot for the better: oft Fortune, in fitful visits, has
made him her mock, then established him foursquare. There is
no succour for us in the Aetolian and his Arpi: but in Messapus
there is, in blest Tolumnius, and in those many captains whom
the nations have sent; nor small shall be the glory, to attend the
chosen of Latium and the Laurentine fields. And Camilla we

have, of the glorious Volscian race, leading her mounted squadron and troops resplendent in brass. But if it is I alone whom the Teucrians demand for battle, – if such is your will, and I so impede the common good, – Victory has not used to flee with such utter loathing from these hands, that I should shun to adventure any deed with so fair a hope before me! High of heart I will front him, though he match the great Achilles and accoutre him in harness such as his, wrought by the hands of Vulcan. To you, and to the sire of my bride, have I devoted this life – I, Turnus, brave as the bravest of my fathers. *Aeneas calls on him alone.* And God send that so he may call! nor let Drances, in my stead, atone with his blood this wrath of Heaven, – if wrath of Heaven it be, – nor, if valour and glory be all, bear that palm away!'

Thus they, in mutual conflict, debated the dubious issue: Aeneas moved his embattled lines from the camp. Suddenly, amid dire confusion, a messenger came running through the royal halls and filled the city with wild alarms: the Teucrians, he cried, and the Tyrrhene host, were drawn in array of battle, and sweeping down from Tiber river over all the plain. Instant all minds were wildered; the heart of the people was shaken, and their anger roused by no gentle spur. With outstretched hands they clamoured for arms: for arms their youth cried, while the despairing fathers wept and muttered. And now, on all hands, a wild din rose to the heavens in motley notes of discord: – even as when bands of birds light haply on some towering grove, or when, by Padusa's fish-haunted stream, the hoarse-throated swans give tongue amid the vocal pools. 'Ay, citizens,' cried Turnus, seizing the moment, 'convene your council and sit lauding peace, while they rush on our realm in arms!' Nor farther he said, but leapt up, and rushed, hot-footed, from the high halls. 'Thou, Volusus,' he cried, 'bid the Volscian squadrons arm; and lead out the Rutulians! Thou, Messapus, and, Coras, thou with thy brother, extend our horse under arms over the spreading plains! Let part strengthen the approaches of the town and man the towers: the rest of our host charge at my side, where my word shall point the way!'

Straight men ran to the battlements from all the city. Latinus himself, grey-headed king, abandoned his conclave and high designs, and, unmanned by that disastrous hour, deferred them to other season; and much he accused himself that he gave not unforced welcome to Dardan Aeneas, nor bestowed a bridegroom

upon his child, a son upon his city! Others entrenched the gates,
or brought up stakes and stones; and the raucous clarion sang the
murderous note of war. Then mothers and boys – a motley coro-
nal – encircled the walls; the last agony left none uncalled! Nor
less, amid a matron retinue, the queen moved charioted to Pallas'
temple and tower-capped hill, gifts in her hand, and at her side
the maid Lavinia, – well-spring of all that woe, – her sweet eyes
riveted on earth. Entering, the mothers darkened the shrine with
smoking incense, and from the stately threshold poured the voice
of lamentation: 'Queen of the sword, arbitress of war, Tritonian
maid, break with thine hand the spear of the Phrygian pirate, hurl
him prone to earth, and stretch him prostrate beneath our lofty
portals!' – For Turnus, he accoutred him with furious speed for
the fray. And now he had donned his red-flashing corselet, and
stood horrent in brazen scales, his ankles encased in gold, his
brows yet bare, and the sword girded to his side. Glittering he
ran, an aureate vision, from the citadel-height, with heart on fire,
and in hope already assailed the foe: – even as, when some steed
has burst his bonds and fled the stalls, free at length, and master
of the open plain, either he races to the pastures and the banded
mares, or, wont to bathe in the water of his familiar stream,
flashes past and neighs, with head high-tossed in wanton joy,
while the mane plays waving over neck and over shoulder!

Face to face Camilla met him, with the Volscian lines behind
her, and, fast beneath the gates, leapt queenlike from her
charger, while all the observant band quitted the saddle and
vaulted to earth. Then she: 'Turnus, if the brave may justly rest
any faith in themselves, I both dare and promise to front Aeneas'
cavalry and ride alone to encounter the Tyrrhene horse. Grant
me to brave the war's first perils with this hand: do thou, on foot,
stay by the walls and guard the town!' To this Turnus, with eyes
fixed on the dread maid: 'O virgin glory of Italy, what thanks
shall I assay to speak or render? But now, since that soul of thine
rises outtopping praise, share thou the toil with me! Aeneas –
thus fame and the scouts I have sent avouch – has dispatched,
with felon thought, his light-armed horse in the van, to thunder
athwart the plains, while he, scaling the mountain's desert steep,
marches fast upon the town. For him I weave the toils of war in
the deep forest-gorge, intent to beset the double pass with men
and swords. Do thou, with advancing banners, encounter the
Tyrrhene horse. With thee shall ride fierce Messapus, the
squadrons of Latium, and Tiburtus' bands: assume thou, too, a

leader's charge!' He said, and with like words spurred Messapus and the allied captains to battle; then advanced to meet the foe.

There is a glen with sinuous curve, fit site for the deceits and wiles of war, confined on either hand by a wall obscure with serried foliage. Thither a narrow path leads, and a straitened gorge and ungenerous approach give access. Above, on the towerlike cliffs and the mountain's topmost crest, lies an unfrequented plain, a retreat sequestered and secure, whether thou wouldst front the battle to left or right, or stand hard upon the ridges and roll down the giant rocks. Hither the prince hastened along a familiar line of road, and, seizing the post of vantage, lay waiting in the traitorous woods.

Meantime, in the halls of Heaven, Latona's daughter addressed fleet Opis, one of her maiden sisterhood and sacred band, and opened her lips in these sad accents:

'Ah, maiden, Camilla is marching to the cruel war, and vainly she girds our arms upon her, – Camilla, whom I loved as none besides! For this is no new love that has come upon Diana, and stirred her heart with sweet thrill and sudden! When, driven from his realm through hatred of his tyrant power, Metabus turned from Privernum's immemorial town, he took with him his infant babe to share his exile, as he fled through the midmost battles of war, and, from her mother's name Casmilla, called her – with light change – Camilla. He, carrying her before him on his breast, sought the long mountain-ridges of solitary forest, while on every side pressed angry javelins, and hovering clouds of Volscian soldiery encircled him. And, lo, midway in his flight, Amasenus was foaming in flood over the summit of his banks: so fierce a rain had burst from the clouds. He, in act to breast the stream, was checked by love for his babe and dread for that dear burden. And, as in spirit he pondered every course, suddenly his unwilling resolve was made! In his strong hand haply he bore a huge spear, in warrior mode, all solid with knotted and fire-tempered oak: to this he affixed his child, encased in bark of the forest cork, and bound her fairly to the centre of the shaft; then, poising it in his giant hand, thus cried to the heavens: "O gracious queen, dweller in the woods, Latonian maid, this babe a father's voice devotes to thy service! Thine is this earliest weapon she holds, flying – thy suppliant – through the air from the enemy's hand. Goddess, I adjure thee, receive for thine own this little child, whom now I commit to the uncertain breeze!" He said, and, with arm drawn back, launched the whirling lance: the waters shrieked, and over the racing river poor Camilla fled on the strident steel. But Metabus, now that a great band pressed closer upon him, sprang into the stream, and, the victory achieved, plucked spear and maid – his gift to Trivia – from out the green sward. Him no cities received to their hearths, nor to the shelter of their walls; nor would that fierce soul have brooked submission: on the shepherds' lorn hills he lived out his life! There amid brakes and tangled coverts, he nurtured his daughter at the breast of a herded mare on the wild sustenance of her milk, draining the teats into her tender lips. And, soon as she had begun to plant the footsteps of her baby feet, he armed her hands with trenchant javelin, and hung bow and shafts from her infant shoulder. In lieu of gold to bind her tresses, in lieu of the long mantling robe, the skin of a tiger slain drooped from her crown and down her back. Even then she flung her childish spears from that tender hand, whirled the smooth-thonged sling round her head, and struck down the crane of Strymon or the snowy swan. In the Tyrrhene towns full many a mother has sought her for her son in vain: content with Diana alone, unsullied she cherishes the undying love of arms and maidenhood! I would she had not been swept away in this tide of war, nor striven to smite the Teucrians: so had she now been dear to me, and one of my sister-train! But since the pangs of doom are hard upon her, go, Nymph of mine, glide from the empyrean, and repair to the Latin borders, where, under boding star, they join the disastrous fray. Take these, and draw from my quiver the avenging shaft: by it let the foe – Trojan or Italian alike – whose wound shall violate that conse-crated flesh, pay me blood for blood! Then, in sheltering cloud, I will bear her piteous clay and her unspoiled arms to sepulture and lay her again in her native earth.' She said, and Opis shot hurtling down through the light airs of heaven, the black whirl-wind shrouding her form.

But meantime the Trojan powers neared the walls, with the Etruscan captains and all their mounted array marshalled into squadrons according to their tale of men. Over all the plain neighed prancing horses, veering hither and thither as they fought against the tight-drawn rein: the iron field bristled far and wide with spears, and the champaign blazed with lifted arms. Nor less, in counter-menace, Messapus and the fleet Latians, and Coras with his brother, and maid Camilla's squadron, rose into view upon the plain in adverse lines, with vibrant javelins and spears far-extended from backdrawn hands: and the marching of men and the neighing of steeds grew hot and furious. And now either advancing host had halted within the cast of a spear: with sudden cry they dashed forth, spurring their frantic chargers; like snowflakes the frequent javelins showered from all hands, and the heavens were veiled in shade. Instant Tyrrhenus and fierce Aconteus charged with utmost effort of levelled spears, and closed in the first great thunderous crash, so that the chest of either horse broke and shattered on opposing chest. Like bolted thunder or ponderous mass hurled from some engine of war, Aconteus was flung precipitate far away, and scattered his life to the winds.

Straight confusion seized the embattled lines; the Latins broke, and, throwing their shields behind them, galloped to the city walls. The Trojans gave chase, Asilas leading the vanward bands. And now they approached the gates, when the Latins raised their battle-cry again, and turned their coursers' facile necks, while the pursuers fled, and retreated far as they might, with slackened rein. As when ocean, advancing with alternate flood, now dashes to earth, flings its wave high over the rocks in foam, and drenches the extreme sands with its crested surge; now flees racing back, drawing the spinning stones in its reabsorbent tide, and with ebbing waters quits the strand: – even so the Tuscans twice drove the routed Rutules to their city; twice, repelled, glanced back and slung their protecting shields behind them! But when, closing for the third encounter, their whole hosts stood interlocked and man marked man, then in truth rose the moans of the dying, and arms, and bodies, and stricken horses mingled with butchered riders, weltered in deep pools of blood; and the bitter fray surged high. Orsilochus flung his lance at Remulus' steed – its lord he quailed to face! – and left the steel lodged beneath the ear. At the blow the charger reared frantic, and, under the intolerable wound, lifted his chest and flung his feet high: Remulus, unseated, rolled on earth. Catillus brought low Iollas, and Herminius, giant in courage, giant in body and arms: – bare that head with the yellow hair, bare those shoulders (wounds had no terrors!), and bare the great frame that challenged the steel! Through his ample shoulders the driven spear came quivering, and, piercing through, bent him double with agony. Everywhere the red blood flowed; conflicting swords dealt slaughter, and men sought a glorious death by wounds!

But amid the thickest carnage, fierce as the Amazon, raged Camilla, the quiver at her back and one breast bared for the fray;

and now the tough javelins rained from her hand, now, with unwearied arm, she snatched a mighty twy-bill; while from her shoulder rang the bow – Diana's armament. Nay, were she ever driven back in retreat, she turned her bow, and, fugitive, yet sped her shafts! Around stood her chosen friends, maiden Larina, and Tulla, and Tarpeia shaking her brazen axe – Italians all, whom high-souled Camilla herself chose, to add lustre to her glory, true servants in peace and war. Such the Amazons of Thrace, when they spurn Thermodon's icy stream and war in painted arms, or round Hippolyte or when grim Penthesilea returns in her car; and, amid wild tumultuous shrieks, the women-warriors rave exultant with crescent-shields!

Whom first, whom last, dread maid, did thy steel lay low? How many a bleeding frame didst thou stretch dying on earth? First Euneus, Clytius' son; for, as he fronted her, she gored his unharnessed breast with the long spear of pine! Vomiting streams of blood he fell, bit the ensanguined earth, and, dying, writhed upon his wound. Then Liris, and Pagasus above him. Headlong and side by side they fell, – the one, while, flung from his stabbed horse, he gathered up the reins; the other, while he came to the rescue and stretched a weaponless hand to his falling friend. Amastrus, Hippotas' son, she sent to crown the tale; then, pressing on the rout, overtook with distant spear both Tereus and Harpalycus, Demophoon and Chromis; while, for every hurtling dart sped from her maiden hand, a warrior of Phrygia bled. At distance Ornytus, mighty hunter, rode, strangely dight, on Apulian steed: the hide stripped from a bullock draped his broad shoulders in the fray, a wolf's wide-grinning jaws and white fangs decked his head, and a rustic pike armed his hand; himself he moved in the midmost throng, a full head taller than all. Him she caught, – a light task, when the column fled, – pierced him, and thus, with fierce heart, taunted the fallen: 'Tuscan, and didst thou dream thou wert chasing wild-beasts in thy forests? The day is come that shall refute Etruria's vaunts by a woman's sword. Yet shalt thou carry no slight renown to the shades of thy fathers – that thou didst fall under Camilla's steel!'

Followed Orsilochus and Butes, two Teucrians of giant mould! But Butes she transfixed from the rear, between corselet and helm, where his neck gleamed white as he sat in the saddle, and the shield hung on his left arm. Orsilochus she fled, and, wheeling in wide orbit, baffled him, took the inner circle, and pursued the pursuer; then, rising to greater height, drove her strong axe with reiterate blow through armour and through bone, though he pleaded mercy with many a prayer: and the warm brain gushed down his face from the wound! Now crossed her path – and paused in terror at the sudden vision! – the warrior son of Aunus of the Apennine, not meanest in Liguria, while Fate allowed him to deceive! He, when he saw that by no speed of foot could he escape the conflict, nor turn aside the pursuant queen, assayed to spin his toils by policy and craft, and so began: 'What unwonted chivalry is thine, if – woman though thou art – thou trustest in thy gallant horse? Resign that means of flight; dare to front me hand to hand on the impartial earth, and gird thee for battle on foot: full soon shalt thou know on whom the penalty of vain-glory shall fall!' He said; but she, flaming infuriate with fierce resentment, passed her horse to a comrade, and stood facing him in equal arms, unterrified and on foot, with naked sword and maiden shield. But the youth, deeming his wiles had conquered, fled on the instant and galloped fugitive away, with rein reversed, and iron heel goring his fleet charger. 'False Ligurian, vainly elated with misproud heart, bootlessly has thy trickster brain had recourse to thy native arts; nor shall thy fraud convey thee unscathed to lying Aunus!' Thus the maiden, and with fire-swift feet ran crossing the horse; then, seizing the bridle, met him face to face, and exacted vengeance from her enemy's blood: – lightly as the falcon, bird of prophecy, stoops from a towering cliff, and overtakes on the wing some dove, high-soaring amid the clouds, then holds her in the clutch and tears out her heart with crooked talons, while blood and rent plumage come falling from the sky.

But not with unseeing eye the Sire of gods and men sat viewing the scene, high-throned on Olympus' summit: he roused Tyrrhenian Tarchon to the fierce fray, and woke his ire by no gentle stings! Therefore, amid the carnage and wavering columns, Tarchon spurred, and goaded his ranks with manifold rebuke, calling each warrior by his name and rallying the routed to battle:

'O hearts that will never feel – men that are ever sluggards! – Etruscans, what panic, what utter cowardice has come upon your souls? A woman drives you in disarray, and breaks these ranks! To what end bear we the steel? or why these futile blades in our right hands? But no laggards ye in love's midnight fray, nor when the curved pipe has proclaimed the Bacchic rout! Look to the feast and the cups on the laden board (this your passion, this your delight!), till the seer's auspicious voice announce the sacrifice and the fat victim call you to the deep groves!' So saying, he spurred his charger into the throng, ready himself to bleed, and dashed storm-like upon Venulus, gripped the foe with his right, tore him from his steed, and bore him off before his saddle bow with fiery speed and giant strength! A shout went up to heaven, and all the Latins turned their eyes. Like fire Tarchon flew over the plain, the arms and the man within his grasp; then broke the steel from the head of his enemy's lance, and searched the unguarded flesh where he might implant the fatal stroke: he, in counter-struggle, held the hand from off his throat, and foiled force by strength. And as when a tawny eagle, high-soaring, flies with a captured serpent, and her feet bind it fast, and her talons cling firm-fixed; but the wounded snake rolls his sinuous coils, horrent with erected scales, and hisses from his mouth, rising and towering; she, undismayed, presses her reluctant foe with crooked beak, while her pinions beat the air: – even so Tarchon bore his prey in triumph from out the Tiburtian line! Fired by their captain's example and success, the sons of Lydia charged. Then Arruns, the claimed of Fate, circled in the van of fleet Camilla with javelin and deep-pondered guile, and explored how occasion might most lightly be won. Wherever the infuriate maid rode amid the ranks, there Arruns crept up, and silently tracked her steps: wherever she returned in triumph and withdrew from out the foe, there stealthily he bent his rapid reins. Now this approach he assayed, now that, traversed the whole circuit on every hand, and, remorseless, shook his destined spear.

It chanced that Chloreus – priest, once, and holy, on Cybelus' peaks – glittered, far-resplendent in Phrygian arms, and spurred his foaming charger, which a gold-clasped skin covered with feathery brazen scales. Himself he shone in foreign purple of darkened hue, and from Lycian horn sped his Cretan shafts: a golden bow was on his shoulders, a golden helm on his sacred head: his saffron scarf and its rustling folds of linen were gathered into a knot by yellow gold; and his tunic and barbaric hose were broidered by the needle. Him, – whether in hope to affix his Trojan arms to her temple-gates, or to follow the chase, dight in his captive gold, – the maiden, with unforeseeing heart, pursued alone out of all the conflicting war, and swept, reckless, throughout the ranks, flaming with a woman's passion for prey and spoils: when, the moment gained at last, Arruns sped his lance from the ambush, and thus prayed aloud to Heaven:

'Apollo, highest of gods, guardian of holy Soracte, – in whose
worship we are first, in whose honour the blazing heap of pine is
fed, while we, thy votaries, walk faith-supported through the fire
amid many a living ember! – grant, Sire omnipotent, that my
steel may cancel this our shame! I seek no prize of war, no trophy
from the defeated maid, nor any spoils: exploits to come shall
bring me fame. Let but this dire scourge fall vanquished beneath
my stroke, and inglorious I will return to the cities of my
fathers!'

Phoebus heard, and in thought vouchsafed that half his vow
should prosper: half he scattered to the fleet winds. That he
should overthrow Camilla and strike her down in sudden death,
he yielded to his prayer: that his high motherland should view his
return, he granted not; and the storm merged his accents in the
southern gales. Thus, when, sped from his hand, the lance hur-
tled through the air, each eager Volscian mind, each eye, was
turned upon the queen. She alone heeded neither air, nor sound,
nor weapon descending from the skies, till the spear winged its
way, and, fixed beneath the bare breast, drank, deep-driven, her
maiden blood. In wildered haste her companions ran and lifted
their falling queen. More terrified than all, Arruns fled, fear mingling with his joy; and no more he dared to trust his lance, nor to
front the maiden's arms. And as the felon wolf – when he has
slain a shepherd or great steer – ere the hostile steel takes up the
pursuit, plunges incontinent into the shelter of the high hills,
afar from the ways of men, and knows the boldness of his deed,
and, drooping his craven tail, whips it beneath his belly, and
races to the woods: – even so Arruns rushed, unmanned, from
the view, and, contented to escape, was lost amid the weaponed
throng! She, with dying hand, strained at the spear: but, lodged
by her ribs, the pointed steel stood between the bones, deep
within the wound. Bloodless she sank; her eyes sank, chill in
death; and the once radiant hue deserted her cheeks. Then, as
her life ebbed, she turned to Acca, one of her maiden company
and loyal above the rest, sole participant in Camilla's cares, then
so spoke: 'Thus far, sister Acca, have I availed: now the cruel
wound undoes me, and all grows dim and dark around. Hie thee
hence, and bear my latest message to Turnus: let him replace me
in the fray and ward the Trojans from the town. And now, fare
thee well!' And, with these words, she dropped the reins, and
sank perforce to earth. Then, as she grew chill in death, little by
little she freed herself from all the burden of her clay, drooping

her languid neck and that head which Fate had touched: the steel fell from her grasp, and, moaning, the indignant life fled beneath the gloom! – Then, in truth, an infinite clamour rose striking the golden stars: on Camilla's fall the fray waxed hotter, and in serried battalions there charged at once the full Teucrian powers, and the Tyrrhene captains, and Evander's Arcadian horse.

But Opis, Trivia's sentinel, had long sat high-throned on the mountain-crests, and, unterrified, surveyed the battle. And when from far she discerned Camilla, thus ruthlessly done to death amid the din of raging combatants, she sighed and so spoke from the depths of her heart: 'Alas, poor girl! too, too cruel the penalty thou hast paid for assaying to attack the Teucrians with the sword! And naught has it availed thee, in thy day of desolation, to have served Dian in the woods and borne our quiver upon thy shoulder! Yet not, in this last hour of death, has thy queen left thee unhonoured; nor shall thy doom be unsung on earth, nor thyself brook the fame of the unavenged. For be he who it may, whose wound has profaned thy flesh, – his guilty blood shall pay the forfeit!' Under the mountain-height stood a vast tomb of mounded earth, embosomed in shadowing oaks, where Dercennus slept, Laurentum's whilom king. Here first, on rapid pinion, the goddess alighted, all beautiful, and gazed from the hillock's summit in quest of Arruns. Then, as she beheld him refulgent in arms and puffed with vanity: 'Why,' she cried, 'wilt thou stray so far? Turn thy step hither – come hither to thy doom, and receive the overdue reward for Camilla slain! Shall even such as thou bleed by Dian's shafts?' – Thus she of Thrace, and drew the fleet arrow from her golden quiver, stretched the bow with grim intent, and drew it afar, till the curving ends met each with other, and at length, with levelled hands, she touched the pointed steel with her left, her breast with her right and the string. Straight, at one and the selfsame moment, Arruns heard the whistling of the dart and the rustling of the air, and the iron lodged in his breast. Him, gasping and moaning his last, his oblivious comrades left on the unknown dust of the plain, while Opis winged her departure to Olympus the skies!

First, their mistress reft, fled Camilla's light-accoutred horse: the Rutulians fled in rout, bold Atinas fled, and scattered captains and devastated troops sought safety, and turning their chargers, raced to the walls. Not a man availed to sustain in arms the death-dealing onslaught of Troy or to abide the brunt, but, on languid shoulders, retreating they bore their slackened bows, and galloping hooves of four-footed steeds shook the crumbling champaign. Dust rolled to the ramparts in black and turbulent clouds, and, from their watch-towers, matrons with beaten breasts uplifted the cry of women to the stars of the firmament. On those, who, at full speed, first broke through the opening gates, followed multitudinous foes, mingling with their ranks: nor might they escape a piteous death; but, on verge of the threshold, within their ancestral walls, and amid the shelter of their homes, they were pierced, and sobbed away their lives. Part closed the gates, nor dared to open to their comrades, nor to receive the suppliants within the town: and a woeful carnage arose, of them that guarded the entry in arms, and them that dashed upon their arms! Shut out before eye and visage of their weeping parents, part rolled headlong into the moats before the pursuant ruin: part, with frantic rein, charged blindly against the gates and the firm-barred doorways. Even the matrons on the walls, in hot rivalry – true love of country their guide, Camilla before their eyes! – hurled down spears from eager hands, and, in fiery haste, did the work of the steel with poles of stubborn oak and seared stakes, and burned to be first to die for their city!

Meantime the bitter tidings filled Turnus' ear in the woods, and Acca brought to the prince her tale of giant turmoil: – the Volscian lines destroyed, Camilla fallen, the enemy pressing his assault, sweeping all before him in victorious war, and panic already driving to the walls. He, infuriate – and thus the stern will of Jove required! – abandoned the ambuscaded hills and quitted the rough woods. Scarce had he passed from view and issued upon the plain, when father Aeneas entered the unwatched defile, surmounted the ridge, and marched out from the shadowy forest. Thus both at speed hastened with their full powers to the ramparts, not long the distance between: and at one moment Aeneas descried afar the dust-smoking plains, and saw the Laurentine hosts, and Turnus was ware of dread Aeneas in arms, and heard the coming of their feet and the snorting of their steeds. And in that hour they had begun the fray and tried the issue of battle, had not roseate Phoebus begun to lave his weary coursers in the Iberian flood, and to restore the night in place of the waning day. – Thus they encamped before the town, and fortified their ramparts.

BOOK XII

WHEN TURNUS SAW the Latins broken and fainting in War's adversity, saw his promise now claimed, and himself the cynosure of all eyes, he burned with heart yet more implacable, and his pride surged yet higher. As, in Punic fields, the lion, whose breast the hunters have stricken with heavy wound, rallies at last to battle, and, exultant, bids the hirsute muscles start from his neck, snaps unterrified the brigand's implanted spear, and roars from lips incarnadined: – even so, as Turnus kindled, his vehemence grew! Then thus he bespoke the king, and, storm-like, began: 'In Turnus lies no impediment! it needs not that craven Troy should retract her word and renounce her pact: I go to the encounter! Bring the vessels, sire, and solemnize the terms of truce. Either with this arm I will hurl the Dardan renegade from Asia down to hell – let Latium sit by and watch! – and with unaided sword cancel our nation's shame, or let him rule where he has conquered, and Lavinia's hand be his!'

To whom Latinus, with soul unruffled: 'Great-hearted prince, the higher thy fierce courage towers, the more heedfully it befits that I should counsel and anxiously balance every chance! Thou hast the realms of Daunus thy sire, thou hast many a town that thy hand has captured, and Latinus has gold and a generous heart. There are unwed maidens else in Latium and our Laurentine fields, and they of no unhonoured line. Grant me – the mask removed – to make this ungentle saying plain; and take this to thy thought no less: Without sin I might not ally my child to any of her old-time wooers – so sang the inspired voice of both gods and men! Conquered by my love for thee, conquered by our kindred blood, and the tears of my mourning queen, I severed all bonds, snatched the betrothed from her bridegroom, and drew the unrighteous sword! From that day, Turnus, thou seest what perils, what wars, pursue me – what calamities thyself art first to suffer. Twice vanquished in the stricken field, hardly we protect the hopes of Italy behind our battlements: the streams of Tiber are yet warm with our blood, and the far-spread plains yet white with our bones. Why do I drift with every wind? What madness works on my brain? If, with Turnus dead, I stand prepared to welcome their alliance, why do I not annul the conflict while Turnus lives? What shall our Rutulian kin, what the rest of Italy, say, if (Fortune refute my word!) I betray thee to death, while thou suest for my daughter and our espousals? Bethink thee of war's inconstancy: pity thy white-haired father, who now sits sorrowing in his native Ardea, far-estranged from thee!'

But not all his words could assuage Turnus' passion: it swelled yet higher, and the leech's touch lent fury to the fever! Soon as he found voice, he thus began: 'The care, gracious sire, which thou bearest for me, for me – I entreat thee – resign, and suffer me to purchase honour, though it be at the price of death. We, too, my king, scatter spears and no weakling steel from our right hand; and blood flows when our sword, too, has smitten! No goddess-mother will be at his side to enshroud in mist her fugitive son with woman's wile, and conceal herself in traitorous shadows!'

But the queen, dismayed by the new terms of conflict, wept, and clung to her fiery son, resolved to die: 'Turnus, by these my tears, by any reverence for Amata that yet may touch thy soul – thou art now our only hope, the solace of my joyless years – the honour and sovereignty of Latinus are in thy hands, and on thy shoulders rests all the incumbent weight of our sinking house, – one guerdon I entreat: forbear to join encounter with Troy! Whatever hazards await thee in this thy conflict, await me also, Turnus: with thee I will quit this hated day, nor look – a captive queen – on Aeneas wedded to my child!' With burning cheeks bathed in tears, Lavinia heard her mother's voice; deep blushes kindled their fires, and mantled in her glowing face. As when the artist has stained ivory of Ind with sanguine purple, or white lilies are red with many an intermingled rose – such the hues that her maiden countenance revealed! He, lost in love's turmoil, fixed his gaze upon her, then, fired yet more for the fray, shortly addressed Amata: 'Mother mine, give me not tears, I pray thee, nor thus sad omens, to attend me as I march to the strife of relentless war: for Turnus is not free to delay his doom. Idmon, be thou my herald, and bear to the Phrygian tyrant this message that shall like him not: So soon as the morrow's Dawn shall ride blushing through the skies above her encrimsoned wheels, let him forbear to urge the Teucrians against the Rutules: Rutulia and Troy – let their swords have peace; with our own blood let us decide the war, and Lavinia be wooed and won in yonder lists!

So said, he rushed within the palace; then called for his steeds, and with quickening joy surveyed them, as they neighed before his face – those steeds that Orithyia herself gave in guerdon to

Pilumnus, to outshine the snows and outstrip the winds. Around stood the eager charioteers, caressing their breasts with hollowed palms and combing their flowing manes. Next he threw upon his shoulders the hauberk rugged in golden scales and pallid orichalc, and, with the act, adjusted his blade and buckler and the horns of his ruddy crest: – that blade the celestial Lord of Fire had himself wrought for his father Daunus and dipped glowing in the Stygian wave. Then – where, leaning on a giant column, it stood in his central halls – he seized with strong hand his mighty spear, the spoil of Auruncan Actor, and shook it quivering, while he cried: 'O thou, my lance, never false to my call, now – now – is the hour come! Once greatest Actor bore thee, as now the hand of Turnus bears: grant that I may smite down the body of the Phrygian – the woman-man! – that I may tear his corslet and rend it away in this strong hand, and defile in dust his love-locks, curled by the warm iron and dank with myrrh!' Such the frenzy that spurred him on: sparks flashed from all his blazing visage, and flame shot from his angry eyes: – even as a bull, ere the fray begins, raises dread bellowings, and, dashing against some forest-bole, instructs his horn to anger, while his blows defy the gales, or with scattered sand he marks the prelude of battle!

Nor less, meantime, Aeneas, grim in the arms his mother gave, edged his valour and roused himself with the whips of anger, rejoicing that offer of truce abridged the war; then solaced his comrades and the fears of mourning Iulus, expounded the decrees of Fate, and bade an embassage convey his settled answer to king Latinus, and announce the terms of peace.

The risen morn was scarce sprinkling the mountain-peaks with light, what time the coursers of the Sun first rise from the unfathomed flood, and breathe the day from uplifted nostrils, when already Teucrians and Rutulians were preparing the measured plain for conflict beneath the stately city's walls, with hearths in the midst, and turf-clad altars to their common deities. Others were bringing water from the fount and fire, draped in the ritual apron, and with brows wreathed in vervain. Forth marched Ausonia's array, and bands of pikemen came streaming through the crowded gates. From other quarter rushed all the Teucrian and Tyrrhene host, accoutred in steel, as though War's stern encounter called them. Nor less, amid their thousands, the captains glanced here and there in the splendour of gold and purple: Mnestheus of Assaracus' line, gallant Asilas, and Messapus, the tamer of steeds, the Neptune-born. So soon as, at given signal, each had retired to his own ground, they planted their spears in earth and reclined their shields against them. Matrons, eager and uncontained, the old and feeble, and the unweaponed vulgar, took their posts on tower and roof, while yet others stood by the frowning gates.

But Juno, gazing forth from the summit of that eminence which is now styled *Alban*, – then a hill unnamed, unhonoured and inglorious, – viewed the plain, and the twin hosts of Laurentum and Troy, and Latinus' town. Instant, goddess to goddess, she spoke to Turnus' sister, mistress of lakes and sounding rivers – such honour Jove, throned in the empyrean, made consecrate to her, in recompense for her reft maidenhood: 'Nymph, glory of the stream, best-beloved of our heart, thou knowest how I have preferred thee alone before all that ever ascended to the ingrate couch of high-souled Jove, and how full willingly I have yielded thee a place in Heaven: learn, Juturna, what sorrow is thine – nor censure me! Where Fortune seemed to permit, and the Three allowed the star of Latium to prosper, I have shielded Turnus and thy city: now I behold the prince ranged against a destiny that is greater than his; and the hour of fate and the enemy's stroke draw nigh. This battle, this truce, mine eyes cannot brook. Do thou, if thou darest aught of avail for thy brother's sake, proceed: it is thy part. Perchance a kindlier lot may yet attend the unhappy! Scarce had she said, when the tears gushed from Juturna's eyes, and thrice and four times she smote on her fair breast. 'This is no season for tears,' cried Saturn's daughter; 'hasten, and – if any mode be found – snatch thy brother from death; or wake the battle again, and strike the compacted league from their grasp. It is I that warrant thee to dare!' Thus having counselled, she left her wavering and stricken in soul by the cruel wound.

Meantime the kings came forth: – Latinus' ample frame drawn in four-horse car, his brows resplendent in a diadem of twice six golden rays, emblem of his ancestral sun; while Turnus rode behind a snowy pair, waving in his hand two spears pointed with broad steel. On the other hand came father Aeneas, source of the Roman line, flaming in starry shield and celestial arms, and at his side Ascanius, second hope of queenly Rome, moving from the camp; while the white-stoled priest had brought the young of a bristled boar with an unshorn ewe of two summers, and set his flock by the burning altars. With gaze turned to the orient sun, they sprinkled the salted corn from their hand, marked the foreheads of the cattle with the knife, and from goblets poured libation on the altar-stones.

Then, with drawn brand, good Aeneas preferred his prayer: 'Now be the Sun witness to my call, and this Earth, for whose sake I have availed to support such weight of woe, and the almighty Sire, and thou his consort, Saturnian queen (now – my prayer is – now at last of kindlier soul!); and thou, famed Mavors, who governest all battles under thy lordly sway; and the Fountains and Rivers I invoke, and the deity of the high Empyrean, and the powers that tenant the azure sea: – if chance will that victory shall fall to Ausonian Turnus, we assent that the vanquished shall retire to Evander's city; Iulus shall quit your soil, not ever in days to come shall the people of Aeneas return in rebellious arms, or assail this realm with the sword. But if Victory shall make the field our own – as I rather deem, and as I pray the heavenly will may rather confirm! – I shall not bid Italy stoop beneath the Teucrian sway, nor seek I the crown for my head: under equal law let each unconquered nation enter on everlasting league! I will prescribe but the gods and their worship: my father Latinus shall bear the sword, and bear his wonted sceptre. For me, the Trojans shall raise my city-walls, and Lavinia lend her name to the town!'

Thus first Aeneas: and thus Latinus followed in order, with eyes uplifted to heaven, and hand outstretched to the stars: 'By the same powers I swear, Aeneas – by Earth, and Sea, and Stars, and Leto's twin progeny, by Janus of the double face, by the might of the nether gods, and the shrines of cruel Dis: may the Father hear my words, whose bolted thunder sanctions treaty! I touch the altars, I attest the flames and sacred powers betwixt me and thee: on the part of Italy no lapse of time shall break this peace and this league, let the issue fall as it may; nor shall any violence bow my will, not though, in universal deluge, it spill earth into ocean and blend heaven with hell, – even as this sceptre' (for a sceptre by chance his right hand bore) 'shall never again be dressed in light foliage and put forth branch and shade, since once in the forest it was hewn from the nether stem, and, motherless, resigned its verdant sprays beneath the steel – once a tree: now the workman's hand has sheathed it in fair bronze and given it to the Latin sires to bear!' With such interchange of pledges they confirmed the treaty, full in view of the princes: then slew the doomed creatures above the flame, tore out the entrails while they still breathed, and piled the altars with laden trenchers.

But to the Rutulians the battle had long seemed unequal, and their breasts throbbed with conflicting impulse: and now all the more, when they beheld the combatants at closer view. Their mood was quickened by Turnus, as he advanced with quiet step and humbly adored the altar with downcast eye, – quickened by his wasted cheeks, and the pallor of his youthful frame! Soon as his sister Juturna marked that these whispers spread and the hearts of the multitude were wavering and hesitant, into the midmost ranks, in feigned semblance of Camers – great his ancestral house, lustrous the renown of his father's worth, and dauntless himself in arms! – into the midmost ranks she flung herself, with no dubious intent, sowed a motley harvest of rumour, and so cried: Think ye not shame, Rutulians, to hazard a single life for thus many and thus brave? In numbers – or in might? – are we less than their peers? Behold, all Troy is here with Arcady, and Etruria's fated powers, bent upon Turnus' doom. If but the half of us charge, scarce may each man find a foe! He, indeed, shall ascend on the wings of fame to that Heaven for whose altars he vows himself to the death, and shall live and move on the lips of men: we, our country lost, shall obey perforce our haughty lords – we, who on this day sat listless upon the field!'

More and yet more her words incensed the warriors' resolve, and a murmur crept along their lines. Even the Laurentines, even the Latians, felt that change; and they who of late hoped only repose from battle and safety for their fortunes, now yearned for the sword, prayed that the league might be annulled, and pitied Turnus' unjust fate! To these Juturna added another, and more potent, spur: in the heights of heaven she gave a sign, than which none more powerful blinded their Italian hearts with lying miracle. For, winging the crimson sky, Jove's golden-hued bird was chasing the fowls of the strand and the noisy rout of their plumed array, when, suddenly stooping to the waves, he bore off in felon claws a swan, passing fair. The Italians stood alert, and – wondrous to see! – all the birds turned clamorously from flight, their pinions obscuring heaven, and in massed cloud pursued their foe through the air, till, overborne by their assault and overweighted by his prey, he yielded the struggle, flung the victim from his eagle-talons into the stream, and fled far within the clouds!

Then, in truth, the Rutulians hailed the omen with acclaim, and threw up their hands. And first Tolumnius, the augur: 'This it was, this,' he cried, 'that my vows so often have sought! I receive the sign, and acknowledge the hand of Heaven. With me – even me – at your head, grip the steel, oh hapless people, whom yon rapacious alien affrights with his battle like weakling birds, and by the strong hand harries your coasts. He, too, will take to flight and spread his sails far out to the deep. Do ye, with single soul, close your squadrons, and defend with the sword your ravished king!' He said, and, running forward, cast his spear against the confronting foe: the strident cornel sped hurtling on, and cleft the air in no dubious course. Instant upon the deed followed a wild clamour, and all their ranks were disarrayed, and the tumult fired their hearts. The spear flew on, where it chanced that nine brothers of goodly frame stood opposite – those nine, whom one faithful Tuscan wife had borne to Arcadian Gylippus. On one of these – a comely youth in shining arm – it lit, hard by the waist, where the sewn belt chafes upon the belly and the clasp bites the juncture of either side. Through his ribs it drove, and flung him prone on the yellow sand! But his brethren – a gallant band, and kindled by grief – drew their blades or snatched at the missile steel, and rushed blindly on. In counter-charge ran the Laurentine columns; while, in adverse tide, streamed Trojans, and men from Agylla's town, and Arcadians with painted shields. Thus fierce the one passion in every breast – to decide the issue by the sword! Incontinent they stripped the altars; the storm of weapons passed glooming over all the sky, and the iron rain fell fast. Altar-fires and wine-bowls were swept away; and Latinus himself fled, bearing back his defeated gods from the barren league. Others reined their cars, or flung themselves at a bound upon their steeds, and made in with unsheathed brands.

Messapus, aflame to break the truce, spurred with threatening mien full against Tuscan Aulestes, a king and wearing the ensign of a king: he, in precipitate retreat, stumbled – luckless wight! – amid the altars that stood in his path behind, and fell upon head and shoulders. Lance in hand, Messapus flew up like fire, and, towering on his charger, smote heavily down with the beaming spear, as he pleaded and pleaded again; then cried: 'The blow has sped: the high gods have gained a better victim! The Italians ran swarming round, and stripped his warm limbs. – As Ebysus came, in act to wound, Corynaeus fronted him, snatched a smouldering brand from the altar, and dashed the flames in his face: the great beard caught the blaze, and a stench of burning arose. Then, pursuing his blow, he grasped the hair of the bewildered foe in his left, bent him to earth by the pressure of his knee, and so struck him in the side with stark blade. Podalirius, in chase of shepherd Alsus, as he rushed through a rain of darts in the van, was hard upon him with imminent, naked steel; when he, swinging back his axe, sundered brow and chin full in front, and bathed the armour in broad streams of gushing blood. Ungentle rest and iron sleep sank heavily on his eyes, and his lids closed to eternal night.

But good Aeneas stood with weaponless hand outstretched and head unhelmed, calling loudly on his host: 'Whither will ye rush? What means this swelling tide of discord? Oh, bridle your ire! Truce is already sealed, and all its terms fixed: the right of combat is mine alone. Give me way, and resign your terrors; this hand shall confirm the league; these rites even now make Turnus mine!' While yet he spoke, while the accents were still on his lips, lo, an arrow came flying to him on strident wing – by what hand driven, in what blast sped, none knows, nor who (whether chance or deity!) conferred that glory on Rutulia: the lustre of that high deed is dark, and no man made his vaunt in the wounding of Aeneas!

When Turnus descried Aeneas withdrawing from the lines, and the captains in confusion, he burned with sudden hope and ardent, called for his steeds and called for his arms, leapt agile and triumphant into the car, and set his hand to the reins. Many a stout warrior-frame he consigned to doom or his flying course, many a man he left rolling in the throes of death, crushing their ranks beneath his wheels, or flinging their captured spears on the fugitive rout. Even as, when he whirls along the stream of icy Hebrus, red Mavors thunders on his shield and gives rein to his frantic steeds, waking War: they, on the open plain, fly before the South-wind and the Zephyr, while farthest Thrace moans under the trampling of their feet, and around him whirl the faces of black Fear, and Anger, and Treachery, attendant on the god: – such was Turnus, as eagerly through the mid fray he urged his smoking coursers, spurning – woeful sight – the hostile slain, while the racing hooves scattered bloody dews, and trampled on gore and commingled sand! And now he had delivered Sthenelus to death, and Thamyrus and Pholus, that and this in close encounter, the first from far; and from far the two Imbrasidae, Glaucus and Lades, whom Imbrasus himself had nurtured in

Lycia and equipped in equal arms, whether to join battle hand
against hand, or, mounted, to outstrip the winds.

Elsewhere Eumedes rushed into the midmost battle, Eumedes,
the war-famed scion of ancient Dolon, – in name his grandsire
come again, in heart and hand his sire of old, who dared to claim
the chariot of Peleus' son for his guerdon, did he approach the
Danaan camp as spy: but with far other guerdon the seed of
Tydeus requited his emprize, and now his hope aspires no more
to Achilles' steeds! Him when Turnus descried from far on the
open plain, first hurling his fleet javelin in pursuit through the
void expanse, he stayed his twin coursers, leapt down from the
car, and descended on the fallen, dying man; then, with foot
planted on his neck, wrenched the blade from his right, dyed its
lustrous edge deep in his throat, and with such taunt crowned his
blow: 'Lie, Trojan! – lie and measure those fields and that Hesperia which thou soughtest in war: such the meed that falls to
them who dare to tempt me with the sword; thus do they found
their city-walls.' With flung spear he sent Asbytes to join him in
death, and Chloreus, and Sybaris, and Dares, and Thersilochus,
and Thymoetes, flung over the neck of his stumbling horse. And
as the blast of the Edonian North sounds on the deep Aegean,
chasing the rollers to the beach, and the clouds flee through
heaven before the incumbent gales: so, where Turnus cleft his
path, the columns yielded and the battled lines turned to flight:
the impulse bore him on, and the breeze that met the car shook
his streaming plume. Phegeus brooked not his onset, nor the fury
of his pride: he flung himself before the chariot and with his
right hand swung aside the jaws of the careering steeds, as they
foamed upon the bit. While he was dragged pendent from the
yoke, the broad lance found his unguarded frame, pierced,
implanted, the double corselet, and grazed the surface of his flesh
with slight wound. Yet he, with opposing buckler, turned and
made upon his foe, seeking succour from the naked blade; when
the wheel and the axle, spinning in forward course, flung him
headlong and rolled him on the plain, and Turnus, with follow-
ing sword, severed his head betwixt the nethermost helm and the
breastplate's upper marge, and left the trunk to cumber the sand.

And while Turnus' conquering hand thus spread death upon
the plains, Mnestheus, meanwhile, and loyal Achates, with Ascanius at their side, lodged Aeneas within the camp, bleeding and
with alternate step supported on his tall lance. Raging, he strove
to pluck forth the dart with its broken shaft, and demanded the

speediest mode of cure, bidding them cut the wound with broad sword, tear apart the weapon's ambuscade to its depths, and send him again to battle! And now Iapyx, Iasus' son, was come, dearest of men to Phoebus; to whom once, under the poignant spell of love, Apollo offered his own arts, his own powers – his augury, his lyre, and his fleet arrows. He, to prolong the span of his sire who lay sick to death, chose rather to know the virtue of herbs and the practice of healing, and to meditate inglorious a silent art! Bitterly impatient, Aeneas stood propped on his mighty lance, with a great concourse of warriors and weeping Iulus at his side, himself unmoved by their tears. The aged man, his robe rolled back and girt high in the Healer's mode, strove much with the leechcraft of his hand and the potent herbs of Phoebus – in vain: in vain his hand assayed the dart and his gripping pincers grasped at the steel! No fortune guided his course, Apollo lent not counsel nor aid: and higher and higher the dread alarm surged over the plains, and disaster stood nearer now. Already they saw heaven beset with dust: the horsemen came riding up, and shafts were falling thickly in the midst of the camp; while starward rose the woeful clamour of battling men and men that fell under the iron doom of War.

In that hour, Venus, heart-stricken by her son's unmerited anguish, plucked with maternal hand dittany from Cretan Ida, a stem with downy leaves and crowned by a lustrous flower; not strange that herb to the wild goat when the fleet arrows have pierced his flank! This Venus brought to earth, her face veiled in obscure halo: this, secretly infused, she steeped in the river-water outpoured in the ewer's glittering brim, then sprinkled the healthful juices of ambrosia and fragrant panacea. With that water ancient Iapyx laved the wound, nor knew what he did: and suddenly all pain fled from the body, and the blood was stanched deep in the wound. And now, obsequious to his hand, the shaft fell out under no constraint, and the hero's new-born strength returned to its whilom vigour. 'Bring him arms with instant speed! Why linger ye?' cried Iapyx, foremost to incense their spirit against the enemy. 'This comes not by mortal aid nor by my preceptress art: not this the hand that preserves thee, Aeneas! A greater god works herein, and restores thee to greater deeds.' He, thirsting for battle, had enclosed his thighs in the circling gold, and, loathing delays, stood brandishing his spear. Soon as the shield was adjusted to his side and the corselet to his back, he clasped Ascanius in armed embrace, and, but touching his lips through the helm, thus said: 'Learn valour and true endurance from me, my child, – fortune from others! Now my right hand shall hold thee secure in war, and lead thee through the paths where high honour may be won: thy care be it to remember this, when soon thy years shall have grown to ripeness; and, while thy soul dwells on the example of thy kindred, let Aeneas and Hector – sire and uncle – wake thy prowess!'

So said, he passed through the gates – a mighty man shaking a massy spear. With him Antheus and Mnestheus rushed in serried array, and all the host streamed from the forlorn camp. The plain was a turmoil of blinding dust, and the startled earth quaked under their trampling feet. From an opposing mound Turnus saw their coming: the Ausonians saw, and a chill tremor ran through their very marrow. Before all the Latians else, Juturna heard and knew the sound, and quailed and fled. The prince flew on, and swept his dusk column athwart the open champaign. As when a storm cloud bursts from the stars and sweeps to earth over the mid seas ay me, the swain's prescient heart trembles from far: for it shall wreak ruin on his trees and destruction on his crops, and all things shall be whelmed both far and near! – and in its van fly the winds, wafting the roar to the strand: – such was the Rhoeteian chief as he urged his squadrons full on the foe, and, one and all, they closed their battalions and gathered thickly to his side! Thymbraeus smote ponderous Osiris with the sword, Mnestheus Arcetius: Epulo Achates slew, Ufens Gyas; and Tolumnius himself, the augur, bled, who had first hurled his lance on the enemy's line. The din rose up to heaven, and, routed in turn, the Rutulians gave back in flight along the plain amid clouds of dust. Himself he deigned not to strike the fugitives down in death, nor assailed those who met him fairly upon foot, nor them that bore the lance: Turnus alone he tracked and sought through the gathered gloom – Turnus alone he claimed for battle!

Heart-stricken by such terror, Juturna – warrior-maid – hurled Metiscus, Turnus' charioteer, full betwixt the reins, and left him at distance, fallen from the pole: herself she took his seat and with her own hands guided the flowing reins, wearing all that Metiscus wore – his voice, his frame, and his arms. As a black swallow flits through the ample halls of some wealthy lord and wings her way round his stately courts, gathering her tiny crumbs of food to regale the twitterers in her nest; and now her pinions sound in the vacant colonnades, now round the water-ponds: –

such was Juturna, as she whirled behind her steeds through the enemy's midst, and flew over all with racing chariot, and now here, now there, displayed her brother in triumph, – yet suffered him not to close in battle, but shot far away! Nor less, while he sought encounter, Aeneas threaded the mazy circle, tracking his steps and calling him with mighty voice across the shattered squadrons. But often as his glance was cast on his foe and his foot assayed to match the flight of those winged steeds, so often Juturna swerved with retreating car. Alas, what might he do? Vainly he tossed on inconstant tide, and discordant cares racked his breast with call and counter-call. On him Messapus – whose left hand haply bore two stout shafts tipped with steel – levelled and flung the one with nimble charge and unerring stroke. Aeneas halted, and, sinking on his knee, crouched behind his arms: yet the rapid spear bore his helmet's peak away and smote the topmost plumes from the summit. Then in truth his wrath surged high; and, patience overborne by treachery, he watched steeds and chariot vanish in retreat, then – much adjuring Jove and the altars of the broken truce – plunged at last into their midmost ranks, and, clothed in terrors, moved under the War-god's smile, wreaking a fierce promiscuous carnage and casting loose all reins of passion.

And now what god shall hymn me those woeful deeds, that counterchange of slaughter, and the death of the captains, whom Turnus now – now Troy's hero – drove in their turn over all the plain? King of Heaven, and was it thy will that in thus ruinous shock two nations should close, destined to dwell ·in endless peace? Aeneas, met by the Rutule Sucro (that fray first stayed the Teucrian onslaught!), caught him in the side after brief delay, and, where death comes speediest, drove the stark sword through his ribs and the fabric of his chest. Turnus, in foot-encounter, smote Amycus, hurled from his horse, and his brother Diores – this with long spear as he rushed on, this with the sword-edge – then hung each severed head from his car, and bore them off dripping with sanguine dews. The one sent Talors and Tanais and brave Cethegus down to death, three met at once, and sad Onites, Peridia's child, of the Echionian name: his foe the brothers sent from Lycia and Apollo's fields, and young Menoetes of Arcadia, who shrank from war in vain: round the streams of fish-haunted Lerna, where his cottage stood, he had plied his art, unversed in the employments of the great, while his father sowed on hired soil. And as fires let loose from diverse quarters on a parched forest and rustling thickets of bay; or as foaming rivers, when, in dizzy career, roaring they descend from the mountain-tops and race to the plain, each in its own wide-wasting path: – with equal fury Aeneas and Turnus alike rushed through the battle: now, now the tide of wrath seethed within them; their unvanquished hearts were strained to breaking; now with utmost force they dashed upon wounds!

This hurled Murranus from his chariot and flung him prone to earth with the whirling stone of a vast rock, Murranus, whose loud tongue vaunted the immemorial names of grandsires and grandsires' sires, and all his long line descending through so many a Latian king! Under rein and yoke the wheels rolled him forward, and he lay trampled beneath the quick-beating hooves of galloping steeds that forgot their lord. That met Hyllus, charging in giant fury, and flung the spear at his gold-bound forehead; and, piercing the helm, the point stood fixed in his brain. Nor, Cretheus, bravest of the Greeks, could thy strong hand deliver thee from Turnus! nor did Cupencus' deities shield their worshipper when Aeneas came: he laid his breast bare to the steel, and his buckler's brazen rampart availed not the victim. Thee, too, Aeolus, the Laurentine plains saw bleed, covering supine a great breadth of earth. Fallen thou wert laid whom nei-ther Argos' legions nor Achilles, the destroyer of Priam's realm, could overthrow! Here didst thou find thy mortal goal: thy stately home stood under Ida, – at Lyrnesus thy stately home, on Laurentine soil thy sepulchre! The whole lines were flung into utter turmoil, and all Latium and all Troy – Mnestheus and bold Serestus, Messapus, tamer of steeds, and stout Asilas; and the Tuscan phalanx, and Evander's Arcadian horse – fought every man for his own hand with utmost effort of their powers. Nor rest nor respite: they strained in titanic struggle!

And now his fairest mother inspired Aeneas to march on the walls, fling his column swiftly against the town, and confound the Latins with unhoped blow. While he, tracking Turnus through the diverse ranks, swept his glance to left and right, he descried the city immune from the raging war, quiet and unamerced. Incontinent the vision of a greater battle fired him; he summoned his captains, Mnestheus and Sergestus and gallant Serestus, and ascended a mound, round which the rest of the Teucrian host came thronging in serried array, yet resigned not shield or spear. Then, standing in their midst on the earthen eminence, he spoke: 'Let no delay retard my command: – Jove fights with us. Nor let any advance more slowly because the emprize is sudden. To-day – save they agree to admit our yoke, and, conquered, to obey their conquerors – I will raze this town, the wellspring of the war, the very seat of Latinus' empire, and lay its smoking roofs level with the ground! What, shall I delay till it be Turnus' pleasure to brook our sword and the vanquished again find heart to abide the encounter? Men of my country, this is the head, this the sum, of the accursed war! Bring torches with hot speed, and with fire reclaim the treaty!' He ceased; and all, their hearts kindling with equal zeal, formed a wedge and poured in serried mass to the walls. Ladders and unexpected flames rose into sudden view: part ran to the various gates and slew the foremost sentinels; part hurled the steel and overshadowed the sky with javelins. Himself in the van, Aeneas uplifted his hand to the city-walls, and loudly impeached Latinus, calling heaven to witness that he was again driven into battle – that Italy was twice his foe, and this treaty broken as the first! Among the bewildered citizens faction rose high: some bade unbar the city and fling the gates wide for the Dardans, and dragged their king himself to the battlements: some brought arms, and assayed to defend the ramparts. As when some swain has discovered bees in covert of the rock, and filled their hive with bitter smoke; they within, alarmed for their estate, flit scattering through the waxen fortalice, and edge their anger with loud hummings: the black fume rolls through their chambers, the inner rocks sound with murmurous confusion, and the vapours mount to the void air!

And now this last blow fell on weary Latium, shaking the whole city to her base with woe. For when, from her palace, the queen saw the enemy's advance, the walls assaulted, and fires flying to the roofs, yet nowhere Rutulia's opposing spears, nor any lines of Turnus, she deemed (unhappy!) her prince dead in combat, and – her brain reeling under the sudden agony – cried out that she was the cause, the guilt-stained fountain-head of ill; then, with many a brain-sick utterance of her melancholy frenzy, rent, death-resolved, her purple robes, and from lofty beams hung the knot of a ghastly death. Soon as the sad Latian dames learned that calamity, first her child Lavinia, – her flowery tresses and roseate cheeks all torn, – then the rest of their throng around her, broke into wild sorrow; while the halls rang far and wide with lamentation. Thence the disastrous rumour was noised through the town: hearts sank, and Latinus, his robes rent, went thunder-blasted by the doom of his consort and the ruin of his city, defiling his white hairs with showers of unclean dust!

Meanwhile Turnus, warring on the extreme plain, pursued the scant stragglers, slacker now, and less and less exulting in his steeds' victorious course. To him the air bore that cry blended with unknown terrors, and on his eager ears smote the sound of the stricken city and its joyless murmur. 'Alas, why are the walls a turmoil of loud sorrow? Or what this great cry ringing from the distant town?' He said; and, distraught, halted with drawn reins. Then his sister, – as, changed to the semblance of Metiscus the charioteer, she governed car and steeds and reins, – thus met his doubt: 'Turnus, pursue we the sons of Troy by this path where victory first opens way: there are others whose hand can guard their homes! Aeneas assails the Italians in mingled mellay: let our sword, no less, wreak dread carnage on his Teucrians! Neither in number of the slain nor in honours of the fray shall he surpass thee when thou retirest!' To this Turnus: 'Sister, I both knew thee long ago, when thy arts first shattered the truce and thou didst fling thee into this war, and now vainly thou wouldst hide thy deity! But who willed thee to descend from Olympus and endure these toils? Was it that thou mightest view thy brother's cruel death? For what may I do? or what chance can now give me hope of safety? Before these eyes I beheld Murranus – none dearer left to me! – fall, a great man conquered by a great wound, while his voice called on me! Unhappy Ufens has bled, that he might not behold our shame: the Teucrians hold his corpse and arms! Shall I suffer their homes to be razed to earth – the last drop to fill the cup! – nor refute Drances' taunts with this right hand? Shall I turn my back, and shall this earth see Turnus in flight? Is it so hard a thing to die? Be kind to me, ye powers below, for they above regard me not. A stainless soul, ignorant of that guilt, I will descend to you – I whom no day shall have argued unworthy of my great forefathers!'

Scarce had he spoken, when, lo, Saces came spurring through the enemy's throng on foam-covered horse, – the front of his face bleeding from an arrow, – and rushed on, imploring Turnus by his name: 'Turnus, our last hope is stayed on thee: pity thou thy people! Aeneas thunders in arms, and threatens to hurl down Italy's topmost towers and give them to destruction: even now brands are flying to the roofs. To thee Latium turns – to thee with look and eye! Even Latium's king mutters doubt – whom he shall bid to his daughter's hand, or to which alliance he shall incline! More, the queen – thy surest trust – has fallen by her own hand and fled in terror from the day. Alone before the gates Messapus and gallant Atinas uphold our battle. Around these, on each side, throng serried legions, and the iron harvest stands horrent with naked blades: and thou wheelest thy car over the deserted sward!' Aghast, and bewildered by the changing picture, Turnus stood in mute gaze: in his one heart surged the great tides of shame, grief mixed with madness, love stung by fury, and conscious valour! Soon as the shadows were banished and light dawned again on his mind, storm-tossed he turned his blazing orbs to the battlements and looked back from his car to the spacious city.

But, lo, a fiery crest, flame-rolled betwixt the storeys, was flickering to heaven and preying upon a turret – a turret which himself had built of compacted beams and set on wheels, and overlaid with lofty bridges. 'Now, now, my sister, fate proves too potent : forbear thy delays; let us follow where God and Fortune's stern dictates call! My purpose stands to join encounter with Aeneas: it stands to endure in death whatever bitterness resides therein; and no longer, my sister, shalt thou view me disgraced! Yet suffer me first, I pray, to be mad with this madness.' He said; and leapt quickly from his car to the ground, rushed through foes and through spears, and, leaving his sister to her sorrow, broke in swift course through the midmost lines. And as a rock falls precipitate from some mountain-crest, torn thence by the wind, or washed forth by the swollen rains, or loosened by the stealthy lapse of years; under mighty impulse the destroying cliff crashes in abrupt descent and bounds over earth, involving in its train forests and herds and men: – so, through the cloven ranks, Turnus rushed to the city-walls, where the ground was deepest-dyed with spilt blood and the air hissed with spears; then, with a gesture of his hand, began in loud tones: 'Desist now, Rutulians; and, ye Latians, check your darts! Whatever fortune comes is mine. It is juster that I alone should expiate the broken truce in your stead, and decide the issue by the steel!' All that intervened gave ground, and yielded him space.

But father Aeneas, when he heard Turnus' name, abandoned the walls and abandoned the battlements' height, cast all delays aside, broke off all his toils, and – his heart leaping with joy – rang dread thunder on his arms: great as Athos, great as Eryx, or great as Father Apenninus himself, when he roars with quivering holms and exultant lifts his snowy head in air. And now, indeed,

Rutulians and Trojans and every Italian turned their gaze upon them, and undid the armour from their shoulders; – both they who manned the ramparts on high and they whose ram battered the walls below. Even Latinus marvelled to see those mighty men, born in distant regions of earth, met each with other and ridding their quarrel by the steel. And they, when the lists were clear in the deserted plain, ran forward with swift pace, first flinging their spears from distance, and rushed on the fray with shields and sounding brass. Earth moaned; their swords showered recurrent blows, and chance and valour were blended in one. And as, in great Sila or upon Taburnus' crown, when two bulls dash to mortal encounter with adverse front, the timorous hinds withdraw, the whole herd stands mute with dread, and the heifers mutter doubt – who shall be the forest-lord, whom all their bands shall follow: they, with vehement fury, deal promiscuous wounds, infix their conflicting horns, and bathe neck and shoulders in streaming blood, while the moaning wood bellows again: – even so Aeneas of Troy and Daunia's hero met under shield, and the ruinous crash filled heaven! Jove himself upheld two scales in levelled balance and imposed the diverse fates of both, – whom the struggle should doom, and on which side the weight of death should sink.

And now Turnus, deeming himself immune, shot forward, rose with all his frame to the uplifted sword, and smote. Trojans and expectant Latins cried loud, and the ranks of either host held their breath. But the traitorous blade shivered, and forsook its fiery lord in the mid stroke – did not flight come to his succour. Swifter than the East he fled, when he descried a strange hilt in his unweaponed hand. Fame tells that in headlong haste, when he mounted his yoked steeds for the first affray, he left his father's brand behind, and seized the steel of Metiscus his charioteer; and for long that sufficed, while the Teucrians were turning their recreant backs: but, when it came to the divine Vulcanian arms, the mortal glaive flew apart at the blow like brittle ice, and the fragments lay shining on the yellow sand. Sense bereft, therefore, Turnus fled afar over the plain, wheeling in aimless circle, now hither, now thither: for on all hands the serried ring of Teucrians enclosed him, and here the great morass, there the frowning battlements confined him.

Nor less Aeneas, – though his knees, retarded yet by the arrow wound, impeded him at whiles and denied him their speed, – still pursued, and pressed him with foot hard upon racing foot. As when the hunter has caught a stag, shut in by some stream or pent within the feather-hung line of scarlet, and chases him with running, barking hound: he, in dread of the toils and lofty banks, flees a thousand ways, and fleeing returns; but the quick Umbrian clings open-mouthed to his trail, and now – now – he seems to hold him, and, as though he held, snaps his jaws, and baffled bites at nothingness! Then, in truth, the clamour rose loud: the encircling banks and lakes gave answer, and all heaven thundered with the tumult. The one, even in act of flight, upbraided his Rutulians all, invoking each by name and demanding his wonted sword. Aeneas, in countermand, threatened death and instant doom, should any approach; terrified their trembling hearts with menace of destruction to the city; and, despite his wound, pressed on. Round five full circles they raced, and unthreaded as many more, this way and that; for they sought no light or sportive meed, but ran for Turnus' life and blood!

Here, it chanced, a wild olive of bitter leaf had stood, consecrate to Faunus, a venerable bole erewhile in the mariner's sight; whereon, preserved from the wave, they were wont to affix their gifts to the Laurentine god and suspend their votive weeds: but the Teucrians, with unregarding zeal, had hewn down its sacred stem, that the combatants might encounter in clear lists. There the spear of Aeneas stood: thither its force had borne and lodged it, and now held it in the tough root. Bending, the Dardan assayed to pluck the steel forth in his hand, and pursue with javelin-cast him whom his speed availed not to reach. Then Turnus, distraught with fear: 'Faunus,' he cried, 'have pity, I pray thee; and thou, gracious Earth, hold the iron fast, if always I have observed your honours, which Aeneas' people, in other sort, have made profane with war!' He said; and called the celestial aid to no unavailing vow. For, though he struggled long, and lingered over the stubborn trunk, by no effort could Aeneas unlock the biting timber. While fiercely he strove and strained, the Daunian goddess, changed again to semblance of Metiscus the charioteer, ran forward and restored the blade to her brother. Then Venus, indignant that such licence was granted the bold Nymph, approached and plucked the spear again from the deep root. Towering in arms and refreshed in spirit, – this reliant on his sword, that fierce and erect with spear in hand, – the champions stood fronting War's breathless strife!

Meanwhile the King of all-puissant Olympus bespoke Juno, as from a lurid cloud she surveyed the battle: 'What now shall be

the end, my consort? What remains at the last? Thou knowest –
self-avowed thy knowledge! – that the skies claim Aeneas, as hero
made divine, and the Fates exalt him to the stars. What devising,
or what hoping, lingerest thou in the chill clouds? Was it meet
that mortal wound should profane a god? or that his reft blade –
for without thee what could Juturna avail? – should be restored
to Turnus, and might rise high in the vanquished? Cease at long
last, and bow to our entreaty, that thy great sorrow may no
longer prey on thee in silence, nor gloomy cares come coursing
on me so oft from thy sweet lips! The bourne is reached. Power
has been thine to toss the Trojans over land or sea, to kindle an
unblest war, to dress a palace in mourning, and to dissolve a
bridal in tears: farther to attempt I forbid!' Thus Jupiter spoke;
and thus, with downcast look, Saturn's goddess-child returned:
'In truth, great Jove, because thy pleasure was known to me,
unwillingly I abandoned both Turnus and the earth: nor else
wouldst thou behold me now alone on my aery seat, enduring
fair and foul; but flame girt would I stand even by their embattled lines, dragging the Teucrians to the fatal fray. That I counselled Juturna to succour her hapless brother I confess, and
sanctioned her to dare yet more in the cause of life, – but sanctioned not the levelled shaft nor the drawn bow! Thus much I
swear by the implacable fount of the Stygian wave – that awful
name which alone may bind the upper gods! And now I yield and
with loathing resign the war. One guerdon – banned by no fatal
law – I entreat from thee, for Latium's sake and the majesty of
thy kindred: when soon they establish peace with a happy bridal
(so be it for me!), when they shall unite in law and league, command not the native Latins to change their name, to become
Trojans, or to bear the Teucrian style, – command them not to
change their tongue nor to resign their garb: let there be a
Latium still, let there be kings at Alba throughout the ages, let
there be a Roman race strong in Italian valour! Troy lies fallen,
and fallen let her lie – herself and her name!'

To her – with a smile – the author of men and things: 'True
sister of Jove thou art, and Saturn's other seed: so fiercely the
waves of passion roll in thy breast! But come, allay thy fury conceived in vain: I grant thy wish, and, submissive and unreluctant,
surrender to thee! Ausonia's sons shall preserve their ancestral
speech and customs; and as their name is, so it shall be: the Teucrians shall but mingle and merge in the body of their realm.
Myself will assign the mode and ritual of their worship, and I will

make them all *Latins* of one speech. Thence thou shalt see a race arise from admixture of Ausonian blood, surpassing men and surpassing gods in piety; nor shall any people celebrate thy honours with equal zeal!' Juno yielded assent, and with new-born joy reversed her purpose. – Meanwhile she departed from the sky and abandoned her cloudy throne.

This sped, the Sire revolved other purpose in his breast, and prepared to withdraw Juturna's succour from her brother's sword. There are twin fiends, – *Furies* styled, – whom, with hellish Megaera, Midnight bore in one and the selfsame travail, and swathed them in viperous coils, and gave them wind-swift wings. Before Jove's throne and the threshold of the grim King they start to view, whetting the terrors of suffering men, what time Heaven's monarch plies pestilence and dreadful death, or affrights guilty towns with war. The one of these Jove sent swiftly down from the empyreal height, and bade her confront Juturna, charged with his omen. Forth she flew, borne earthward in rushing whirlwind. Even as a cloud-piercing arrow launched from the string – an arrow which Parthian (Parthian or Cydonian) has armed with gall of deadly venom and shot, a leech-proof shaft – leaps whistling and unseen through the fleeting shades: – so sped the daughter of Night, as she hied to earth! Soon as she discerned the Ilian lines and Turnus' array, shrinking with sudden change to the form of that little bird which oft, perched at night on tomb or deserted roof, sings, with boding voice, her belated descant through the dusk, – in such transmuted semblance the fiend passed and repassed, rustling before Turnus' face, and beat his buckler with her wings. A strange palsy unstrung his limbs with fear; his hair rose with horror, and the voice clove to his throat.

But when from far Juturna knew the Fury's strident pinions, she rent – hapless maid! – her dishevelled tresses, and, sister-like, tore her cheeks and smote her breast: 'What succour, my Turnus, can thy sister now lend? What more is left to me – cruel that I am? What art of mine may prolong thy day? Can I front that presence of dread? Now, now, I quit the field. Ye hellish birds, forbear to appal my quaking heart: I know the beating of your wings and their sound fraught with death – I hear the haughty mandate of great-souled Jove. Is it thus he requites my maidenhood reft? Why gave he eternal life? Why lost I the mortal's privilege? Then, certes, at this hour I might annul my anguish, and journey through the shadows at the side of my poor

brother? Immortal – I? Can aught that is mine be sweet to me
without thee, my brother? O what earth may yawn deep enough
for me and send me down – a goddess to the nethermost shades?'
So far she spoke; then shrouded her head in the grey robe, and,
with many a moan, plunged her celestial frame into the river's
depth!

Against his foe pressed Aeneas, brandishing his vast tree-like
spear, and thus spoke from unpitying heart: 'What now for thy
next delay? Turnus, why shrinkest thou still? Not with swift foot,
but hand to hand with fatal steel must this contest be waged!
Turn thee into all shapes soever, and muster all thy powers
whether of courage or art: choose, if thou wilt, to wing thy flight
to the exalted stars, or to hide thee in shelter of the cavernous
earth!' He, with shaken head: 'Thy fiery words dismay me not,
fierce as thou art: the gods dismay me, and Jove my foe!' And,
without further parle, he looked round on a mighty rock, a
mighty rock and ancient, which haply lay on the plain, set there
as landmark to ward dispute from the fields. Scarce twice six
chosen men could uplift it on their shoulders, – men of such
mould as earth produces in these days: – then the hero caught it
with hasty hand and hurled it against the foe, rising to his height
and running at speed. But he knew not himself as he ran, nor as
he moved, nor as he raised his hand, nor as he stirred the gigantic
rock: his knees tottered, and his chill blood froze as ice. The very
stone that he flung whirled through the void inane; but traversed
not all the space, nor bore the stroke to its goal. And even as in
dreams, when languid sleep has oppressed our eyes, we seem to
strive in vain to extend our eager course, and, in the mid effort,
sink swooning down; our tongue is palsied, our wonted strength
of limb avails not, and voice and word obey not our summons: –
so to Turnus, with whatever valour he sought the means, the dire
fiend denied the issue! And now vague phantasies whirled
through his soul: he looked to his Rutulians and the town; he
wavered in fear, and trembled at death's pursuant step, but saw
not whither he might escape, nor how nerved he might advance
against the foe, nor anywhere his car, nor his sister that drove the
car!

As he wavered, Aeneas brandished the fate-charged spear,
choosing occasion with alert eye, and hurled it from far with all
the might of his frame. Never stone sped from mural engine, so
roars: never crash follows so loud on the rending thunderbolt!
Like sable whirlwind flew the lance on its dread errand of doom,

and opened the corselet's edge and the extreme orb of the seven-fold shield; then, singing, pierced full through the thigh. Smitten by that blow, Turnus, with doubled knee, fell to earth in his mighty stature. Groaning the Rutulians rose as a man, and all the mountain round re-echoed, and far and near the forests profound flung back the cry. He, in humble suppliance, raised his eyes and beseeching hand: 'I have merited,' he said, 'and I cry not mercy: use thy fortune to the full! Yet, if any thought of a father's misery can touch thee – in Anchises thou, too, hadst such a sire! – pity, O pity, Daunus' white hairs, and restore to my kindred me, or, if so thou wilt, my breathless clay! Thou hast conquered, and, conquered, the Ausonians have seen me outstretch these palms. Lavinia is thine to wed: strain not thy hatred farther!' Rolling his eyes, Aeneas stood grim in arms, and refrained his hand. And more, and yet more, that speech had begun to sway his hesitant resolve, when the ill-starred belt met the view high on his shoulder, and the baldrick of youthful Pallas flashed with the familiar studs, – Pallas, whom Turnus had vanquished and laid bleeding on earth, and now bore on his shoulders the ensign of his foe. He – soon as his eyes drank in the memorials of his cruel grief and those ravished spoils – incensed with fury and terrible in his wrath: 'And shalt thou, clothed in the trophies of my friend, escape me hence? It is Pallas – Pallas immolates thee with this wound and exacts vengeance from thy guilty blood!' So saying, like fire he buried the steel full in his breast. The chilling limbs relaxed, and the indignant life fled moaning beneath the shades.

WORDSWORTH CLASSICS

REQUESTS FOR INSPECTION COPIES Lecturers wishing to obtain copies of Wordsworth Classics, Wordsworth Poetry Library or Wordsworth Classics of World Literature titles on inspection are invited to contact: Dennis Hart, Wordsworth Editions Ltd, Crib Street, Ware, Herts SG12 9ET; E-mail: dennis.hart@wordsworth-editions.com. Please quote the author, title and ISBN of the titles in which you are interested; together with your name, academic address, E-mail address, the course on which the books will be used and the expected enrolment.

Teachers wishing to inspect specific core titles for GCSE or A level courses are also invited to contact Wordsworth Editions at the above address.

Inspection copies are sent solely at the discretion of Wordsworth Editions Ltd.

JANE AUSTEN
Emma
Mansfield Park
Northanger Abbey
Persuasion
Pride and Prejudice
Sense and Sensibility

ARNOLD BENNETT
Anna of the Five Towns
The Old Wives' Tale

R. D. BLACKMORE
Lorna Doone

M. E. BRADDON
Lady Audley's Secret

ANNE BRONTË
Agnes Grey
*The Tenant of
Wildfell Hall*

CHARLOTTE BRONTË
Jane Eyre
The Professor
Shirley
Villette

EMILY BRONTË
Wuthering Heights

JOHN BUCHAN
Greenmantle
The Island of Sheep
John Macnab
Mr Standfast
The Thirty-Nine Steps
The Three Hostages

SAMUEL BUTLER
Erewhon
The Way of All Flesh

LEWIS CARROLL
Alice in Wonderland

M. CERVANTES
Don Quixote

ANTON CHEKHOV
Selected Stories

G. K. CHESTERTON
*The Club of Queer
Trades*
*Father Brown:
Selected Stories*
*The Man Who Was
Thursday*
*The Napoleon of
Notting Hill*

ERSKINE CHILDERS
The Riddle of the Sands

JOHN CLELAND
*Fanny Hill – Memoirs of
a Woman of Pleasure*

WILKIE COLLINS
The Moonstone
The Woman in White

JOSEPH CONRAD
Almayer's Folly
Heart of Darkness
Lord Jim
Nostromo
Sea Stories
The Secret Agent
Selected Short Stories
Victory

J. FENIMORE COOPER
The Last of the Mohicans

STEPHEN CRANE
The Red Badge of Courage

THOMAS DE QUINCEY
*Confessions of an English
Opium Eater*

DANIEL DEFOE
Moll Flanders
Robinson Crusoe

CHARLES DICKENS
Barnaby Rudge
Bleak House
Christmas Books
David Copperfield
Dombey and Son
Ghost Stories
Great Expectations
Hard Times
Little Dorrit
Martin Chuzzlewit
The Mystery of Edwin Drood
Nicholas Nickleby
The Old Curiosity Shop
Oliver Twist
Our Mutual Friend
Pickwick Papers
Sketches by Boz
A Tale of Two Cities

BENJAMIN DISRAELI
Sybil

FYODOR DOSTOEVSKY
Crime and Punishment
The Idiot

ARTHUR CONAN DOYLE
*The Adventures of
Sherlock Holmes*
*The Case-Book of
Sherlock Holmes*
*The Return of
Sherlock Holmes*
*The Best of
Sherlock Holmes*
*The Hound of the
Baskervilles*
*The Lost World &
Other Stories*
Sir Nigel
*A Study in Scarlet & The
Sign of Four*
The Valley of Fear
The White Company

GEORGE DU MAURIER
Trilby

ALEXANDRE DUMAS
*The Count of
Monte Cristo
The Three Musketeers*

MARIA EDGEWORTH
Castle Rackrent

GEORGE ELIOT
*Adam Bede
Daniel Deronda
Felix Holt the Radical
Middlemarch
The Mill on the Floss
Silas Marner*

HENRY FIELDING
Tom Jones

RONALD FIRBANK
*Valmouth &
Other Stories*

F. SCOTT FITZGERALD
*The Diamond as Big as
the Ritz & Other Stories
The Great Gatsby
Tender is the Night*

GUSTAVE FLAUBERT
Madame Bovary

JOHN GALSWORTHY
*In Chancery
The Man of Property
To Let*

ELIZABETH GASKELL
*Cranford
North and South
Wives and Daughters*

GEORGE GISSING
New Grub Street

OLIVER GOLDSMITH
The Vicar of Wakefield

KENNETH GRAHAME
The Wind in the Willows

G. & W. GROSSMITH
Diary of a Nobody

H. RIDER HAGGARD
She

THOMAS HARDY
*Far from the Madding
Crowd
Jude the Obscure
The Mayor of
Casterbridge*

*A Pair of Blue Eyes
The Return of the Native
Selected Short Stories
Tess of the D'Urbervilles
The Trumpet Major
Under the Greenwood
Tree
The Well-Beloved
Wessex Tales
The Woodlanders*

NATHANIEL
HAWTHORNE
The Scarlet Letter

O. HENRY
Selected Stories

JAMES HOGG
*The Private Memoirs and
Confessions of a Justified
Sinner*

HOMER
*The Iliad
The Odyssey*

E. W. HORNUNG
*Raffles: The Amateur
Cracksman*

VICTOR HUGO
*The Hunchback of
Notre Dame
Les Misérables*
IN TWO VOLUMES

HENRY JAMES
*The Ambassadors
Daisy Miller &
Other Stories
The Europeans
The Golden Bowl
The Portrait of a Lady
The Turn of the Screw &
The Aspern Papers
What Maisie Knew*

M. R. JAMES
*Ghost Stories
Ghosts and Marvels*

JEROME K. JEROME
Three Men in a Boat

JAMES JOYCE
*Dubliners
A Portrait of the Artist
as a Young Man*

OMAR KHAYYAM
The Rubaiyat
TRANSLATED BY E. FITZGERALD

RUDYARD KIPLING
*The Best Short Stories
Captains Courageous
Kim
The Man Who
Would Be King
& Other Stories
Plain Tales from
the Hills*

D. H. LAWRENCE
*The Plumed Serpent
The Rainbow
Sons and Lovers
Women in Love*

SHERIDAN LE FANU
*In a Glass Darkly
Madam Crowl's Ghost &
Other Stories*

GASTON LEROUX
The Phantom of the Opera

JACK LONDON
*Call of the Wild &
White Fang*

KATHERINE MANSFIELD
Bliss & Other Stories

GUY DE MAUPASSANT
The Best Short Stories

HERMAN MELVILLE
*Billy Budd & Other
Stories
Moby Dick
Typee*

GEORGE MEREDITH
The Egoist

H. H. MUNRO
*The Collected Stories
of Saki*

SHIKH NEFZAOUI
The Perfumed Garden
TRANSLATED BY
SIR RICHARD BURTON

THOMAS LOVE
PEACOCK
*Headlong Hall &
Nightmare Abbey*

EDGAR ALLAN POE
*Tales of Mystery and
Imagination*

FREDERICK ROLFE
Hadrian VII

SIR WALTER SCOTT
*Ivanhoe
Rob Roy*